Barbara Clay Finch

Lives of the Princesses of Wales

Vol. II

Barbara Clay Finch

Lives of the Princesses of Wales
Vol. II

ISBN/EAN: 9783337168575

Printed in Europe, USA, Canada, Australia, Japan

Cover: Foto ©Raphael Reischuk / pixelio.de

More available books at **www.hansebooks.com**

LIVES OF THE PRINCESSES OF WALES.

BY

BARBARA CLAY FINCH.

IN THREE VOLUMES.

VOL II.

London:

REMINGTON AND CO.,

NEW BOND STREET, W.

1883.

CONTENTS.

KATHARINE OF ARAGON

(continued.)

CHAPTER IV.

The Princess Mary—Execution of Buckingham—Marriage of Maria de Rojas—Description of the King—Of the Queen—Her piety—Visit of Charles V.—His betrothal to the Princess Mary—Her education—Katharine's ill-health—Her letter to Wolsey—Henry Fitzroy—Mary sent to Ludlow—First rumours of a divorce—Wolsey's instigation of it—Anne Boleyn—Katharine's letter to Charles V.—Her interview with Henry—Fisher's view of the case—Letter of the Emperor to Katharine—Embassy to the Pope—Popularity of the Princess Mary—Behaviour of the Queen 1

CHAPTER V.

Illness of Anne Boleyn—The King's letters to her—Letter of Erasmus to Katharine—Arrival of Campeggio—Interviews of the Queen and Cardinal—Address of the Council to the King—Conversation between the King and Queen—The King's address at Bridewell—Audience of Wolsey and Campeggio with the Queen—Warham and Tunstall question Katharine—The brief of dispensation—Henry's embassy to the Pope—Exhibition of the brief to the English ambassadors—Katharine's letter to Muxetula—Henry's treatment of the Queen—Splendour of Anne Boleyn—Letter of the Emperor to Katharine—The Court of Inquiry—The Queen's Speech—Her popularity—Her reception of Wolsey and Campeggio—Letters of the English nobles to the Pope—His reply—Adjournment of the Court of Inquiry—Fall of Wolsey—Letter of the Queen—Thomas Cranmer—His embassy to the Pope—Bribery of the French Universities—Christmas at Greenwich—Illness of the Princess Mary . . . 34

CHAPTER VI.

Thomas Cromwell—Deputation to the Queen—Her reply—Separation of Henry and Katharine—Her departure from Windsor—Letter to the Princess Mary—Interview of the King and Reginald Pole—Elevation of Anne Boleyn to the peerage—Her

journey with Henry to Calais—Letters of Queen Katharine—
Marriage of Henry and Anne Boleyn—Cranmer's Court at
Dunstable—Katharine's refusal to be present—Her marriage
pronounced invalid—Her reception of the announcement—
Coronation of Anne Boleyn—Her unpopularity—Sermons of
the Friars at Greenwich—The King's Proclamation—Katharine's
removal to Bugden—Her heavy sorrow—Her forgiveness of
Anne Boleyn—Her letters to her daughter—Birth of Eliza-
beth—Interview of Mary and Anne Boleyn—Letter of the
French Ambassador—Visit of Lee and Tunstall to Katharine—
Her inflexible resolution—Her letter to the Emperor—Refusal
of her servants to take the oath of allegiance—Her wishes respecting them—Refusal to go to Fotheringay—Removal to
Kimbolton—Traces of her residence there   .   .   . 84

CHAPTER VII.

Persecution of Father Forrest—Attachment of her servants to
Queen Katharine—Illness of the Princess Mary—The bull of
excommunication –Queen's letter to the Emperor—Threats of
Anne Boleyn—Non-publication of the bull—Letter of Katharine to the Pope—Illness of the Queen—Her request to see her
daughter—Henry's refusal—His resolve to enforce her submission—Opinion of Katharine's physician—Her renewed
entreaty to see her child—Her last letter to the Emperor—
Devotion of Lady Willoughby—Queen's message to the Emperor—Her letter to the King—Her death—Reception of the
news at Greenwich—The general sorrow—Letter of the King
to Lady Bedyngfeld—Funeral of Queen Katharine—Her will—
Her character—Her memory preserved at Kimbolton .   . 123

CAROLINE OF ANSPACH.

CHAPTER I.

England in the eighteenth century—Birth of Caroline—Sophia
Charlotte — Charlottenburg — Caroline's education—An Im-
perial suitor — Her marriage —Her husband—The Electress
Sophia—Marriage of the Princess of Hanover—Caroline's
children — Herrenhausen — Royal matchmaking—Death of
the Electress—Death of Queen Anne—Caroline's arrival in
England—Coronation of George I,—Poetical address to the
Princess of Wales—Quarrel between the King and his son—
Leicester House—Caroline's popularity—Mrs. Howard—Mrs.
Clayton—Anecdotes of the Princess of Wales—Buckingham
House—Richmond Lodge—Pope at Hampton Court—Hunting
in Belsize Park—Birth of Princess Mary—Inoculation of the

Princesses—Reconciliation of the King and Prince—Caroline and
Sir Woolston Dixie—Rudeness of Dean Swift—The King's
Cockcrower—Death of Sophia Dorothea—Death of George I.—
Reception of the news by George II.—The Queen and Sir
Robert Walpole—Caroline's allowance—Her reception of Lady
Walpole 149

CHAPTER II.

Coronation of George and Caroline—Drury Lane Theatre—Royal
Visit to the City—Queen's patronage of authors—Her muni-
ficence to Elizabeth Elstob—Frederick Prince of Wales—
Thomson's " Sophonisba " — " The Beggars' Opera " — The
Duchess of Queensberry—The Queen's Birthday — Horace
Walpole—Lord Hervey—Caroline's immense influence—Self-
importance of the King—Queen's love for her husband—
Mrs. Howard—Mrs. Howard's husband—Caroline Regent—
Stephen Duck — Royalty at home — The Duke of Grafton—
The Princess Royal—Her ambition—Her betrothal to the
Prince of Orange—His appearance—Arrival—Illness — Pre-
sents to the Princess—The Royal Marriage—Extraordinary
ceremonies—The Drawing-room—Opinion of the Princesses—
Departure of the Prince and Princess—Address of the House
of Lords to the Queen 180

CHAPTER III.

The Excise Bill—Caroline's great influence—Her support of
Walpole — Resignation of Lady Suffolk — Arrival of the
Princess of Orange—Her conversation with Lord Hervey—
Her wish to remain in England—Her reluctant farewell—
King's treatment of the Prince of Wales—Return of the
Princess of Orange—Her final departure—Queen's liking for
Lord Hervey—Her conversations with him—Her power over
the King—Her ill-health—Her endurance—The importance
of her life—Her opinion of a second marriage—Departure of
the King for Hanover—Caroline appointed Regent—·King's
extraordinary letters—Lord Hervey's imaginary diary—His
drama of Court life—The King's return—His ill-humour—
Lord Hervey's account of an evening with the King and
Queen—Conversation of the Queen and Sir Robert Walpole
—Her remark on the Triple Alliance 219

CHAPTER IV.

Marriage of the Prince of Wales—King's return to Hanover—His
prolonged absence—The Queen and Walpole—Her letter to the
King—His reply—His return—A stormy voyage—Letter of
Princess Amelia—The Queen's birthday—Dissensions between

the King and Prince of Wales—Queen's estrangement from her son—Her illness—Her imprudence—King's want of consideration—Affection of the Princess Caroline—Queen's injunctions concerning the Prince of Wales—Her state pronounced hopeless—Her superstition regarding Wednesday—Her farewells to her children—Her last gift to the King—His extraordinary conduct—His grief—His irritability—Queen's interview with Sir Robert Walpole—With the Archbishop of Canterbury—Her death—Her funeral—Behaviour of the King—Character of the Queen—Verses on her death—Her children—Death of the King 247

AUGUSTA OF SAXE-GOTHA.

CHAPTER I.

Description of Frederick Prince of Wales—Queen Caroline's scheme for his marriage—Lady Diana Spencer—Augusta of Saxe-Gotha—Mission of Lord Delaware—Journey of the Princess—Meeting of Frederick and Augusta—A royal water-party—Augusta's reception at St. James's—Criticisms upon her—Marriage of the Prince and Princess—Congratulations of the Lord Mayor—Augusta's visit to the Theatre—Her feigned illness—Her visit to the city—Her attendance at the Lutheran Chapel—The Queen's opinion of her—Her childishness—Lady Archibald Hamilton—Extraordinary conduct of the Prince—Danger of the Princess—Birth of the Lady Augusta—Visits of the Queen to the Princess of Wales—Christening of the Royal infant—Removal of the Prince and Princess to Kew—Princess Caroline's opinion of Frederick—Birth of George III.—Birthday of the Prince of Wales—Birth of the Duke of York—Of Princess Elizabeth—Visit of Frederick to St. Bartholomew's Fair—Leicester House—Reconciliation of the King and Prince—Birth of the Duke of Gloucester—Of the Duke of Cumberland—Anecdotes of Prince George—Royal theatricals—Princess Elizabeth—Reception of Vertue at Carlton House—Birth of Princess Louisa—Of Prince Frederick—His christening—Visit of the Prince and Princess of Wales to Spitalfields—The Princess's birthday . . . 281

LIVES OF THE PRINCESSES OF WALES.

KATHARINE OF ARAGON.

(*Continued.*)

CHAPTER IV.

The Princess Mary—Execution of Buckingham—Marriage of Maria de Rojas—Description of the King—Of the Queen— Her piety—Visit of Charles V.—His betrothal to the Princess Mary—Her education—Katharine's ill-health—Her letter to Wolsey—Henry Fitzroy—Mary sent to Ludlow— First rumours of a divorce—Wolsey's instigation of it—Anne Boleyn—Katharine's letter to Charles V.—Her interview with Henry—Fisher's view of the case—Letter of the Emperor to Katharine—Embassy to the Pope—Popularity of the Princess Mary—Behaviour of the Queen.

DURING their absence the King and Queen had been kept constantly informed by the Privy Council of the health and general well-being of their precious only daughter. She was a lively, merry child, rosy-cheeked and brown-eyed, and her beauty, vivacity, and healthfulness reconciled the King, ostensibly at least, to his want of male heirs. While her parents were away she was living in royal state at Richmond. Though only four years old, she was required to give audience to three Frenchmen of rank then visiting England, and the Privy Council sent a minute and highly laudatory account of her manner of receiving and entertaining them. "After they had been shown everything notable in London, they were conveyed in a barge, by the Lord Berners and the Lord Darcy to Richmond, where they repaired to the Princess, and found her right honourably accompanied with noble personages, as well spiritual as temporal, and her house and chambers furnished with a proper number of goodly gentlemen and tall yeomen. Her presence-chamber was attended, besides the lady governess and her gentlewomen, by the Duchess of Norfolk and her three daughters, the Lady Margaret, wife to the Lord Herbert, the Lady Gray, Lady Neville, and the Lord John's wife. In the great chamber were many other gentlewomen well apparelled. And when the gentlemen of France came into the presence-chamber to the Princess, her grace in such wise showed herself unto them, in welcoming and entertaining them with most goodly countenance, proper communication, and pleasant pastime in playing on the virginals, that they greatly marvelled and rejoiced at the same, her tender age considered."

In another letter the Council mentions that they have several times seen the little Princess, "your dearest daughter, who, God be thanked, is in prosperous health and convalescence; and like as she increaseth in days and years, so doth she in grace and virtue."

When the King and Queen returned she accompanied them to Greenwich, and remained with them until after her birthday in the following February. She received many Christmas gifts, amongst others a pair of silver snuffers from the Duke of Norfolk, and a bush of rosemary covered with gold spangles, brought her by a poor woman of Greenwich. But the Queen's attention was diverted from this beloved child in the spring of 1521, when the Duke of Buckingham, who had always been a staunch and loyal friend to her, was arrested and executed for treason, mainly through the agency of Cardinal Wolsey. " Then has the butcher's dog pulled down the fairest buck in Christendom," cried Charles V., when he heard the news. Katharine did all she could to save his life, and did not attempt to conceal her opinion of Wolsey's share in his death.

She was a woman of strong attachments, and very faithful to old friends. Her maid of honour, Maria de Rojas, who had attended her on her first coming to England, was loved by her with deep and unshaken affection, which was as warmly returned. " I wish," the Queen had written to her father, before her marriage with Henry, " to keep Maria near my person, and the girl desires of all things to remain with me."

" She loves Maria more than any living thing," Caroz, the Spanish Ambassador, had written to the Spanish King; and the maid of honour deserved the friendship she had inspired, being in good truth noble and devoted, and loyal to the death. Of noble Spanish blood, the child of the Count of Salinas, the Captain General of Castile, and envoy at the Papal and Imperial Courts, she was not likely to lack suitors; but, like her mistress, she had elected to take England as her home, and wedded for love William Willoughby, Baron Willoughby d'Eresby, the seventh of his line. The union did not last long, and in her widowhood Lady Willoughby left her country seat at Parham, and returned to the Queen, her only child, a daughter, Katharine, having, as an heiress, been taken from her care. Of the other ladies who had been with her when she came as Princess of Wales, the Queen now had none remaining with her. Inez de Vargas had married William Blount, fourth Baron Montjoy, the friend of Erasmus. They had fallen in love with each other during the idyllic summer following the royal love-match, and both the King and Queen were well pleased with the marriage. Maria de Salazar had married in Flanders; and the rest had returned to Spain.

The personal appearance of the King about this time is described by the Venetian Ambassador, Guistinian, in a letter not meant for Henry's eye, and which, therefore, need not be accused of undue praise. " His Majesty is," he says, " about twenty-nine years of age, as handsome as nature could form him, above any other Christian Prince; handsomer by far than the King of France. He is exceedingly fair, and as well-proportioned as possible. . . . He is an excellent musician and composer, an admirable horseman, and wrestler. He possesses a good knowledge of the French, Latin, and Spanish languages, and is very devout. On the day on which he goes to the chase he hears mass three times, but on the other days as often as five times. He has every day service at the Queen's chamber at vespers and compline. He is uncommonly fond of the chase, and never indulges in this diversion without tiring eight or ten horses. These are stationed at the different places where he purposes to stop. When one is fatigued he mounts another, and by the time he returns home they have all been used. He takes great delight in bowling, and it is the pleasantest sight in the world to see him engaged in this exercise, with his fair skin covered with a beautifully fine shirt. He plays with the hostages of France, and it is said they sport from 6,000 to 8,000 ducats in a day. Affable and benign, he offends no one. He has often said to the ambassador, he wished that every one was content with his condition, adding, ' We are content with our islands.' "

Of the Queen, Miss Strickland gives some interesting particulars. " In the portrait most commonly recognized as Katharine of Aragon she appears a bowed-down and sorrow-stricken person, spare and slight in figure, and nearly fifty years old. But, even if that latest picture of Holbein really represent Katharine, it must be remembered that she was not near fifty all her life, therefore she ought not to be entirely identified with it, especially as all our early historians, Hall among them (who was present at the Field of Gold), mention her as a handsome woman. Speed calls her ' beauteous,' and Sir John Russell, one of Henry's Privy Council, puts her in immediate comparison with the triumphant beauties, Anne Boleyn and Jane Seymour, declaring she was not to be easily paralleled when in her prime. Her portrait, engraved in the first volume of Burnet, from the miniature of Strawberry Hill, is very different from the one usually known ; and there is a fac-simile of it, as a whole-length oil painting, in the gallery at Versailles, though it is called by a different name. This portrait represents her as a very noble-looking lady of thirty ; the face oval, the features very regular, with a sweet, calm look, but somewhat heavy, the forehead of the most extraordinary height—phrenologists would say with benevolence greatly developed. The oil painting at Versailles has large, dark eyes and a bright brunette complexion. The hood cap of five corners is bordered with rich gems, the black mantilla veil depends from the back of the cap on each side, for she never gave up the costume of her beloved Spain; clusters of rubies are linked with strings of pearl round her throat and waist, and a *cordelière* belts of the same jewels hangs to her feet. Her robe is dark blue velvet, with a graceful train broidered with sable fur; her sleeves are straight, with ruffles, and slashed at the wrists. Over them are great hanging sleeves of sable fur, of the shape called rebras. She draws up her gown with her right hand; the petticoat is gold-coloured satin, barred with gold. Her figure is stately, but somewhat column-like and solid. It realized very well the description of an Italian contemporary, who said that her form was *massive.* . . . The routine of Katharine's life was self-denying. Her contemporaries held her in more estimation for her ascetic observances than for her highest practical virtues. She rose in the night to prayers, at conventual hours; she dressed herself for the day at five in the morning. Beneath her royal attire she wore the habit of St. Francis of the third order, of which community she was an admitted member. She was used to say that she considered no part of her time so much wasted as that passed in dressing and adorning herself. She fasted on Fridays and Saturdays, and on the vigils of saints' days. She confessed at least weekly, and received the Eucharist every Sunday. For two hours after dinner one of her attendants read to her books of devotion. Notwithstanding this rigorous rule of self-discipline, Katharine delighted in conversation of a lively cast; she often invited Sir Thomas More to her private suppers with the King, and took the utmost pleasure in his society."

Sir Thomas More was not the only thoughtful and cultivated man who thought well of Katharine. Erasmus had a high opinion of her. He dedicated to her his treatise on "Christian Matrimony," instanced her as an example to womankind, and asks, in speaking of the King and Queen, "What household is there among the subjects of their realms that can offer an example of such united wedlock? Where can a wife be found better matched with the best of husbands?" He was no fair-weather friend; for after the trouble of her life began, and sycophants and flatterers were deserting her, Erasmus had the courage to call the attention of Henry himself to his wife's virtues. "Your noble wife," he wrote to the King, "spends that time in reading the sacred volume which other Princesses occupy in cards and dice." Katharine, in her turn, warmly appreciated the scholar; and would gladly have made him her Latin master had he continued in England.

Her studies did not prevent her becoming a proficient in needlework, the universal feminine accomplishment in all times and ages.

> With stole and with needle she was not to seek,
> And other practicisings for ladies meet
> For pastimes, as tables, tric-trac, and gleek,*
> Cards and dice,

writes an old English versifier; and Taylor, writing in the reign of James I., thus commemorates her skill:—

> I read that in the 7th King Henry's reign,
>   Fair Katharine, daughter to the Castile King,
> Came into England with a pompous train
>   Of Spanish ladies, which she thence did bring.

* Chess, backgammon, and whist.

She to the eighth King Henry married was
    (And afterwards divorced) when virtuously
(Although a Queen) yet she her days did pass
    In working with the needle curiously.
As in the Tower, and places more beside,
    Her excellent memorials may be seen
Whereby the needle's praise is dignified
    By her fair ladies and herself a Queen.
Thus for her pains, here, her reward is just:
Her works proclaim her praise though she be dust.

In the year 1523, Charles V. again visited England. He was brought by the King to Greenwich Palace, where Katharine received him at the hall door, holding by the hand her little daughter, the Princess Mary. Charles bent his knee, and asked her blessing, and was introduced to his little cousin, whom he had come to betroth. Mary was at that time but six years old, but, according to the fashion of those days, she was considered none too young to be solemnly affianced. A solemn treaty of matrimony was signed at Windsor, whereby the Emperor engaged to marry her when she had completed her twelfth year; and the visit of her bridegroom-elect, with the accompanying festivities, raised the expenditure of the little maiden's establishment to £1,139 6s. 1½d. Charles wished that his future bride should be sent to Spain to complete her education; but this her parents would not consent to, though they promised that she should be brought up in all things as a Spaniard. "As to the education of the Princess Mary," said the King, "if the Emperor should search all Christendom for a mistress to bring her up, and frame her after the manner of Spain, he could not find one more meet than the Queen's grace, her mother—who cometh of the royal house of Spain, and who, for the affection she beareth to the Emperor, will nurture her, and bring her up to his satisfaction.

But the noble person of the young Princess is not meet as yet to bear the pains of the sea, nor strong enough to be transplanted into the air of another country."

"The care of Mary's excellent mother," says Miss Strickland, "was now sedulously directed to give her child an education that would render her a fitting companion to the greatest sovereign of modern history, not only in regard to extent of dominions, but in character and attainments. To Dr. Linacre, the learned physician, who had formerly been one of Prince Arthur's, was entrusted the care of the Princess Mary's health, and some part of her instruction in Latin; the Queen, her mother (as appears by her own written testimony) often examining her translations and reading with her. Linacre died when the Princess was but eight years of age, having first written a Latin grammar for her use. It was dedicated to her, and he speaks with praise of her docility and love of learning, at that tender age. The copy belonging to the Princess is now in the British Museum. Queen Katharine requested Ludovicus Vives, a Spaniard of deep learning, who was called by his contemporaries the second Quintillian, to draw up a code of instructions for the education of Mary. He sent a treatise in Latin, dedicated to the Queen, from Bruges, and afterwards came to England, and at Oxford revised and improved it. He thus addresses Katharine of Aragon:—'Govern by these my monitions Maria, thy daughter, and she will be formed by them; she will resemble thy domestic example of probity and wisdom, and, except all human expectations fail, holy and good will she be by necessity.' Vives points out with exultation the daughters of Sir Thomas More as glorious

examples of the effects of a learned and virtuous
female education. His rules are rigid: he im-
plores that the young Princess may read no idle
books of chivalry or romance. He defies and
renounces such compositions, in Spanish, as
'Amadis de Gaul,' 'Tirante, the White,' and
others burnt by the curate in 'Don Quixote.'
He abjures 'Lancelot du Lac,' 'Paris et Vienne,'
'Pierre Provençal,' and 'Margalone and the
Fairy Melusina.' In Flemish he denounces
'Florice and Blanche,' and 'Pyramus and Thisbe.'
All these, and such as these, he classes as *libri
pestiferi*, corrupting to the morals of females. In
their places he desires that the young Princess
Mary may read the Gospels, night and morning,
the Acts of the Apostles, and the Epistles, selected
portions of the Old Testament, and the works of
Cyprian, Jerome, Augustine, and Ambrose; likewise Plato, Cicero, Seneca's maxims, Plutarch's
Euchiridion, the Paraphrase of Erasmus, and the
Utopia of Sir Thomas More. Among the works
of classic poets, he admitted the Pharsalia of
Lucan, the tragedies of Seneca, with selected
portions of Horace. He deemed cards, dice, and
splendid dress as pestiferous as romances. He
gave rules for her pronunciation of Greek and
Latin, and advised that lessons from these
languages should be committed to memory every
day, and read over two or three times before the
pupil went to bed. He recommended that the
Princess should render English into Latin frequently, and likewise that she should converse
with her preceptor in that language. Her Latin
dictionary was to be either Perotti or Colepin.
He permitted some stories for her recreation, but
they were all to be purely historical, sacred, or
classic. He instanced the narrative of Joseph

and his brethren, in the Scriptures; that of
Papyrus in Aulus Gellius, and Lucretia in Livy.
The well-known tale of Griselda is the only
exception to his general exclusion of fiction, and
that perhaps he took for fact. It is a curious
coincidence that Griselda was afterwards considered, in England, as the prototype of Queen
Katharine."

In 1523, the health of the Queen began to give
way. She had been sorely tried by the death of
her infants, and perhaps English air was anything
but a restorative to a native of Granada. Her
delicacy seemed chronic ; and from 1523 to 1526
she is but rarely mentioned by chroniclers of her
Court. She herself believed the end of her life
was drawing nigh. Perhaps it would have been
better for her, poor soul, if her belief had been
true ; if she had died as honoured wife and un-
doubted Queen, with no stain resting on her
daughter's name. Death would not have seemed
to her devout nature so hard to meet as the
lonely agony, the stinging humiliations of her
later years. In the January of 1524, or 1525, she
wrote the following letter to Cardinal Wolsey,
touching the wedding of one of her attendants, in
which her strong impression of the slight tenure
on which she held her life is evident :—

"My Lord,

"It hath pleased the King to be so good
lord unto me as to speak unto Arundel the heir,
for a marriage to be had between him and one of
my maids, and upon this I am agreed with him,
having a sum of money which, being offered unto
him, he shall make her sure jointure, during her
life, the which she cannot be sure of without the
licence and goodwill of his father being on live·

[alive]. For the which cause I beseech you to be good and gracious lord to the said Arundel, for business which he hath now to do before you, to the intent that he may have time to go to his father, and make me sure of her jointure in this present term time.

"And if this be painful [inconvenient] to you, I pray you, my lord, pardon me, for the uncertainty of my life, and the goodness of my woman, causeth me to make all this haste, trusting that she shall have a good husband and a sure living, and if God would call me the next day after, the surer it shall appear before him, that I intend to help them that be good, and taketh labour doing me service. And so I make an end, recommending me unto you.

"KATHARINE THE QWENE.
"At Ampthill, the xxv day of January."

These years of ill-health did not pass without events occurring which were of necessity of great interest to Katharine. On June 25th, 1525, Henry Fitzroy, the King's illegitimate son by Elizabeth Blount, then a boy of six years old, was created Duke of Richmond with infinite pomp and splendour. "A month afterwards," says M. du Boys, "the King added the dignity of Lord Admiral of England, and afterwards made him large grants of land. . . . The same deed that created the boy Duke of Richmond gave him precedence over all the English nobility, and over the Princess, his sister, herself. This last favour was too significant; it must have been a severe wound to a mother like Katharine, jealous for the preservation of her daughter's rights to the crown. But it is said that the Queen only mentioned her resentment to three Spanish ladies of her household. These ladies had sympathized with her grief; they were accused of having aroused and kept up her resentment, and the King instantly dismissed them from the Court. It was a harsh and cruel proceeding, says the Venetian Ambassador, who mentions the fact, but the Queen was obliged to submit patiently." It was about this time she wrote a sad, little note to her nephew, Charles V.:—

"MOST HIGH AND POWERFUL LORD,

"I cannot imagine what may be the cause of your Highness having been so angry, and having so forgotten me that for upwards of two years I have had no letters [from Spain], and yet I am sure I deserve not this treatment, for such are my affections and readiness for your Highness's service, that I deserve a better reward."

This epistle seems to have had little effect on the Emperor, as, in the same year, 1525, he broke his contract with the Princess Mary, and married Isabel of Portugal. It is said that already rumours of a meditated divorce were afloat, and that the Emperor was bitterly angered by such an insult to his aunt; but it is possible that the English were not very anxious to see their King's only child and heiress married to a great continental power, among whose vast estates England would become a mere appanage. The little lady was treated entirely as the heiress-apparent, created Princess of Wales, and given a splendid establishment; and, in the autumn of the same year that witnessed the breaking of her betrothal, was taken to Ludlow Castle for residence and education, according to the usual custom of the heirs to the crown—that castle where her mother

had spent the brief season during which she bore
that title which was yet again to be bestowed on
her.   The Princess bade adieu to her parents at
Langley, in Herefordshire, in September, arrived
safely at her destination, and was noticed as being
" joyous and decorous " in manners.   A new set
of instructions regarding her education was given
to her council, framed, it is apparent, chiefly by
the Queen.

" First, above all other things, the Countess of
Salisbury, being lady-governess, shall, according
to the singular confidence that the King's highness hath in her, gives most tender regard to all
that concerns the person of the said Princess, her
honourable education and training in virtuous
demeanour ; that is to say, to serve God, from
whom all grace and goodness proceedeth.   Likewise, at seasons convenient, to use moderate exercise, taking open air in gardens, sweet and wholesome places, and walks (which may conduce unto
her health, solace, and comfort), as by the said
lady-governess shall be thought most convenient.
And likewise to pass her time most seasons at her
virginals, or other musical instruments, so that
the same be not too much, and without fatigation,
or weariness, to attend to her learning of Latin
tongue and French.   At other season to dance, and
among the rest to have good respect to her diet,
which is meet to be pure, well prepared, drest, and
served with comfortable, joyous, and merry communication, in all honourable and virtuous manner.
Likewise, the cleanliness and well-wearing of her
garments and apparel, both of her chamber and
person, so that everything about her be pure, sweet,
clean, and wholesome, as to so great a princess
doth appertain ; all corruptions, evil airs, and
things noisome and unpleasant, to be eschewed."

"It hath been asserted," says Miss Strickland,
" by all contemporaries, that Queen Katharine, at
one time of her life, cherished an ardent desire
that her daughter Mary should be united in
marriage with Reginald Pole, son of the Countess
of Salisbury, the noble kinswoman who had constantly resided with the young princess. All the
biographies of Reginald Pole declare that Mary
manifested the greatest partiality to him from her
earliest childhood. This might have been ; yet
the difference of their ages, Reginald being born
in 1500, was too great for any partiality to have
subsisted between them, in early life, as lovers.
While there was hope of her daughter becoming
the wife of the Emperor, it was not probable that
Queen Katharine, who loved her nephew exceedingly, could have wished her to marry Reginald
Pole. But when Reginald returned to England at
the same time that the imperial match was broken
off, and appeared in her court, in his twenty-fifth
year, possessing the highest cultivation of mind,
and the grandest person and features, of that
perfect mould of beauty which revived the memory
of the heroic Plantagenets, his ancestors, it is
possible that the wise Queen, weighing the disad-
vantages of wedlock with a foreign monarch,
might wish her Mary united to such a protector.
The match would have been highly popular among
the English, as the national love for the memory
of the Plantagenet kings was only equalled by the
intense national jealousy of foreign alliances;
besides which the personal qualities of Reginald
rendered him the pride of his country. He had,
however a mistrust of the atmosphere of the
English court, as portentous of storm and change ;
he reminded his royal relatives that he had been
educated for the Church, and withdrew himself into

the seclusion of the Carthusian Convent of Sion. Here Reginald abstracted himself from the world, by sedulous attention to books, but it was observed that he neither took priest's orders nor monastic vows."

But we must turn from the pleasant details of Katharine's love and care for her precious only child to matters which concerned her as deeply, but which, alas! were cruelly different to those fond cares of motherhood. Hitherto, in spite of the loss of her children, she had been an exceptionally happy Queen. Though not immaculate, Henry had given her but little cause for grief or jealousy, in comparison with the conduct of many other monarchs; and she had the good fortune to have gained not only his love, but his respect—the first and last woman who ever did so. For nearly twenty years she had been a beloved and honoured wife, a noble and respected queen ; her daughter, acknowledged as the heiress of England, was growing into girlhood; her passionately-loved husband was still, to all appearance, kind and loving to her ; when the cloud came down upon her that was to ruin her fame, to break her heart, and, bitterest of all, to taint her daughter's name.

Who first whispered the possibility of a divorce, must always remain a mystery. For the honour of mankind, we must hope that the oft repeated assertion that the King, already captivated by Anne Boleyn's charms, hit on this expedient for removing Katharine, is false ; but whether another version, that Henry, conscience-stricken, consulted his confessor, Dr. Longland, and heard from him that his scruples were correct, we cannot tell. "The truth is," says Holinshed, "that whether this doubt was first moved by the Cardinal

[Wolsey], or by the said Longland, being the King's confessor, the King was not only brought in doubt, whether it was a lawful marriage or no, but also determined to have the case examined, cleared, and adjudged by learning, law, and sufficient authority. The Cardinal verily was put most in blame for this scruple now cast into the King's conscience; for the hate he bare to the Emperor, because he would not grant to him the archbishopric of Toledo, for the which he was a suitor, and therefore he did not only prevent the King of England to join in friendship with the French King, but also sought a divorce betwixt the King and the Queen, that the King might have in marriage the Duchess of Alençon, sister to the French King, and, as some have thought, he travailed in that matter with the French King at Amiens, but the Duchess would not give ear thereto." Probably this was really the commencement of the case; and the King's confession of doubts and misgivings to Longland most likely occurred after the wily Cardinal had first whispered his crafty words in his ear. To do Wolsey justice, it is unlikely that any personal grudge against Charles V., such as that mentioned by Holinshed, was the sole cause of his scheming. No doubt, arrogant and ambitious as he was, it rendered him more eager in his movements; but, in spite of his many faults, he was really loyal and patriotic enough to honestly strive for the welfare of the King and the country, and he seems to have sincerely believed that such a move would be a benefit to both, heedless that it would be doing evil that good might come, and ignorant that it would strike the first blow at his own safety. How, in all likelihood, the beginning was made of that debate which broke the Queen's heart and shortened her life, Miss Yonge tells in the following words :—

"Mary Tudor remained the only child of her parents, and her sex was beginning to be felt as a great misfortune. To marry her to a subject would be to aggrandize one family, and make all the others jealous; and to give her to a foreign prince might lead to England being swamped in some great continental power. Therefore, Cardinal Wolsey recollected with satisfaction that Queen Katharine's former espousals with Prince Arthur might form a pretext for declaring the marriage with the King as invalid, and thus leaving him free to take another wife, with more hope of male offspring. It was true that the wedding had only been the outward ceremony often performed to bind children together, and that a dispensation had been duly obtained for her wedlock with Henry; but such dispensations had often been given, and as often set aside when reasons of state made an excuse convenient for putting asunder what God had joined together; and Wolsey expected no scruples from the Pope that could not be overcome by a handsome bribe, while as to the King, he had already shown inconsistency to the Queen by admiration of more than one lady of the court, and was likely to be pleased to be free to marry a younger bride. Little did Wolsey think, when he thus conceived a cruel and godless expedient of state policy, what a stone he set rolling, and how he would be one of the first it would overwhelm! Meantime the ratification of the Holy League in the early spring of 1527, brought two French Ambassadors to England, who proposed that Mary should be married either to King Francis himself or to his second son, Henri, Duke of Orleans, not to the

Dauphin, because it was the great object to prevent England being united with France. All went smoothly, when in the midst the Bishop of Tarbes, without orders from his master, asked Henry and the Cardinal if the Princess's legitimacy was beyond a doubt. There is very little question but that Wolsey thought this was the best way of suggesting his plan to the King. However, he pretended that it was the shock to him that it really was to Henry."

A magnificent entertainment was given to the two French Ambassadors at Greenwich, May 5th, 1527, by way of farewell; first a tournament, where three hundred lances were broken, a supper, and a dance, when the King, Turenne, and four other gentlemen, were habited as Venetians, and selected each a lady for his partner. Henry chose the lady whose name is inextricably connected with his own—one of the Queen's maids of honour, Anne Boleyn.

It was not the first time he had met her. She had returned from France some five or six years before, and had had a little romance which, through Wolsey's interference, had been nipped untimely in the bud—a love-affair with Earl Percy, Northumberland's heir. He had been made to break his troth and marry another; and Anne never forgot or forgave the Cardinal who had marred her early dream. Her father was Sir Thomas Boleyn, her mother Lady Elizabeth Howard, daughter of the Duke of Norfolk; and she was a wonderfully attractive creature, not lovely, but with a fascination more powerful than beauty, and with all her natural gifts refined and heightened by her French education. "She possessed," says Chateaubriant, "a great talent for poetry, and when she sang, like a second

Orpheus, she would have made bears and wolves attentive. She likewise danced the English dances, leaping and jumping with infinite grace and agility. Moreover, she invented many new figures and steps, which are yet known by her name, or by those of the gallant partners with whom she danced them. She was well skilled in all games fashionable at Courts. Besides singing like a syren, accompanying herself on the lute, she harped better than King David, and handled cleverly both lute and rebec. She dressed with marvellous taste, and devised new modes, which were followed by the fairest ladies of the French Court, but none wore them with her gracefulness, in which she rivalled Venus." Even her devoted admirer, Wyat, could hardly call her beautiful, though he extolled " her favour, passing sweet and cheerful," and remarked that " in this noble imp, the graces of nature, adorned by gracious education, seemed even at the first to have promised bliss unto her in after times." Saunders gives a picture of her that shows her charms must have been more those of vivacity and grace than actual comeliness. " Anne Boleyn was in stature rather tall and slender, with an oval face, black hair, and a complexion inclining to sallow; one of her upper teeth projected a little. She appeared at times to suffer from asthma. On her left hand a sixth finger might be perceived. On her throat there was a protuberance, which Chateaubriant describes as a disagreeably large mole, resembling a strawberry; this she carefully covered with an ornamented collar band, a fashion which was blindly imitated by the rest of the maids of honour, though they had never before thought of wearing anything of the kind. Her face and figure were in other respects symmetrical; beauty and sprightliness sat on her lips; in readiness of repartee, skill in the dance, and in playing on the lute, she was unsurpassed." The King was said to have met her some time previously at her father's place, Hever Castle, in Kent; and to have declared she had the wit of an angel; and Wolsey, who thought his admiration one of the passing follies of royalty, was quite ready to give him opportunities of meeting her at his masques and banquets. Anne herself, fond of admiration, excitable, with a dangerous love of coquetry, and yet with quite enough prudence to refuse any overtures but those which pointed to ring and crown, received the royal attention readily. With all her outward polish, there was a curious lack of true refinement in her nature, which made her willing to encourage her mistress's husband in his pursuit of her. Hepworth Dixon pleads in her behalf that her family had always regarded the Queen's union as illegal, and that she had imbibed their views; but even if this were so, no really modest woman would have given countenance to attentions which, as she knew, must mean either an insult to herself or a cruel repudiation of the royal lady whom she served. "Your wife I cannot be," she told the King, "both in respect of my unworthiness, and also because you have a Queen. Your mistress I will never be." The speech sounds noble and spirited; but our admiration is lessened when we find that she still allowed his wooing, and received and answered enthusiastic love-letters, in which she figures as the King's "darling" and "sweetheart," and he as her "servant and friend." As Miss Strickland says, "it is difficult to imagine any woman of honourable principles receiving and treasuring such letters from a married man."

Perhaps it was the remembrance of Anne's determined words that made Henry willing to follow Wolsey's lead in consulting his council about what was called " the King's secret matter " —the question of the validity of his marriage. Wolsey was anxious to press on the conclusion of the case, and see his master wedded to Renée of France ; never dreaming of the possibility of the maid of honour being elevated to the throne. The Cardinal had long kept spies near the Queen's person. " If the Queen," says Tindal, " was intimate with any lady, to that person he was familiar in his conversation and liberal in gifts, in order to make her reveal all she said and did. I know one lady who left the Court, for no other reason than that she would no longer betray her majesty." But, in spite of all his spies, he could never learn how news of " the secret matter " then under debate came to Katharine's ears. Only a day or two after the banquet at which the fair Boleyn had completed her conquest of the already fascinated Henry, the Queen wrote to her nephew the Emperor. " She does not," says M. du Boys, " venture upon the question of the divorce ; but her deep mental grief may be perceived."

" MOST HIGH AND POWERFUL LORD,

" I hardly know how to confess the many obligations in which I stand towards your Highness for the many favours conferred upon me. I hold it to be that your Highness has chosen to show sorrow for my death, perceiving that neither my existence nor my services are such as to deserve being recalled to your memory. And yet, trusting in your Highness's innate kindness and virtue, I will, with the help of God, employ my life in the furtherance of those objects which may be for your Highness's service, though my abilities be scanty and my powers small.

" As Francisco Poynes, gentleman, and esquire of the household of the King my lord, bearer of this letter, will inform your Highness, I take this opportunity to write and request that he may be credited in whatever he may say in my name; the said Poynes being a person whom I entirely trust, and to whom I bear much goodwill, and am, besides, under great obligations on account of his many virtues.

" As I fear that my letter may be tedious to your Highness, as written by one inexperienced in these matters, I shall say no more here than try and entreat your Highness to have pity on so much bloodshed and perdition of souls, so costly, and redeemed at such a price; bearing in mind that this world is perishable and of short duration, and the next one eternal. There is urgent need that peace between Christian princes be concluded before God sends down his scourge, which cannot tarry if these quarrels and disagreements continue between Christian princes.

" If, in the expression of these my sentiments, I have given the least offence, I beg your Highness to pardon me; my ignorance alone is the cause. God, etc.

" Your good Aunt,
" CATHARINE.
" Grannuiche [Greenwich], 10th of May."

Growing more alarmed as time went on, the Queen, with both her own right and her child's to defend, took prompt measures. She despatched her trusty servant, Francisco Felipo, whose name had been anglicized as Francis Phillipps, into Spain, ostensibly to see his mother, but really to bear

a letter to her nephew the Emperor.   Wolsey
heard of her intentions, and did his best to prevent
the journey.   " He feigns to go," he wrote to the
King, " to visit his mother, now sickly and aged ;
but your Highness taketh it surely in the right
that it is chiefly for disclosing your secret matter
to the Emperor, and to devise means and ways
how it may be impeached.   Wherefore your
Highness hath right prudently devised so that
his passage into Spain should be letted and stopped;
for if the said matter should come to the Emperor's
ears, it should be no little hindrance to your
grace's particulars ; howbeit, if he pass by sea
there can be nothing devised."   In spite of King
and Cardinal, however, Felipo accomplished his
mission, and placed the letter in the Emperor's
hands.   Charles, indignant at the meditated
insult to his aunt, and uneasy also on account of
political considerations, wrote at once to his
ambassador in London.   " It is not our intention
to desert her," he said ; " on the contrary, we
mean to do what we can in her behalf. . . . .
Entreat his Highness to take what we say in good
part, as coming from our love, and from our
sense of what is best for him and for ourselves ;
to put an end, as soon as may be, for the honour
and service of God, to this affair ; and to arrange
the matter with as much reserve and secrecy as it
demands."

Her nephew was not the only one to whom
the Queen appealed.   She turned for help to
Fisher, Bishop of Rochester, her confessor, and
one of her staunchest friends ; and then she resolved to speak to her husband himself.   Perhaps
the King had enough of his old tenderness for
her left to wish to cause her as little pain as
possible; at all events, he made light of the

matter to her, and assured her it was but a mere
formal inquiry, instituted to set at rest for ever
all doubt of Mary's legitimacy; and after what
one old chronicler calls " a brief tragedy," she
allowed herself to be soothed into tranquility.
Wolsey, in a letter to the King, makes some
mention of the interview. "The first night," he
writes, " I lodged at Sir John Wiltshire's house,
where met me my lord of Canterbury [Warham],
with whom, after communication on your grace's
secret matter, I showed him that the knowledge
thereof is come to the Queen's grace, and how dis-
pleasantly she taketh it, and what your Highness
hath done for the staying and pacificaiton of her,
by declaring to her that your grace hath nothing
intended nor done, but only for the searching
and trying out of the truth upon occasion given
by the doubts moved by the Bishop of Tarbes.
And noting his countenance, gesture, and manner,
I perceive he is not much altered from his first
fashion; expressly affirming that, however dis-
pleasantly the Queen might take it, yet the truth
and judgment of the law must have place. He
somewhat marvelled how the Queen should come to
the knowledge thereof, and by whom, thinking your
grace might constrain her to show her informers."

Growing more infatuated with Anne Boleyn
every day, and, there is little doubt, strongly
urged forward in the prosecution of the " secret
matter " by his inamorata, Henry resolved on
explaining all his real or pretended scruples to
Katharine; perhaps hoping that her scrupulous
conscience might be so impressed by his arguments that she would consent to a separation
with very little trouble. " The King," says M.
du Boys, " having virtually separated from the
Queen from the date of the 20th or 22nd of June,

gave her his reasons for this determination by revealing to her for the first time that they had both been in a state of mortal sin all the long years they had lived together. This was, he said, the opinion of many prelates and men learned in the canon law whom he had consulted; and, therefore, as the continuance of such a life troubled, and even tortured, his conscience, he had taken the unalterable resolution of obtaining a separation from her, *a mensa et thoro,* so she had only to name the place where she would take refuge."

Mendoza, the imperial ambassador, sent the Emperor an account of this interview, in a despatch written July 13th, 1527. "The Queen, bursting into tears, and being too much agitated to reply, the King said to her, by way of consolation, that all should be done for the best, and begged her to keep secrecy upon what he had told her. This the King must have said, as it is generally believed, to inspire her with confidence, and prevent her seeking the redress she is entitled to; for so great is the attachment that the English bear to the Queen that some demonstration would probably take place in her household. Not that the people of England are ignorant of the King's intentions, for the affair is as notorious as if it had been proclaimed by the public crier, but they cannot believe that he will ever carry so wicked a purpose into effect. However this may be, though people say that such an iniquity cannot be tolerated, he (Mendoza) attaches no faith to such popular asseverations, especially as they have no leader to guide them, and, therefore, should the King carry out his design, and the suit now commenced go on, the people will most probably content themselves with grumbling."

Hearing that the Queen had sought the counsel of Fisher, Wolsey spoke of the matter to him, and would fain have persuaded him that her cause was hopeless, and her marriage illegal; but the resolute old Bishop, in no wise daunted by the Cardinal's pride of speech, or haughtiness of demeanour, kept to his own opinion. " On looking into such authorities as lie at hand," he said, " I find they differ very much ; some holding that the thing is not lawful, others that it is. On full reflection, I see an easy answer to the first, and none at all to the second. It is not, I think, clearly forbidden by the Divine law for a brother to marry the wife of a childless brother; and considering the plenary power given by our Lord to the Pope, who can deny that the Pope can grant a dispensation for any serious cause? Even if the arguments were balanced, my opinion would be that since it is the Pope's province to clear ambiguous passages of Scripture, his decision rules the question. I have no scruple in asserting that the dispensation lies within the papal power." But Fisher's honest opinion was of little use to Queen Katharine; for both King and Cardinal were determined the divorce *should* be right.

In the midst of her distress, the Queen found some comfort in an affectionate and encouraging letter from Charles V.:—

" MADAME AND MY AUNT,

" Your letter by Francisco Phs [Phillipps], bearer of this present, came duly to hand. I have perfectly well understood the verbal message he brought from you respecting the affair [of the divorce], and the reason why you sent him to me. After him came your own physician, Vitoria, with whom I had also a long conversation on the subject. You may well imagine the pain this intelligence caused me, and how much I felt for you. I cannot express it otherwise than by assuring you that, were my own mother concerned, I should not experience greater sorrow than in this, your case, for the love and affection which I profess to your serene Highness is certainly of the same kind as that of a son towards his parent.

"I have immediately set about taking the necessary steps for the remedy [of your case], and you may be certain that nothing shall be omitted on my part to help you in your present tribulation. But it seems to me that in the meantime your serene Highness ought not to take this thing so much to heart as to let it impair your bodily health, for, if this is preserved, all other matters will be remedied, with God's help. I beg you to bear in mind this my recommendation, and I have no doubt that in this, as in other matters, your serene Highness will act much better than I could counsel. As I do, however, presume that before the receipt of this my letter you will have heard my intentions through Don Inigo de Mendoza, I shall say no more here than to refer you to my letter to that ambassador, as well as to the message now conveyed by the abovementioned Francisco, which is, no doubt, what your serene Highness most wishes to know. Most earnestly entreating you to inform me as soon as possible of the course of this affair, that I may do all that is necessary for your protection, as well as of your health, I remain, etc.,

"In the hand of your good nephew,

"CHARLES.

"Valencia, the 27th of August."

In the early part of 1528, the King and Cardinal made another move. "Wolsey sent a learned ecclesiastical lawyer, Stephen Gardiner, with Edward Fox, the King's almoner, to Orvieto, to demand of Pope Clement V. what was called a decretal bull—namely, a sentence on his own authority that the command in the law of Moses forbidding a man to marry his brother's widow, was, like the great moral law, so binding that the dispensation of Julius II. was null and void, so as to prevent the long delay of the regular trial of the case before the two Cardinals—which, as Henry apprehended, might last far beyond his lifetime. But for one Pope to reverse the formal sanction of another would have been contrary to all precedent, unless there could be proved to have been false evidence laid before the first; and Gardiner could only obtain that the commission to examine should at once be set forth, and empowered to separate the parties if expedient."*

Even had he wished, the Pope would hardly have dared to act more decisively in the matter for fear of offending the Emperor; but the answer given appeared to satisfy Henry, who requested that Cardinal Campéggio should be joined with Wolsey in the inquiry. This Cardinal held the Bishopric of Salisbury, and the King hoped to easily induce him to give judgment on his side; and Anne Boleyn showed exultation at once premature and unwomanly. But now Wolsey, who had all along been so eager in the cause, began to hesitate and waver. For the first time he seems to have perceived that, if the divorce were granted, no French Princess, but Anne Boleyn, of whose bitter enmity to himself he was

* C. M Yonge.

well aware, in spite of the dissimulation she had
practised while he seemed a likely person to
smooth her way, would become Queen of England.
He tried to check the King's eagerness, telling
him that it was a matter of conscience, and that,
if he honestly thought his marriage valid, he
ought not to seek for it to be annulled; but
Henry, utterly enthralled by Anne Boleyn's charms,
received his speeches with a burst of anger, and
Wolsey comprehended on what very slippery
ground he stood.   To obtain the divorce on
which the King had set his heart was the only
thing that would secure his safety; and this
accordingly he strove to do. " He sent off fresh
letters to Rome, beseeching the Pope to save him
from ruin by signing the decretal bull, promising
to conceal it from everyone but the King. The
Pope was very unwilling; but Gardiner and the
other English emissaries harassed him unceasingly,
and at last he signed it, giving it, however, to
Cardinal Campeggio, with orders never to let it out
of his own possession, but to read it to the King
and Cardinal and then burn it. The fact seems to
have been that Wolsey wanted the bull to set his
own conscience at rest; but after all, it could say
no more than that if Katharine had been Arthur's
wife she could not be Henry's, and the whole
matter turned on whether they had been mere
children or really husband and wife."*

Campeggio, although believed by the King to
be likely to be favourable to him, was really
inclined to the Queen's side, and this view was
backed by the strong influence of the Emperor;
and thus he delayed his journey to England on
various pleas of illness, leaving Henry and Anne
in the utmost impatience. While the matter was

* C. M. Yonge.

thus pending, the Queen was treated with all respect and honour; and her unfortunate daughter was still regarded as the heiress of the kingdom. The King seemed much perplexed with regard to this latter. Until another child was born, she was his only heir; and he wished to have her looked upon as legitimate, while at the same time he was feverishly anxious to have his marriage with her mother declared null and void. She was very popular with the people, who declared " that King Henry might marry whom he would, yet they would acknowledge no successor to the crown but the husband of the Lady Mary,"* and expressed their affection for her, and indignation against Wolsey as the originator of the divorce, in lines of more genuine heartiness than poetry :—

> Yea, a princess whom to describe
> It were hard for an orator;
> She is but a child in age,
> And yet she is both wise and sage—
> And beautiful in favour.

> Perfectly doth she represent
> The singular graces excellent
> Both of her father and mother.
> Howbeit, this disregarding,
> The carter of York is meddling
> For to divorce them asunder.

The following rhymes, celebrating the dancing together of the young princess and her royal sire were probably written not later than this year :—

> Ravished I was, that well was me,
> O Lord! to me so fain,
> To see that sight that I did see
> I long full sore again.

> I saw a king and a princess
> Dancing before my face,
> Most like a god and a goddess,
> (I pray Christ save their grace!)

* Hall.

This king to see whom we have sung,
        His virtues be right much,
But this princess, being so young,
        There can be found none such.

So *facund* fair she is to see,
        Like to her is none of her age,
Withouten grace it cannot be
        So young to be so sage.

This king to see with his fair flower,
        The mother standing by,
It doth me good, yet at this hour,
        On them when that think I.

I pray Christ save father and mother,
        And this young lady fair,
And send her shortly a brother,
        To be England's *right* heir.

It will be seen by this specimen that courtly versifiers of Tudor times possessed fully as much adulatory instinct, if not quite the same amount of poetical polish, as those of our more enlightened age.

The Queen behaved all through this bitter time of doubt and hesitation, while her husband was writing vehement love-letters to another woman, and striving his utmost to be rid of her, with singular dignity and endurance, and indeed with a meekness hardly to be expected from a daughter of Castile, which made Cavendish liken her to " a very patient Grissel." With her rival she condescended to no reproof or altercation, and is only known once to have made any allusion to Anne Boleyn's position. They were playing cards together, and the Queen addressed her. " My Lady Anne, you have the good hap ever to stop at a king; but you are like others, you will have all or none." Shakespeare makes Anne speak pityingly and gently of the Queen—

So good a lady that no tongue could ever
Pronounce dishonour of her,—by my life,
She never knew harm-doing;—O now, after
So many courses of the same enthron'd,
Still growing in a majesty and pomp,—the which
To leave's a thousandfold more bitter, than
'Tis sweet at first to acquire,—after this process,
To give her the avaunt ! it is a pity
Would move a monster.

And Wyat, her poet adorer, mentions that "the love she bare ever to the Queen," made her unwilling to usurp her mistress's place; but both dramatist and lover flattered the lady by ascribing to her virtues she did not possess ; for in truth Anne seems to have had little heed of aught but the following out of her own ambition.

CHAPTER V.

Illness of Anne Boleyn—The King's letters to her—Letter of Erasmus to Katharine—Arrival of Campeggio—Interviews of the Queen and Cardinal—Address of the Council to the King—Conversation between the King and Queen—The King's address at Bridewell—Audience of Wolsey and Campeggio with the Queen—Warham and Tunstall question Katharine—The brief of dispensation—Henry's embassy to the Pope—Exhibition of the brief to the English ambassadors—Katharine's letter to Muxetula—Henry's treatment of the Queen—Splendour of Anne Boleyn—Letter of the Emperor to Katharine—The court of inquiry—The Queen's speech—Her popularity—Her reception of Wolsey and Campeggio—Letter of the English nobles to the Pope—His reply—Adjournment of the court of inquiry—Fall of Wolsey—Letter of the Queen—Thomas Cranmer—His Embassy to the Pope—Bribery of the French Universities—Christmas at Greenwich—Illness of the Princess Mary.

IN the summer the terrible epidemic known as the sweating sickness broke out in England. The Queen and the Princess Mary were with the King at Greenwich for the mayings—mayings, alas, sadly different to the gladsome festivals of Katharine's early wedded life—when it first appeared; but they quickly removed to Tittenhanger, where the King, in a fit of compunction, shared the Queen's devotions, made thirty-nine wills, and turned his attention to the compounding of quack medicines. Anne Boleyn had gone to Hever Castle, where both she and her father were attacked by the plague; and she was for some days in great danger. Henry's pretence was not so profound as to prevent him sending the tenderest of notes to his "entirely beloved," and reminding her that, "wherever he was, he was hers," and that "the anguish of absence is so great, that it would be intolerable, were it not for the firm hope he has of her indissoluble affection towards him." One can but think a little curiously, as one reads the words, of the equanimity with which he bore the final parting with her, consummated by the headsman's sword.

Campeggio, unwilling as he was, had been obliged to set forth for England; and Anne Boleyn was impatient for tidings of his coming. Henry, no less anxious than she, answered her "reasonable requests" for news. "The legate, which we most desire, arrived at Paris on Sunday or Monday last past, so that I trust by next Monday to hear of his arrival at Calais; and then I trust, within a little while after to enjoy that which I have so long longed for, to God's pleasure and both our comforts. No more to you at this present, mine own darling, for lack of time; but that I would you were in my arms, and I in yours, for I think it long since I kissed you."

With the husband whom, to her unhappiness, she loved as deeply as ever, thus madly pursuing another—with her name and rank questioned, her title of wife doubted, her child looked on as of doubtful birth—Katharine must have sorely needed the consoling words sent her by Erasmus in the previous spring. " It is most rare to find a lady born and reared in courts, who binds her hope on acts of devotion, and finds her solace in the word of God. Would that others, more especially widows, would learn to follow your example; and not widows only, but unmarried ladies too, for what so good as the service of Christ? He is the Rock—the spouse of pious souls—and nearer than the nearest human tie. A soul devoted to this Husband is at peace, alike in good and evil times. He knows what is best for all; and is often kindest when He seems to turn the honey into gall. Every one has His cross to bear; without that cross no soul can enter into rest!"

At last, late in the autumn, Campeggio arrived. "Now I hear that Cardinal Campeggio is going to England," wrote the Emperor to his aunt on the 1st of September, "but I am certain, because the Pope writes me so, that nothing will be done to your detriment, and that the whole case will be referred to him at Rome, the Cardinal's secret mission being to advise the King, your husband, to do his duty." As we have seen, Campeggio was averse to a question of divorce; but he sought to cut the Gordian knot by striving to persuade the Queen to enter a convent, and he exerted himself to the utmost to induce her to do so at their first interview on October 22nd. It would have been much the shortest way out of the difficulty, and, if she would consent, the King was ready to allow her to retain her rents, pensions, and ornaments, and the title of Queen, and to pronounce her daughter heiress of England in the absence of heirs male. But Katharine, with her own honour and her child's rights to defend, though far too dignified to be demonstrative, was firm as adamant. "I know, most reverend lord," she said to the Cardinal, "the sincerity of my own heart. I wish to die in the Holy Faith, and in obedience to God and His Church; but I desire to state the business to His Holiness. I have heard you would persuade me to enter a religious house?" Campeggio did his best to enforce that persuasion. "By so doing," he answered, "your Majesty will satisfy God, preserve your conscience, and sustain the glory of your name. You will avoid public scandal, retain your dowry, and support your daughter's rights." "I enforce these arguments," writes the legate, "by the example of a Queen of France who did the same, and is still honoured by God and that kingdom. The same arguments were enforced by the Cardinal of York, who begged her to ponder them well, and hoped she would resolve for the best. Then he ventured to mention Henry's conscientious scruples to her, to be taken into account. That, since her Highness had already reached the third and last period of natural life, and had spent the first two setting a good example of virtue to the world, she would thus put a seal to all the good actions of her life, and would besides, prevent, by such religious profession, the many and incalculable evils likely to arise from such matrimonial discord."

The Queen, at the conclusion of this exhortation, which must surely have tried her patience to the utmost, at first turned angrily to Wolsey, implying that she looked on him as the author of all her misfortunes ; but presently she regained all her wonted calm, and addressed the legate with her accustomed dignity. "She held," she said, "her husband's conscience and honour in more esteem than anything else in this world, but that as she entertained no scruple at all about her marriage, but considered herself the true and legitimate wife of the King her husband, the proposal just made in the name of his Holiness was inadmissible. She knew for certain that if his Holiness, instead of listening to the arguments and suggestions of her enemies, had heard what she had to say in her defence, such a proposal would never have been made. She was, however, so dutiful a daughter of the Church that nothing would make her swerve from the path of obedience. So we left her, assuring us that she would make known to our lord (the Pope) the sincerity of her conscience. To this I replied that I had been sent by the Pope to hear whatever she chose to explain to me, and I would faithfully report to him my opinion, and by his reply she would learn that I had done my duty sincerely. She concluded the conference by saying she was a lone woman and a stranger, without friend or adviser, and intended to ask the King for councillors, when she would give us audience." The legate was obliged to leave her unconvinced. No argument prevailed with Katharine. With all the dauntlessness and high spirit of her Castilian birth, she would maintain her own rights and her daughter's to the last.

" Soon after a remarkable incident took place ; the Queen, with the King's permission, requested Campeggio to hear her confess, and the legate thought he ought not to refuse. While Katharine found in this the means of quieting her conscience, her intention was to inform the Cardinal legate, who was to be her judge as well as confessor, of several of the details of her private life that he could not have suspected. She wanted to lay bare her whole soul before him. It was the best way— she saw it instinctively—to gain and keep his confidence. At the end she released him from the absolute secrecy that should have enfolded the information of the confessional, and, indeed, formally requested him to communicate it to the sovereign pontiff. The precise information she gave concerning her former marriage could leave no doubt upon Campeggio's mind as to the nature of her relations with Prince Arthur. At the end of this confidential conference she insisted that everything should be judicially decided, and she assured Campeggio that, if a legal and final decision were given annulling her marriage, and sanctioned by the Pope, she would submit, and look upon herself

as free as Henry VIII. himself." * The Cardinal
again tried to induce her to enter some convent of
St. Clare.

" Never ! " said the Queen ; " I will never do it.
I will die as I have lived, in that estate of matrimony to which God has called me." " The Italian
hoped she would relent. Hinting that some of
her friends were indiscreet, and that the Council
might indite them for conspiracy to imagine the
King's death, he tried to frighten her by saying
the charge would ruin her, whether she were guilty
or not guilty. Death by the axe might be her
sentence. Mary would be buried in a convent.
Surely she would change her attitude ! ' No,'
said Katharine, with a slow and solid emphasis, ' I
shall never change.' In vain Campeggio pointed
out how much her obstinacy would hurt her
nephew and disturb the Church. A sense of
personal injury buoyed her up. The question
should be tried; the world should know her
wrongs.

" If judgment passed against her marriage, she
would be free, even as the King was free. Change
that opinion? Never! If the greatest punish-
ment were threatened she would never flinch.
Were she condemned to be torn limb from limb
she would not alter; nay, if after death she could
return to life, rather than change, she would prefer to die again. So said the Queen."† " I
assure you," writes Campeggio, " that from all her
conversation and discourse, I have always judged
her to be a prudent lady, and now more so. But
as she can without prejudice, as I have said above,
avoid such perils and difficulties, her obstinacy in
not accepting this sound counsel does not much
please me."

* M. du Boys.   † Hepworth Dixon.

That Campeggio's warning to the Queen was not given without ample foundation is evident from an address from his obsequious council to the King. "They were informed," it ran, "of a design to kill the King and the cardinals, in which conspiracy, if it could be proved the Queen had any hand, she must not expect to be spared. That she had not shown either in public, or in the hours of retirement, as much love for the King as she ought; and, now that the King was very pensive, she manifested great signs of joy, setting all people to dancing and other diversions. This she did out of spite to the King, as it was contrary to her temper and ordinary behaviour. She showed herself much abroad, too, and by civilities and gracious bowing of her head (which was not her custom formerly), she sought to work upon the affections of the people. From all which the King concluded that she hated him. Therefore, as his council in their consciences thought his life was in danger, they advised him to separate himself from the Queen, both at bed and board, and, above all, to take the Princess Mary from her."

A few days later Henry himself had another interview with his wife, and told her that "she was not married to him, and that all the priests of England had subscribed a declaration to that effect with their own names. The Pope had condemned her at Rome, and the legate Campeggio had come for the sole purpose of having the sentence executed." "How," asked Katharine, "can the Pope condemn me without a hearing?" "The Emperor has answered for you," said the King, "and consequently the Pope has decided against you." He added, after various other incorrect statements, that he advised her to embrace a religious life voluntarily, as otherwise she would be compelled to do so. Tears came into the Queen's eyes. "May God forbid," she cried, "my being the cause of that being done, which is so much against my soul, my conscience, and my honour! I know very well that if the judges are impartial, and I am granted a hearing, my cause is gained, for no judge will be found unjust enough to condemn me." She begged that she might be allowed to plead her own cause. "I am quite willing," said the King, "that it should be so. A counsel shall be appointed for your defence, and, moreover, you may send to Flanders for a jurist; but this must be done forthwith, for the affair admits of no delay."

After twenty years of married life, it was remarkable that the royal conscience should have suddenly grown so tender that any delay in the effort to cast off the faithful wife should be inadmissible. The poor Queen, however, was glad of the concession, and wrote at once to Margaret, Regent of the Netherlands, to provide her with two skilled lawyers.

As Katharine steadily refused to cut the matter short by retiring into a convent, a court of inquiry had perforce to be held. She chose as her counsellors Warham, Fisher, Clerk, and Tunstall, and she was also allowed to send for Vives, whom, in happier days, she had consulted concerning the education of her child. He came to her, and undertook to write in defence of her position. But, ere the formal court was opened, Henry held a meeting on his own account. Assembling all his council, nobility, and judges, in the great hall at Bridewell Palace, the King made a long statement to them. "Our trusty and well-beloved subjects," he began, "it is not unknown to you how we have reigned over this realm for nearly twenty years,

during which time we have so ordered us, thanked
be God, that no outward enemy hath oppressed
you or taken anything from you; but when we
remember that we must die, we think that all our
doings in our lifetime are effaced, if we leave you
in trouble at the time of our death." After this
rather hypocritical prelude, in which, be it noticed,
all mention of Anne Boleyn is studiously ignored,
he proceeded to inform them of his doubts of the
validity of his marriage. "If it be adjudged," he
hastened to add, "that the Queen is my lawful
wife, nothing will be more pleasant or more
acceptable to me, both for the clearing of my conscience, and also for the good qualities and con-
ditions I know to be in her. For I assure you all,
that besides her noble parentage, she is a woman
of most gentleness, humility, and buxomness; yea,
and of all good qualities pertaining to nobility she
is without comparison. So that if I were to marry
again I would choose her above all women. But
if it is determined in judgment that our marriage
is against God's law, then shall I sorrow parting
from so good a lady and loving companion. These
be the sores that vex my mind! These be the
pangs that trouble my conscience, for the declaration of which I have assembled you together. And
now you may depart." His "well-beloved subjects" received this communication in various
ways. Some grieved that the King was troubled
in his conscience; some regretted that aught
should arise inimical to the Queen; and some said
nothing, probable wondering by what strange com-
bination of circumstances so affectionate and
conscientious a husband could by any possibility
appear as the ardent lover of Anne Boleyn.

A few days later both the cardinal legates,
Wolsey and Campeggio, had an audience of the

KATHARINE OF ARAGON. 43

Queen at the same palace, and announced to her that the court of inquiry was about to be held. Katharine answered them in words which, says Hall, " were spoken in French, and written down by Campeggio's secretary, who was present, and then I translated them as well as I could."

" Alas! my lord," said she, " is it now a question whether I be the King's lawful wife or no, when I have been married to him almost twenty years and no objection made before? Divers prelates and lords, privy councillors of the King, are yet alive who then adjudged our marriage good and lawful; and now to say it is detestable is a great marvel to me, especially when I consider what a wise prince the King's father was, and also the natural love and affection my father, King Ferdinand, bare unto me. I think that neither of our fathers were so unwise and weak in judgment, but they foresaw what would follow our marriage. The King, my father, sent to the Court of Rome, and there obtained a dispensation, that I, being the one brother's wife, might, without scruple of conscience, marry the other brother lawfully, which licence under lead [under leaden seal] I have yet to show, which makes me say and surely believe (as my first marriage was not completed) that my second is good and lawful. But of this trouble," she added, turning to Wolsey, " I may only thank you, my lord of York, because I ever wondered at your pride and vain glory, and abhorred your voluptuous life, and little cared for your presumption and tyranny, therefore of malice have you kindled this fire, especially for the great grudge you bear to my nephew the Emperor, whom you hate worse than a scorpion, because he would not gratify your ambition by making you Pope by force; and therefore have you said, more than once, you would trouble him and his friends—and you have kept him true promise; for of all his wars and vexations, he may thank only you. As for me, his poor aunt and kinswoman, what trouble you put me to by this new-found doubt, God knoweth, to whom I commit my cause."

Towards the end of October, "the Queen," says M. du Boys, " received a strange visit, and had to submit to an interrogatory that she was far from expecting.   As the legates, in their last conference with her, had asked for any papers she had in her possession which might be useful in her suit, she had given them a copy of the brief of dispensation [for her marriage with Henry VIII.], the original having been at the time sent to Queen Isabella of Castile.   Katharine had received this copy from Mendoza some time before.   In the month of October she gave audience to two prelates who had been named as her counsel—Warham, Archbishop of Canterbury, and Tunstall, Bishop of London, with some other persons of distinction.   They told her that two questions had been put to them by the other party, and that they were obliged to refer them to her.   Thereupon they had to ask her, first, whether she had desired the King's death, and had conspired against his life, so that she might be free, she herself and her daughter, to marry as they pleased; secondly, whether she had any special reason for not having sooner exhibited the brief of dispensation for her marriage which she had lately placed in the legates' hands, and wished to know how she had procured it.

" The answer was, as to the first question, ' that she could not imagine how such an abominable accusation could come from the King, her lord, for he well knew that she prized his life more than her own, and that therefore there was no need for

her to answer such a question as that; and respecting the copy of the brief of dispensation,
she had not exhibited it before because she had
never imagined that it would be required. As to
who had given it to her, she stated that Don Inigo
de Mendoza had sent it to her six months ago.'

"When the bishops had gone the Queen sent
Mendoza a message to tell him what had passed,
and, as she was not sure of the exact date when
the copy was given her, she told him what her
answer had been, so that, if he were asked, his
reply might agree with hers. This shows how
prudent Katharine was, cautious, and attentive to
the smallest circumstances; she would not expose
a flank in any quarter to her accusers. Mendoza
afterwards says :

"'The reason why they interrogated the Queen
as to whether it was true that she had attempted
the King's life, that she and her daughter, the
princess, might afterwards marry whomsoever they
pleased, was solely from the King's impatience to
have the separation hastily pronounced by Legate
Campeggio before proceedings had been even
commenced. Most likely the Queen's enemies
could not think of a more gratuitous or false
accusation to serve their purpose than to make
this King believe that he could not live with her
except at the risk of his life. So great, however,
are the avarice of the English people and the
King's violence, that I am very much afraid
witnesses will in the end be found to testify to
anything whatsoever. Your imperial Majesty
may judge how difficult the Queen's position is
when accused of the very crime which has perhaps
been attempted against her, and that in the name
of the King, her husband, who must know her
innocence.'"

In the same letter the imperial ambassador expresses his fear that Campeggio would be bribed by the King to give judgment in his favour. "For," he says, "though this King is generally very careful of his money, such is his passionate love for the Lady [Anne] that he will spare nothing to see his wishes accomplished, and will put all his fortune at stake." Henry did indeed offer the Cardinal the bishopric of Durham, but it was promptly declined; and, for a year after the refusal, the revenues, in all about twenty thousand pounds, were given by the enamoured monarch to Anne Boleyn. The Cardinal was found incorruptible, and therefore the objection to the brief produced by the Queen was fastened on with all the greater eagerness.

"We must first explain," says M. du Boys, "that the terms of the bull of dispensation granted by Julius II. had been held to be quite insufficient, and that Wolsey had contrived a fresh plan of attack on this ground. But the copy of the brief furnished by Katharine upset this plan completely, for the brief had provided for all the omissions of the bull. Neither the Cardinal nor Henry VIII. suspected that this document had been sent into Spain to Ferdinand and Isabella, and that the original was safe in Charles V.'s hands. Then the divines and doctors attendant on the King did not scruple to raise objections against the authenticity or fidelity of the copy produced by Katharine. They said that if the brief had really been the work of Julius II. a minute of it must be found on the registers in the Vatican, and the King sent instructions to his ambassadors to make inquiries for it; but in addition they said that the Emperor had only to send the original of the brief, as it was in his possession, to London, and an examination could be made whether it bore the marks of authenticity. Mendoza informed the Emperor of these fresh facts. He said some friends of the Queen were afraid that the last English ambassador sent to Rome in great haste, with his hands full of gold, might be intended to bribe the Cardinal datery [Giberto], and to purloin the register, or to falsify the original brief of dispensation, so as to destroy its force. He says:

" 'The Queen has sent me a message to this effect, requesting that I would communicate the intelligence to the Imperial ambassador at Rome. I have complied with her wishes and written to him [Muxetula], not by special messenger, owing to the roads in Italy being, as I am told, intercepted by the Venetians, but through a merchant of this place. May my letter reach him in safety, that the Imperial agents near the Pope may be warned against the designs of these people, who, after accusing the poor Queen of attempting the life of her husband, will not certainly scruple to falsify the draft of the dispensation brief, or cause the original register to be conveyed where it will never be found again. As I have said over and over again, had the attested copy arrived [from Spain], or were it to come soon, much mischief might be avoided; but such is the King's impatience, and the pressure he puts upon those who are conducting this affair, that I am very much afraid, unless at the moment I write the document is already on its way, it will come too late.'

" In another place he insists that the original of the brief must be carefully retained and preserved at Madrid. He thought that Henry VIII. would be capable of making it disappear as soon as he got it into his possession. He suggested that a new certified copy should be made in Spain in the presence of the ambassadors. Wolsey, on the other hand, wishing to procure the original document at any price, thought it would be a masterpiece of cleverness to get it demanded from Charles V. by the Queen herself. So he managed to indoctrinate her chief advisers, telling them that an inspection of the original of the brief would dissipate all doubts and prove its authenticity, and also that a simple copy would have no weight before a regular tribunal. The Queen's advisers, therefore, prepared a very curious document, published entire by Professor Brewer in his collection. They begun by repeating the arguments suggested by Wolsey, representing to their august client that, if she did not do as she was asked, she ran the risk of having her marriage annulled and her daughter declared illegitimate.

"'This may easily be done if you write to the Emperor that your counsel has shown you that the original of the brief must be produced. The lacking thereof might be the extreme ruin of your affairs, and no little danger to the inheritance of your child. You shall further say you have promised to exhibit the original here within three months; failing which, sentence will probably be given against you. If you do not succeed in this, it will be much to your hindrance, for if we ourselves were judges in this matter, and should lawfully find that where ye might did not do your diligence for the attaining of the said original, surely we would proceed further in that matter as the law would require, tarrying nothing, therefore, as if never any such brief had been spoken of.

"'It is desirable also that you should write to the Emperor's ambassador, from whom you had the copy, to support your application. If the Emperor utterly refuses, then the Queen must protest that as it is her own she will sue to the Pope for compulsories, and adopt other remedies as shall be thought convenient; but she hopes she will not be driven to use such extremities. And to the intent that the King and his counsel shall not think that she intends any frivolous delay, it will be expedient that she declare, in the presence of a notary, that she intends not to use any delay, but will recover it with all diligence, *bonâ fide*, and when it is sent it shall be exhibited.'

" This last demand, showing an insulting want of confidence, was no doubt also suggested by Wolsey. We do not know if such a declaration was made by the Queen, according to her counsel's advice, drily enough expressed as may be seen. But what is certain is that she wrote a letter to the Emperor, of the kind the prelates, her advisers, wished, desiring him to be satisfied with keeping a certified copy for himself, and sending her the original brief. This letter was entrusted to her chaplain, Thomas Abel, for transmission to her nephew, Charles V. But Abel, in the same parcel and the same conveyance, sent another letter to the Emperor, written by himself, and informing his Majesty that, in claiming the original of the brief, the Queen did not express her real desire, but had acted under pressure of a sort of moral violence. He added that she begged him to do everything in his power to have the suit transferred to Rome, for she could expect no justice in England. Lastly, he requested, in the name of the Queen, that the Imperial Ambassador at Rome, Muxetula, should be informed of her real situation, her almost complete want of liberty; and that he should be requested to tell all this to the Pope, in explanation of the Queen's silence."

Nor was this the only precaution taken by the Queen's friends. "After Katharine's agent, Philipps, had returned to London, she obtained the King's permission to send an officer of her household, named Montoya, into Spain. She gave him no letter, either in ordinary writing or in cipher. She only sent a verbal message, and Mendoza made him almost learn by heart what he was to say confidentially to the Emperor. Montoya was to enlighten the Emperor as to the moral constraint that Henry VIII. was exercising over the Queen, and repeat to him that no account was to be taken of her last letter, nor of the wish she expressed to be judged in England as soon as possible." *

The English Ambassadors, Gardiner and Fox, had already been sent to Rome to attempt to facilitate the divorce; but all their efforts seemed unavailing, and Campeggio's mode of procedure was so tardy that Henry suspected he had received private instructions to impede the affair as much as possible—a suspicion that was not ungrounded, as the Pope's secretary had indeed written to the Cardinal, forbidding him to move a step further in the matter without fresh instructions, and telling him "that he was especially to endeavour to make Henry VIII. renounce his plan of divorce, and persuade him to restore his affection to the Queen." The King, growing impatient, determined to send two fresh ambassadors to the Pope—Vannes and Sir Francis Bryan—"well provided," says Mendoza, "with false tales and every possible means of corruption;" and adds that the poor Queen was, as well she might be, "greatly alarmed."

* M. du Boys.

With these Ambassadors were sent a set of instructions, signed by the King himself, which are, perhaps, the most extraordinary specimens of the kind to be met with in history. The Ambassadors were to represent to his Holiness that Charles V. was desirous of becoming master of Italy, to contrast his selfish designs with the *devotion and disinterestedness* of the English King; to inquire, with great caution and respect, how it was that the Papal legate was allowed to delay for so long the business of the divorce; and to call the Pope's attention to the alleged brief of which Katharine spoke. They were also directed to retain the best advocates and canonists to be found in Rome; "and to learn from them whether, if the Queen can be induced to enter into lax religion, the Pope may, *in plenitudine potestatis*, dispense with the King to proceed to a second marriage, with legitimation of the children; and, although it is a thing that the Pope perhaps cannot do in accordance with the Divine and human laws already written, using his ordinary power, whether he may do it of his mere and absolute power, as a thing in which he may dispense above the law; what precedents there have been, and how the Roman Court shall define or determine, and what it doth use or may do therein, so that no exception, scruple, or doubt may be hereafter alleged in anything that shall be affirmed to be in the Pope's power. Similarly, as the Queen will probably make great difficulty in entering religion or taking the vow of chastity, means of high policy must be used to induce her thereunto; and, as she will perhaps resolve not to do so unless the King will do the like, the ambassadors must find out from their counsel if, to ensure so great a benefit to the King's succession and realm,

and to the quiet of his conscience, he takes such
a vow, whether the Pope will dispense with him
for the said promise or vow, discharging him
clearly of the same, and thereupon to proceed,
ad secunda vota cum legitimatione prolis, as is
aforesaid.

"Furthermore to provide for everything, as well
propter conceptum odium as for the danger that
may ensue by continuing in the Queen's company,
they shall inquire whether the Pope will dispense
with the King to have "duas uxores," making
the children of the second marriage legitimate as
well as those of the first; whereof some great
reasons and precedents, especially of the Old
Testament, appear!"

"Happily," says M. du Boys, "Henry, in a
kind of postscript, desired Bryan and Vannes not
to execute the last part of his instructions until
they should have conferred with two fresh Ambassadors, who, he said, would soon arrive—Knight,
his private secretary, and Dr. Benett. Indeed,
in his impatience to end the matter, the King had
chosen to add these two diplomatists to the others
who had only started a few days sooner. Benett
and Knight themselves took with them Dr.
Taylor, and as they went through France they
all waited on Francis I." Their instructions
were almost as original as those given to Bryan
and Vannes. They were to say "that the King,
having his mind fixed on the certainty of eternal
life, hath in this case put before his eyes the light
and shining brightness of truth, as the best
foundation for the tranquillity of his conscience,
knowing, as the Apostle says, that there is no
good foundation except that which Christ has
laid ; and that the King, finding his conscience
touched by plain suspicion of the falsity in the

brief, has recourse to the only fountain of remedy
on earth, the Pope himself. They shall desire
him to set aside all vain allegations, and in this
matter bring the truth to light; and, considering
the importance of the thing, how many may
be touched by it to urge that by consenting to
put an end to the cause, as he may do by the
plenitude of his power, all suspicions may be
removed. They shall also obtain a commission
decretal to the legates to pronounce the breve
forged. If the Pope will not consent, they shall
deliver to his Holiness the other letters of the
two legates desiring the avocation of the cause,
and a written promise from the Pope to give
sentence in the King's favour, on certain grounds
of which a summary is sent, *e.g.*, that the Emperor
will not send a brief, that the brief is false on the
face of it, and that the King is in great perplexity,
and his health in danger, etc. But they shall
obtain a promise from the Pope before the avocation."

Armed with these instructions, the Ambassadors
journeyed to Rome, where their first proceedings
were " directed against the brief so unexpectedly
produced by Katharine. They said they could
not understand how the document could have
been sent to Ferdinand in Spain, unknown to
anyone, while the authentic copy of the bull had
been addressed to Henry VII. in England, at his
request. What was the use of this double process? They were anxious to search the Vatican
registers, and did not find a minute of the brief.
Besides, they said, that the two documents pur-
porting to be written the same day, at the
beginning of the year, could not have been signed
by Julius II., for the ecclesiastical year of Rome
begins on the 25th of December of our common

calendars, and at that time Julius II. had not become Pope. But this objection proved too much; for it applied to the bull as well as the brief, and the fact of the bull was not contested. As to Clement VII., in the preparation of a brief, perhaps only a few hours later than the bull itself, he only saw Julius II.'s deliberate intention to confirm, and perhaps explain, the dispensation already given. Besides, he thought he could not decide a point of fact like a forgery in an authentic document in virtue of his infallibility, since that ought to be reserved for doubt in points of doctrine and morality. He said that the Emperor's explanation must be awaited; for that Prince had sent information to Rome that he was in possession of the original of the brief in question in Spain, that he would exhibit it to several ambassadors, especially the English, and that, until a formal demand had been made upon the Spanish Government to thus produce it, no accusation of forgery could be brought against King Ferdinand or the Emperor Charles V." *

So little progress did these envoys make, in spite of their elaborate directions, that Gardiner was again sent out to assist them; and soon after his arrival Clement VII. fell seriously ill, and was for some days in a dangerous condition. "He had hardly become convalescent," says M. du Boys, "when the English agents made their way even to his bedside, and tried to take advantage of his physical weakness to obtain what they wanted from him. But all their threats and prayers were wrecked against the Pope's wisdom and fairness. He said he could not deprive Katharine of the privileges allowed by canon law to every accused person or defendant in any suit.

* M. du Boys.

That the *plenaria potestas* did not authorize him to change the true into false, nor the just into the unjust. He was greatly devoted to the King, but could only do him services compatible with reason and equity. His expression was that the King had a good place in his Paternoster, but none in his Credo. All the expedients of the English diplomatists fell impotent, all their hopes failed. Thus Vannes wrote that, even if the Queen were to take the veil, the Pope, having consulted with the most learned canonists at Rome, had declared that, according to their advice, he would have no right to allow the King to contract a second marriage. As to the supposed forgery, Clement wrote himself to Henry VIII. on the 29th of April, 1529, that he could not give a decision on this point till he had heard both sides. The Pope had offered to send a special delegate to Spain to examine the original on the spot, and compare it with the copy, in concert with the English Ambassador. But Gardiner and his colleagues would not consent; time pressed, and an immediate decision was needful. Gardiner did not spare the wretched Pontiff some violent scenes, even while he was writhing with pains that seemed to be the agony of death. Yet Gardiner could get nothing out of that valiant spirit which continually rose above bodily suffering. In vain did he and his colleagues demand the publication of the bull of decretal, containing the original commission, and insist on a promise of ratification of the legate's sentence at Rome, in case of its being unfavourable to the Queen. They had to be contented with further powers from the Cardinals, and as this first *pollicitation* did not appear sufficient, a second was obtained, more distinct and more extended, under specious

pretexts.   But as the Pope in this document did
not renounce the right of receiving an appeal
from the adverse party, nor of transferring the
cause, if need arose, the Ambassadors' success
was very incomplete.   One of the number,
Bryant, a cousin of Anne Boleyn's, wrote her a
letter, disguising a portion of the truth, so as not
to discourage her.   But in his correspondence
with Wolsey he more frankly lamented that the
dexterity displayed by Gardiner, Vannes, and
Gregory Casale had been useless, and that their
efforts, as well as his own, had been thrown away.

"On their side Charles V. and his ambassadors
did not remain inactive.   In order to cut short
the arguments of the English agents, the Emperor
had proposed to furnish the original brief, the
copy of which had been impeached, but to show
it to the Pope alone.   Gardiner and his colleagues
would not take any account of this offer, but it
produced a great effect upon the mind of Clement
VII.   The Emperor, in his letters to his diplo-
matic agents, in the beginning of the year 1529,
Mendoza in England, and Muxetula and Micer
Mai at Rome, had never ceased to stir up their
zeal in his Aunt Katharine's cause.   In one of
these letters, February 5th and 6th, after accusing the English ministry and courtiers of per-
verting the King Henry's mind by vile artifices
and low intrigues, he tells Mendoza that it is
necessary to demand that the decision of the
divorce case should be transferred to the Apostolic
Holy See, even though the Queen, under the
influence of fear, and even of violence, should
oppose this measure, ' protesting, of course, the
nullity of action, and appealing to Rome, and,
if necessary, to the next general council, citing
and summoning each and every one of them

individually, and by their own names, to appear at the Court of Rome, or before the said general council, as it may be.' On the 16th of February following, he writes to Muxetula, his ambassador at Rome : ' It is our duty, though the Queen, desirous of avoiding scandal, had not applied for it, to claim in this instance the protection and favour of the Holy See, and to request that the case be tried before his sacred consistory, and the commission given to Cardinal Campeggio revoked. We, therefore, command you to beg his Holiness, in our name, to have the cause brought before his Court, notwithstanding any contrary steps taken by the new English ambassadors to prevent a thing so just and reasonable.'

" Meanwhile Micer Mai, the Spanish envoy to the Pontifical Court, had returned with all speed to his post, and had taken several steps there. On March 6th he wrote to his master: ' With regard to the Queen of England's case, he (Mai) hopes that the first brief put for the Pope's signature will be that for the adjudication of the suit at Rome.' This hope was premature; for though the Pontifical Court and the Cardinals seemed inclined for the transfer of the cause to the Court of Rome, their good intentions were paralysed by the Queen herself not having expressed a wish, although Charles V. and his agents had acted for her, and in her name. This obstacle was soon to vanish.

" By the 16th of March it is clear that events are drawing on. Cardinal Santa Croce wrote the following letter to the Emperor, and it must have considerably advanced the solution of the question,

" ' To-day, the 6th of March, a packet of letters has been received from the Imperial ambassador

in England of the 25th of February. There is,
inside, one from the Queen to the Pope, closed
and sealed, asking him, as it is presumed, to
have her case tried here [at Rome]. The Queen
having complained that she had no liberty to
defend herself in England, it was resolved that
she herself should write an autograph letter to
the Pope, stating her wishes. That has been
done, as it would appear, with great difficulty,
and is, most probably, the subject of her missive.
The Queen writes to him (Santa Croce), commanding him to put the letter into the Pope's
hands with the greatest possible secrecy, as she
does not want anyone to know it. The Pope,
however, is not well enough now to treat affairs
of this kind. As soon as he recovers, the letter
shall be given to him.
    "'Rome, 16th of March, 1529.'"

While the Queen was taking this step, her
nephew was seeking to strengthen her cause by
the exhibition of the brief concerning which there
had been so much doubt and suspicion. "The
King of England's ambassadors to Charles V.,"
Dr. Lee and Ghinucci, Bishop of Worcester,
having expressed to Catalayud their desire to
see the original brief of dispensation sent by
Julius II. to Queen Isabella, his Majesty the
Emperor gave orders for the document to be
exhibited to them in presence of some notaries
nominated for the purpose, and several grandees
of Spain. In this solemn meeting, Nicholas
Perrenot, Sieur de Granvelle, and the Chancellor
of the Empire, explained how the Emperor had
done all he could to preserve friendly relations
with his ally, the King of England, but that
this Prince had cast doubts upon the authenticity

of the copy of the brief of dispensation of which
Queen Katharine had made use, the original
being in the possession of her nephew, Charles
V. Then the Sieur de Granvelle took the document in his hands, unsealed, opened it, and gave
it to the English Ambassadors to read, and to copy
if they chose. The Ambassadors, visibly em-
barrassed, refused to take cognisance, on the
pretext that the question of forgery having been
referred to the Pope they did not think themselves
authorised to interfere in the question. On the
invitation of the Bishop of Osma, and the Bishop
of Elma, Nicholas Perrenot read the precious
document aloud in presence of the two above-
named Bishops, Henry, Count of Nassau, the
lord chamberlain of the Emperor, the Count de
Pont-de-Vaux, grand-master of the King's household, the Sieur de la Chaux, prefect of the palace,
and Louis of Flanders, Sieur de Praël. A minute
of this meeting was drawn up in Latin by the
notaries, containing a copy of the brief, and the
minute was signed by the witnesses present,
except the English Ambassadors. This ought to
have put an end to the miserable quibbles
advanced against the sincerity and fidelity of the
copy presented to the legates by Queen Katharine.
  " Charles V. himself wrote to Mendoza that the
English ambassadors, after the meeting, having
asked him to allow them a private examination of
the brief he immediately consented. 'And an
authentic copy of it made, properly revised, and
collated with the original, in order to show that
we omit nothing that is likely to preserve the
friendship of their King, and that, if he will but
attend to the letter of the brief, his scruples will
at once vanish.'
  " Is it credible that the two ambassadors, in

their official correspondence, still found reasons
for suspecting the validity of the original document?"

The poor Queen herself, in the midst of her
distress, was not unmindful of, or ungrateful for,
the exertions displayed by her friends on her
behalf. To Muxetula, the Emperor's Ambassador
at Rome, who had shown great zeal and vigilance
in her cause, she wrote the following gracious and
grateful letter :—

"AMBASSADOR,—

"Your letter enclosing papers has come to
hand. I thank you very much for the diligence
and care you display in my affairs, without my
having directly applied to you. Be sure that you
will always find a true friend in me to do you any
favour within my power. I beg you to continue
in future as hitherto, and follow up this cause as
it has begun. Let me know what answer his
Holiness makes to your representations and
petitions on my behalf. I shall feel grateful for
this and any other service you may render me,
and will not fail to apprise the Emperor, your
master, of any further steps taken in my defence.
In all other matters you shall give full credence
to Don Inigo de Mendoza, the Emperor's ambassador at this Court, to whom I am as much
indebted as I am to yourself, for the trouble and
pains you have taken in my affairs. His letters
will inform you of the proceedings.

"Anton Court (Hampton Court), this 25th of
January, 1529."

Her grief is sadly indicated in her confidences
to Vives, whom we have seen her consulting in
happier days regarding the education of her child.

"The Queen began to open to him—as her countryman—her distress that the man whom she loved more than herself should think of marrying another; which was the greater grief the more she loved him. The Queen desired him to ask the Imperial ambassador to write to the Emperor to do what was just with the Pope, lest she should be condemned without being heard."

The man whom "she loved more than herself" avenged himself on the wife of whom he was weary for the bands that chafed him. "He would not give her liberty of defence nor power of appeal, which he would not have refused to the least of his subjects. He had sent away the Spanish advocates associated with Katharine's counsel, as being harder to influence than natives of his kingdom. Now he made use of the legates themselves to procure the Queen's submission, persuading them to employ in turn cajolery and menaces. Most odious espial was directed on the details of her private life. Thus, when Henry had abolished the household, and dismissed the court of the Princess Mary, she had returned to her mother. Now Katharine was accused of a habit of savage and morose devotion unseasonable to the youth around her. The Queen, thinking she ought to give her daughter some diversion, so as to prove that her piety was not so narrow, without having anything that could be called an entertainment, let her dance sometimes with her companions. The opportunity was seized for blaming her for this great impropriety. The legates were to tell her that she ought not to amuse herself while the King was sad and pensive, on account of all that was going on. And what was Henry about? He was going, no doubt, without much publicity, it is true, to lighten his sorrow and cheer his pensiveness by Anne Boleyn's side, in her fine apartments at Greenwich. That was not all! He caused reproaches to be made to Katharine on account of the acclamations in her favour that met her when she showed herself in London, and the dislike of the people to Wolsey and the King himself. He pretended to see in it proofs of a secret conspiracy against the whole English government!"*

While Katharine was thus harassed, calumniated, and neglected, the Lady Anne was already experiencing the foretastes of her future triumph. "Greater court is now paid to her," writes Du Bellay, the French Ambassador, "every day than has been to the Queen a long time. I see they mean to accustom the people by degrees to endure her, so that when the great blow comes it may not be thought strange. However, the people remain quite hardened, and I think they would do more if they had more power; but great order is continually taken."

What agony this divorce was costing Katharine it is, perhaps, difficult to realize. "Let it be borne in mind," says Reed, "that when she came to England, betrothed to the heir of England's throne, she brought, as the daughter of Ferdinand and Isabella, not only her splendid dowry, but the pride of the proudest monarchy in Europe. She came from the palace that had lately rejoiced in those wondrous achievements by which the spaces of Christendom were enlarged; for in one and the same year did Ferdinand and Isabella remove from the soil of Spain the long-enduring dynasty of the Saracens, and send forth Columbus to search the dark waters of the west. For near

* M. du Boys.

twenty years was this proud Castilian woman
Queen of England, the honoured wife of Henry
VIII." Imagine such a character, with all the
lofty pride, the stately dignity of her race, with
all the love for husband and child of an intensely
deep and tender nature, suddenly confronted
with the prospect of disgrace, repudiation, ruin;
threatened with separation from her daughter;
and knowing, with what keen anguish it is almost
impossible to describe, that he of whom she had
written that "she loved him more deeply than
she loved herself," was eager and anxious to be
rid of her, and was impatiently awaiting the
hour that should leave him free to wed her rival
—her own maid of honour! Be it always remembered that, whatever view may now be taken
of her marriage, Katharine herself believed, from
the bottom of her heart, that she was the King's
true wife and Queen; and that she upheld her
rights, and fought out her cause so fearlessly,
with the strongest consciousness that in so doing
she was following the plain dictates of duty. We
have all heard, as Reed tells us, " of Constance
wildly clamouring for her son's royal claim, and
of Margaret of Anjou indomitably warring for
her son's inheritance; but the noblest matron of
them all is Queen Katharine, in whom are seen
all the feelings of the wife, the mother, and the
Queen—the pride of birth and of place—the consciousness of irreproachable purity—the anguish
of the bitterest wrong—all sinking down with
something of placid piety into the most piteous
dejection."

The spring of 1529 was now well advanced, but
in those days communication between Italy and
England was what would seem to us intolerably
slow, and Katharine had heard little of the pro-

ceedings at Rome. "It is true she must have received a letter from her nephew, Charles V., dated April 23rd, and concluding thus : 'As a case of this sort must be referred to our Most Holy Father in his Holy Apostolic See, we have earnestly requested him not to allow it to be tried elsewhere than at his Court, inasmuch as your honour, and that of all our relatives and friends, is deeply concerned in the issue. You may be sure, most Serene Queen, and our dearest and most beloved aunt and sister, that I shall not fail in what I consider to be my duty.' But it is not known whether this letter had reached the Queen in the month of May. Certainly she did not know that the protests and petitions mentioned by Charles V. had been made ; and lastly, Mendoza, who had always been her faithful support, and kept up her communications with Spain and Rome, being greatly injured in health by the English climate, had persuaded the Emperor to recall him, in order to save his life. The loss of this able and devoted adviser left a great void for the unhappy Katharine." *

She went again to see Campeggio, and he once more entreated her to take the veil, thus showing that he had not as yet learned the opinion of the Roman canonists, which declared, that even were she to do so the King could not legally re-marry. But the Queen was inflexible. "Her Christian devotion, her gentle humility, were not inconsistent with an impregnable Spanish tenacity and unbending royal pride ; she never would voluntarily have yielded her place to the clever manœuvrer who wished to usurp her rights as wife and Queen. She did not understand this inversion of any idea of justice

* M. du Boys.

and turn of the cards to make the King's mistress
a legitimate wife, and his legitimate wife a
concubine. And so Campeggio, after his conference with the Queen, could not help praising
her sincerity, her firmness, and greatness of
soul." *

Meanwhile, proceedings in the matter of the
divorce went on. " In the great hall of the palace
at Blackfriars," says Miss Strickland, " was prepared a solemn court; the two legates, Wolsey
and Campezzio, had each a chair of cloth of gold
placed before a table, covered with rich tapestry.
On the right of the court was a canopy, under
which was a chair and cushions of tissue for the
King, and on the left a rich chair for the Queen.
It was not till the 28th of May, 1529, that the
court summoned the royal parties. The King
answered the two proctors; the Queen entered,
attended by four bishops and a great train of
ladies, and, making an obeisance with much
reverence to the legates, appealed from them, as
prejudiced and incompetent judges, to the Court
of Rome; she then departed. The court sat every
week, and heard arguments on both sides, but
seemed as far off as ever from coming to any decision. At last the King and Queen were cited
by Dr. Sampson to attend the court in person on
the 18th of June." Both obeyed the summons.
The court was full. There sat the two Cardinals
as judges; Archbishop Warham and all the
bishops except Fisher and Standish, were on the
bench; Gardiner was chief clerk; and behind the
bar stood the advocates and proctors—Sampson,
Bell, and Tregonell, on the King's side; Fisher,
Standish, and Ridley, on the Queen's. Silence
was ordered, the Pope's commission read, and the

* M. du Boys.

crier raised his voice. "Henry, King of England, come into the court!" "Here, my lords!" answered the King. "Katharine, Queen of England, come into the court!" The Queen did not speak; "but rose up incontinent out of her chair, where she sat, and because she could not come directly to the King for the distance which severed them, she took pain to go about unto the King, kneeling down at his feet in the sight of all the court and assembly, to whom she said in effect, in broken English, as followeth : *

"'Sir, I beseech you for all the loves that hath been between us, and for the love of God, let me have justice and right, take of me some pity and compassion, for I am a poor woman and a stranger born out of your dominion, I have here no assured friend, and much less indifferent counsel; I flee to you as to the head of justice within this realm. Alas! sir, wherein have I offended you, or what occasion of displeasure? Have I designed against your will and pleasure; intending (as I perceive) to put me from you? I take God and all the world to witness, that I have been to you a true humble and obedient wife, ever comformable to your will and pleasure, that never said or did anything to the contrary thereof, being always well pleased and contented with all things wherein you had any delight or dalliance, whether it were in little or much; I never grudged in word or countenance, or showed a visage or spark of discontentation. I loved all those whom you loved only for your sake, whether I had cause or no; and whether they were my friends or my enemies. This twenty years I have been your true wife or more, and by me ye have had divers children, although it hath pleased God to call them out of

* Cavendish's Life of Wolsey.

the world, which hath been no default in me.
And when ye had me at the first, I take God to
be my judge, I was a true maid; and whether it
be true or no, I put it to your conscience. If
there be any just cause by the law that ye can
allege against me, either of dishonesty or any
other impediment to banish and put me from you,
I am well content to depart to my great shame
and dishonour; and if there be none, then here I
most lowly beseech you let me remain in my
former estate, and receive justice at your hands.
The king your father was in the time of his reign
of such estimation through the world for his
excellent wisdom, that he was accounted and
called of all men the second Solomon; and my
father Ferdinand, King of Spain, who was
esteemed to be one of the wittiest princes that
reigned in Spain, many years before, were both
wise and excellent kings in wisdom and princely
behaviour. It is not therefore to be doubted,
but that they elected and gathered as wise
counsellors about them as to their high discre-
tions was thought meet. Also, as me seemeth,
there was in those days as wise, as well learned
men, and men of as good judgment as be at
this present in both realms, who thought then
the marriage between you and me good and
lawful. Therefore it is a wonder to hear what
new inventions are now invented against me,
that never intended but honesty. And cause me
to stand to the order and judgment of this new
court, wherein ye may do me much wrong, if ye
intend any cruelty; for ye may condemn me for
lack of sufficient answer, having no indifferent
counsel, but such as be assigned me, with whose
wisdom and learning I am not acquainted. Ye
must consider that they cannot be indifferent

counsellors for my part which are your subjects,
and taken out of your own council before,
wherein they be made privy, and dare not, for
your displeasure, disobey your will and intent,
being once made privy thereto.   Therefore I most
humbly require you, in the way of charity, and
for the love of God, who is the just judge, to
spare me the extremity of this new court, until
I may be advertised what way and order my
friends in Spain will advise me to take.   And
if ye will not extend to me so much indifferent
favour, your pleasure then be fulfilled, and to
God I commit my cause!' "

As the Queen finished, she rose from her
kneeling posture.   All thought she was returning to her seat, but, making a low courtesy to
the King, she took the arm of her receiver-
general, Griffith, and left the court.

"Recall her Highness," said the King.

"Katharine, Queen of England, come into
court," commanded the crier.

"Madam," said Griffith, "you are called."

"1 hear it," she answered, "but on—on—go
you on—for this is no court wherein I can have
justice."

Then the King, forgetting apparently, or
thinking it wiser to ignore, the murderous
imaginings of which he had allowed his council,
unrebuked, to accuse his wife, spoke of her in
terms of high eulogy to the judges and bishops
assembled.   "As the Queen is gone," he said,
"I will, in her absence, declare unto you all,
my lords here presently assembled, she hath been
to me as true, as obedient, and as conformable
a wife as I could in my fantasy desire.   She
hath all the virtuous qualities that ought to be
in a woman of her dignity!"   Cardinal Wolsey

"ever watching for a sign of change, and thinking that his hour was come, made haste to get
himself excused, asserting that he had never
been a mover in this great affair."* Henry, in
an elaborate speech, declared that his first doubts
had been excited, not by Wolsey, but by the
Bishop of Tarbes, at the negociations for his
daughter's marriage. "I moved this matter
first," added the King, "to you, my Lord of
Lincoln, my ghostly father; and, forasmuch as
you then were in some doubt to give me counsel,
moved me to ask farther counsel of all of you, my
lords"—an assertion curiously at variance with
the emphatic statement of Longland, that Henry
had been continually urging him upon the subject; but the Tudor nature could readily adapt
awkward facts to its own liking—"wherein I
moved you first, my Lord of Canterbury, asking
your license (as you were our Metropolitan) to put
this matter in question; and so I did of all of you,
my lords, to the which you have all granted by
writing under your seals." Warham and most of
the other bishops admitted it; but Fisher declared
he had never signed.
"Here is your hand and seal," said Henry.
"It is a forgery," said Fisher.
Warham declared Fisher had permitted him to
sign it for him; but Fisher firmly denied it,
asking—"If he wished it to be done, why could
he not have done it himself?" and the King,
losing all his scanty patience, dissolved the court,
and from that day looked on his old tutor as his
enemy.
Katharine's popularity was manifest, when, on
this memorable 18th of June, she set forth from
Baynard's Castle to Blackfriars. "The women as

* Hepworth Dixon.

she passed encouraged her, and shouted to her to care for nothing. 'If the matter was to be decided by the women, the King would lose the battle,' says Du Bellay, with some spirit, and then he adds ironically, 'She recommended herself to these good prayers, with other Spanish tricks.'" *

The female part of the nation was indeed so entirely with her, and the unpopularity of Anne Boleyn so great, that on one occasion, when the latter was on a pleasure expedition in the country, a mob of women assailed her, and she escaped with difficulty from personal violence.

On June 25th the Queen was again summoned before the court, but she refused to appear, though she sent in an appeal to the Pope, signed with her own hand on every page. She was pronounced contumacious, and the trial went on till July, when, following the Roman custom, the legates declared they must cease to sit till October. "At this delay," says Miss Strickland, "Anne Boleyn so worked upon the feelings of her lover that he was in an agony of impatience. He sent for Wolsey, to consult with him on the best means of bringing the Queen to comply with his wishes. Wolsey remained an hour with the King, hearing him storm in all the fury of unbridled passion. At last Wolsey returned to his barge; the Bishop of Carlisle, who was waiting in it at Blackfriars Stairs, observed, 'that it was warm weather.' 'Yea, my lord,' said Wolsey, 'and if you had been chafed as I have been, you would say it was *hot.*'"

Both Wolsey and Campeggio were ordered to repair to Bridewell Palace early the next morning, in order to try and persuade the Queen to settle the matter by retiring into a convent. They

* M. Du Boys.

went, and Katharine, who was at work with her ladies, came to them in the presence chamber with a skein of red silk round her neck. With stately courtesy she thanked them for coming, and said, " She would give them a hearing, though she imagined they came on business which required much deliberation, and a brain stronger than hers."

"You see," she added, pointing to the silk, "my employment; in this way I pass my time with my maids, who are indeed none of the ablest councillors, yet have I no other in England; and Spain, where there are those on whom I could rely, is, God knoweth, far off."

"If it please your grace," said Cardinal Wolsey, "to go into your privy chamber, we will show you the cause of our coming."

"My lord," answered the Queen, "if you have anything to say, speak it openly before all these folks; for I fear nothing that ye can say or allege against me, but that I would all the world should both hear and see it; therefore I pray you speak your minds openly."

Wolsey began to address her in Latin.

"Pray, good my lord," said Katharine, "speak to me in English, for I can, thank God, speak and understand English, though I do know some Latin."

"Forsooth then," said the Cardinal, "Madam, if it please your grace, we come both to know your mind, how ye be disposed to do in this matter between the King and you, and also to declare secretly our opinions and our counsel unto you, which we have intended of very zeal and obedience that we bear to your grace."

Poor Katharine! she had learnt to be cautious of such "zeal and obedience" as was now offered, and her answer was at once dignified and prudent. " My lords, I thank you then of your good wills ; but to make answer to your request I cannot so suddenly, for I was set among my maidens at work, thinking full little of any such matter, wherein there needeth a longer deliberation, and a better head than mine, to make answer to so noble wise men as ye be ; I had need of good counsel in this case, which toucheth me so near ; and for any counsel or friendship that I can find in England, [they] are nothing to my purpose or profit.   Think you, I pray you, my lords, will any Englishman counsel or be friendly unto me against the King's pleasure, they being his subjects ? Nay forsooth, my lords ! and for my counsel in whom I do intend to put my trust be not here; they being in Spain, in my native country.   Alas, my lords ! I am a poor woman lacking both wit and understanding sufficiently to answer such ap- proved wise men as ye be both, in so weighty a matter.   I pray you to extend your good and in- different minds in your authority unto me, for I am a simple woman, destitute and barren of friendship and counsel here in a foreign region ; and as for your counsel, I will not refuse, but be glad to hear."

" And with that," says Cavendish, " she took my lord by the hand and led him into her privy chamber with the other cardinal; where they were in long communication ; we, in the other chamber, might sometime hear the Queen speak very loud, but what it was we could not understand.   The communication ended, the cardinals departed and went directly to the King, making to him relation of their talk with the Queen; and after resorted home to their houses to supper."

" When the King of England saw," says M. du

Boys, "public opinion arising in favour of
Katharine, and the zeal of the legates entrusted
with the trial declining more and more, he perceived that he must make some sort of diversion,
and give his suit a colour of material interest.
So he tried to attach the English nobility to his
cause, and induced them to take a kind of initia-
tive in the matter by a direct address to the sovereign pontiff. Doubts having been raised as to
the illegitimacy of the Princess Mary, even though
these doubts were ill-founded, pretenders to the
crown would make them an excuse to exalt their
claims over those of a young girl incapable from
her sex of defending her own. Then there would
be the spectacle of a renewal of civil war, like
those which had seen the Houses of York and
Lancaster in arms, and had caused English blood
to flow in torrents during the fifteenth century.
Henry, his ministers, and all his friends or
favourites, dexterously put forward these considerations, and managed to get the nobles of the kingdom, or a certain number of them, to write a
letter to the Pope, entreating him to give their
sovereign satisfaction by declaring the nullity of
his former marriage, so that he might contract a
second, and have an heir male, whose rights
should be incontestable. Policy does not always
agree with justice, and it prompted a number of
lords spiritual and temporal to write a letter to
the sovereign pontiff, of which this is the substance. They said that not only the King but the
whole realm of England were complaining of the
interminable delays that had arisen in the decision
of an affair that was in the highest degree
interesting to the whole country. His Holiness
had received incontestable services from the English government, and really ought to give a

favourable hearing to their prayers, and remedy their grievances, as he could not be ignorant of them. That the most learned universities of Europe had examined the question of the validity of the King's marriage, and are said to have found that Henry VIII. had reason to require a declaration of nullity; 'therefore all England beseeches His Holiness to give his sanction to this general opinion that the voiding of this marriage would be equitable and advantageous. This would be the only means of ensuring the peace of England and preventing the horrors of civil war, into which it would certainly again fall, if the King were to die without male offspring; and therefore supplication is made to His Holiness to enable him to have hopes. Having always considered the sovereign pontiff as our father, we beseech him to look upon us as his children, and not to abandon us. If His Holiness should indefinitely defer to grant our request, we shall take too long a delay as a refusal, and shall, in consequence, find ourselves obliged to seek a remedy elsewhere, and perhaps come to some melancholy extremity, to our great regret; but finally a sick man seeks comfort wherever he thinks he can find it.' The date of this letter is July 13th, 1529. It is signed by Cardinal Wolsey, the Archbishop of Canterbury, the Dukes of Norfolk and Suffolk, two marquisses, thirty earls, four bishops, twenty-five barons, twenty-two abbots, and twelve members of the House of Commons.

"The 29th September following, Clement VII. made a calm and dignified reply to this petition. He said he forgave the English lords the harsh language they had used in the end of their letter, and attributed the improper expressions to their affection for their King. He begged them, as a

fond father, not to think of seeking remedies
elsewhere than in the bosom of the church. He
pointed out to them that it is not the physician's
fault when the sick man is impatient, and will do
nothing he dislikes; that, if Henry VIII. had the
opinion of some doctors and some universities on
his side, the Queen could appeal to the law of
God, and high authorities found in the writings of
learned divines; that Europe would not understand that a marriage could be disputed which
had been contracted and completed so many years
ago on a dispensation from the Pope, asked for by
two great kings, and after the birth of several
children. He said he had no greater wish than
to gratify the King as far as he could, without
violating the most sacred claims of justice; and
he did not think that, as the King was so pious,
he would approve of the letter of these lords.
The King expressed great discontent at this
letter, though the Pope had taken pains to speak
with the greatest kindness of him personally."

In October the legates resumed their sitting,
and Henry pressed impatiently for judgment.
Then, in Hepworth Dixon's graphic language,
"Compeggio threw aside his mask. 'I will give
no judgment in this cause until I have made relation to the Pope of our proceedings. Wherefore
I adjourn the Court.' Every one stood amazed,
and Suffolk gave the wonder and the fury voice.
With lofty mien and flashing eye he strode into
the centre of the group, and cried, ' It was never
merry in England while we had cardinals among
us !' Wolsey retorted sharply, ' Sir ! of all men
within this realm you have least cause to be
offended with cardinals; for if I, a simple cardinal, had not been, you should have had at this
moment no head on your shoulders.' Henry left

the court abruptly, while the peers and prelates looked into each others' faces for a sign. All felt that something great and striking had occurred, but few conceived the greatness of that hour. The revolution had commenced."

A fortnight later it was generally known that on the previous 18th of July the Pope had transferred the suit to Rome by a Bull of Revocation ; and Anne Boleyn's chance of queenship seemed by such an edict gravely lessened. Neither she nor the King, however, gave up hope ; and if poor Katharine trusted that she might now retain her crown, she knew well that she had lost her husband's love for ever.

The next great event was the fall of Cardinal Wolsey, for whom none were sorry. The great nobles hated him as a pretentious upstart ; and Anne Boleyn and her followers were glad to have so great an obstacle removed, while the common people had disliked him for his extortions and his advocacy of the divorce—the cause of Katharine being generally popular, especially with the women, who universally espoused her claims. She was still recognised as Queen ; and Henry permitted her to accompany him on a royal progress to the More, a manor in Hertfordshire, and Grafton in Northamptonshire—the place where Wolsey had his last interview with his master. " The Bishop of Bayonne," says Miss Strickland, " in his letters, affirms, that there was no apparent diminution of affection between the King and Queen ; and though they were accompanied by Anne Boleyn, the Queen showed no marks of jealousy or anger against her." Henry still treated his wife with outward deference, and she never sullied her dignity with useless recrimination. " They pay each other the best attentions,"

wrote the Italian Scarpinello, " and his Highness
makes her many compliments in the Spanish
fashion. Peace appears to reign, as though there
had never been a question in dispute between
them. Katharine affirms with warmth that
everything her lord, the King, has done, has been
inspired by true and holy doubt, and not by
preference for another love." In spite of her
haughty Castilian blood, the poor Queen was a
very woman ; and resolutely closed her eyes, with
pathetic obstinacy, to all the flaws and errors of
her love.

Katharine had a strong impression that if once
a papal confirmation of her marriage was issued,
all idea of the divorce would at once drop. For
this confirmation she wrote in impassioned
language to her Roman agent, Dr. Ortiz, in the
following letter, which is translated from the
original Spanish :—

" DOCTOR— I have had much pleasure and comfort from the letters, seeing that thou tellest me of
the good and evil which is passing where thou art ;
and I know full well the pains thou art at, and
the affection and good will thou hast for the good
of this business, and the manner in which thou
dost recommend it to His Holiness, so that he may
do justice and with brevity, taking it into his
conscience which is the best road and most certain
for those who have to fill that holy seat. And in
all and everything that may be done by His Holiness, such as thou dost see them, I do not, however, perceive any other road but that of recommending to God, and I pray to Him that He may
remedy the evils of which this kingdom and
Christendom through this business seems to have
no end. I fear that God's vicar on earth does not

wish to remedy them. I do not know what to think of His Holiness; but on this side, the heretics who are in the Christian world, seeing that this cause, as it is in suspense, gives room that there should be more suspense; and he being the head and protector of the Church, he wishes the Church to have a great fall. I cannot do more, as I have written to His Holiness, than to inform him of the truth, and have represented to him the evils I see if they follow the course of not bringing to an end this cause, and procure that there shall be an end to it through the means which appear to me the proper ones. And if these are of no avail, I will complain to God because here on the earth in His ministers there is no faith and charity, for His mercy will not abandon me. I entreat thee to endeavour to continue the same course as thou hast done heretofore. I have seen a copy of the brief which His Holiness has issued, and I have shown it to learned persons, and they have told me that the medicine which is to cure this wound must be stronger, and that the remedy is the sentence, and anything else will bring anger and little profit for a few days only. God give thee much health. 14th of April [1530]. To His Holiness communicate what I have written to thee in this letter.

"(Signed)   CATHERINA."
"To Dr. Ortiz in Rome."

While poor Katharine was thus passionately pleading her cause with the Pope, Henry was planning how he could rid himself of her for ever. After Wolsey's fall, he chose to have none but laymen in his council, thinking they would stand less in awe of the Pontiff; and while the Queen was writing her letter, the King was resolved to send a last appeal to Rome. The man appointed to plead the royal cause was Thomas Cranmer. That name, so familiar to our ears, had not then long been known. Two years before, in 1528, he was a Fellow of Jesus College, Cambridge, and had fled from there with two of his pupils, when the sweating sickness broke out. They took refuge at Waltham ; and, it being the time when the King and Queen were at Tittenhanger, the royal suite had been scattered up and down the neighbourhood. Dr. Stephen Gardiner and Dr. Fox, the King's secretary and almoner, found quarters in the house where Cranmer was living; and the conversation in the evening turned on the universal subject of the King's divorce.

"Cranmer, who had a peculiarly clear legal mind, said the point was this :—The Pope had the power to dispense with the laws of the Church, but not with the laws of God. Was marriage with a brother's widow contrary to the law of God? That was a question for universities and canonists. If so, had Arthur and Katharine been really husband and wife? Fox and Gardiner carried the report to the King, who was delighted. 'Who is this Dr. Cranmer?' he cried. 'Where is he? Is he still at Waltham? Marry, I will speak to him! Let him be sent for out of hand. This man, I trow, has got the right sow by the ear.' Cranmer was brought to the court, made to write out his argument, and appointed one of the royal chaplains. The King asked him if he would undertake to maintain his argument at Rome; and he answered that he would. In the meantime he defended his treatise both in Oxford and Cambridge, and won over several distinguished men to his view of the question."*

* C. M. Yonge.

The time for sending Cranmer to lay his arguments before the Pope seemed now to have arrived. Charles V. was at Bologna for his double coronation as Emperor of the West and King of Lombardy; and both he and the Pope were dwelling under the same roof.   The King formed an embassy to proceed thither, of which Cranmer was one member, and at the head of which was the father of Anne Bolèyn, lately advanced to the dignity of Earl of Wiltshire, who was empowered to make a full explanation to Charles of the King's demand, "adding hints of his power and bribes up to £300,000, if the Emperor's consent could be gained."* Many objected that Lord Wiltshire was not a fit person for the post allotted him; but Henry overruled the difficulty by saying no other man had so strong an interest in the cause; and the embassy set forth, and found themselves graciously received by the Pope, but unable to gain any advantage; and the Emperor was quite as impenetrable, and not gracious at all.

" Stop, sir," he said, as Lord Wiltshire began to address him.   " Allow your colleagues to speak—you are a party concerned."

" I am here," Wiltshire replied, "not in the name of my child, but in that of my sovereign. If your Majesty agrees to what I ask, my master will rejoice; if not, your disapproval will not prevent the King of England demanding and receiving justice."

He ventured to add the proposal of Henry to restore Katharine's marriage portion if the divorce were pronounced; but the answer was haughty and decisive.

" I am no merchant to sell the honour of my

* C. M. Yonge.

aunt; " and judging nothing was to be gained by
further delay, the Earl returned to England.
"Cranmer visited Rome, and then travelled
through Germany, trying to interest the reform-
ing Princes in his master's cause; but Luther
saw no charms in the 'defender of the faith,' who
only wanted to get rid of his lawful wife, and he
gained no sympathy. Luther even wrote to
Barnes, the royal agent, that he had rather let the
King have two wives at once than get rid of his
lawful one. The universities of Germany were
still less willing to decide in the King's favour.
Much was hoped from the fourteen universities of
France. Indeed, Henry had the assurance to write
François I. to interfere in his favour; but the
King of France replied that he could not offend
the Emperor, while his sons were still in his
power, nor could they be released till he had paid
2,000,000 crowns to the Emperor, and redeemed
for them the lily of gold which Maximilian had
pawned for Henry VII. This made Henry forgive
the debt, make a present to him of the pledge, and
lend a large sum, for which consideration the
Count of Montmorency canvassed the doctors of
the university of Paris one by one; and though
the consciences of the majority were against it,
dexterous management obtained a decision in the
King's favour. A few of the others were also won
over, and Oxford and Cambridge were subservient,
so that Henry had outward justification, though
every one knew how dishonestly it had been
obtained. Armed with these decisions, such as
they were, Henry applied again to the Pope, but
with no better success; indeed, Clement had
gathered courage to make what was tantamount to
a refusal to meddle any more with the matter, and
a representation that if he were afraid of a dis-

puted succession this was no means of preventing it."*

The whole of this year of 1530 the Queen had
the company of her daughter. Threats had, as
we have seen, been already held out, of separating
them if Katharine continued "contumacious," but
as yet these had not been carried into effect.
Henry's disappointment on finding himself still
bound at the end of the year was keen. "The
King sore lamented his chance," says Hall; "he
made no mirth or pastime, as he was wont to do,
yet he dined with and resorted to the Queen as
accustomed; he ministered nothing of her estate,
and much loved and cherished their daughter, the
Lady Mary." Christmas was passed by the royal
pair at Greenwich, and the usual gaieties of
masques and banquets went on as usual, Katharine
being treated with all the deference due to her
rank. Great efforts were made to induce her to
withdraw her appeal to Rome, but in vain. The
Queen steadily refused to retreat an inch from the
position she had taken up. Perhaps, if there had
been only herself to think of, she might have sur-
rendered, though her high spirit, and her keen
consciousness of her rights, would have rendered
it doubtful even then; but with her child's name
to defend, she was inflexible. She refused to give
up in any way her station of Queen. She insisted
on accompanying the King wherever he went; and
even when Mary fell ill away from her, and she
longed to go and nurse her, she would not do so,
for fear advantage should be taken of her absence
to prevent her return. She entreated that her
daughter might be brought to her. "If you
desire it," said Henry, "you can go to her, and
stay with her." But Katharine knew with whom

* C. M. Yonge.

she had to deal too well to acquiesce. "Neither for my daughter, nor for any person in the world, will I separate from you, or lodge in any other house than that in which you live." She had done all she could for her own honour and her daughter's; she had bent her pride to follow her husband to his own apartments, and beseech him to give up the hope of a divorce—in vain; but she would never

> Make herself so guilty
> To give up willingly that noble title,

which she believed with all her heart was rightly hers; and she was resolved to fight on to the last.

> Nothing but death
> Should e'er divorce her dignities.

CHAPTER VI.

Thomas Cromwell—Deputation to the Queen—Her reply—
Separation of Henry and Katharine—Her departure from
Windsor—Letter to the Princess Mary—Interview of the
King and Reginald Pole—Elevation of Anne Boleyn to the
peerage—Her journey with Henry to Calais—Letters of
Queen Katharine—Marriage of Henry and Anne Boleyn —
Cranmer's court at Dunstable—Katharine's refusal to be
present—Her marriage pronounced invalid—Her reception
of the announcement—Coronation of Anne Boleyn—Her
unpopularity—Sermons of the Friars at Greenwich—The
King's Proclamation—Katharine's removal to Bugden—Her
heavy sorrow—Her forgiveness of Anne Boleyn—Her letter
to her daughter—Birth of Elizabeth—Interview of Mary and
Anne Boleyn—Letter of the French Ambassador—Visit of
Lee and Tunstall to Katharine—Her inflexible resolution—
Her letter to the Emperor—Refusal of her servants to take
the oath of allegiance—Her wishes respecting them—
Refusal to go to Fotheringay—Removal to Kimbolton—
Traces of her residence there.

THE year 1531 opened gloomily for Henry and
Anne Boleyn. For nearly five years the lady had
been waiting for the crown—for nearly five years
the King had been waiting with eager impatience
to offer it to her; and the looked-for day seemed
as far off as ever. But suddenly a new actor
appeared in the ever-shifting Tudor drama,
whose coming opened the way summarily to the
attainment of the royal wishes.

This new comer, Thomas Cromwell, was a man
of lowest origin. " Born in Putney, son of a
smith and ale-wife, he had been much abroad in
early life ; at Antwerp in the days of Philip and
Juana ; at Rome in the days of Julius II. He
had borne a pike in the Italian wars, and written
letters in the rooms of a Venetian trader. Watching in his tent he got the New Testament by

heart, and riding in the saddle he conned the lessons of Machiavelli's Prince. On marrying he had won the notice of Russell, and entered the service of Wolsey, acting as the Cardinal's secretary, and collecting many facts about those priories and convents which his master meant to spoil. When Wolsey's household staff was carried to the King, Cromwell went with it; and the King perceiving in him a man of fertile brain and ready fingers, kept him near his side."* He it was who now suggested an expedient which Henry was only to glad to adopt. "Nothing was to be done with the Pope. Why should not Henry be his own Pope? England was a monster now with two heads, King and Pope. Cut off one, and let the King be alone. Had not the German Protestants renounced Rome. Henry might do the same, not in faith, but in power."† The advice was not unpalatable to the imperious Tudor, with whom it was an imperative necessity that he should always have his own way; but, before going all the length that Cromwell advised, he sent a deputation to the Queen at Greenwich, entreating her to quiet both his conscience and her own by submitting the case to four English bishops and four nobles. Katharine received the deputation in her chamber, and heard this message. Then she made her reply.

"God grant the King a quiet conscience! This, my lord, shall be your answer: I am his wife; lawfully married to him by order of Holy Church; and so I will abide until the Court of Rome, which was privy to the beginning, shall have made an end."

But the King was tired of waiting for a decree from Rome. He took the law into his own hands. He and Katharine were both staying at

* Hepworth Dixon. † C. M. Yonge.

Windsor Castle after the feast of Trinity; and on the 14th of June he departed, leaving her there alone. From the despatches of Chapuys, the Imperial Ambassador who had replaced Mendoza, we learn the details of the time. "The Queen," he writes to Charles V. on the 17th of July, "complained of not being allowed to speak with her husband at his departure, as it would have been a consolation at least to bid him adieu; and Henry sent her a bitter answer, after taking counsel with the Duke of Norfolk and Gardiner, that he was very much offended at her for causing him to be cited personally to Rome, and for refusing a reasonable offer he had made her by his council to allow the cause to be decided by some other tribunal."

On the 31st Chapuys reports that Anne Boleyn "goes along with the King to the chase; and the Queen, who used to follow, has been commanded by the King to stay at Windsor." On the 19th of August the poor Queen was still at the Castle. "The Princess is now with her," says Chapuys. "They amuse themselves by hunting, and visiting the royal houses around Windsor." But the final crash was soon to come. "The King," writes the Ambassador, on September 10th, "under pretence of hunting about Windsor, has ordered the Queen to dislodge, and retire to More, a house belonging to St. Alban's, and the Princess to Richmond." "Go where I may," said the forsaken Queen, "I am his wife, and for him will I pray."

She never saw either husband or child again. Henry, anxious to be rid of her at any cost, had not been ostensibly ungenerous in his provision for her. All the manors settled on her by Prince Arthur were hers, and a list of other places to which she might retire was drawn up; but in reality the choice of her residence rested entirely with the King, as we find from a remark of Chapuys' some months later, that " the Queen is exceedingly sorry the King has refused her certain houses to which she wished to retire, and has commanded her to go to one of the worst in England."

From More she wrote to inform the Pope how she had been expelled from her husband's home; and from thence removed to Ampthill, near Woburn.

" An utter silence," says Miss Strickland, " is maintained, alike in public history, and in state documents, regarding that agonizing moment when the Princess Mary was reft from the arms of her unfortunate mother, to behold her no more. No witness had told the parting, no pen has described it; but sad and dolorous it certainly was to the hapless girl, even to the destruction of health. In the same month that Henry VIII. and Queen Katharine finally parted, Mary had been ill, for a payment is made by her father, to Dr. Bartelot, of £20 in reward for giving her his attendance." The forsaken Queen yearned after her daughter; but, in the following letter, written at this time, she had sufficient self-forgetfulness and tender consideration to say nothing that would add to the grief of the lonely and desolate girl. She had hitherto taught Mary Latin herself, with occasional help; and she was anxious that the Princess should continue her studies with her new tutor, Dr. Featherstone, hoping perhaps that they would divert her mind from sadder thoughts.

" DAUGHTER,

" I pray you, think not that forgetfulness has caused me to keep Charles so long here, and answered not your good letter, in the which I perceive ye would know how I do. I am in that case that the absence of the King and you troubleth me. My health is metely good; and I trust in God that He who sent it me doth it to the best, and will shortly turn all to come with good effect. And in the meantime, I am very glad to hear from you, specially when they shew me that ye be well amended. I pray God to continue it to His pleasure.

"As for writing in Latin, I am glad that ye shall change from me to Maister Federston ; for that shall do you much good to learn from him to write right, but yet sometimes I would be glad when ye do write to Maister Federston of your enditing, when he hath read it that I may see it; for it shall be a great comfort to me to see you keep your Latin, and fair writing, and all. And so I pray to recommend me to my Lady of Salisbury.

"At Woburn, this Friday night.

"KATHARINE THE QWENE."

"The last part of this letter," says M. du Boys, "betrays the pupil of Peter Martyr, the distinguished classical scholar who had attracted the attention of Erasmus in his youth. It is beautiful to see how this persecuted Queen is able to control the expression of her sorrow and personal anxiety thus to watch from a distance over her daughter's welfare, and procure for her a solid education which offers so many resources and consolations in all occurrences of life."

The desolate Queen was not left wholly undefended. Reginald Pole, on whom the King wished to confer the See of York, wrote a letter so strongly worded against the divorce that the King sent for him to the great gallery in Whitehall Palace to explain himself. He trembled and shed tears, but held to his words, and would not see the King's specious arguments. Henry left him in fierce anger, and Reginald returned to Italy, and heard no more of the Bishopric of York. Katharine appears to have returned to More after sojourning at Ampthill, as we find that she addressed a letter from thence to her nephew, on the 15th of December. Soon after Pope Clement sent a private message to the King, warning him to put away " one Anna," and take back his lawful wife and Queen ; but the King took no notice of the admonition, unless the appropriation of the Annates, or first fruits, hitherto always paid to the Pope, to his own private use, and the commanding the Queen to remove to a house further off, and with much worse accommodation, could be so called.

On the 1st of September, 1532, Anne Boleyn, robed in crimson velvet and ermine, was brought into the State apartment at Windsor Castle, and solemnly created Marchioness of Pembroke by the King, with a pension of £1,000 a year— no insignificant sum in those days—wherewith to maintain her dignity. When Henry met François I. at Calais in October, she accompanied him ; and on Sunday evening, October 28th, danced before both sovereigns, " in masking apparel, of strange fashion, made of cloth of gold, slashed with crimson tinsel satin puffed with cloth of silver, and knit with laces of gold."*　What Queen Katharine's feelings were concerning this event can best be gathered from a letter, written by her to the Emperor, of September 18th :—

" MOST HIGH AND MIGHTY LORD,

" Although your Majesty is occupied with your own affairs, and with your preparations against the Turk, I cannot, nevertheless, refrain from troubling you with mine, which perhaps in

* Hall.

substance and in the sight of God are of equal importance. Your Majesty knows well that God hears those who do Him service, and no greater service can be done than to procure an end in this business. It does not concern only ourselves —it concerns equally all who fear God. None can measure the woes which will fall on Christendom if his Holiness will not act in it, and act promptly. The signs are all around us in new printed books, full of lies and dishonesty—in the resolution to proceed with the cause here in England—in the interview of these two Princes, where the King, my lord, is covering himself with infamy through the companion which he takes with him. The country is full of terror and scandal; any evil may be looked for if nothing be done, and inasmuch as our only hope is in God's mercy, and in the favour of your Majesty, for the discharge of my conscience, I must let you know the strait in which I am placed.

"I implore your Highness, for the service of God, that you urge his Holiness to be prompt in bringing the cause to a conclusion. The longer the delay the harder the remedy will be.

"The particulars of what is passing here are so shocking, so outrageous against Almighty God, they touch so nearly the honour of my lord and husband, that for the love I bear him, and for the good that I desire for him, I would not have your Highness know of them from me. Your ambassador will inform you of all."

Meanwhile, Anne felt that now her success was nearly certain, her end well-nigh attained; and the dancing and dressing, which became every day more gorgeous, was only the outward expression of her inward satisfaction.

While her rival was thus further bewitching the King, Katharine, who had been at "the Bishop of Ely's house, seventeen miles from London,"* was at "Arforde Castel," as she wrote Hertford Castle, from whence she sent the following letter in Spanish to her nephew the Emperor, to whom she always clung with affection and deference as the child of her sister, and the head of her house :—

"MOST HIGH AND MOST POWERFUL LORD,

"God knows how much pleasure and comfort I have had in knowing of the victory which in Hungary and in other parts over the enemy of our faith your Majesty has had, and likewise the going of your Majesty to Bologna to see his Holiness to arrange as to what is to be done in future. I hold this for certain that these things are of God, and not made and directed by human means, as our Lord in His mercy, by the hand of your Highness, has wished to do so much good to all the Christian world. God has enlightened you, so that you should see his Holiness on which account all this kingdom and myself have hopes, certain it was with the grace of God that his Holiness may stay the second Turk, which is the business of the King, my lord, and my own. I call him second Turk because the ills, an end not being made by his Holiness to this cause in time, there has followed, and still follows each day, great and such bad examples that I do not know which is the worst, this business or that of the Turk.

"I have suffered much pain in importuning your Majesty so many times with this matter, for I am sure you desire the same ending of it as I do; but seeing so much ill, which the tardiness

* Chapuys.

occasions to this my suffering life with so little
quietude, and the time to make an end (of the
business) so expedient, it appears that God in
His bounty has wished that his Holiness and
your Majesty should meet to cause so great a
good that I am forced to be so importunate.
For the love of the passion of our Lord Jesus
Christ, I supplicate your Highness, since that by
the good works ye do, God will shed on thee
signal mercies and benefits each day that you
are occupied in doing this good so signal, before
you part from his Holiness, because in any other
my remedy will remain with God, and I shall
enter into another purgatory, from which I do
not hope to leave until it shall please Him, in the
absence of your Highness, recollect when at
another time he pronounced in that same city, and
also what was done.   I certify that your Majesty
being present or absent, it is all the same, that
here it is known the truth, and thus losing the
hope of those who persuade my King and lord to
make this a perpetual case, all will be at an end.
And believe me, your Highness, that there is no
one who knows this better than I do; and thus I
end, hoping good news for her who is most
affectionate to your Majesty, and supplicating
and praying to our Lord that He may give you
the health that your good work merits, and grace
to bring the enemy of our faith to the true conversion, repentance, and glory of your royal estate.
Such is my prayer.

"Arforde, 5th November.

"The humble Aunt of your Majesty,

"and your servant,

"CATHARINA."

Inscribed, "To the most high and most powerful Emperor and King, my lord and nephew."

Two other Spanish letters written by Katharine about this time are extant; the first, to the Grand Commander of Leon, dated from "Vichefarfil," which probably stands for Bishop's Hatfield :—

"ESPECIAL FRIEND,

"For the good and benefit that God has done to all Christendom by the hands of your sovereign in delivering it from the enemy of our faith, we all see the obligation under which we are to continue to do good works; and thou knowest that a greater thou canst not do than to procure from his Majesty that he may lose no opportunity in that his Holiness makes an end and termination of the business of the King, my lord, and mine, the which has brought and will bring so much evil to all Christendom for all the time it may be pending. And because I know how good a friend thou art to me in doing me kind acts, I return to pray most affectionately now that God who has been pleased to bring this cause of such high merits, that you will not forget me, but continue by the love you have of me, and what you have done, and be thou certain that thou hast in me a good friend to do for thee what may be in my power.

"Vichefarfil, 6th of November.

"Through want of quietude of heart, I have not power in my hand to write all that I would have wished, that if the remedy of his Majesty now fails me when he was with the Pope to make an end of my business, I am now unassisted, so now let God in His mercy do with me as seemeth fit, which is what I desire.

"(Signed) CATHARINA."

The second letter is to the Emperor, written after hearing of the meeting of François and Henry at Calais :—

" MOST HIGH AND MOST POWERFUL LORD,

" After having written the letter which your Majesty will see, a friend of mine informed me that it was very 'certain that the King, my lord, and the King of France in these interviews have determined to obtain [their wishes] from his Holiness through the Cardinals they send there, and because I am certain that your ambassador will make known to your Highness what he observes in this matter. I do not wish to give you more trouble with my letters in reference to those of the said ambassador. And returning to supplicate in regard to the contents of the letter I have written to your Majesty, and what you are to do for me, and know that the thunder of this land does not cost lightning except to wound me by the will of God.

" I pray that you see fit to make the effort, for it is just that his Holiness, for already the whole world knows well the necessity that something should be done, and it was represented that he (his Holiness) would not impede the good that from your Majesty this kingdom, and I hope for. And that the letters go safely and in time, I send by this post, by which I hope through our Lord to have so good a reply that it will comfort my life. Our Lord help the royal estate of your Majesty, and guard and increase your State.

" Hertford Castle, the 11th of November, 1532.
" The humble Aunt of your Majesty,
" (Signed)   CATHARINA."
Inscribed, " To the most high and powerful lord the Emperor and King, my nephew."

Meanwhile, Henry had resolved to wait no longer for any decree of Pope or Cardinal. He had appointed Cranmer to the See of Canterbury, vacant by the death of Warham; but before the new Archbishop could return from Germany, Dr. Rowland Lee was called to say mass in a garret chamber at Whitehall, on St. Paul's day, January 25th, 1533, and was there commanded by the King to wed him to Lady Anne, who was present with one lady in her train. This lady, Anne Savage, with two grooms of the chamber, Norreys and Heneage, were the only witnesses of the rite which gave Anne Boleyn the rank and crown for which she had waited and hungered so long. Immediately afterwards, Cromwell " obtained an Act of Parliament, reaffirming the old one, which forbade appeals from being carried out of the kingdom, thus closing up Katharine's appeal to Rome. Then Convocation was shown the opinion that Montmorency had elicited from the University of Paris, and called on to say whether the Pope could grant a dispensation to marry his brother's widow. Only three Bishops at first gave answer on the King's side, and thirty-six Abbots. But when the further question came on whether Katharine had been Arthur's wife or not, two more Bishops came over to the King's party, the clergy had as a body declared their assent, and there was nothing to do but to pronounce sentence." *

Accordingly the new Archbishop, accompanied by four Bishops, established his court at a priory of black canons at Dunstable, six miles from Ampthill, where the repudiated Queen was then residing. She was served with a citation to appear before him on Saturday, the 10th of May.

* C. M. Yonge.

"The bearers of the summons," says Froude, "were Sir Francis Bryan (an unfortunate choice, for he was cousin of the new queen, and insolent in his manner and bearing), Sir Thomas Gage, and Lord Vaux. She received them like herself with imperial sorrow. They delivered their message; she announced that she refused utterly to acknowledge the competency of the tribunal before which she was called; the court was a mockery; the Archbishop a shadow. She would neither appear before him in person, nor commission any one to appear on her behalf." She was accordingly pronounced contumacious, and on the day after Ascension Day, May 23rd, 1533, Cranmer, in the Lady Chapel at Dunstable Priory, solemnly declared that the marriage had never been good, and that both Henry and Katharine were free to marry again!

The tidings were brought to Katharine by Lord Montjoy, her former page, on July 3rd. How she received them is told in the messenger's account, published among the State Papers of Henry VIII., under William IV's commission. "She commanded her chamberlain should bring into her privy chamber as many of her servants as he could inform of her wishes; 'for,' she said, 'she thought it a long season since she saw them.' Her grace was then lying upon her pallet, because she had pricked her foot with a pin, so that she might not well stand or go, and also sore annoyed with a cough. Perceiving that many of her servants were there assembled, who might hear what should be said, she then demanded, 'Whether we had our charge to say by mouth or by writing?' We said 'Both;' but as soon as we began to declare and read that the articles were addressed to the princess dowager, she made exception to that name, saying, she was ' not princess dowager, but the queen, and, withal, the King's true wife ; had been crowned and anointed queen, and had by the King lawful issue, wherefore the name of queen she would vindicate, and so call herself during her lifetime.' "

By the King's orders, a bribe of increased income was offered if she would resign her rank, but she treated all such offers with royal scorn. Then they warned her that, " if she retained the name of queen, she would (for a vain desire and appetite of glory) provoke the King's highness, not only against her whole household to their hindrance and undoing, but be an occasion, that the King should withdraw his fatherly love from her honourable and dearest daughter, the lady princess Mary, which ought to move her, if no other cause did."

But Katharine's lofty resolution was unshaken. " As to any vain glory, it was not that she desired the name of a queen, but only for the discharge of her conscience to declare herself the King's true wife, and not his harlot, for the last twenty-four years. As to the princess, her daughter, she was the King's true child, and as God had given her unto them, so, for her part, she would render her again to the King, as his daughter, to do with her as should stand with his pleasure, trusting to God that she would prove an honest woman, and that neither for her daughter, her servants, her possessions, or any worldly adversity, or the King's displeasure, that might ensue, she would yield in this cause to put her soul in danger ; and that, they should not be feared, that have power to kill the body, but He only that have power over the soul."

The commissioners left her that day, but re-

turned again on the morrow, only to find her as
inflexible as ever. "She exerted her queenly
authority," says Miss Strickland, " by commanding the minutes of this conference to be brought
to her, and drew her pen through the words
'princess dowager' wherever they occurred. The
paper still remains in our national archives with
the alterations made by her agitated hand. She
demanded a copy that she might translate it into
Spanish; and the scene concluded with her pro-
testations, that she would 'never relinquish the
name of queen.'" "I would rather be a poor
beggar's wife," she cried, "and be sure of
heaven, than queen of all the world, and stand in
doubt thereof by reason of my own conceit. I
stick not so for vain glory, but because I know
myself the King's true wife—and while you call
me the King's subject, I was his subject while he
took me for his wife. But if he take me not for
his wife, I came not into this realm as merchandise, nor to be married to any merchant; nor do
I continue in the same but as his lawful wife, and
not as a subject to live under his dominion otherwise. I have always demeaned myself well and
truly towards the King—and if it can be proved
that either in writing to the Pope or any other, I
have either stirred or procured anything against
his Grace, or have been the means to any person
to make any motion which might be prejudicial to
his Grace or to his realm, I am content to suffer
for it. I have done England little good, and
I should be sorry to do it any harm. But if I
should agree to your motions and persuasions, I
should slander myself, and confess to have been
the King's harlot for twenty-four years. The
cause, I cannot tell by what subtle means, has
been determined here within the King's realm,

before a man of his own making, the Bishop of
Canterbury, no person indifferent I think in that
behalf; and for the indifference of the place, I
think the place had been more indifferent to
have been judged in hell; for no truth can be
suffered here, whereas the devils themselves I
suppose do tremble to see the truth in this cause
so sore oppressed."

" The implicit obedience Henry's agents paid
Katharine, even when they came to dispute her
title, proved how completely she was versed in the
science of command. Her servants had been
summoned by Montjoy to take an oath to serve
her, but as Princess of Wales, which she forbade
them to do; therefore many left her service, and
she was waited upon by a very few, whom the
King excused from the oath."*

Meanwhile Anne Boleyn was tasting all the
sweets of that queenship just wrested from
Katharine. On the 19th of May she was brought
with much rejoicing from Greenwich up the
Thames to the Tower, "conducted thither in
state by the Lord Mayor and the City Companies,
with one of those splendid exhibitions upon the
water which, in the days when the silver Thames
deserved its name, and the sun could shine down
upon it out of the summer sky, were spectacles
scarcely rivalled in gorgeousness by the world-
famous wedding of the Adriatic."† On the 31st
she made the progress through the city customary
to all queens on the coronation eve, amid pomp
and splendour such as had never been surpassed—
through streets draped in scarlet and crimson,
cloth of gold and velvet; past pageants which
rivalled each other in gorgeous compliment to the
queen; surrounded by knights and ladies, and

* Strickland.   † Froude.

with a guard in coats of beaten gold. In the midst of all this magnificence, a white chariot approached, "drawn by two palfreys in white damask, which swept the ground, a golden canopy borne above it making music with silver bells: and in the chariot sat the observed of all observers, the beautiful occasion of all this glittering homage—Fortune's plaything of the hour, the Queen of England—Queen at last, borne along upon the waves of this sea of glory, breathing the perfumed incense of greatness which she had risked her fair name, her delicacy, her honour, her self respect to win: and she had won it."*

The following day, Whit Sunday, June 1st, she was solemnly crowned with all state and splendour in Westminster Abbey, the crown of St. Edward and then the crown made for her being set upon her head, her train borne by the Duchess of Norfolk, and all the noble ladies of the kingdom following her in scarlet velvet and ermine. "Did anything of remorse," asks Froude, "any pang of painful recollection, pierce at that moment the incense of glory which she was inhaling? Did any vision flit across her of a sad mourning figure, which once had stood where she was standing, now desolate, neglected, sinking into the darkening twilight of a life cut short by sorrow? Who can tell? At such a time, that figure would have weighed heavily upon a noble mind, and a wise mind would have been taught by the thought of it, that although life be fleeting as a dream, it is long enough to experience strange vicissitudes of fortune. But Anne Boleyn was not noble and was not wise, too probably she felt nothing but the delicious, all-absorbing, all-in-

* Froude.

toxicating present; and if that plain suffering face presented itself to her memory at all, we may fear that it was rather as a foil to her own surpassing loveliness. Two years later she was able to exult over Katharine's death; she is not likely to have thought of her with gentler feelings in the first flush and glow of triumph."

In spite of the grace and fascination of the new Queen, and the splendour which marked her coronation, the marriage was very unpopular with the lower classes. "We'll have no Nan Bullen! Nan Bullen shall not be our Queen!" was the common cry; and in Wales a rising took place in favour of the repudiated Queen. Even the House of Commons were partizans of Katharine, and presented a petition to the King, moved by a member called Tems, that he would take Queen Katharine home. Sir Thomas More, who was invited to be present at the coronation, and to whom twenty pounds had been sent to provide himself with a suit for the occasion, refused to appear; and Reginald Pole wrote indignantly of the "sorceress" and "Jezebel," as he politely termed Anne. On the 11th of July, Clement VII., published a decree commanding Henry to separate from Anne before September, and take back Katharine, on pain of excommunication if he disobeyed. At Greenwich, Peto, a Friar of the Order of Observants, preaching before the royal pair, boldly denounced their crime, threatened them with awful judgments, compared the King to Ahab, and finished by declaring that "like that accursed Israelitish king, his blood would be licked by dogs." Wonderful to relate, Henry listened in silence, and let the friar go; but the next Sunday a certain Dr. Curwen preached, and reviled Peto. "Another friar, named Elstow, defended Peto in his absence, and called Curwen a lying prophet. Both friars were brought before the Council, and Cromwell told them they ought to be tied up in a sack, and thrown into the Thames. Elstow smiled and said, 'Such threats may move those clad in purple and fine linen. We know the way to heaven by water as well as by land, and care not which way we go.' The two friars were banished, their house broken up, and Curwen shortly after made a Bishop. Other sermons took the same course, and the other Bishops actually forbade all preaching for a time, and Cranmer, issuing new licenses to preach, forbade anything to be said on this question."*

"On one hot midsummer Sunday in this year 1533," says Froude, "the people gathering to church in every parish through the English counties read, nailed upon the doors, a paper signed Henry R., setting forth that the Lady Katharine of Spain, heretofore called Queen of England, was not to be called by that title any more, but was to be called Princess Dowager, and so to be held and esteemed." The proclamation, we may suppose, was read with varying comments. Of the reception of it in the northern counties the following information was forwarded to the Crown. The Earl of Derby, lord lieutenant of Yorkshire, wrote to inform the Council that he had arrested a certain "lewd and naughty priest," James Harrison by name, on the charge of having spoken unfitting and slanderous words of his Highness and the Queen's Grace. He had taken the examinations of several witnesses, which he had sent with his letter, and which were to the following effect:—

"Richard Clark deposeth that the said James

* C. M. Yonge.

Harrison, reading the proclamation, said that Queen Katharine was Queen, Nan Bullen should not be Queen, nor the King should be no King but on his bearing.

" William Dalton deposeth that in his hearing the above-named James said, ' I will take none for Queen but Queen Katharine. Who the devil made Nan Bullen Queen ? I will never take her for Queen,' and he, the said William, answered, ' Hold thy peace ; thou wot'st not what thou sayest. But that thou art a priest I should punish thee, that others should take example.' "

In this summer Katharine moved from Ampthill to Bug·len, now Buckden, which belonged to the Bishop of Lincoln—" a forest lodge standing on the Great North Road, four miles from Hunting-don—a spacious edifice of brick, with gardens, ponds, and orchards, nestling in the shadow of an ancient church." * Here, writes Dr. Harpsfield, " Queen Katharine spent her solitary life in much prayer, great alms, and abstinence ; and when she was not this way occupied, then was she, and her gentlewomen, working with their own hands something wrought in needlework, costly and arti-ficially, which she intended, to the honour of God, to bestow on some of the churches. There was, in the said house of Bugden, a chamber with a window that had a prospect into the chapel, out of the which she might hear divine service. In this chamber she enclosed herself, sequestered from all other company, a great part of the night and day, and upon her knees used to pray at the same window, leaning upon the stones of the same. There were some of her gentlewomen who curiously marked all her doings, and reported that oftentimes they found the said stones where her

* Hepworth Dixon.

head had reclined wet as though a shower had
rained upon them. It was credibly said that at the
time of her prayer she removed the cushions that
ordinarily lay in the same window, and that the
said stones were imbrued with the tears of her
devout eyes, when she prayed for strength to
subdue the agonies of wronged affections."
Strength was won both for endurance and forgiveness, and she learned to pardon even the
prime cause of her miseries, the usurper of her
name and place. "I have credibly heard," says
the just-quoted authority, "that, at a time of her
sorest troubles, one of her gentlewomen began to
curse Anne Boleyn. The Queen dried her stream-
ing eyes, and said earnestly, 'Hold your peace!
Curse not—curse her not, but rather pray for her,
for even now is the time fast coming when you
shall have reason to pity her, and lament her case.'
And so it chanced indeed."

The following letter from Katharine to her
daughter Mary was probably written from Bugden
during this summer—apparently in August :—

" Daughter, I heard such tidings this day, that
I do perceive (if it be true) the time is very near
when Almighty God will provide for you, and I
am very glad of it ; for I trust that he doth handle
you with a good love. I beseech you to agree to
his pleasure with a merry [cheerful] heart, and
be you sure that without fail he will not suffer
you to perish if you beware to offend him.

" I pray God that you, good daughter, offer
yourself to him. If any pangs come over you,
shrive yourself, first make you clean ; take heed
of his commandments, and keep them as near, as
he will give you grace to do, for there are you sure
armed.

"And if this lady do come to you as it is spoken, if she do bring you a letter from the King, I am sure in the self same letter you will be commanded what to do. Answer with very few words, obeying the King your father in everything—save only that you will not offend God, and lose your soul, and go no further with learning and disputation in the matter. And wheresoever, and in whatever company you shall come, obey the King's commandments, speak few words, and meddle nothing.

" I will send you two books in Latin; one shall be, De Vita Christi, with the declarations of the gospels; and the other the Epistles of St. Jerome, that he did write to Paula and Eustochium, and in them, I trust, you will see good things.

" Sometimes, for your recreation, use your virginals or lute, if you have any. But one thing specially I desire you, for the love you owe to God and unto me, to keep your heart with a chaste mind, and your person from all ill and wanton company, not thinking or desiring of any husband, for Christ's passion; neither determine yourself to any manner of living, until this troublesome time be past. For I do make you sure you shall see a very good end, and better than you can desire.

" I would God, good daughter, that you did know with how good a heart I write this letter unto you. I never did one with a better, for I perceive very well that God loveth you. I beseech him, of his goodness, to continue it.

" I think it best you keep your keys yourself, for whosoever it is [that is, whosoever keeps her keys] shall be done as shall please them.

" And now you shall begin, and by likelihood I shall follow. I set not a rush by it, for when they have done the utmost they can, then I am sure of amendment.

"I pray you recommend me unto my good lady of Salisbury, and pray her to have a good heart, for we never come to the kingdom of heaven but by troubles. Daughter, wheresoever you come, take no pain to send to me, for, if I may, I will send to you.

"By your loving mother,
"KATHARINE THE QUENE."

"Hitherto," says Miss Strickland, "this letter has been deemed a mystery. It is evidently written with conflicting feelings, under the pressure of present calamity, but with the excitement of recently awakened hope of better days. The Queen has privately heard of some great, but undeclared, benefit to her daughter, which she hints at to cheer her. Meantime she expects that a lady is to summon Mary by a letter from the King, and that she is shortly to be introduced into trying scenes, where the divorce will be discussed, and her opinions demanded. On these points, she disinterestedly and generously exhorts her not to controvert her father's will. The Queen expects her daughter to be surrounded by dissipated company, where temptations will sedulously be brought to assail her, against which she guards her. She likewise anticipates that enemies will be near her, and warns her to keep the keys herself, dreading the surreptitious introduction of dangerous papers into her escritoire. Lady Salisbury is still Mary's protectress, but that venerable lady is in trouble, and looking darkly forward to the future. The kind Queen sends her a message of Christian consolation, the efficiency of which she had fully tried. All that has been considered mysterious in the letter of Queen Katharine vanishes before the fact preserved in the pages of the Italian Pollino, who declares that Mary was present at Greenwich Palace, and in the chamber of Anne Boleyn, when Elizabeth was born. Setting aside the religious principles of the historian, the simple fact that Mary was there is highly probable. Till some days subsequent to the birth of Elizabeth, Henry did not disinherit his eldest daughter, lest, if anything fatal had happened to Queen Anne and her infant, he might have been left without legitimate offspring of any kind. It is very likely that the laws of England required then, as now, that the presumptive heir of the kingdom should be present at the expected birth of an heir apparent to the crown. If Katharine of Aragon's letter be read with this light cast on it, how plain does it appear. The good mother endeavoured to fortify her daughter's mind for the difficult situation in which she would find herself, in the chamber of Anne Boleyn, at the birth of the rival heir. Then the beneficial change in Mary's prospects, hinted at by her mother, has reference to the recent decree of the Pope (soon after made public), who in July, 1533, had annulled the marriage of Henry VIII. with Anne Boleyn, and forbade them to live together under pain of excommunication—a sentence which likewise illegitimated their offspring, and confirmed Mary in her royal station—this sentence was published in September, as near as possible to the birth of Elizabeth, and secret intelligence of this measure had evidently been given to Katharine of Aragon when she wrote to Mary. She knew that the decision of Rome had previously settled all such controversies, and it was natural enough that she should expect the same result would take place."

The child, at whose birth Mary was present, was christened with much pomp by the name of the King's mother, and created Princess of Wales in Mary's stead; and the disinherited elder sister was domiciled with the baby heiress at Hatfield Lodge. A bitterer lot can hardly be imagined than that of the poor young princess, deprived of her rank, forced to see another in her place, keenly conscious of her mother's wrongs, and of the unjust elevation of that mother's rival. Anne came occasionally to see her child, and during one of her visits tried, with questionable wisdom and good feeling, to induce Mary to recognize her queenly rank.

"Treat me as Queen," she said. "Submit yourself to the King, and I will do my best to reconcile you to his Grace, and see that things are made more pleasant for you."

Mary was a Tudor, and her answer was as imperious as any utterance of King Hal himself:—

"Madam, I know no other Queen in this realm than my lady, my mother. If you will tell the King, my father, what I say, you will oblige me." She had all the courage of her race, and an absorbing devotion to her mother. "And while Katharine of Aragon lived, Mary of England would have suffered martyrdom rather than make a concession against the interest and dignity of that adored parent."*

How great was the popularity of the disinherited young princess and her repudiated mother with the English people, may be gathered from the following letter, addressed by the French Ambassador, M. D'Inteville, to Cardinal Tournon, and written apparently in the autumn of 1533.

* Strickland.

" The project for the marriage of the Princess Mary," says Froude, " with the Dauphin, had been revived by the Catholic party ; and a private arrangement, of which this marriage was to form the connecting-link, was contemplated between the Ultramontanes in France, the Pope, and the Emperor."

" MY LORD,

" You will be so good as to tell the Most Christian King that the Emperor's Ambassador has communicated with the old Queen. The Emperor sends a message to her and to her daughter, that he will not return to Spain till he has seen them restored to their rights.

" The people are so much attached to the said ladies that they will rise in rebellion, and join any prince who will undertake their quarrel. You probably know from other quarters the intensity of this feeling. It is shared by all classes, high and low, and penetrates even into the royal household.

" The nation is in marvellous discontent. Every one but the relations of the present Queen is indignant on the ladies' account. Some fear the overthrow of religion ; others fear war and injury to trade. Up to this time, the cloth, hides, wool, lead, and other merchandise of England have found markets in Flanders, Spain, and Italy ; now it is thought navigation will be so dangerous that English merchants must equip their ships for war if they trade to foreign countries ; and besides the risk of losing all to the enemy, the expense of the armament will swallow the profits of the voyage. In like manner, the Emperor's subjects and the Pope's subjects will not be able to trade with England. The coasts will be blockaded by the ships of the Emperor and his allies; and at this moment men's fears are aggravated by the unseasonable weather throughout the summer, and the failure of the crops. There is not corn enough for half the ordinary consumption.

"The common people, foreseeing these inconveniences, are so violent against the Queen, that they say a thousand shameful things of her, and of all who have supported her in her intrigues. On them is cast the odium of all the calamities anticipated from the year.

" When the war comes, no one doubts that the people will rebel as much from the fear of the dangers which I have mentioned, as from the love which is felt for the two ladies, and especially for the Princess. She is so entirely beloved that, notwithstanding the law made at the last Parliament, and the menace of death contained in it, they persist in regarding her as Princess. No Parliament, they say, can make her anything but the King's daughter, born in marriage; and so the King and every one else regarded her before that Parliament.

" Lately, when she was removed from Greenwich, a vast crowd of women, wives of citizens and others, walked before her at their husbands' desire, weeping and crying that notwithstanding all she was Princess. Some of them were sent to the Tower, but they would not retract.

" Things are now so critical, and the fear of war is so general, that many of the greatest merchants in London have placed themselves in communication with the Emperor's Ambassador, telling him, that if the Emperor will declare war, the English nation will join him for the love they bear the Lady Mary.

" You, my Lord, will remember that when you

KATHARINE OF ARAGON. **111**

were here, it was said you were come to tell the
King that he was excommunicated, and to demand
the hand of the Princess for the Dauphin. The
people were so delighted that they have never
ceased to pray for you. We, too, when we arrived
in London, were told that the people were praying
for us. They thought our embassy was to the
Princess. They imagined her marriage with the
Dauphin had been determined on by the two
Kings, and the satisfaction was intense and universal.

"They believe that, except by this marriage,
they cannot possibly escape war; whereas can it
be brought about, they will have peace with the
Emperor and all other Christian princes. They
are now so disturbed and so desperate that, although at one time they would have preferred a
husband for her from among themselves, that they
might not have a foreign King, there now is
nothing which they desire more. Unless the
Dauphin will take her, they say she will continue
disinherited; or, if she come to her rights, it can
only be by battle, to the great incommodity of the
country. The Princess herself says publicly that
the Dauphin is her husband, and that she has no
hope but in him. I have been told this by persons
who heard it from her own lips.

"The Emperor's Ambassador inquired, after you
came, whether we had seen her. He said he knew
she was most anxious to speak with us; she
thought we had permission to visit her, and she
looked for good news. He told us among other
things, that she had been more strictly guarded
of late, by the orders of the Queen that now is,
who, knowing her feeling for the Dauphin, feared
there might be some practice with her, or some
attempt to carry her off.

" The Princess's ladies say that she calls herself
the Dauphin's wife. A time will come, she says,
when GOD will see that she has suffered pain and
tribulation sufficient ; the Dauphin will then
demand her of the King her father, and the King
her father, will not be able to refuse.

" The lady who was my informant heard, also,
from the Princess, that her governess, and the
other attendants whom the Queen had set to
watch her, had assured her that the Dauphin
was married to the daughter of the Emperor; but
she, the Princess, had answered it was not true—
the Dauphin could not have two wives, and they
well knew that she was his wife; they told her
that story, she said, to make her despair, and
agree to give up her rights; but she would never
part with her hopes.

" You may have heard of the storm that broke
out between her and her governess when we went
to visit her little sister. She was carried off by
force to her room, that she might not speak with
us; and they could neither pacify her nor keep
her still, till the gentleman who escorted us told
her he had the King's commands that she was
not to show herself while we were in the house.
You remember the message the same gentleman
brought to you from her, and the charge which
was given by the Queen.

" Could the King be brought to consent to the
marriage, it would be a fair union of two realms,
and to annex Britain to the Crown of France
would be a great honour to our sovereign ; the
English party desire nothing better; the Pope
will be glad of it; the Pope fears that, if war
break out again, France will draw closer to England on the terms which the King of England
desires; and he may thus lose the French tribute

as he has lost the English. He therefore will urge the Emperor to agree, and the Emperor will assist gladly for the love he bears to his cousin. "If the Emperor be willing, the King of England can then be informed ; and he can be made to feel that, if he will avoid war, he must not refuse his consent. The King, in fact, has no wish to disown the Princess, and he knows full well that the marriage with the Dauphin was once agreed on.

"Should he be unwilling, and should his wife's persuasions still have influence with him, he will hesitate, before he will defy, for her sake, the King of France and the Emperor united. His regard for the Queen is less than it was, and diminishes every day. He has a new fancy, as you are aware."

Dwelling at Bugden, Katharine's patience brought her peace, and she in some degree regained her cheerfulness. The people living near, as they learned to know her, began to love her well. According to Harpsfield, "they visited her frequently out of pure respect, and she received the tokens of regard they daily showed her most sweetly and graciously." But she was not long left in quiet. Archbishop Lee, and Tunstall, Bishop of Durham, came to see her, and read to her six articles, setting forth why she ought to be looked on as the Princess Dowager of Wales, and how she ought to relinquish the title of Queen. "We admonished her," they wrote to the King, "not to call herself your Highness' wife, for that your Highness was discharged of that marriage made with her, and contracted new marriage with your dearest wife Queen Anne, and forasmuch (as thanked be God) fair issue has already sprung of this marriage and more is likely to follow by God's grace." "My lords!" said Katharine, "I am the King's wife, and I shall be his wife until I die. Why you, my lord of Durham," she added, turning to Tunstall, "and the other members of my council, always told me that my cause was just!" The Bishop tried to excuse his change of front. "The question was the validity of the papal brief and bull; not the question of marrying with a brother's wife. Since then, the universities in Europe have pronounced, and Pope Clement, when at Marseilles, sent a message to the King, that he was ready to pronounce the dispensation bad, the marriage null and void"—a message of which none but Tunstall had ever heard. "I have now," he continued, "changed my former opinion. I would exhort you to do the same, and cease to usurp the name of Queen." Such exhortations were too much for the high spirit of the outraged matron; and she vowed, in pain and pride, that "she would never quit the title of Queen, which she would persist to retain till death;" concluding by declaring that "she was the King's wife and not his subject, and therefore not liable to his Acts of Parliament." And from this neither threats nor persuasions could move her.

On the 15th of November Katharine wrote to her nephew, congratulating him on the success of his recent campaign against the Turks, and then alluded to the subject that was nearest to her heart in the following terms:—

"And as our Lord in His mercy has worked so great a good for Christendom by your Highness's hands, so has He enlightened also His Holiness; and I and all this realm have now a sure hope

that, with the grace of God, his Holiness will
slay this second Turk, this affair between the
King my lord and me. Second Turk, I call it,
from the misfortunes which, through his Holiness's long delay, have grown out of it, and are
now so vast and of so ill example that I know not
whether this or the Turk be the worst. Sorry am
I to have been compelled to importune your
Majesty so often in this matter, for sure I am you
do not need my pressing. But I see delay to be
so calamitous, my own life is so unquiet and so
painful, and the opportunity to make an end now
so convenient, that it seems as if God of His goodness had brought his Holiness and your Majesty
together to bring about so great a good. I am
forced to be importunate, and I implore your
Highness for the passion of our Lord Jesus
Christ, that in return for the signal benefits which
God each day is heaping on you, you will accom-
plish for me this great blessing, and bring his
Holiness to a decision. Let him remember what
he promised you at Bologna. The truth here is
known, and he will thus destroy the hopes of
those who persuade the King my lord that he will
never pass judgment."

The air of Bugden was too damp to suit the
Queen, and she requested that she might be
moved to some place nearer London. The King
in answer sent orders that she should be taken to
Fotheringay Castle, which belonged to her as part
of her dower as Prince Arthur's widow, and
which she had, Leland tells us, " done great costs
in refreshing." But thither she positively refused to go. In taking up her residence there,
she would appear to accept the position of
Princess Dowager; and not even thus tacitly
would she compromise her cause. The Duke of

Suffolk was nevertheless sent to break up her household at Bugden, to take her if she still declined to go to Fotheringay, to Somarsham, a house belonging to the Bishop of Ely, and to cause her servants to take the recently framed oath of allegiance—"Ye shall swear to bear faith, troth, and obedience, only to the King's grace, and to the heirs of his body, by his most dear and entirely beloved lawful wife, Queen Anne." This declaration was not easily administered to Katharine's retainers. "They were very earnest in entreaties to be dismissed rather than retained in her service, if they were forced to abjure their oaths to her as Queen; for they could not take the second oath without perjury, neither could any inducement prevail on Katharine to say she should consider them as her dutiful servants if they called her the Princess Dowager. Both her almoner and receiver implored her to yield on this point, yet she persisted in her determination. The rest of the household refused to take the oath against her wish, and the commissioners questioned them regarding the persons who had persuaded them so earnestly that Katharine was Queen."* At length it was discovered that the Queen's chaplains, Barker and Abell, had thus influenced them. The latter was, says Hepworth Dixon, "the boldest champion in her cause, and his Invicta Veritas was making no light stir in college walls." These two were called before the Commissioners, who wrote to Henry that "we found them stiffly standing in their conscience, that she was Queen, and the King's lawful wife, and that no man sworn to serve her as Queen might change that oath without perjury, and they acknowledged they had shown the same to as

* Strickland.

many as asked their counsel; whereupon we have
committed them to the porter's ward, with liberty
to speak to no one but their keeper." Abell had
been Katharine's confessor, and there was no
little difficulty in supplying his place. "In a confessor she required two things: first, that he
should speak Castilian well, for she would not
confess her sins in any other tongue; second,
that he should go with her in all she had done, in
all she was doing, and in all she meant to do."*
Such a man was not easily found; but at last the
post was given to Atequa, Bishop of Llandaff, an
old Spanish priest who had accompanied her from
Spain—"a man of meek appearance and opinion,
who desired to live in peace and keep the revenues
of his see. As Bishop of Llandaff he had subscribed the Act of Appeals, the Act of Supremacy,
and the Act of Succession. Though he loved the
Queen, he was not likely to involve himself in
plots. So he was suffered to remain a bishop, and
to act as Katharine's spiritual guide."†

Sir Edmund Bedyngfeld, nominally steward of
her household, but really "the castellan who held
her in custody,"‡ wrote to the Privy Council a
minute account of a conversation the Queen held
with him at this time regarding her household.
"She wished to retain her confessor, her physician, and her potecary; two men servants, and as
many women as it shall please the King's grace to
appoint; and that they should take no oath, but
only to the King and to her, but to none other
woman."

"As to my physician and potecary," she continues, "they be my countrymen; the King
knoweth them as well as I do. They have continued many years with me, and have (I thank

* Hepworth Dixon. † *Ibid.* ‡ Strickland.

them) taken great pains with me; for I am oft times sickly, as the King's grace doth know right well. And I require their attendance for the preservation of my poor body, that I may live as long as it pleaseth God. They are faithful and diligent in my service, and also daily do they pray that the King's royal estate may long endure. But if they take any other oath than they have taken to the King and me (to serve me) I shall never trust them again, for in so doing I should live continually in fear of my life with them. Wherefore I trust the King, of his high honour and goodness, and for the great love that hath been betwixt him and me (which love in me now is as faithful to him as ever it was, so take I God to record it), will not use extremity with me, my request being so reasonable."

Her wishes were so far complied with that the physician and apothecary did remain; but, as we have already seen, the confessor was removed. She remained as resolute as ever about the change of residence, as the following letter, written by the Duke of Suffolk to the Duke of Norfolk for the information of the Privy Council, testifies:—

"MY LORD,

"Because we have written to the King's highness, we shall only advertise you, that we find here the most obstinate woman that may be; insomuch that, as we think, surely there is no other remedy than to convey her by force from hence to Somersame [Somarsham]. Concerning this, we have nothing in our instructions; we pray your good lordship that with speed we may have knowledge of the King's express pleasure, at the furthest by Sunday night [December 21st], or else there shall not be time before the feast

[Christmas Day] to remove her. My lord, we have had no small travail to induce the servants to take the new oath. Notwithstanding, now many of them are sworn with promise to serve the King's highness according to his pleasure. My lord, we found things here far from the King's expectation, we assure you, as more at our return you shall know.

" Moreover, whereas Tomeo was appointed to be clerk comptroller here in this house, and Wilbrahim with my lady princess [Elizabeth]; we understand that your lordship hath taken Tomeo to serve my lady princess, and discharged Wilbrahim, whereby this house is disappointed of that necessary officer.

"Bugden, Friday, 19th of December."

The Queen told Thomas Vaux, one of her officers, and a spy of Cromwell's, "that she had no mind to go to Fotheringay, and that she would not go thither, though all provisions were made for her, yet from the place where she was she much wished to go." In a despatch from " R. Sussex," dated December 31st, 1534, it is complained that " against all humanity and reason she still persists that she will not remove, saying, that although your grace have the power, yet ne may she, ne will she go, unless drawn with ropes ; " and instructions are asked for, " what to do if she persisteth in her obstinacy, and that she will, we surely think, for in her wilfulness she may fall sick and keep her bed, refusing to put on her clothes." The Duke of Suffolk treated her with such insolence that she left his presence, refusing to see him again ; and after his departure she was left a short time in peace, and lived in such exceeding retirement that she never left her room, where she even took her meals, except to sit in an adjoining gallery opening on the chapel, to hear mass. In the beginning of the new year of 1535 she was, however, taken to Kimbolton Castle, whence she was not again to be removed till she took her last journey of all to Peterbro' Cathedral.

"Kimbolton," writes the Duke of Manchester,* " may be considered a secluded spot. Even after the corn counties have been opened up by train, and telegraph, and mail, the castle is eight miles from a post town, nine miles from a railway line, no less than thirty miles from Peterborough, the city in which Katharine was buried, now the nearest station at which an express from London to York finds it worth while to stop. The Castle, with the hamlet at its gates, was built by the ancient race of the Mandevilles in a broad hollow at the crossing of two great roads, under the grey shadow of Stonely Priory, a convent founded by the Bigrames, of whom, and of whose doings in the early time, a few stones, a mound of earth, a green road, a clump of trees, and the name of a field and spinney, alone remain. Kimbolton rose in the heart of a saintly district, near St. Neots, St. Ives, and Swinstead Abbey, on the edge of the monastic regions of the fen. The soil is hard, the river sluggish, the underwood dense, the population thin."

The traces of Katharine's residence there are still distinctly marked. The place abounds in memories of her. "The room in which she passed away, a room on the ground floor, looking into the deer park, and across the moats towards the Castle Hill and the keeper's lodge, still bears her name. The boudoir which she occupied, on the

* "Society from the Reign of Elizabeth to Anne."

walls of which she hung her pictures and tapes-
tries, adjoins it. A travelling chest in which she
kept her clothes and jewels, and which bears her
cypher on the lid, remains at the foot of the
grand staircase. A secret passage leading from
the white drawing-room into the chapel is said to
have been the means by which she eluded the
observation, and escaped from the presence of her
husband's spies; a tradition that is in keeping
with all that we know from Sir Edmund Bedyngfeld's reports of her reserved and secluded ways
of life while there. Though all the fronts of
Kimbolton Castle were renewed by Sir John
Vanburgh, and the white drawing-room was
added by that nimble wit and heavy builder to the
pile, the wing which Katharine occupied is still
the same in block as when the Mandevilles raised
it in an angle of the cross roads from Bedford to
Huntingdon, from St. Neots to Oundle; the same
as when Katharine, tiring of the close gardens
and damp ponds of Buckden, chose it for her last
home, in preference either to Somarsham near St.
Ives, or Fotheringay Castle on the Nene. That
wing is of hoar antiquity. The inner and outer
moats, it is true, have been filled up; the gates
have been rebuilt by the architect of Blenheim
and Castle Howard; the castle has been squared,
and faced, and trimmed ; yet behind the
facings and finishings a good deal of strong
Plantagenet and of very fine Tudor work may
still be traced. For although the writer of the
'Relapse' and the 'Provoked Wife' did a good
deal to improve the pictorial aspects of the castle,
he left the frame of it intact, much as it had
come down from Mandeville, Bohun, and Stafford,
into the hands of Wingfield and Montagu. No
fancy is required to animate once more the silent

rooms. The corridor along which Bastien and Antonio helped their royal mistress into chapel, the gallery in which she sat to hear Atequa chant masses and complines, still, after a lapse of three hundred years, whisper to the imagination of her presence. From a window of her boudoir you may see the portal at which Lady Willoughby, splashed and fainting, knocked on that winter night, and through which her tears and eloquence forced a way to the bedside of her dying friend. There is the chamber into which the Spanish ambassador, Eustachio Chappius, the Capucius of Shakespeare, was introduced by Bedyngfeld in times to see the aunt of an Emperor expire. On the walls hang portraits of the time, which are said to have belonged to her; portraits which may have been brought by her from Buckden, and left with her travelling trunk by Rich, and the royal officers, when they carried away her plate, with 5000 marks, as trifles unworthy of their care. These pictures are on panel; some of them by Holbein; those which are known being her nearest friends or associates. One is of her mother, Isabel the Catholic. Two are of her nephew Charles V. One is of the Archduke Philip, husband of her unhappy sister, Crazy Jane. There are portraits of Sir John Cheeke, William, first Lord Paget, and Thomas Cromwell, Earl of Essex. One of the known portraits is the Count of Nassau. . . . . This collection of Queen Katharine's kinsmen and associates has been at Kimbolton time out of mind; and until recently hung in the Queen's boudoir."*

* " Society from the Reign of Elizabeth to Anne."

CHAPTER VII.

Persecution of Father Forrest—Attachment of her servants to
Queen Katharine—Illness of the Princess Mary—The bull of
excommunication—Queen's letter to the Emperor—Threats
of Anne Boleyn—Non-publication of the bull—Letter of
Katharine to the Pope—Illness of the Queen—Her request
to see her daughter—Henry's refusal—His resolve to enforce
her submission—Opinion of Katharine's physician—Her
renewed entreaty to see her child—Her last letter to the
Emperor—Devotion of Lady Willoughby—Queen's message
to the Emperor—Her letter to the King—Her death—
Reception of the news at Greenwich—The general sorrow—
Letter of the King to Lady Bedyngfeld—Funeral of Queen
Katharine—Her will—Her character—Her memory preserved
at Kimbolton.

KATHARINE'S nominal income as Princess Dowager
of Wales was £5,000 a year; but this was so
irregularly paid that Sir Edmund Bedyngfeld
bears witness that the household was more than
once utterly without money. But this was the
least of her troubles. A far bitterer sorrow was
the persecution of her old confessor, Father
Forrest, who had been thrown into Newgate, and,
says Pollino, "for two years had remained among
thieves and persons of infamous characters, and
had endured the cruellest torments. Queen
Katharine, who considered herself the cause of his
intolerable miseries, felt herself obliged to write to
him, saying 'how much the thought of his sufferings grieved her and moved her to pity, and to
write him a letter of comfort, although she
dreaded lest it should be intercepted and occasion
his death.'" "Since you have always shown
yourself ready," she wrote, in words that were the
echo of her own courage, "to give good counsel to
others, you will know very well what to do, and

that you are called to bear witness for the love of
Christ and the truth of His Catholic Faith. If
you will hold up against the few brief torments
which have been prepared for you, you will receive,
as you well know, eternal gains. I should esteem
a man bereft of sense and reason who, to save
himself some passing pains on earth, would lose
his great reward in heaven." The "Signora
Lisabetta Ammonia," as Pollino Italianizes the
name of Elizabeth, Lady Hammond, also wrote to
Forrest on behalf of the Queen, "informing him of
the continual tears and grief that oppressed Queen
Katharine on his account, ever since his sentence.
That the Queen could feel no ease or comfort till
she had sent to him to know ' whether there was
aught she could do to avert from him his fate ? '
adding that she was herself languishing under
incurable infirmity, and the fury and rage of the
King would infallibly cut short her life. It was
but last Monday the King had sent some of his
council to the Queen's house to make search for
persons or things he thought were hidden there ;
and his agents, with faces full of rage and angry
words, had exceedingly hurried and terrified Queen
Katharine." *

Father Forrest replied to Katharine's letter and
messages in the following epistle :—

" SERENEST QUEEN AND DAUGHTER IN CHRIST,

" Your servant Thomas gave me your
Majesty's letter, which found me in great affliction,
yet in constant hope of release by means of death
from the captivity of this miserable body. Not
only did your letter infinitely comfort me, but it
excited in me patience and joy.

" Christ Jesu give you, daughter and lady of

* Strickland.

mine, above all mortal delights which are of brief
continuance, the joy of seeing His divine presence
for evermore.

"Remember me in your most fervent oraisons;
pray that I may fight the battle to which I am
called, and finally overcome, nor give up for the
heavy pains and atrocious torments prepared for
me! Would it become this white beard and hoary
locks to give way in aught that concerns the glory
of God? Would it become, lady mine, an old man
to be appalled with childish fear, who has seen
sixty-four years of life, and forty of those has worn
the habit of the glorious St. Francis? Weaned
from terrestrial things, what is there for me if I
have not strength to aspire to those of God? But
as to you, lady of mine, and daughter in Christ,
sincerely beloved, in life and death I will continue
to think of you, and pray God in His mercy to send
you from heaven, according to the greatness of
your sorrows, solace and consolation. Pray to God
for your devoted servant, the more fervently when
you hear of horrid torments prepared for me.

"I send your Majesty for consolation in your
prayers my rosary, for they tell me that of my
life but three days remain."

The "horrid torments" the old man anticipated
did, indeed, come to him; but it was not till
two years after Katharine's troubles had been
ended that he sealed his fidelity to her with his
life. He is an instance, among many others,
of the wonderful power the unhappy Queen had
of attaching people to her. In her dignity,
meekness, and courage there seems to have been
a charm which made all those who came in
contact with her steadfast friends. There was
nothing to be gained, and much to be lost, by
friendship with her, and bluff King Hal was not

a pleasant person to offend; but in spite of all difficulties and penalties she owned adherents who, as we have seen, were loyal and true to her to death itself. Even the poor people around her learnt to love her. At Bugden, as before mentioned, the peasants were warmly attached to her, and at Kimbolton they were not slow to pay her homage. " A poor man ploughing near Grantham found a huge brass pot, containing a large helmet of pure gold, set with precious stones, with some chains of silver, and ancient defaced rolls of parchment, all of which he presented, says Harrison, in his description of England, to Queen Katharine, then living near Peterborough."*

In March, Katharine had another sorrow to bear in the illness of her daughter. She wrote to Chapuys imploring that she might be permitted to have her with her, and take charge of her till her health improved. " Dr. Butts, the King's physician, who was secretly Katharine's friend, backed her request, adding that the Princess's disorder might prove dangerous if she was longer parted from her mother. The King, though otherwise anxious that she should have proper assistance, would not hear of it. He reproached Butts with disloyalty. He said he would take good care how he allowed those two ladies to get together. The Queen was of such high mettle that with her daughter at her side she might assemble a force about her, take the field, and make war upon him with as much spirit as her mother Isabella." †

When Clement VII. would have published a bull of excommunication against Henry VIII., his persecuted wife had interferred to avert the blow. " I understand," Reginald Pole wrote to

* Strickland.   † Froude.

his friend Priuli, "that if the Queen, the aunt of Cæsar, had not interfered, the anathema would have already gone out against the King." But now the tenderness and patience of the outraged wife were worn out, and the remedy from which she had shrunk in horror she now regarded as the only means of rescuing herself, her child, and her Church from the peril and persecution under which they suffered. She did not seek assistance without just cause. Her rival was the triumphant Queen of England; that rival's babe was the acknowledged heir; Mary was branded as a child of shame; and the Church, which claimed all the devotion of the daughter of Isabel the Catholic, was being set at naught by King and nation. Driven to despair by all she saw and suffered, Katharine wrote to the Emperor on the 8th of April, entreating his help. She cannot, she says, "but urge and insist to your Majesty, as I have always hitherto done, that you should bear in mind our Holy Catholic faith, and the peril in which this realm is standing for want of the sentence. I entreat for it with all my energy. I am a Christian woman, and stand bound to sue for it in the presence of such scenes as I am obliged to witness. My daughter has been ill, and has not yet recovered. Her treatment is such that were she well it would break her constitution, far less being sick can she regain her health, and if she perish it will be a double sin. Your Majesty will think of means to do us good. . . . . Care not for me; I am accustomed to bear any burden, but I must let your Highness understand that I am as Job, waiting for the day when I must go sue for alms for the love of God."

If Chapuys is to be trusted, the peril in which

Katharine and Mary stood was in truth no imaginary one. According to his account—and though he was strongly prejudiced in the Queen's favour, it must not be forgotten that his position at the Court gave him such opportunities of ascertaining what occurred that we are not justified in discrediting his assertions—Anne Boleyn was at this time " crying incessantly to the King that he does neither well nor prudently in allowing the Queen and Princess to live, seeing they have deserved death far more than those who have been executed, and are the cause of all the trouble ; " and furthermore telling " that it was a shame to himself and to the realm to spare them, and that they ought to be punished as traitoresses under the form of the statute."

With her own life and her daughter's thus menaced, it cannot be wondered that Katharine took every means possible for defence and safety. Among others she wrote to Mary, the Regent of the Netherlands, her niece, entreating her to use her influence with her sister Leonor, wife of François I., to persuade that King "to show himself a true friend of his brother of England, by assisting in delivering him from a state of sin."

At length, on the 30th of August, 1535, the Pope, Paul III., sealed a bull, " summoning Henry to appear in sixty days and answer for his offences, and in default excommunicated him, deprived him, and his children by Anne, of the crown, absolved his subjects from their oaths of allegiance, and called on Christian princes to dethrone him. It was as strongly worded as any bull of Innocent III. against John or Philippe Auguste ; but the days when it could have been carried out were gone by. All good men had felt with the Popes in the contests of the eleventh and twelfth centuries, spiritual and moral conscience went together; but now the moral sense had so often been outraged, and the more lucrative forms of superstition so put forward, that in the re-action many religious men thought freedom again, however brought about. There was no mighty feudal nobility to delight in any sanction to attack their Prince, and as to stirring up foreign sovereigns to punish the offender, the Emperor had already quite enough on his hands, and François I. was Henry's friend. So Paul, though he had sealed the bull in his first indigna-tion, decided, on second thoughts, not to publish it, since it could not be executed, and would only increase the difficulties and dangers of those who still held to them in England ; but it was laid up in the Vatican, to be put forward when ex-pedient." *

But this unpublished bull did little good, while Anne Boleyn still worked by every means in her power to have both mother and daughter murdered. "She thinks of nothing but to get them des-patched," wrote Chapuys ; "it is she who com-mands and governs all, and the King will not contradict her." In despair, Katharine wrote on October 10th, to the Pope, imploring him to "apply the remedy."

"MOST HOLY AND MOST BLESSED FATHER,

"I kiss your Holiness's hands. My letters have been full of importunities and complaints, and thus have been more calculated to give you pain than pleasure. I have, therefore, for some time ceased to write to your Holiness, or to petition you, though I have burdened my con-

* C. M. Yonge.

science by silence, to pay more attention to what is passing in this realm. I have but one satisfaction in thinking of these things. I have never ceased to thank our Lord Jesus Christ for having appointed—now in a time when Christendom is in such straits—a vicar like your Holiness, of whom from all sides I hear so much good. God in His mercy has preserved you for this hour. Once more, therefore, like an obedient child of the Holy See, as all my ancestors have been, I do entreat you to bear in special memory this realm, the King, my lord and husband, and my daughter. Your Holiness and all Christendom know what things are done here, with how great offence to God, how great scandal to the world, how great reproach to your Holiness. If a remedy be not shortly applied there will be no end to condemning souls and to making martyrs. The good will be constant and will suffer. The lukewarm, seeing none to aid them, may possibly fall, and the rest will stray out of the way like sheep that have lost their shepherd. I lay these things before your Holiness because I know not any one on whose conscience the martyrdom of these holy and virtuous persons and the ruin of so many souls ought to lie more heavily than on yours, in that your Holiness neglects to encounter so great an evil, which the devil, as we see, has sown among us.

"I write frankly to your Holiness for the discharge of my own conscience, as to one who, as I hope, can feel [with me] and my daughter the deaths of these holy men. It is a mournful pleasure to me to think that we shall follow them in the manner of our torments . . . . [a few words are here illegible] otherwise we shall sing Gloria in Excelsis Deo. And so I end,

waiting for the remedy from God and from your
Holiness; and may it come speedily, else the time
will be past. Our Lord defend your Holiness's
person."

The "remedy from God" was soon to come;
but in a different guise to what the suppliant
Queen looked for. Weary and heart-broken as
she was—

Cast off, betray'd, defamed, divorced, forlorn—

the hour of her long sorrow would soon be past,
and all her tears and troubles calmed in the "holy
dawn of death." She was already ill, and, as
the autumn wore on, she yearned to have her
child near her. That she would be allowed
to see her she hardly hoped; but the King
might let mother and daughter breathe the same
air. She wrote to Cromwell, entreating for this
boon. In this letter, "she promises solemnly,"
says Miss Strickland, "'that if Mary may be
resident near her, she will not attempt to see
her, if forbidden.' She adds, that such measure
was 'impossible, since she lacked provision
therefore;' meaning, she had neither horse nor
carriage to go out. Yet she begs the King may
be always told, that the thing she most desires is
the company of her daughter; 'for a little comfort
and mirth she would take with me should undoubtedly be a half health unto her. For my
love let this be done.' Doleful would have been
the mirth, and heartrending the comfort, had
such an interview been permitted, between the
sick daughter and the dying mother; but it was
no item in the list of Henry's tender mercies."

While Katharine was thus rapidly fading into
her grave, Henry was resolving to use more

decided measures for subduing her and her daughter. "On November 6th," writes Froude, "Chapuys learnt from the Marchioness of Exeter that the King had determined that the two poor ladies should either break or bend. He had been heard to say to one of his most intimate advisers that he would endure no longer the alarm and anxiety which the Queen and Princess caused him. Parliament was about to meet, and the matter should then be considered. He swore peremptorily that he would wait no further."

Towards the end of the same month, Chapuys begged an audience with the King, and told him that Katharine lay sick to death at Kimbolton. "To death," said Henry, surprised, and not ill pleased; "if she were but to die my quarrels with the Emperor would cease." He was anxious to learn the truth, and Cromwell wrote to Bedyngfeld, rating him sharply "because foreigners heard intelligence from the King's own castles sooner than himself." Sir Edmund made the best excuse he could in reply to this remonstrance. "His fidelity in executing the orders of the King," he wrote, "rendered him no favourite with the lady dowager, therefore she concealed everything from him." He questioned the Queen's Spanish doctor as to her health, and forwarded the latter's answer:—

"'Sir, she doth continue in pain, and can take but little rest; if the sickness continueth in force, she cannot remain long.'

"I am informed," continued Sir Edmund, "by her said doctor, that he had moved her to take some more counsel of physic; but her reply was—

"'I will in no wise have any other physician, but wholly commit myself to the pleasure of God.'"

She was glad to die; but she sent again an urgent and moving entreaty that her child might come to receive her last blessing. Mary likewise implored to go to her mother; but it was the King's will they should never see each others' faces again. The sole cause was that reasonless Tudor cruelty that was in the blood.

"On December 13th," says Froude, "Katharine wrote her last letter to the Emperor. Her handwriting, usually remarkably bold and powerful, had become feeble and tremulous, and in the staggering and barely legible lines I make out with difficulty only that she expected something desperate to be attempted against her in the approaching Parliament, which would be a scandal to the world and her own and her daughter's destruction. After this there are no more traces of her pen."

Her old friend, Lady Willoughby—she who had accompanied her from Spain, and loved her faithfully all her life—entreated Cromwell for permission to go to her. Cromwell delayed giving her a written licence, implying that a verbal message was sufficient. "Without I have a letter of his grace, or else of you, to show the officers of my mistress's house, my licence shall stand to no effect," she answered. She was put off again, and, growing desperate, resolved to start without her papers, and trust to her woman's wit to gain access to the Queen.

"New Year's morning, 1536," says Hepworth Dixon, "found her in the saddle at the Barbican. The ride was long, the air inclement, the track a waste. Unused to riding, she was thrown to the ground and badly bruised. Still she pressed on. Some persons on the road dissuaded her from going forward, telling her the good old Queen was dead; but neither icy winds, nor smarting wounds, nor fatal news, sufficed to turn her back. Long after dark, a noise of hoofs was heard before the castle gates. Bedyngfeld went down to see the new arrival; but the Spanish lady was unknown to him by sight. She gave her name, and told her errand. He required to see her warrant for admission. Fearing to say she had no papers, Lady Willoughby pointed to her hurts, her freezing limbs, her chattering teeth, and begged him, for love of Jesus and for Christian charity, to lift her in and set her by the fire. What was he to do? Cromwell's commands were strict. No person was to pass those gates without a written licence. Yet, in that wild country, on that winter night, could he repel this faint and pleading woman from his gate? Stonely Priory stood a mile off; with a brook to cross, a hill to climb. His heart gave way, the door swung back, and Lady Willoughby was carried in; but here the chamberlain meant to stop, since he might have to pay for breach of Cromwell's orders with his head. When warmth had soothed her limbs, and loosed her tongue, she told the warder she had come to see the Princess Dowager by Cromwell's wish, and on the morrow, when her trunks were opened, she would place her papers in his hands. Her use of the words 'Princess Dowager,' removed Bedyngfeld's suspicion, and on a promise of showing her papers next day he let her pass to Katharine's room, and saw no more of her until the Queen was dead."

The following day, January 2nd, Chapuys arrived, and, after dinner, was taken to Katharine's room, where he stayed about a quarter of an hour. Bedyngfeld was present, but as both

Queen and envoy spoke in Spanish, he was
unable, much to his disappointment, to report
the conversation in his despatches to the Privy
Council. At five the same afternoon, Katharine
sent her doctor to fetch Chapuys to her again;
and the next day she received him more than
once. It was at one of these visits that she
charged him with a message to her nephew and
other friends. "Make my excuses to the Emperor,
to Monsignor Granvelle, and the great commander
for my not writing to them, and beg them, for
the love of God, and by either one means or
another, to make an end of this affair. It is this
waiting for a cure that never comes, together
with the misery which this waiting causes both
of us to suffer, that throws everything into disorder."

She dictated to one of her maidens her last
letter to her husband—a letter which shows the
undying love she bore him, in spite of all his
faithlessness and cruelty:—

"MY MOST DEAR LORD, KING, AND HUSBAND,
"The hour of my death draweth nigh. I
cannot choose but out of the love I bear you to
put you in remembrance of your soul's health,
which you ought to prefer before all considerations
of the world, and before the care and tendering
of your own body, for which you have cast me
into many miseries, and yourself into many cares.
But I forgive you all, and devoutly pray that
God will forgive you also. For the rest, I com-
mend unto you Mary, our daughter, beseeching
you to be a good father unto her, as I have always
desired. I entreat you also to consider my maids,
and to give them marriage portions, which is not
much, they being but three. For all my other

servants I ask you for one year's pay more than their due, lest otherwise they should be in want. Lastly, I vow that mine eyes desire you above all things. Farewell!"

Shakespeare, "that mighty genius, nearly her contemporary, who has done her the noblest justice,"* has set before us the last words of Katharine in a scene surpassingly pathetic and beautiful. Few can read without faltering the tender, simple appeal of the dying Queen to her husband on her child's behalf:—

> A little
> To love her for her mother's sake, that lov'd him
> Heaven knows how dearly—

Or the saintly forgiveness of her last message :—

> Remember me
> In all humility unto his Highness;
> Say his long trouble now is passing
> Out of this world: tell him, in death I bless'd him.

But yet Katharine's own letter, brief as it is, seems even more touching than the words in which the great dramatist, in his poet-sympathy for that high heart, immortalizes her memory.

After the arrival of her faithful friend, Lady Willoughby, the Queen seemed calmer and easier; and on the 5th of January Bedyngfeld thought it possible she might rally; but all the next day she gradually sank, and on the 7th the priest was called at ten in the morning to perform the last rites of her Church. At two, supported by Lady Willoughby's faithful arms, she ended, without a struggle, the long sorrow of her life. "She changed," says Dr. Harpsfield, " this woeful, troublesome existence for the serenity of the

* Strickland.

celestial life, and her terrestrial ingrate husband for that heavenly spouse who will never divorce her, and with whom she will reign in glory for ever."

When the long-looked for tidings reached Greenwich, Henry, hardened and debased as he had grown, was nevertheless keenly affected by Katharine's death. He told her friends " he would have to her memory one of the goodliest monuments in Christendom," meaning the Abbey Church of Peterborough, which he spared, in the universal destruction of monasteries, on her account. He had solemn obsequies performed at Greenwich on the day of her funeral, and commanded all his Court to attend in mourning; but Anne Boleyn—who, when told of her old mistress's death, had exclaimed triumphantly, " Now I am indeed a Queen ! " and had bidden her parents rejoice that now the crown was firmly on her head—had no inclination to obey this mandate, but " in sign of gladness dressed herself and all the ladies of her household in yellow. And amidst them all exalted for the death of her rival. ' I am grieved,' she said, ' not that she is dead, but for the vaunting of the good end she made.' She had reason to say this, for nothing was talked of but the Christian death-bed of Katharine, and numberless books and papers were written in her praise, blaming King Henry's actions, and all the world celebrated the obsequies of Queen Katharine." *

This was no mere form of speech; for the English resident at Venice wrote to a divine in Henry's Court that " Queen Katharine's death had been divulged there, and was received with lamentations, for she was incredibly dear to all

* Pollino.

men for her good fame, which is in great glory among all exterior nations;" adding that her death had occasioned great obloquy, and that much sympathy was expressed for her daughter, whom it was feared would soon follow her mother. Even now the King chose to speak of her as his brother's widow, and so mentioned her in a letter relating to her funeral, addressed to Lady Bedyngfeld, Sir Edward's wife :—

"HENRY REX.

"To our right dear and well-beloved Lady Bedyngfeld.

"Forasmuch as it has pleased Almighty God to call to his mercy out of this transitory life the right excellent Princess, our dearest sister the Lady Katharine, relict of our natural brother Prince Arthur, of famous memory, deceased, and that we intend to have her body interred according to her honour and estate. At the interment whereof (and for other ceremonies to be done at her funeral, and in the conveyance of her corpse, from Kimbolton, where it now lieth, to Peterborough, where the same is to be buried) it is requisite to have the presence of a good many ladies of honour. You shall understand, that we have appointed you to be there one of the principal mourners; and, therefore, desire you to be in readiness at Kimbolton the 25th of this month, and so to attend on the said corpse till the same shall be buried. Letting you further wit that for the mourning apparel of your own person we send you by this bearer (a certain number) of yards of black cloth, and black cloth for two gentlemen to wait upon you, and for two gentlewomen and for eight yeomen; all which apparel you must cause in the meantime to be made up, as shall appertain. And concerning the habiliment of linen for your head and face, we shall before the day limited send the same to you accordingly.

"Given under our signet, at our manor at Greenwich, January 10th.

"P.S.—For saving of time, if this order is shown to Sir William Poulett, living at the Friars, Augustine's, London, comptroller of our household, the cloth and linen for the head shall be delivered."

On the 26th of January the funeral procession set forth from Kimbolton for Peterborough, approaching the city, according to an old tradition, by a way known as Bigrame's Lane. John Chambers, the last Abbot of Peterborough, performed the service, and she was buried near the altar, on the north side of the choir, her grave, marked only by a small brass plate, being long pointed out by Scarlett, the centenarian sexton, who lived to bury another Queen—Mary Stuart—in the same Cathedral. A hearse covered with a pall of black velvet, on which was wrought a large silver cross and silver scutcheons of Spain, stood for some years over the spot, surrounded by tapers, which, wrote one of Cromwell's agents, "the day before the Lady Anne Boleyn was beheaded kindled of themselves, and after matins were done to Deo Gratias the said tapers quenched of themselves; and that the King had sent thirty men to the abbey where Queen Katharine was buried, and it was true of this light continuing from day to day." The perpetrator of this trick was never discovered; but it is not unlikely that it was the same person who stole the rich pall from the hearse, and left in its stead a mean one, which, in the year 1543, likewise disappeared. More than twenty years after Katharine's death her daughter Mary, herself in a dying state, left directions in her will that "the body of my most dear and well-beloved mother, of happy memory, Queen Katharine, which lieth now buried at Peterborough, shall, within as short a time as conveniently it may after my burial, be removed, brought, and laid nigh the place of my sepulture; in which place I will my executors cause to be made honourable tombs, for a decent memory of us." This, however, was never done; and mother and daughter repose far apart, one in the chapel her grandfather raised at Westminster, the other in the old abbey church in Northamptonshire.

Katharine's will, evidently, from the foreign idioms her own composition, is as follows :—

"In the name of the Father, and of the Son, and of the Holy Ghost, I, Katharine, etc., supplicate and desire King Henry VIII., my good lord, that it may please him of his grace, and in alms, and for the service of God, to let me have the goods, which I do hold, as well in silver and gold as in other things; and also the same that is due to me in money for the time past, to the intent that I may pay my debts and recompense my servants, for the good services they have done for me. The same I desire, as affectuously as I may, for the necessity, wherein I am ready to die, and to yield my soul unto God.

" First, I supplicate that my body be buried in a convent of Observant Friars. Item, that for my soul be said 500 masses. Item, that some personage go to our Lady of Walsingham on pilgrimage, and in going by the way to deal [distribute in alms] twenty nobles. Item, I appoint to Mistress Darrel £20 for her marriage. Item, I ordain the collar of gold, which I brought out of Spain, be to my daughter. Item, I ordain to Mistress Blanche £100. Item, I ordain to Mrs. Margery and to Mr. Whyller, to each of them £40. Item, I ordain to Mrs. Mary, my physician's wife, and to Mrs. Isabel, daughter to Mr. Marguerite, to each of them £40 sterling. Item, I ordain to my physician the year's coming wages. Item, I ordain to Francisco Phillippo all that I owe him, and besides that £40. I ordain to master John, my apothecary, his wages for the year coming; and besides that, all that is due to him. I ordain, that Mr. Whyller be paid his expenses about the making of my gown, and besides that £20. I ordain to the little maidens £10 to every one of them. I ordain my goldsmith to be paid his wages, for the year coming, and besides that, all that is due to him. I ordain that my lavenderer [laundress] be paid that which is due to her, and her wages for the year coming. I ordain to Isabel de Vergas £20. Item, to my ghostly father his wages for the year coming.

"Item, it may please the King, my good lord, to cause church-ornaments to be made of my gowns which he holdeth, to serve the convent thereas I shall be buried, and the furs of the same I give to my daughter."

"This will," says Miss Strickland, "proves how slight were the debts of the conscientious Queen, yet she felt anxiety concerning them. On her just mind even the obligations she owed her laundress had their due weight. It furnishes, too, another instance of the pitiful meanness of

Henry VIII. The sentence alluding to the disposal of her gowns 'which he holdeth,' will not be lost on female readers; and shows plainly that he had detained the best part of his wife's wardrobe, it is likewise evident that the gold collar brought from Spain was the only jewel in her possession; Will it be believed that, notwithstanding Henry shed tears over her last letter, he sent his creature, Lawyer Rich, to see whether he could not seize all her property, without paying her trifling legacies and obligations? The letter of Rich, dated from Kimbolton, January 19th, is extant. It is a notable specimen of legal chicanery. 'To seize her grace's goods as your own,' he says, 'would be repugnant to your Majesty's own laws; and, I think, with your grace's favour, it would rather enforce her blind opinion while she lived than otherwise,' namely, that she was the King's lawful wife. He then puts the King into an underhand way of possessing himself of poor Katherine's slender spoils, by advising him to administer by means of the Bishop of Lincoln for her as Princess Dowager, and then to confiscate all as insufficient to defray her funeral charges! Whether the debtors and legatees of the brokenhearted Queen were ever satisfied is a doubtful point; but, from a contemporary letter of a privy councillor, it seems that one of her three faithful ladies, Mrs. Elizabeth Darrel (the daughter of an ancient line still extant in Kent), was paid her legacy. The other ladies, Blanche and Isabel de Vergas, were from Spain—a fact Shakespeare has not forgotten. The name of Patience, remembered in his scene as Katharine's sweet songstress, does not occur; perhaps she was reckoned among the *little* maidens, who are likewise the legatees of their unfortunate patroness. The property Katharine could claim for the liquidation of her debts and obligations to her faithful servants, was, even by Henry's own arbitrary decisions, considerable, being the arrears of the £5000 per annum due to her from her jointure as Arthur's widow. This stipend, either from malice or poverty, had not been paid her. A scanty maintenance was all that Katharine received from her faithless spouse; and when the noble portion she had brought into England is remembered, such dishonesty appears the more intolerable. Even a new gown, it will be observed by the will, was obtained on trust. It appears likely that Katharine possessed no more of her jewels than were on her person when she was expelled from Windsor Castle by the fiat of her brutal lord."

"Born," says M. du Boys, "under the brilliant sky of Andalusia, passing her earliest years amid the splendours of Isabella's court, this princess had scarcely passed beyond childhood before her lot was cast in a far different spot, not only to endure the fogs of England, but, after Prince Arthur's death, she had to undergo the capricious and uncertain moods of King Henry VII., who reduced her to moral and physical distress, and clouded the fairest years of her youth with most tyrannical acquisitions. Her riper years had still more bitter agonies in store for her. The material privations she had to undergo towards the decline of her life were as nothing compared with the most acute anguish that could poison married life. Yet besides her great qualities, she is shown to have had those of a domestic and accomplished woman. A Protestant writer says :* 'She loved

* Larrey.

work and quiet, and took great care of her house;
her gentleness was invariable, and she showed the
most perfect obedience to her husband.' Her
heart was also most charitable, warm, and tender,
and, as we have seen, excited almost fabulous
devotion even to the last moments of her life.
It is remarkable how she managed to preserve her
self-possession in the most difficult circumstances.
In her words, in her actions, in her letters, is
always to be found the simplicity that is a mark
of real greatness. At certain times she becomes
sublime, quite naturally, and without effort; it is
only the spontaneous expression of her inner
thoughts. She made a point of claiming the pre-
rogatives of her rank to the very end, and not
allowing a single one to be invaded. Her modest
abode became a kind of little independent state
within great England, where she could preserve
all the majesty and inviolability of her crown. It
was the will of Heaven that she should pass her
life without reproach, and even without suspicion.
There was never the least failure in this pure and
great soul. The King's desertion was to remain
without pretext or excuse.   .

"There was mourning all over the Continent
when the death of the daughter of Isabella of
Castile, the real Queen of England, became
known. The learned composed prodigious eulo-
gies; many preachers made funeral orations. Even
the very Protestant writers who were the apolo-
gists of Anne Boleyn never venture to assume the
part of detractors of Katharine." In England the
people lamented for this good Queen, and never
ceased to pity her as being unjustly divorced and
persecuted. Round her last moments there arose
one of those legends that crown some heads with

a mysterious halo, a kind of popular consecration
that nothing can prevent, neither the triumph of
the adverse cause nor the pressure of suspicious
despotism. These traditions were kept up in
families in after generations, and Shakespeare
gave them an eloquent shape. In his play of
Henry VIII., the Queen is presented dying like
a saint. And the English poet, in verses as
vigourous and lofty as the most beautiful lines of
Dante, describes a celestial vision as sent to the
Queen in her last hour; she is suddenly roused
from stupor with her attendants around her, and
exclaims—

> ' No ? saw ye not even now a blessed troop
> Invite me to a banquet ; whose bright faces
> Cast thousand beams upon me like the sun ?
> They promised me eternal happiness,
> And brought me garlands, Griffith, which I feel
> I am not worthy yet to wear : I shall
> Assuredly.'

"A modern author says, 'She draws this
assurance from the increasing peacefulness that
her reconciliation with her two great enemies
gives her in the sight of Heaven. She wins her
greatest victory in forgiving Wolsey, and sends
her blessing to Henry VIII. before her death. . .
. . . Alas ! the most unproductive blessing that
ever was.' "*

Her memory yet clings around the old pile
wherein, with husband and child both absent,
and with no one nearer and dearer than her
loyal lady to receive her last word and glance, she
breathed her last. "The tale of her arrival at Kimbolton Castle, of her secluded habits while living
there, of the departure of her funeral cortege for

* Larrey.

Peterborough, has not yet faded from the peasant. Few of these hedgers and ploughmen have seen a theatre or read a play; they know nothing about Shakespeare or his drama; yet the spirit of that tender and solemn scene in *Henry VIII.* may be said to lie upon their hearts in the wintry evenings when they whisper to each other how the unhappy lady glides in the dusk of twilight through the rooms of Kimbolton, pauses on the stairs, or kneels in the chapel, a beautiful and mournful figure, in flowing white, and wearing a regal crown." *

* " Society from the Reign of Elizabeth to Anne."

CAROLINE OF ANSPACH.

CAROLINE OF ANSPACH.

CHAPTER I.

England in the eighteenth century—Birth of Caroline—Sophia
Charlotte—Charlottenburg—Caroline's education—An Im-
perial suitor—Her marriage—Her husband—The Electress
Sophia—Marriage of the Princess of Hanover—Caroline's
children—Herrenhausen—Royal matchmaking—Death of
the Electress—Death of Queen Anne—Caroline's arrival in
England—Coronation of George I.—Poetical address to the
Princess of Wales—Quarrel between the King and his son—
Leicester House—Caroline's popularity—Mrs. Howard—
Mrs. Clayton—Anecdotes of the Princess of Wales— Buck-
ingham House—Richmond Lodge—Pope at Hampton Court
—Hunting in Belsize Park—Birth of Princess Mary—
Inoculation of the Princesses—Reconciliation of the King
and Prince—Caroline and Sir Woolston Dixie—Rudeness
of Dean Swift—The King's cockcrower—Death of Sophia
Dorothea—Death of George I.—Reception of the news by
George II.—The Queen and Sir Robert Walpole—Caroline's
allowance—Her reception of Lady Walpole.

THE next on the list of royal ladies who have
borne the title of Princess of Wales lived out her
life in an age far removed and widely differing
from the splendid yet half barbaric days of the
earlier Tudors. Splendour indeed and glitter
enough there was throughout that portion of the
eighteenth century which bounds the history of
Caroline, Princess of Wales, and Queen of England; and the world had so far progressed that it
was now no longer possible to bring a queenly
wife to the block in fulfilment of her husband's
craving for liberty, or to fill the throne with a
succession of more or less victimized consorts;
but the brilliancy stood in place of solid worth,

and the splendour was but the veneer hiding the all pervading corruption and looseness of morals which were unhappily the order of the day.

During the two hundred years which had elapsed since the days of the ill-fated Katharine of Aragon, the whole condition of society had materially changed. The national religion was no longer dependent on the views of the reigning sovereign; but the tenure of office of the reigning sovereign depended on his acceptance of the national faith. Literature, still in its infancy in Tudor times, had now grown into strength and glory, and the names of Shakespeare, Milton, and Bacon, were among the greatest of their country's treasures; the people, realizing their own power, had measured themselves against their rulers, had been victorious, and of their own free will had called those rulers back; Scotland had been united to the English kingdom, and the country had developed into one of the most renowned and important on the face of the globe. The England which welcomed the young German Princess as its heiress apparent, was a different England to that which had received the stately Spanish bride of the early-doomed Arthur Tudor.

Throughout these years not one lady had borne the title of Princess of Wales. Edward VI., had died young as one of the few bachelor Kings of England; Mary and Elizabeth had left no sons; James I., saw his eldest heir perish in early youth, and his second son remained unwedded until he mounted the throne. Charles II., likewise waited for his kingship before he sought a bride; and the next Prince of Wales, James Francis Edward, had ceased to bear that title ere he married the Polish lady whom he hoped to bring to England as his Queen. Since 1509 the title which has so

gracious a sound in our ears had not been heard
in England, till the accession of George I., in
1714, bestowed it on the lady who is the subject
of these pages.

Caroline Wilhelmina Dorothea, daughter of
John Frederick, Marquis of Brandenburg Anspach,
by his second wife, Eleanor Erdmuth Louisa,
daughter of John George, Duke of Saxe-Eisenach,
was born March 1st, 1683. Her father died while
she was still very young, and, her mother, con-
tracting a second marriage with George IV.,
Elector of Saxony, the young Princess was removed by her guardian, Frederick, Elector of
Brandenburgh, afterwards first King of Prussia,
to his own Court. Here Caroline was brought up
under the superintendence of the Electress Sophia
Charlotte, the sister of George I., a clever and
sensible woman, whose character is thus drawn
by her great grand-niece, Caroline Matilda of
Denmark—

"Her Court was a temple where was preserved
the sacred fire of the vestals, the asylum of arts
and sciences, and the seat of elegance, taste, and
politeness. That Princess had the genius of a
great man, and the knowledge of the most learned;
she thought it was not below the dignity of a
Queen to honour a philosopher. This was
Leibnitz; and as those who have received from
heaven privileged souls, raise themselves on the
level with sovereigns, she admitted Leibnitz to
her conversation with that freedom which
characterizes true merit and discernment. She
proposed him as the only man capable to lay the
foundation of her new academy. Leibnitz, who
had more than one soul, if I may be allowed to
use the expression, was worthy of being the first
president of a society which he might have repre-

sented alone. All the learned in Europe mourned at her death. This celebrated Princess joined to all the exterior accomplishments and the most endearing charms, the graces of the mind and the most superior understanding. She had travelled in her youth in France and Italy with her august parents. She was destined for the throne of France. Louis XIV. was struck with her beauty, but political reasons prevented this marriage. She brought into Prussia the spirit of society, true politeness, and the love of the fine arts. She seated upon her throne the Muses; and her curiosity was such in philosophical inquiries, that she aspired to know the principles of things. Leibnitz, whom she pressed one day upon that subject, said to her Majesty—' Madam, it is not in my power to give a satisfactory answer to your sublime questions; you want to know what no mortal is capable to explain.' Charlottenburg was the rendezvous of men of exquisite taste and literature; all sorts of feasts and entertainments, diversified with that splendour and magnificence which stamped all her public diversions, made this abode delightful, and her Court more brilliant than any in Europe."

Under the guardianship of this Princess, Caroline of Anspach grew up " a very accomplished young lady. If," says Dr. Doran, " the instructress was able, the pupil was apt. She was quick, enquiring, intelligent, and studious. Her application was great, her perseverance unwearied, and her memory excellent. She learned quickly and retained largely, seldom forgetting anything worth remembrance; and was an equally good judge of books and individuals. Her perception of character has, perhaps, never been surpassed. She had no inclination for trivial subjects, nor

affection for trivial people. She had a heart and
mind only for philosophers and philosophy; but
she was not the less a lively girl, or the more a
pedant on that account. She delighted in lively
conversation, and could admirably lead or direct
it. Her knowledge of languages was equal to that
of Sophia of Hanover, of whom she was also the
equal in wit and in repartee. But therewith she
was more tender, more gentle, more generous."
While still in early youth, the hand of the
Princess Caroline was asked in marriage by an
Austrian archduke, afterwards the Emperor
Charles VI. "It must be told to the honour of
Caroline of Anspach," says Thackeray, "that, at
the time when German princes thought no more
of changing their religion than you of altering
your cap, she refused to give up Protestantism
for the other creed, although an archduke, afterwards to be an emperor, was offered to her for a
bridegroom. Her Protestant relations in Berlin
were angry at her rebellious spirit; it was they
who tried to convert her (it is droll to think that
Frederick the Great, who had no religion at all,
was known for a long time in England as the
Protestant hero), and these good Protestants set
upon Caroline a certain Father Urban, a very
skilful Jesuit, and famous winner of souls. But
she routed the Jesuit; and she refused Charles
VI.; and she married the little Electoral Prince
of Hanover, whom she tended with love, and with
every manner of sacrifice, with artful kindness,
with tender flattery, with entire self-devotion,
thenceforward until her life's end."
This marriage took place in 1705, when both
bride and bridegroom were twenty-two years of
age. George Augustus, the Electoral Prince of
Hanover, and heir presumptive of the British

crown, was fortunate in his choice of a wife who
was "remarkable for beauty, for cleverness, for
learning, for good temper—one of the truest and
fondest wives ever prince was blessed with,"* a
fact the more remarkable when we consider how
little there was in his appearance or demeanour
likely to attract a beautiful young Princess. He
was little, red-faced, choleric, but not altogether
bad-hearted—"il est fougueux, mais il a du
cœur," his father used to say of him—coarse in
his tastes, obstinate, and caring nothing for the
intellectual pleasures of which she thought so
much. Where lay the fascination none could
divine; but "love will still be lord of all;" and
while scores of her sister Princesses made "mar-
riages de convenance" with men infinitely superior
to her bridegroom, Caroline loved and obeyed and
tended him with changeless devotion to the day
of her death. The new relations whom she gained
by her marriage were her sister-in-law, Sophia
Dorothea, a fair, blue-eyed beauty; her father-in-
law, George Louis, afterwards George I.; and
her husband's grandmother, the Electress Sophia,
noticeable as the foundress of our present royal
line. This lady, who, by the recently passed Act
of Succession, was now the heiress to the crown
of England, was, as may well be supposed, a personage of no small importance in Caroline's new
home; and the following description of her,
written by Toland, when, in 1700, he accompanied
the Earl of Macclesfield in his presentation of the
Act of Succession will not be uninteresting—

"The Electress is three-and-seventy years old,
which she bears so wonderfully well that, had I
not many vouchers I should scarce dare venture
to relate it. She has ever enjoyed extraordinary

* Thackeray.

health, which keeps her still very vigorous, of a cheerful countenance, and a merry disposition. She steps as firm and exact as any young lady, has not one wrinkle in her face, which is still very agreeable, nor one tooth out of her head, and reads without spectacles, as I have often seen her do, letters of a small character, in the dusk of the evening. She is as great a worker as our late Queen (Mary), and you cannot turn yourself in the palace without meeting some monument of her industry, all the chairs of the presence-chamber being wrought with her own hands. The ornaments of the altar in the Electoral chapel are all of her work. She bestowed the same favour on the Protestant abbey, or college, of Lockurn, with a thousand other instances, fitter for your lady to know than for yourself. She is the most constant and greatest walker I ever knew, never missing a day if it proves fair, for one or two hours, and often more, in the fine garden at Herrenhausen. She perfectly tires all those of her Court who attend her in that exercise but such as have the honour to be entertained by her in discourse. She has been long admired by all the learned world, as a woman of incomparable knowledge in divinity, philosophy, history, and the subjects of all sorts of books, of which she has read a prodigious quantity. She speaks five languages so well, that by her accent it might be a dispute which of them was her first. They are Low Dutch, German, French, Italian, and English, which last she speaks as truly and easily as any native ; which to me is a matter of amazement, whatever advantages she might have in her youth by the conversation of her mother; for though the late King's (William's) mother was likewise an Englishwoman, of the same royal family;

though he had been more than once in England before the Revolution; though he was married there, and his Court continually full of many of that nation, yet he could never conquer his foreign accent. But, indeed, the Electress is so entirely English in her person, in her behaviour, in her humour, and in all her inclinations, that naturally she could not miss of anything that peculiarly belongs to our land. She was ever glad to see Englishmen long before the Act of Succession. She professes to admire our form of government, and understands it mighty well, yet she asks so many questions about families, customs, laws, and the like, as sufficiently demonstrate her profound wisdom and experience. She has a deep veneration for the Church of England, without losing affection or charity for any other sort of Protestants, and appears charmed with the moderate temper of our present bishops and others of our learned clergy, especially for their approbation of the liberty allowed by law to Protestant dissenters. She is adored for her goodness among the inhabitants of the country, and gains the hearts of all strangers by her unparalleled affability. No distinction is ever made in her Court concerning the parties into which Englishmen are divided, and whereof they carry the effects and impressions whithersoever they go, which makes others sometimes uneasy as well as themselves. There it is enough that you are an Englishman; nor can you ever discover by your treatment which are better liked, the Whigs or the Tories. These are the instructions given to all the servants, and they take care to execute them with the utmost exactness. I was the first who had the honour of kneeling and kissing her hand on account of the Act of Succession; and she said, among other discourse,

that she was afraid the nation had already re-
pented their choice of an old woman, but that she
hoped none of her posterity would give her any
reasons to grow weary of their dominion. I
answered that the English had too well considered
what they did to change their minds so soon, and
they still remembered they were never so happy as
when they were last under a woman's government."

Of Caroline's father-in-law, the same authority,
who seems to have viewed the Electress through
rose-coloured spectacles, remarks that he is " a
proper, middle-sized, well-proportioned man, of
a genteel address, and good appearance; is reserved,
and therefore speaks little, but judiciously." Of
her mother-in-law. the unhappy Sophia Dorothea,
in her living grave at Ahlden, the Electoral
Princess neither heard nor inquired. On that
subject all lips were sealed.

The year after her own bridal, in 1706, Caroline
witnessed the marriage of her sister-in-law, Sophia
Dorothea, with the Crown Prince of Prussia, afterwards the brutal Frederick William I. The ceremony was performed with great splendour; the
Electoral Prince married her by proxy in presence
of the Prussian Ambassador, Count de Finck; her
father, the Elector, loaded her with jewels; three
noted Englishmen — Vanbrugh, Addison, and
Lord Halifax, were present at the nuptials; and
"the Duchess of Orleans was desirous to choose and
give directions for the clothes, and she afterwards
showed them to Louis XIV., who thought them so
rich that he said it were to be wished, for the sake
of the mercers of Paris, that there were more
Princesses that could afford to make such pur-
chases."* The same year Queen Anne created the

* Mrs. Matthew Hall.

husband of Caroline Baron of Tewkesbury, Viscount Northallerton, Earl of Milford Haven, Marquis and Duke of Cambridge, and further decreed that he should enjoy precedence over all the peerage.

On January 20th, 1707, the Electoral Princess gave birth to her first-born child, Frederick Louis —he whom Thackeray speaks of in after years as "their eldest son, their heir, their enemy." It was well that the young mother, bending over her babe, could not look forward to those terrible days when her son was the one being of all others upon earth whom she most hated and found it hardest to forgive. In no long time her nursery was tenanted by two little daughters—Anne, born October 22nd, 1709, and Amelia Sophia, born June 10th, 1711. The elder of these children was the godchild of Queen Anne, who, when the little Princess was about two years old, sent her a present, accompanied by a letter to the Electress Sophia, bearing date November 11th, 1711—both of which were conveyed to their destination by Earl Rivers. The Electress acknowledged their receipt in a letter to the Earl of Strafford, Secretary of State, in which she says that "the gift is infinitely esteemed," and adds—"I would not, however, give my parchment [the Act of Succession] for it, since that will be an everlasting monument in the archives of Hanover, and the present for the little Princess will go, when she is grown up, into another family."

The Electoral family resided chiefly at Herrenhausen, the palace of the reigning Elector, near Hanover. Thackeray draws a not very complimentary picture of it—

" Put clumsy High Dutch statues in place of the marbles of Versailles: fancy Herrenhausen waterworks in place of those of Marly : spread the table with Schweinskopf, Specksuppe, Leber-bruchen, and the like delicacies, in place of the French cuisine ; and fancy Frau von Kielmansegge dancing with Count Kammerjunker Quirini, or singing French songs with the most awful German accent : imagine a coarse Versailles, and we have a Hanover before us."

To this Court came Sophia Dorothea, Princess Royal of Prussia, to visit her father and grand-mother ; and she and the Electoral Princess indulged in visions of matchmaking which seemed rather premature, considering the tender age of the little ones for whom they planned—Frederick Louis being at the time not more than five or six, and Frederica Sophia Wilhelmina, the little Princess of Prussia, two years younger. The project for uniting her with her cousin of Hanover may be said to have existed from her birth.

"I was at Berlin," says Baron de Pöllnitz, "at the ceremony of her baptism, which was per-formed in the chapel of the Castle, in presence of Frederick IV., King of Denmark, Frederick Augustus, King of Poland, and Frederick I., King of Prussia. The birth of this Princess, and the circumstances of three Kings and a Queen attending at her baptism, gave occasion to a great many copies of verses. All the poets said that the presence of these three Kings was a sign that she would one day have possession of three crowns. They had then in view the crowns of Great Britain, that were to devolve to the family of Hanover, in which there was a young Prince who, it was then imagined was to be in time the husband of this Princess."

The Princess herself, in the memoirs written

many years later, when she was Marchioness of
Bareith, speaks at great length of the projects of
the two families, and relates how, after this visit
to Hanover, her mother " brought the bridal rings
to me ; I even opened a correspondence with my
little admirer, and received several presents
from him." " No post-day passed," she further
remarks, " without these Princesses [the Electoral
Princess and the Princess Royal of Prussia]
corresponding about the future union of their
children."

These hopes and plans were not relinquished ;
and we shall hear more of them in the days when
Caroline had attained her regal state.

On May 31st, 1713, was born the third daughter
of the Electoral Princess, Caroline Elizabeth, afterwards honourably distinguished as the " truth-
loving ; " and the following year the dowager
Electress, Sophia, heiress of the Crown of England,
died suddenly, in her eighty-seventh year, on
the 11th of June. She is said to have declared
that " she cared not when she died, if on her
tomb could be recorded that she was Queen of
Great Britain and Ireland "—words which gave
dire offence to Queen Anne, never too much
prepossessed in favour of her Hanoverian
cousins. The particulars of her death are
given by Molyneux, an agent of the Duke of
Marlborough, who, when on his way to her
country palace, was informed of her sudden and
dangerous illness.

" I ran up there and found her fast expiring in
the arms of the poor Electoral Princess, and
amidst the tears of a great many of her servants,
who endeavoured in vain to help her. . . . She
had dressed and dined with the Elector as usual.
. . . She walked and talked very heartily in

the orangery. After that, about six, she went
out to walk in the garden, and was still very well.
A shower of rain came, and as she was walking
pretty fast to get to shelter, they told her she was
walking a little too fast. She answered, 'I believe
I do,' and dropped down on saying these words,
which were her last. They raised her up, chafed
her with spirits, tried to bleed her; but it was all in
vain, and when I came up she was as dead as if
she had been four days so." A shrewd, sensible
woman, with many estimable qualities, as witness
her magnanimity with regard to the exiled Stuarts,
when she heartily hoped "le pauvre Prince de
Galles" might regain his father's inheritance;
and with the almost utter lack of all religious
feeling, so curiously characteristic of her age.
"An agent of the French King's, Gomville, a
convert himself, strove to bring her and her
husband to a sense of the truth; and tells that
he one day asked Madame the Duchess of Hanover,
of what religion her daughter was, then a pretty
girl of thirteen years old. The duchess replied
that the princess *was of no religion as yet.*
They were waiting to know of what religion
her husband would be, Protestant or Catholic,
before instructing her!" * After such an
anecdote it is strange to think of the liberal-
minded mother so nearly becoming Head of the
English Church.

Two months later, on August 1st, Queen Anne,
last of the reigning House of Stuart, died; the
father-in-law of Caroline was proclaimed George
I. of England; and she herself dropped the style
of Electoral Princess of Hanover for the higher
dignity of Caroline, Princess of Wales, and quitted
the Hanoverian Court, where her married life

* Thackeray.

had been "one of some gaiety, if not of felicity." *

"Baron Pöllnitz says in his Memoir, that when the Electoral family of Hanover was called to the throne of this country, she showed more cool carelessness for the additional grandeur than any of the family, whose *outward* indifference was a matter of admiration in the old sense of that word, to all who beheld it. The Princess Caroline, according to the baron, particularly demonstrated that she was thoroughly satisfied in her mind that she could be happy without a crown, and that 'both her father-in-law and her husband were already kings in her eyes, because they highly deserved that title.' " †

Accompanied by her three little daughters, Caroline arrived at Margate on the 13th of October, slept one night there, and one at Rochester, and on the 15th arrived in London, where she was met by the Prince of Wales, and conducted to St. James's Palace; and two days later the gossipping chroniclers of the time tell us that the little Princess Caroline took her first drive. On the 20th George I. was crowned in Westminster Abbey, when "there was much splendour and some calamity, for as the procession was sweeping by, several people were killed by the fall of scaffolding in the Palace Yard." ‡ Three days later, the King, accompanied by the Prince and Princess of Wales, dined with the Lord Mayor and Corporation at Guildhall.

Of course the Princess of Wales did not arrive in England without the Muses being invoked liberally in her behalf. Gray wrote "An Epistle to a Lady, occasioned by the arrival of her Royal Highness the Princess of Wales;" and Addison

* Dr. Doran.   † *Ibid.*   ‡ *Ibid.*

addressed her in strains of fervent eulogy, assuring her that she was

> Born to strengthen and to grace our isle ;

that she

> With graceful ease
> And native majesty is formed to please ;

and that the stage, refined by her influence, will take her as the model for its heroines, intimating further that she herself was

> Skill'd in the labours of the deathless Muse.

Of her eldest daughter, the young Princess Anne, he prophetically remarked that he could

> Already see the illustrious youths complain,
> And future monarchs doomed to sigh in vain.

As soon as he possibly could, George I. visited his beloved Hanover, where he invested his grandson, Prince Frederick, with the Order of the Garter, and did not return until January, 1717. During his absence the Prince of Wales acted as Regent, but the honour was never conferred upon him a second time. "It is probable," says Walpole, "that the son discovered too much fondness for acting the King, as that the father conceived a jealousy of his having done so. Sure it is, that on the King's return, great diversions arose in the Court, and the Whigs were divided —some devoting themselves to the wearer of the crown, and others to the expectant." The Prince and Princess of Wales were turned out of St. James's by the irate monarch, but their children were ordered to remain there. "Father and mother wept piteously at parting from their little ones. The young ones sent some cherries, with their love, to papa and mamma; the parents

watered the fruit with tears."* A daughter of
Lord Portland, afterwards married to Mr. Godolphin, was appointed, without the parents' consent,
governess to the little princesses; and Caroline,
at least, never forgave the lady, and cherished an
unreasonable and unchangeable hatred against
her all her life.

For years after this fracas the King never
addressed a word to his son. For his daughter-
in-law he had an even more cordial dislike, and
politely mentioned her as " cette diablesse Madame
la Princesse." "She was," says Thackeray, "a
very clever woman. She had a keen sense of
humour; she had a dreadful tongue; she turned
into ridicule the antiquated Sultan and his
hideous harem." She did not choose to endure
the treatment her husband submitted to; and when
she and the King met in public, Count Broglie, the
French Ambassador, tells us she would compel
him to answer her remarks; "but even then."
adds the narrator, "he only speaks to her on
these occasions for the sake of decorum." Banished
from the palace, she and her consort established
themselves in Leicester House, and held a court
at which attendance was rigourously prohibited
in the *London Gazette*—a prohibition that
was not very much attended to. "The most
promising of the young gentlemen of the next
party, and the prettiest and liveliest of the young
ladies," according to Walpole, clustered round the
Prince and Princess. There were to be found
Philip Stanhope, Lord Chesterfield, who, had he
lived a century later, would have disputed the title
of "first gentleman in Europe" with George IV.;
John, Lord Hervey, "that mere white curd of
asses' milk;" lovely, witty Mary Lepell, in after

* Thackeray.

time Lady Hervey, of whom some enthusiastic admirer wrote—

> Should the Pope himself go roaming,
> He would follow dear Molly Lepell;

beautiful, audacious Mary Bellenden, whose "face and person were charming; lively she was almost to *etourderie*: and so agreeable she was, that I never heard her mentioned afterwards by one of her contemporaries who did not prefer her as the most perfect creature they ever knew;"* Mrs. Howard, afterwards Lady Suffolk; and Mrs. Selwyn, mother of the famous wit. The Prince of Wales, who thought himself irresistible to the fair sex, would have besieged lovely Mary Bellenden with attentions; but that saucy beauty repelled him *sans cérémonie.* "He had probably been contemplating the engraving of the visit of Jupiter to the Nymph Danae in a shower of gold, when he took to pouring the guineas from his purse in Miss Bellenden's presence. He seemed to her, if we may judge by the comments she made upon his conduct, much more like a villanous little bashaw offering to purchase a Circassian slave; and on one occasion, as he went on counting the glittering coin, she exclaimed, 'Sir, I cannot bear it; if you count your money any more, I will go out of the room.'"† Even this affront was not the worst of her offences in the eyes of her prince; for she actually made a love-match with her handsome suitor, Colonel John Campbell, and treated her royal admirer's anger with the same serene *insouciance* as she had formerly done his gallantry.

Very gay was the new Court. Every morning the Princess held a drawing-room. Every evening

* Walpole.   † Dr. Doran.

there was a grand reception. Spite of the
London Gazette, all the world went there.
" Perhaps the most frolicsome nights at Leicester
House were when the Princess of Wales was in
the card-room, where a dozen tables were occupied
by players, while the Prince, in another room,
gave topazes and amethysts to be raffled for by
the maids of honour, amid fun and laughter, and
little astonishment when the prizes were found to
be more or less damaged." * These fair ladies
used to ride forth with the Prince to Hampton
Court to hunt, and then, returning, and making
their toilettes, would be ready to bandy sweet
nothings with their admirers, while " the Princess
leans on Lady Cowper's shoulder and affects to
admire what she really scorns—the rich dress
of the beautiful Lady Mary Wortley Montague.
On one of the gay nights in Leicester House,
when the Princess appeared in a dress of Irish
silk—a present from ' the Irish parson, Swift '—
the Prince spoke in such terms of the giver as to
induce Lord Peterborough to remark, ' Swift has
now only to chalk his pumps and learn to dance
on the tight-rope to be yet a bishop.' " †

The Princess of Wales speedily gained great
popularity, and began to be looked up to as the
leader of fashion. Her life was not without its
thorns, however—and of these the two principal
ones were Lord Chesterfield and Mrs. Howard.
The former, a born mimic, could never resist
imitating and turning into ridicule his royal
mistress; who, coming to hear of it, rather lost
the dignity which none could assume more grandly
than herself, and told him, a little in jest and
more in earnest, to beware how he fell into her

* " Leicester Fields." *Vide* " Temple Bar," August, 1874.
† *Ibid.*

bad graces, for she had a more bitter tongue than he, and would be careful to repay with heavy interest all he made her endure. The "gentleman" peer, thus arraigned, gravely protested that it was not possible he could ever have dreamt of presuming to ridicule her Royal Highness; and as soon as her head was turned, resumed the audacious mimicry which had won him the warning.

The second "thorn"—Mrs. Howard—probably stung deeper than any raillery of the Earl of Chesterfield. In those bad days we talk of as the good old times, it was held that a King was too exalted a personage to stoop to so bourgeois a virtue as conjugal faithfulness; and the bad eminence to which Mrs. Howard was raised was regarded as no hindrance to her holding the appointment of Woman of the Bedchamber to the Prince's wife; and the morals of the time were so easy, or rather so utterly wanting, that Caroline herself acquiesced in the arrangement, and only manifested every now and then, by some adroitly spoken stab, her knowledge that her servant was her rival. The Prince of Wales, reluctantly aware of his wife's immense mental superiority, thought he had thus satisfactorily proved that he could not be sneered at as under her dominion. No one, perhaps, but the Princess herself quite knew *how* entirely she was the ruling power.

The sycophants of the Court divided their attentions between Mrs. Howard and Mrs. Clayton, another Woman of the Bedchamber, who was supposed to possess unbounded influence over her mistress, and who really did possess some, though by no means in the measureless degree that was rumoured. Never, perhaps, has woman been more whitened and blackened by respective

chroniclers than she—some eulogising her as an
angel of unobtrusive charity, and others vituper-
ating her as the meanest and most avaricious
of bribe-takers.   Her great power was, "that
with her rested to decide whether the prayer of a
petitioner should or should not reach the eye of
Caroline.   No wonder, then, that she was flattered,
and that her good offices were asked for with
showers of praise and compliment to herself,
by favour-seekers of every conceivable class.
Peers of every degree, and their wives, bishops
and poor curates, philosophers well-to-do, and
authors in shreds and patches, sages and sciolets,
inventors, speculators, and a mob of 'beggars'
which cannot be classed, sought to approach
Caroline through Mrs. Clayton's office, and humbly
waited Mrs. Clayton's leisure, while they profusely
flattered her in order to tempt her to be active
in their behalf." *   Both these ladies were retained by Caroline after her accession to the
throne.

In the meantime the Princess made other
interests for herself—one of the interests being
English silkworms.   A Mrs. Gale kept a large
number of these creatures in a mulberry garden
at Chelsea, and from their produce some rich
satin was made for Caroline's use; but the experiment gave so little promise of being profitable
that even her patronage did not aid it.   Another
great wish of hers was to see the charity children
at church on their annual festival.   "It having
appeared that she had not been invited on the
previous occasion, 'upon account of the straitness
of the room,' application was made to the Commissioners for finishing St. Paul's Cathedral for
leave to assemble the schools in that church at

* Dr. Doran.

the ensuing meeting. The Dean and Chapter were applied to, but after an interview with Sir Christopher Wren the scheme was abandoned. It is probable that the Princess attended St. Sepulchre's, notwithstanding 'the straitness of the room;' for she said that 'she would come alone in a hackney chair, rather than not see the charity children upon such an occasion.'"* Her kind-heartedness showed itself strongly on one occasion when she had invited the poet Gay to read his play of "The Captives," at Leicester House. "On being ushered into the august company, Gay, nervous from long waiting, tragedy in hand, bashful and blundering, fell over a stool, thereby threw down a screen, and set his illustrious audience in a comical kind of confusion, amid which the kind-hearted Princess did her best to put Gay at ease in his perplexities." †

The Prince and Princess of Wales had at one time some idea of taking Buckingham House for their town residence, in lieu of Leicester House. Its owner was the Dowager Duchess of Buckingham, "the mad duchess," as she was often called. who thus writes of the negociations to Mrs. Howard :—

"If their Royal Highnesses will have everything stand as it is, furniture and pictures, I will have £3,000 per annum. Both run hazard of being spoiled ; and the last, to be sure, will be all to be new bought whenever my son is of age. The quantity the rooms take cannot be well furnished under £10,000. But if their Highnesses will permit all the pictures to be removed, and buy the furniture as it will be valued by different

* "Charity Children's Day at St. Paul's." *Vide* "Sunday at Home," June, 1868.
† Dr. Doran.

people, the house shall go at £2,000. If the Prince and Princess prefer much the buying outright, under £60,000 it will not be parted with as it now stands; and all his Majesty's revenue cannot purchase a place so fit for them, nor for less a sum. The Princess asked me at the drawing-room if I would not sell my fine house. I answered her, smiling, that I was under no necessity to part with it; yet, when what I thought was the value of it should be offered, perhaps my prudence might overcome my inclination."

Probably the Duchess's ideas were too lavish for her would-be royal tenants, for we hear no more of the matter.

The country house of the Prince and Princess was Richmond Lodge, built on part of the estate forfeited by the Duke of Ormond through his Jacobitism. It must have been, says Dr. Doran, "one of the most pleasant resorts at which royalty has ever presided over fashion, wit, and talent." "At this period," says Croker, "Pope and his literary friends were in great favour at this 'young court,' of which, in addition to the handsome and clever Princess herself, Mrs. Howard, Mrs. Selwyn, Miss Howe, Miss Bellenden, and Miss Lepell, with Lords Chesterfield, Bathurst, Scarborough, and Hervey, were the chief ornaments. Above all, for beauty and wit, were Miss Bellenden and Miss Lepell, who seem to have treated Pope, and been in return treated by him, with a familiarity that appears strange in our more decorous days. These young ladies probably considered him as no more than what Aaron Hill described him—

Tuneful Alexis, on the Thames' fair side,
The ladies' *plaything* and the Muses' pride."

From Pope himself we get a vivid glimpse of this court of a hundred and fifty years since:—

"I went by water to Hampton Court, and met the Prince, with all his ladies, on horseback, coming from hunting. Mrs. Bellenden and Mrs. Lepell took me into protection, contrary to the laws against harbouring Papists, and gave me a dinner, with something I liked better, an opportunity of conversation with Mrs. Howard. We all agreed that the life of a maid of honour was of all things the most miserable, and wished that all women who envied it had a specimen of it. To eat Westphalia ham of a morning, ride over hedges and ditches on borrowed hacks, come home in the heat of the day with a fever, and (what is worse a hundred times) with a red mark on the forehead from an uneasy hat—all this may qualify them to make excellent wives for hunters. As soon as they wipe off the heat of the day, they must simper an hour and catch cold in the Princess's appartment; from thence to dinner with what appetite they may; and after that till midnight, work, walk, or think, which way they please. No lone house in Wales, with a mountain and rookery, is more contemplative than this Court. Miss Lepell walked with me three or four hours by moonlight, and we met no creature of any quality but the King, who gave audience to the vice-chamberlain all alone under the garden wall."

London was smaller in those times. Such an announcement as the following reads strangely to us of the present day, as we recall the trim rows of houses known as Belsize Park and Buckland Crescent:—

"On Saturday their Royal Highnesses the Prince and Princess of Wales dined at Belsize House, near

Hampstead, attended by several persons of quality, where they were entertained with the diversion of hunting, and such others as the place affords; with which they seemed well pleased, and at their departure were very liberal to the servants." *

Four of Caroline's children were born at Leicester House; George William, Duke of Gloucester, born November 2nd, 1717, who died three months later; William Augustus, Duke of Cumberland, always his mother's favourite son, born April 15th, 1721; Mary, born February 22nd, 1723; and Louisa, born December 7th, 1724. The expected birth of the former Princess—the first English-born daughter of the house of Brunswick—was thus alluded to by a rhymer possessing more enthusiasm than good taste—

> Promis'd blessing of the year,
> Fairest blossom of the spring,
> Thy fond mother's wish, appear!
> Haste to hear the linnets sing!
> Haste to breathe the vernal air,
> Come to see the primrose blow;
> Nature doth her lap prepare,
> Nature thinks thy coming slow.
> Glad the people, quickly smile,
> Darling native of our isle.

In the summer succeeding the Duke of Cumberland's birth, the Princess of Wales gained great admiration for her courage by allowing her two daughters, Amelia and Caroline, to be inoculated for the smallpox. Twelve months before, Lady Mary Wortley Montague had reported to the Prince and Princess the good results of the practice as she had observed it at Constantinople; and the Prince had given orders that six condemned criminals should be operated upon, their lives being spared for the purpose. So well did

* " Read's Journal," July 15th, 1721.

the experiment succeed that, in 1721, Caroline allowed Dr. Mead to inoculate the two young Princesses, and he was appointed physician in ordinary to her husband.

A reconciliation had been effected between the King and the Prince and Princess of Wales, and thus the children were once more under the parents' care; but the "old" and "young" Courts still remained distinct, and the Princess did all she could to secure adherents to her husband. Her manner was charming, but occasionally even her tact and courtesy did not save her from making some such unlucky mistake as the following, which occurred after her accession to the throne :—

"The Queen, seeking to make friends, before a reception gathered facts relating to persons who would be presented, on which she might found an agreeable allusion. She heard that Sir Woolston Dixie lived near Bosworth Field, but had not heard that the worthy baronet, a brutal and ignorant man, knew less of the fate of Richard III. than of the ridicule he got in his own parish for having assaulted a tinker one day in crossing Bosworth Field, and made himself a local jest as hero of the Battle of Bosworth. Of all that the Queen knew nothing, when she said with her blandest smile as he came up, 'Oh, sir! it has been related to me your connexion with Bosworth Field and the memorable battle fought there.' The gentleman's face reddened as he broke out with an indecorous vehemence of protestation that all Her Majesty had heard about that battle was a lie, and he would find a way to make those repent who had filled the ears of their sovereign with such gross nonsense. 'God forgive my great sin!' cried the astonished Princess; and Sir

Woolston Dixie left the drawing-room in great agony of wrath"*

In spite of her unfailing efforts to please, the Princess of Wales occasionally met with discourtesy that, in our age, seems almost incredible. Thus Swift, whose manners were always more or less those of a humanized bear, boasted that she sent for him *nine* times to Leicester House before he obeyed the summons. "When he *did* appear before Caroline, he roughly remarked that he understood she liked to see odd persons; that she had lately inspected a wild boy from Germany, and that now she had the opportunity of seeing a wild parson from Ireland."† The gruff dean's rudeness did not prevent the Princess enjoying "Gulliver's Travels." Arbuthnot relates how, when he last saw her, she was reading the book, and "was just come to the passage of the hobbling prince, which she laughed at." Probably she was unaware that the "hobbling prince" was a satire on her husband's supposed wavering between the Whigs and Tories. George himself, though far less acute, would probably have been much quicker to perceive the sarcasm; for, like most little men, he had an inordinate opinion of his own dignity, and not only at once discovered any attempt at ridiculing him, but frequently found an insult where none was intended, as the following anecdote shows:—

"There used to be a curious custom at the English Court, for an officer who was called the King's 'cock-crower,' to crow the hour each night during Lent, within the precincts of the palace, instead of announcing it in the usual manner.

* " The Queen of the Blue Stockings." Vide "All the Year Round," April 20th, 1861.
† Dr. Doran.

On the first Ash Wednesday that George II. was in England, as the Prince was at supper, this official suddenly entered the room, and, following the old usage, crew like a cock in order to announce that it was just ten o'clock. The Prince, not knowing the habits and customs of these so-mad English, thought that this was intended as an insult to him, and it was with the greatest difficulty that the interpreter managed to make him understand, that so far from this being the case, a compliment was intended. However, the practice was discontinued from that time forth, it having been originally intended to recall to mind the fall of St. Peter." *

On the 13th of November, 1726, Sophia Dorothea, the unhappy wife of George I., died at Ahlden; and as some French prophetess had predicted to the King that he would not survive his consort a year, the death of that most hapless lady, the cruel mystery of whose life has never yet been unravelled, caused her phlegmatic widower some uneasy qualms. The impression of coming evil grew upon him; and before setting out in June, 1727, for his last visit to Hanover, he bade farewell to the Prince and Princess of Wales with tears, saying he should never see them again. "It was certainly," says Walpole, "his own approaching end that melted him, not the thought of quitting for ever two persons that he hated." His presentiment proved true; for he died on June 10th, on his way to Osnaburgh; and George and Caroline were King and Queen of England. How the news was conveyed to them can only be told by Thackeray :—

"On the afternoon of the 14th of June, 1727,

* "Weather Wisdom and Folk Lore." Vide "Monthly Packet," March, 1875.

two horsemen might have been perceived galloping along the road from Chelsea to Richmond. The foremost, cased in the jack-boots of the period, was a broad-faced, jolly-looking, and very corpulent cavalier; but, by the manner in which he urged his horse, you might see that he was a bold as well as a skilful rider. Indeed, no man loved sport better; and in the hunting-fields of Norfolk no squire rode more boldly after the fox, or cheered Ringwood and Sweetlips more lustily, than he who now thundered over the Richmond road.

"He speedily reached Richmond Lodge, and asked to see the owner of the mansion. The mistress of the house and her ladies, to whom our friend was admitted, said he could not be introduced to the master, however pressing the business might be. The master was asleep after his dinner; he always slept after his dinner; and woe be to the person who interrupted him! Nevertheless, our stout friend of the jack-boots put the affrighted ladies aside, opened the forbidden door of the bedroom, wherein upon the bed lay a little gentleman; and here the eager messenger knelt down in his jack-boots.

"He on the bed started up, and with many oaths and a strong German accent, asked who was there, and who dared to disturb him.

"'I am Sir Robert Walpole,' said the messenger. The awakened sleeper hated Sir Robert Walpole. 'I have the honour to announce to your Majesty that your royal father, King George I., died at Osnaburgh, on Saturday last, the 10th instant.'

"'*Dat is one big lie!*' roared out his sacred Majesty, King George II., but Sir Robert Walpole stated the fact, and from that day until three and thirty years after, George, the second of the name, ruled over England."

Sir Robert was not a favourite with his newly-made Majesty, or, what was perhaps more important, with the new Queen. On asking the King whom he would select to draw up the address to the Privy Council, George made choice of the Speaker of the House of Commons, Sir Spencer Compton—a polite way of signifying to Sir Robert that his tenure as Prime Minister was ended. The latter "was not pleased at being supplanted, but neither was he wrathfully little-minded against his successor—a successor so incompetent for his task that he was obliged to have recourse to Sir Robert to assist him in drawing up the address above alluded to. Sir Robert rendered the assistance with much heartiness, but was not the less determined, if possible, to retain his office, in spite of the personal dislike of the King, and of that of the Queen, whom he had offended, when she was Princess of Wales, by speaking of her as 'that fat beast, the Prince's wife.' Sir Robert could easily make poor Sir Spencer communicative with regard to his future intentions. The latter was a stiff, gossipping, soft-hearted creature, and might very well have taken for his motto the words of Parmeno in the play of Terence: 'Plenus rimarum sum.' He intimated that on first meeting parliament he should propose an allowance of £60,000 per annum to be made to the Queen. 'I will make it forty thousand more,' said Sir Robert, subsequently, through a second party, to Queen Caroline, 'if my office of Minister be secured to me.' Caroline was delighted at the idea, intimated that Sir Robert might be sure 'the fat beast' had friendly feelings towards him, and then hastening to the King, over whose weaker intellect her more masculine mind held rule, explained to her royal husband

N

that as Compton considered Walpole the fittest man to be—what he had so long been with efficiency—Prime Minister, it would be a foolish act to nominate Compton himself to the office. The King acquiesced; Sir Spencer was made president of the Council, and Sir Robert not only persuaded Parliament, without difficulty, to settle one hundred thousand a year on the Queen, but he also persuaded the august trustees of the people's money to add the entire revenue of the civil list, about one hundred and thirty thousand pounds a year, to the annual sum of seven hundred thousand pounds, which had been settled as proper revenue for a King. Sir Robert had thus the wit to bribe King and Queen, out of the funds of the people; and we cannot be surprised that their Majesties looked upon him and his as true allies."* The jointure of Queen Caroline, granted mainly through Walpole's agency, was thus £100,000 a year, with the dower houses of Somerset House and Richmond Lodge—a larger sum than had ever been previously granted to a Queen Consort. Her Majesty and the Prime Minister were firm allies; but nevertheless the former had not a very high opinion of the latter's moral character. In praising his talents to her husband, she suggested " that Sir Robert was rich enough to be honest, and had so little private business of his own that he had all the more leisure to devote to that of the King. 'New leeches would not be the less hungry;' and with this very indifferent sort of testimony to her favourite's worth, Caroline secured a servant for the King and a minister for herself."†

The King and Queen removed to Leicester House on the very day on which they received the

* Dr. Doran. † *Ibid.*

news of the late King's death; and the following
day held a Court, to which all the great world in
town thronged—"my mother," says Horace
Walpole, "among the rest, who, Sir Spencer
Compton's designation and not his evaporation
being known, could not make her way between
the scornful backs and elbows of her late devotees,
nor could approach nearer to the Queen than the
third or fourth row; but no sooner was she
descried by her Majesty than the Queen said
aloud: 'There I am sure I see a friend!' The
torrent divided, and shrank to either side, 'and
as I came away,' said my mother, 'I might have
walked over their heads, had I pleased.'"

CHAPTER II.

Coronation of George and Caroline—Drury Lane Theatre—Royal Visit to the City—Queen's patronage of authors—Her munificence to Elizabeth Elstob—Frederick Prince of Wales—Thomson's " Sophonisba "—" The Beggars' Opera "—The Duchess of Queensberry—The Queen's Birthday—Horace Walpole—Lord Hervey—Caroline's immense influence—Self-importance of the King—Queen's love for her husband—Mrs. Howard—Mrs. Howard's husband—Caroline Regent—Stephen Duck—Royalty at home—The Duke of Grafton—The Princess Royal—Her ambition—Her betrothal to the Prince of Orange—His appearance—Arrival—Illness—Presents to the Princess—The Royal Marriage—Extraordinary ceremonies—The Drawing-room—Opinion of the Princesses—Departure of the Prince and Princess—Address of the House of Lords to the Queen.

The coronation of the new King and Queen took place on the 11th of October, and was the most gorgeous ceremony which had been seen for many years. " The ceremony was performed," says Lord Hervey, " with all the pomp and magnificence that could be contrived, the present King differing so much from the last that all the pageantry and splendour, badges and trappings of royalty, were as pleasing to the son as they were irksome to the father. The dress of the Queen on this occasion was as fine as the *accumulated* riches of the city and the suburbs could make it; for besides her own jewels (which were a great number and very valuable), she had on her head and on her shoulders all the pearls she could borrow of the ladies of quality at one end of the town, and on her petticoat all the diamonds she could hire of the Jews and jewellers at the other; so the appearance and truth of her finery was a mixture of magnificence and meanness, not unlike the *éclat* of royalty in many other particulars, when it comes to be nicely examined and its sources traced to what money hires and flattery lends." All the jewels mentioned as belonging to the Queen were her private property. Of crown jewels she had none. "At the death of Queen Anne," says Horace Walpole, "such a clearance had been made of her Majesty's jewels, or the new King had so instantly distributed them among his German favourites, that Lady Suffolk told me Queen Caroline never obtained of the late Queen's jewels but one pearl necklace." Her Majesty's attire was a subject of keen interest to the fairer portion of her subjects for some time before the event. "The Queen has upon her pettycoat," says Mrs. Delany, writing on the 5th of October, "for the coronation twenty-four hundred thousand pounds' worth of jewels." The same lively and gossiping lady gives the following entertaining account of her view of the proceedings, written for the benefit of her sister, Anne Granville:—

"Somerset House, the day after the Coronation.

"I was a spectator in Westminster Hall, from whence the procession began, and after their Majesties were crowned, they returned with all their noble followers to dine. The dresses of the ladies were becoming, and most of them immensely rich. Lady Delawar has one of the best figures; the Duchess of Queensborough depended so much upon her native beauty that she despised all adornments, nor had not one jewel, riband, or puff to set her off, but everybody thought she did *not* appear to advantage. The Duchess of Richmond pleased everybody; she looked easy and

genteel, with the most sweetness in her countenance imaginable ; in short all the ladies young
and middle-aged, though not handsome, looked
agreeable and well. The Lords' dress is not
altogether so well, but those that walked well had
the advantage. Lord Sunderland, Lord Albemarle, the Duke of Richmond, Lord Finch, and
my Lord Lichfield were *the top.*

"The Queen never was so well liked; her
clothes were extravagantly fine, though they did
not make show enough for the occasion, but she
walked gracefully and smiled on all as she passed
by. Lady Fanny Nassau (who was one of the
ladies that bore up the train) looked exceedingly
well ; her clothes were fine and very becoming,
pink-coloured satin the gown (which was stiff-
bodied), embroidered with silver, the petticoat
covered with a trimming answerable. Princess
Anne (who is now distinguished by the title of
Princess Royal), and her two sisters, held up the
top of the train. They were dressed in stiff-
bodied gowns of silver tissue, embroidered or quite
covered with silver trimming, with diadems
upon their head, and purple mantles edged with
ermine, and vast long trains; they were very
prettily dressed, and looked very well. After
them walked the Duchess of Dorset and Lady
Sussex, two ladies of the bedchamber in waiting;
then the two finest figures of all the procession—
Mrs. Herbert and Mrs. Howard, the bedchamber
women in waiting, in gowns also, but so rich, so
genteel, so perfectly well dressed that any description must do them an injury. Mrs. Herbert's was
blue and silver, with a rich embroidered trimming; Mrs. Howard scarlet and silver, trimmed
in the same manner, their heads with long
locks and puffs and silver riband.

"I could hardly see the King, for he walked so much *under* his canopy that he was almost hid from me by the people that surrounded him; but though the Queen was also under a canopy, she walked so far forward that she was distinguished by everybody. The room was finely illuminated, and though there was 1800 candles, besides what were on the table, they were all lighted in less than three minutes by an invention of Mr. Heidegger's, which succeeded to the admiration of all spectators; the branches that held the candles were all gilt, and in the form of pyramids. I leave it to your lively imagination after this, to have a notion of the splendour of the place so filled and so illuminated. I forgot to tell you Lady Cartwright looked charmingly, and nothing was ever more beautiful than her fine throat, which appeared to the utmost advantage.

"I went with Mrs. Garland, a particular friend of my Lady Carteret's, and one of a general acquaintance. We went to the Hall at half an hour after four in the morning, but when we came the doors were not opened, which at half an hour after seven they brought us word they were. We then sallied forth with a grenadier for our guide: he conveyed us into so violent a crowd that for some minutes I lost my breath (and my cloak I doubt for ever). I verily believe I should have been squeezed as flat as a pancake if providence had not sent Mr. Edward Stanley to my relief, and he being a person of some authority made way for me, and I got to a good place in the Hall without any other damage than a few bruises on my arms, and the loss of my cloak; but extremely frighted with the mob, so much that all I saw was a poor recompense for what my spirits had suffered.

"I got home without any accident about ten of

the clock at night. It was not disagreeable to be taken notice of by one's acquaintance when they appeared to so much advantage, for everybody I knew came under the place where I sate to offer me meat and drink, which was drawn up from below into the galleries by baskets at the end of a long string, which they filled with cold meat and bread, sweetmeats and wine. I think I have told you as much as I at this time can remember."

Caroline dressed for her coronation in a private room at Westminster. In the early morning she had put on an " undress," " of which everything was new," at St. James's Palace, and had then been carried privately across the park in her chair, preceded by Mrs. Howard and the Lord Chancellor, both in " hack sedans." Mrs. Howard robed her, and Mrs. Herbert, another bedchamber woman, who was ambitious of sharing the honour, was refused, on the ground that as she was already in full dress she could not attire the Queen. When the ceremony was over, the Queen again changed her dress at Westminster, and was carried back to St. James's.

The coronation scene was re-enacted in Drury Lane Theatre, where Mrs. Oldfield appeared in a pageant representing the crowning of Anne Boleyn, which was tacked on to the end of " Henry VIII."—a spectacle on which the manager had expended a thousand guineas. Mrs. Oldfield's magnificence was said to have excelled even that of her Royal mistress; and her beauty, or the gorgeousness of the show, proved so attractive, that the pageant was often played separately from the drama at the conclusion of a comedy or other piece, and the King and Queen went more than once to witness it. In the meantime the new sovereigns paid a visit to the Lord Mayor, of which Mrs. Delany thus writes to her sister :—

"Somerset House,
"31st October, 1727.

"After a Coronation a Lord Mayor's feast cannot presume to make a figure in print, but as I love to keep my word on all occasions, I will, according to my promise, describe as well as I am able what I was yesterday witness of, though with gazing my eyes are so weak to-day, that I fear I shall hardly be able to see my way quite through the crowd. The Duchess of Manchester, Lady Carteret, Lady Fanny Shirley, called on me half an hour after one; the streets were prodigiously crowded with mob and the train-bands, whose ridiculous appearance and odd countenances were very entertaining, and all the windows from the bottom to the top loaded with people. We were in no bustle of coaches, for no hackneys were allowed to pass, and all went the same way; but there was so great a throng they could move but very slowly for fear of trampling the people to death, so that we were a whole hour going from Somerset House to Guildhall. When we came to King Street, the officers upon duty said we must not go any further, but get out of our coaches in Cheapside, for none but the royal family were to drive to the Hall gate, but as the street was well-swept and soldiers planted to keep off the mob, it was very good walking. When we had walked about half way up the street, one of the Lord Mayor's officers with a blue and gold staff met us, and said, with an audible and formal voice, 'Ladies, open your tickets,' which accordingly we did. 'Very well, ladies, you will have admittance into the Hall, and, ladies, *you may tarry until the morning ; indeed from this time until six o' the clock you may tarry.'* Then we were all conducted into the room where my Lady Mayoress and all the Aldermen's ladies were seated. Our names were told, and everybody made a low curtsey to her ladyship, who returned it with a great deal of civility, and told us if we would follow her we should dine at her table—an honour not to be refused, and indeed it was a particular favour. We attended her, and had a very fine dinner, and all the polite men of our acquaintance waited behind our chairs and helped us to what we wanted: I had to my share Sir Robert Sutton and Mr. Stanley.

"As soon as we had dined the Lady Mayoress got up, and we followed her to a very pretty room with a good fire. After that we went back to the first room, at the upper end of which was placed the armed chairs and two stools for their Majesties and the Princesses. All this time my Lord Mayor was performing his part through the City, but *wind and tide* being against him made his return very late.

"The King, etc., were at a house which they say has always been kept for that purpose, over against Bow Church, to see the procession. His own coach and horses, that conveyed him to the Hall, was covered with purple cloth; the eight horses (the beautifullest creatures of their kind) were cream colour, the trappings purple silk, and their manes and tails tied with purple riband; the Princesses' horses were black, dressed with white ribands. The King was in purple velvet; the Queen and Princesses in black, and very fine with jewels. At six o' th' clock my Lord Mayor and Aldermen returned, and in three quarters of an hour after the King came. My Lord Mayor, after having received him, and paid the usual homage at the gate, conducted him, etc., into the room where we sate. He and the Queen and the Princesses stood before the chairs and stools that we placed for them, which were raised four steps, and a very loyal speech was made by one of the Aldermen and an acknowledgment of the honour received. Their Majesties were very gracious, and then the Lady Mayoress and the Aldermen's wives were presented. All that ceremony being over, it was time they should have some refreshment, which they had in a very magnificent manner in the Hall.

"We followed the train, and saw them at dinner. The Lady Mayoress waited at the Queen's elbow. Having satisfied our curiosity so far, we thought it convenient to secure a place in the gallery where the ball was to be, which indeed was much too straight for the purpose, but we solaced ourselves with tea and coffee. About ten the royal folk came where we then were, but the crowd was so insupportable we made the best of our way out of it. I had one glimpse of *our* Alderman, who was endeavouring to get to me, but that was not to be effected, so we were parted and saw no more of him. The King and Queen went about twelve o'clock away, and we stayed an hour and a quarter after them, not being able to get to our coach.

"We got home very well, and I must own I was very well pleased with my day's expedition. The Lady Mayoress and those that *had been*, and the High Sheriff's lady, wore gold chains, but not as a necklace—they were tacked on the robings of their gowns in loose scollops in the manner of a galloon, and looked very pretty upon black velvet. There was a vast many people of quality, and, considering the great number of people, less confusion than I expected."

Willing to patronize the poet Gay, Caroline offered him on her accession the post of Gentleman Usher to the little Princess Louisa, then three years old—a sinecure which was worth £200 a year, and which would have led to other preferment. The offer was ungratefully and scornfully refused; the poet saw in it only an insult; and his fast friend, the terrible Dean of St. Patrick's, was fiercely sarcastic at the idea that Gay would be likely to undertake an office in which he would act as a kind of "male nurse" to the little Princess. The author of "Trivia" acted against his own interests in so declining; for the post of poet laureate falling vacant shortly afterwards, it was offered to Cibber in preference to him. The Queen, who was, says Dean Stanley, "the most discriminating patroness of learning and philosophy that down to that time had ever graced the throne of England," was always ready to befriend literary people. Her own tastes were literary, and she loved reading intensely; but the King so hated the sight of a book that she could only do so in her private room, when he was not present to be displeased with her incomprehensible predilection. It was at her request that Newton compiled an abstract of a work on Ancient Chronology, first published in France, and subsequently in England. She pressed Halley to become tutor to her youngest and favourite son, William, Duke of Cumberland; "but the great perfector of the theory of the moon's motion was then too busy with his syzygies to be troubled with teaching the humanities to little Princes."* Three years after her accession,

* Dr. Doran.

the Queen gave another proof of her willingness to benefit distressed authors by her treatment of Elizabeth Elstob, sister of William Elstob, a noted antiquarian, and herself a good Anglo-Saxon scholar, having written a Saxon Homiliarum and a Saxon Grammar, who being in her old age reduced to poverty, was brought to her Majesty's notice by a letter written by Mrs. Chapon in 1730.

"The Queen," says Mrs. Delany, " was so touched with the letter that she immediately sent for Mrs. Pointz, to inquire into some more particulars about the person mentioned in it, and *the person that wrote it.* The Pointz said she knew no more than what the letter told, but that Mrs. Chapon was a friend of ours. The Queen said she never in her life read a better letter, that it had touched her heart, and ordered immediately an hundred pounds for Mrs. Elstob, and said she 'need never fear a necessitous old age while she lived, and that when she wanted more to ask for it, and she should have it.' I think this was acting like a Queen, and ought to be known, though she ordered that it should not be spoken of, because she has many demands of this kind that it is not possible for her to satisfy. . . Mrs. Chapon's letter was the whole discourse of the drawing-room. The Queen asked the Duke of Portland ' when he should be able to write such a letter.' He answered honestly, ' *never.*' "

Frederick, the eldest son of George and Caroline, now Prince of Wales, had hitherto never been allowed to come to England. To say he had never been a favourite with his parents would not be stating the real fact of the case. Both father and mother had a strong aversion to him, which on Caroline's side was so vehement that she would, says Dr. Doran, "have willingly defrauded him of his birthright. At one time she appears to have been inclined to secure the Electorate of Hanover for William, and to allow Frederick to succeed to the English throne. At another time she was as desirous, it is believed, of advancing William to the crown of England, and making over the Electorate to Frederick. How far these intrigues were carried on is hardly known, but that they existed is matter of notoriety. The law presented a barrier which could not, however, be broken down; but nevertheless, Lord Chesterfield, in his character of the Princess, intimated that she was busy with this project throughout her life." In truth Frederick could not have been an attractive son. He was cunning and spiteful, and precociously dissipated. His tutor complained grievously of his conduct, which his mother tried to excuse by remarking that his faults were mere page's tricks. "Would to Heaven they were no more!" cried the master; "but in truth they are tricks of grooms and scoundrels." On his father's accession the young Prince came to his future kingdom, and encountering a cool reception from his parents, who refused to pay the debts he had contracted in Hanover, soon became the rallying point of the opposition. His dislike to the King and Queen was fully as vehement as theirs for him; and the Court had no more outspoken enemy than the heir to the throne.

In 1729 Thomson, the poet of "Seasons" celebrity, secured the patronage of the Queen for his tragedy of "Sophonisba." She was present at its representation; but not even royal favour could support the unlucky drama, which was ruined by one unfortunate line:—

O, Sophonisba! Sophonisba, O!

Some wicked wit parodied the cry with—

O, Jemmy Thomson! Jemmy Thomson, O!

and all the world laughed at the disconcerted author, whose only consolation was in printing and publishing a copy with a special dedication to Her Majesty. The King and Queen were occasionally anything but well pleased with matters theatrical. Thus Gay's "Beggars' Opera," played in the early part of 1728, gave dire offence at Court, on account of its containing, or being supposed to contain, reflections on the Government.

"The origin of the piece," says Dr. Doran, "was certainly *not* political. It was a mere Newgate pastoral put into an operatic form, and intended to ridicule, what it succeeded in over-throwing for a season, the newly introduced Italian opera. The piece had been refused by Cibber, and was accepted by Rich, who brought it out at Lincoln's Inn Fields, on the 29th of January, 1728, with such success, that it was said of it, that it made Gay rich, and Rich gay. . . . Johnson says of the piece that it was plainly written only to divert—without any moral purpose, and therefore not likely to do good. This is the truth, no doubt; and if Gay put in a few strong passages just previous to representation, it was the public application which gave them double force." It was not the moral teaching of the play which the Queen objected to. "Her own chairmen were suspected of being in league with highwaymen, and probably were; but on their being arrested and dismissed from her service by the master of her household, who suspected their guilt, she was indignant at the liberty taken and insisted on their being restored."* She was

* Dr. Doran.

angry at the political allusions, and at Sir Robert
Walpole's being satirized as a "thief and a friend
of thieves." Accordingly, when Gay produced a
sequel to the offending piece—"Polly"—he
received an injunction from the Lord Chamberlain
forbidding its representation in any theatre—an
edict in the which the author was especially
annoyed, as the piece was his pet creation. He
was a *protégé* of the Duke and Duchess of Queensberry—particularly of the Duchess, whom Prior
has immortalized as

> Kitty, beautiful and young,
> And wild as colt untam'd,

a lovely audacious madcap of a beauty, who spoke
her mind on all possible occasions, and stuck at
nothing. She was violently indignant with the
treatment her favourite had received; "she
thought him much injured ; upon which, to make
him some amends, for he is poor, she promised to
get a subscription for his play if he would print
it."* She not only promised, but performed; for
she asked everyone, literally forced subscriptions
from all her friends, and actually carried her
partizanship so far that she solicited donations in
the royal drawing-room. The King noticed her
eagerness as she was discoursing three or four
gentlemen, and asked her what was the engross-
ing topic. "It is a matter of humanity and
charity," said her intrepid grace, "and I do not
despair but that your Majesty will contribute to it."
The dauntless Duchess had, however, gone a step
too far; and the King and Queen were so much
displeased that she was prohibited, for a time at
least, from appearing in the royal presence—she
was "forbid the Court," as Mrs. Delany puts it;

* "Autobiography and Correspondence of Mrs. Delany."

"a thing," that lady remarks, "never heard of before to one of her rank; one might have imagined *her beauty* would have secured her from such treatment!" The King's vice-chamberlain, Mr. Stanhope, was sent to acquaint her with this decision by a verbal message. The irrepressible lady gave him a note of acknowledgment for the King which certainly cannot be said to err on the side of undue meekness :—

"February 27th, 1728-9.

"The Duchess of Queensberry is surprised and well pleased that the King hath given her so agreeable a command as to stay from Court, where she never came for diversion, but to bestow a civility on the King and Queen; she hopes by such an unprecedented order as this is that the King will see as few as he wishes at his Court, particularly such as dare to think or speak truth. I dare not do otherwise, and ought not, nor could have imagined that it would not have been the very highest compliment that I could possibly pay the King to endeavour to support truth and innocence in his house, particularly when the King and Queen both told me that they had not read Mr. Gay's play. I have certainly done right, then, to stand by my own words, rather than his grace of Grafton's, who hath neither made use of *truth*, *judgment*, nor *honour*, through this whole affair, either for himself or his friends."

This note she gave to Mr. Stanhope to read; and the Court official, horrified at the incisive pirectness of the missive, entreated her to reconsider the matter, and write another epistle. The Duchess demurely took the advice, returned to her desk, and completed another reply, so much more

outspoken and piquant than the first that the
Vice-Chamberlain preferred taking the original
missive. "The Duchess of Queensberry," says
Mrs. Delany, writing on the 14th of March, "is
still the talk of the town. She is going to Scotland; she has great reason to resent her usage,
but she was provoking first, and her answer
though it shows spirit, was not worded as her
friends could have wished; good manners ought
to be observed to our equals, and our superiors
certainly have a right to it. My Lady Hervey
told her the other day, that ' *now she was banished,
the Court had lost its chief ornament,*' the Duchess
replied, ' *I am entirely of your mind.*' It is
thought my Lady Hervey spoke to her with a
sneer, if so her Grace's answer was a very good
one."

This was not the first time the impetuous lady
had fallen under royal displeasure. "She usually
wore an apron, and when this article of attire was
forbidden to be worn at the royal drawing-rooms,
the Duchess appeared in it one day: her entrance
was consequently opposed by the Lord in Waiting. when she tore it off, threw it in his face, and
walked on."*

Mrs. Delany gives a lively account of Queen
Caroline's birthday drawing-room, which she
attended about this time. "On Saturday," she
says, writing from Somerset House on the 4th of
March, 1728-9, "the first day of March, it being
Queen Caroline's birthday, 1 dressed myself in all
my best array, borrowed my Lady Sunderland's
jewels, and made a tearing show. I went with
my Lady Carteret, and her two daughters. There
was a vast Court, and my Lady Carteret got with
some difficulty to the circle, and after she had

* "Autobiography and Correspondence of Mrs. Delany."

made her curtsey made me stand before her. The
Queen came up to her, and thanked her for
bringing me forward, and she told me she was
obliged to me for my pretty clothes, and admired
my Lady Carteret's extremely; she told the Queen
that they were my fancy, and that I drew the
pattern. Her Majesty said she had heard that I
could draw very well (I can't think who could tell
her *such a story*); she took notice of my jewels;
I told her they were my Lady Sunderland's.
'Oh,' says she, '*you were afraid I should think my
Lord Selkirk gave them to you*, but I believe he
only admires, for he will not be so free of his
presents.' (I think it is a great condescension,
after all this to correspond with a country girl!)
. . . . . At night sure nothing but the
Coronation could exceed the squeezing and crowd-
ing that was there, the ball-room was so excessive
full that I could not see one dance, but was thrust
quite from my company. However, a little to
recompense that loss and the fatigue I had undergone, it was my fortune to be thrown in the way
of Guyamore,* who very gallantly got me a seat,
and sate down by me; his aunt, Lady Betty Lee,
was opposite us. I asked him why he would not
go and pay his duty to her? He 'hated to look
at her,' he said, 'she was so confounded ugly;'
and 'that he should be a happy man were I as
ugly.' Miss Tolmash came to the place where I
sate, and I resigned my place and made an
attempt to find my company, but all in vain, I
might as well have attempted to swim across the
sea in a storm; and after having been buffeted
about and crushed to a mummy, my Lord Sunderland espied me out, and made me take his place.
  "The clock struck twelve, the French dances

* Charles, Lord Baltimore.

were just over, and every man took the woman he
liked best to dance country-dances, the Prince set
the example by choosing the Duchess of Bedford,
who is the queen of his fancy at present. Ha Ha *
found me out and entreated me to dance one
dance, but the crowd was so monstrous I had not
courage ; he looked disappointed. *I was sorry* to
refuse him ; but though I would not make use of
him in his own way, I did make a convenience of
him, for by his means I found my Lady Carteret.
We went away at half an hour after one ; and I
was so tired all Sunday, I could hardly hold up
head ; but yesterday I was very well, and dined
with my Lady Carteret ; and went in the afternoon to my Lady Sunderland.

"The King was in blue velvet, with diamond
buttons ; the hat was buttoned up with prodigious fine diamonds. The Queen was in black
velvet, the Court being out of mourning only for
that day. Princess Royal had white poudesoy,
embroidered with gold, and a few colours intermixed ; the petticoat was very handsome, but the
gown looked poor, it being only faced and robed
with embroidery. Princess Amely had a yellow
and silver stuff, the pattern marked out with a
thread of purple, and purple ribbons with pearl in
her head, which became her. Princess Caroline
had pink colour damask, trimmed with silver.
The Prince of Wales was in mouse-colour velvet,
turned up with scarlet, and very richly embroidered
with silver ; he dances very well, especially
country dances, for he has a great deal of spirit.
Lady Carteret's clothes were the finest there —
green and gold, embroidered and trimmed ; Miss
Carteret yellow and silver. Lady Hartford had a
blue manteau, embroidered with gold, and a white

* Hon. Henry Hervey, son of the Earl of Bristol.

satin petticoat; it looked very whimsical, and not pretty."

It has been the lot of few royal personages to have their lives and times chronicled with such gossiping minuteness by two such different observers, as it was of Queen Caroline. Horace Walpole, and John, Lord Hervey, both professors of the highest order in the art of gossip—what a cruel slander it is to make it the vice feminine par excellence!—have left to posterity such graphic and circumstantial details concerning the Queen and all her surroundings that we seem to live again in that world of a century ago, and view with astonished eyes the extraordinary drama of royal life played out under the Second George. Not till we come to read contemporary memoirs do we accurately realize the utter absence of refinement and delicacy, the intense and revolting coarseness of mind and manners, which was so entirely the characteristic of the age that in passing judgment on the persons who then lived, we must consider it less as an individual defect than as a moral leprosy by which all were more or less infected. How widely spread it was may be judged from the fact that Caroline herself, whom Lord Mahon calls "a Queen without a blemish," carried on, purely for pleasure, a correspondence with Elizabeth Charlotte, the Dowager Duchess of Orleans, whose letters are so utterly corrupt that the boldest publisher has never ventured to print them entire, and even the published portions of which are unfit for any pure-minded person to peruse.

Walpole and his "Memoirs" are too well known to need much description. As Thackeray says, his "charming volumes are in the hands of all who love the gossip of the last century. Nothing can be more cheery than Horace's letters. Fiddles sing all through them; wax lights, fine dresses, fine jokes, fine plate, fine equipages, glitter and sparkle there; never was such a brilliant jigging, smirking Vanity Fair as that through which he leads us." Caroline's other chronicler, John, Lord Hervey, is sketched by contemporaries in stronger, darker colours than the pleasant host of Strawberry Hill. Succeeding to the title by the sudden death of his brother, holding the post of Gentleman of the Bedchamber to the King, and the privileged favourite of the Queen, he had ample opportunity for observing the private life of his royal mistress, of which he took advantage to the utmost. The frequent attacks of epilepsy from which he suffered—to prevent which he lived chiefly on asses' milk and biscuits—and the deadly pallor of his complexion, which he used to conceal by rouge, were cruelly satirized by Pope in his " Epistle to Arbuthnot," the peer having in some way offended the fiery little poet. Notwithstanding his ill health, Lord Hervey mixed freely in all the dissipation and vices of the time. " In a lax age his profligacy was notorious. He was a sceptic, and took the greatest delight in wounding the religious susceptibilities of those he came across. In his creed there was nothing great, nothing noble, nothing of good report; all was hollow, artificial, and insincere. As a necessary consequence of this distorted faith, he believed in nothing, except perhaps himself, and in nobody, except perhaps Queen Caroline. Throughout the pages of his " Memoirs " detraction is the principal feature. His enemies are of course painted in the blackest colours, their characters picked out in the *aqua fortis* of hate; but even in his description of his friends there is always something spiteful and malicious, which casts into the shade the praise that may have been bestowed. Everybody is a knave or a sycophant; the world revolves upon the axis of humbug, and between the poles of venality and corruption. A politician is one who identifies his own interests with those of the country; a priest is a scheming hypocrite who makes the best of both worlds, and who would sell his soul for a mitre; justice, truth, morality, and all the other attributes of virtue are only so many masks to conceal motives, and to further the cause of self-advancement."*

From the pages of his " Memoirs " we learn how great was the influence of Queen Caroline over her hot-headed little spouse. Perhaps no woman ever possessed more admirable tact and more unerring skill. Intensely ambitious, and keenly loving power, she practised unflinchingly, says Lord Hervey, " a strict and painful *régime* which few besides herself could have had patience to support or resolution to adhere to." Every day she was *tête-à-tête* with the King for seven or eight hours, " during which time she was generally saying what she did not think, assenting to what she did not believe, and praising what she did not approve; for they were seldom of the same opinion, and he too fond of his own for her ever at first to dare to controvert it. She used to give him her opinion as jugglers do a card, by changing it imperceptibly, and making him believe he held the same with that he just pitched upon. . . She knew it was absolutely necessary to have interest in her husband, as she was sensible that interest was the measure by which people would always judge of her power. To him she sacrificed her time, for him she mortified her inclination.

* " John, Lord Hervey." *Vide* " Temple Bar," October, 1878.

She looked, spake, and breathed but for him, like a weathercock to every capricious blast of his uncertain temper. She governed him by being as great a slave to him thus ruled as any other wife could be to a man who ruled her. For all the tedious hours she spent then in watching him whilst he slept, or the heavier task of entertaining him whilst he was awake, her single consolation was in reflecting she had power, and that people in coffee-houses were saying she governed this country without knowing how dear the government of it cost her."* When Sir Robert Walpole again became Prime Minister, " it was understood by everybody that he was the Queen's minister; that whoever he favoured she distinguished: and whoever she distinguished, the King employed. His reputed mistress, Mrs. Howard, and the Speaker Compton, his reputed minister, were perceived to be nothing ; and Mr. Pulteney and Lord Bolingbroke, in the algebraical phrase, less than nothing."† " The Queen ruled," says Dr. Doran, " without seeming to rule. She was mistress by power of suggestion. A word from her in public, addressed to the King, generally earned for her a rebuke. Her consort so pertinaciously declared that he was independent, and that she never meddled with public business of any kind, that every one, even the early dupes of the assertion, ceased at last to put any faith in it. Caroline 'not only meddled with business, but directed everything which came under that name, either at home or abroad.' It is too much, perhaps, to say that her power was unrivalled and unbounded, but it was doubtless great, and purchased at great cost. That she could induce her husband to employ a man whom he had not yet learnt to like

---

* Lord Hervey's " Memoirs."   † *Ibid.*

was in itself no small proof of her power, considering the peculiarly obstinate disposition of the monarch."

To no one were the lines of Burns:—

> Oh wad some power the giftie give us,
> To see oursels as ithers see us,

more appropriate than to George II. "The tact of the Queen was so admirable that the husband, who followed her counsel in all things, never even himself suspected but that he was leading her. This was the very triumph of the Queen's art, and the crowning proof of the simplicity and silliness of the King. It is said that he sneered at Charles I. for being governed by *his* wife; at Charles II. for being governed by his mistresses; at James led by priests; at William duped by men; at Queen Anne deceived by her favourites; and at his father, who allowed himself to be ruled by any one who could approach him. And he finished his catalogue of scorn by proudly asking, 'Who governs now?'"* Some wit took up the reply the courtiers were too well-bred to offer, and answered the query in the following terms—

> You may strut, dapper George, but 'twill all be in vain;
> We know 'tis Queen Caroline, not you, who reign—
> You govern no more than Don Philip of Spain.
> Then if you would have us fall down and adore you,
> Lock up your fat spouse, as your dad did before you.

Other rhymesters took up the cry, and re-echoed witticisms on—

> So strutting a King and so prating a Queen;

but Caroline's influence remained undisturbed.

Nor must it be supposed that all the Queen's self-sacrifice and exertions were undertaken solely

---

* Dr. Doran.

with a view to attaining the power she longed for. That she dearly loved it, and spared no ends to attain it, is certain ; but that she also dearly loved her husband is just as undoubtedly sure. " One inscrutable attachment," says Thackeray, " that inscrutable woman has. To that she is faithful, through all trial, neglect, pain, and time. Save her husband, she really cares for no created being. She is good enough to her children, and even fond enough of them : but she would chop them all up into little pieces to please him. In her inter-course with all around her, she was perfectly kind, gracious, and natural; but friends may die, daughters may depart, she will be as perfectly kind and gracious to the next set. If the King wants her, she will smile upon him, be she ever so sad ; and walk with him, be she ever so weary ; and laugh at his brutal jokes, be she in ever so much pain of body or heart. With the film of death over her eyes, writhing in intolerable pain, she yet had a livid smile and a gentle word for her master." With all the instincts of imperious autocracy as strong within her heart as in that of the great Catherine of Russia, she had room for wedded love, deep, strong, and faithful, such as the Muscovite Empress never knew.

In spite of her mental powers and love of ruling, Caroline was far too womanly a woman not to take a thoroughly feminine delight in seeing her rival, Mrs. Howard, snubbed, as she occasionally was, by the King. It was this lady's place, until she became Countess of Suffolk in 1731, to dress the Queen's head—a duty which Caroline, who was pleased to subject her to such servile acts, always demanded ; and "it happened more than once," says Walpole, " that the King, coming into the room while the Queen was dressing, has snatched

off the handkerchief, and turning rudely to Mrs.
Howard, has cried, 'Because you have an ugly
neck yourself, you hide the Queen's.'" Caroline
herself was always ready to set down her rival.
The etiquette of the time required that a bedchamber woman should present a basin for her
majesty to wash her hands in, and remain kneeling
until the operation was completed. This service
the Queen exacted from Mrs. Howard, who, said
Caroline, in describing the scene to Lord Hervey,
" proceeded to tell me, with her little fierce eyes,
and cheeks as red as your coat, that, positively,
she would not do it; to which I made her no
answer then in anger, but calmly, as I would have
said to a naughty child:—' Yes, *my dear Howard
I am sure you will. I know you will. Go, go; fie
for shame! Go, my good Howard; we will talk of
this another time.*' Mrs. Howard did come round;
and I told her I knew we should be good friends
again; but could not help adding, in a little more
serious voice, that I owned, of all my servants,
that I had least expected, as I had least deserved
it, such treatment from her; when she knew I
had held her up at a time when it was in my
power, if I had pleased, to let her drop through
my fingers, thus—"

Mr. Howard made more than one attempt to
remove his wife from a Court where her fair fame
was already more than doubtful; and on one occasion had an interview with the Queen, in which
he threatened to take his wife out of her Majesty's
coach if he met her in it. Caroline told him
haughtily to " do it, if he dare;" but the
haughtiness was but a veil to hide her fright,
as she confessed afterwards in her description of
the scene to Lord Hervey:—" I was horribly
afraid of him (for we were *téte-à-téte*) all the time

I was thus playing the bully. What added to my fear on this occasion was, that as I knew him to be *so brutal,* as well as a little mad, and seldom quite sober, so that I did not think it impossible but that he might throw me out of window (for it was in this very room our interview was, and that sash then open, as it is now) ; but as soon as I got near the door, and thought myself safe from being thrown out of the window, I resumed my grand tone of Queen, and said I would be glad to see who would dare to open my coach-door and take out one of my servants ; knowing all the time that he might do so if he would, and that he could have his wife and I the affront. Then I told him that my resolution was positively neither to force his wife to go to him if she had no mind to it, nor to keep her if she had. He then said he would complain to the King ; upon which I again assumed my high tone, and said the King had nothing to do with my servants ; and, for that reason, he might save himself the trouble, as I was sure the King would give him no answer but that it was none of his business to concern himself with my family ; and after a good deal more conversation of this sort (I standing close to the door all the while to give me courage), Mr. Howard and I bade one another *good morning,* and he withdrew."

In May, 1729, George II. left England on a visit to his beloved Electorate ; Caroline was invested with the office of Regent, " and she performed its duties with a grace and an efficiency which caused universal congratulation that the post had not been confided to other, and necessarily weaker hands." * On the King's return the Court amused itself with readings at Windsor Castle.

* Dr. Doran.

These "readings" were the verses of Stephen Duck, the thresher, a Wiltshire labourer, who tried to support his family on wages of four and sixpence a week. Two of his pieces, "The Shunamite" and "The Thresher's Labour," were publicly read in the royal drawing-room by Lord Macclesfield, and the Queen purchased for him the office of yeoman of the guard, and subsequently made him keeper of her grotto, Merlin's Cave, at Richmond. Later, through the same royal patronage, he was raised to the Church, and made Vicar of Kew, but found his new honours so embarrassing that he solved the problem by drowning himself. In the same year as the "readings," 1730, one dark November evening, "the King and Queen, coming from Kew Green to St. James's, were over-turned in their coach, near Lord Peterborough's, at Parson's Green, about six in the evening, the wind having blown out the flambeaux, so that the coachman could not see his way. But their Majesties received no hurt, nor the two ladies who were in the coach with them."

The ordinary life of the Court was not par-ticularly entertaining. "I will not trouble you," says Lord Hervey, writing to Mrs. Clayton, " with any account of our occupations at Hampton Court. No mill-horse ever went in a more constant track, or a more unchanging circle ; so that, by the assistance of an almanac for the day of the week, and a watch for the hour of the day, you may inform yourself fully, without any other intelligence but your memory, of every transaction within the verge of the Court. Walking, chaises, levees, and audiences fill the morning ; at night the King plays at commerce and backgammon, and the Queen at quadrille, when poor Lady Charlotte runs her usual nightly gauntlet— the

Queen pulling her hood, Mr. Schutz sputtering in her face, and the Princess Royal rapping her knuckles, all at a time. It was in vain she fled from persecution for her religion; she suffers for her pride what she escaped for her faith; undergoes in a drawing-room what she dreaded from the inquisition, and will die a martyr to a Court, though not to a Church.

"The Duke of Grafton takes his nightly opiate of lottery, and sleeps as usual between the Princesses Amelia and Caroline. Lord Grantham strolls from one room to another (as Dryden says) '*like some discontented ghost that oft appears, and is forbid to speak;*' and stirs himself about, as people stir a fire, not with any design, but in hopes to make it burn brisker, which his lordship certainly does to no purpose, and yet tries as constantly as if it had ever once succeeded. At last the King comes up, the pool finishes, and everybody has their dismission; their Majesties retire to Lady Charlotte and my Lord Lifford; the Princesses to Bilderbee and Long; my Lord Grantham to Lady Frances and Mr Clark; some to supper, and some to bed; and thus (to speak in the Scripture phrase) the evening and the morning make the day."

The " Lady Charlotte," whose enviable situation Lord Hervey has so graphically depicted, and " my Lord Lifford " were brother and sister. He was by birth Comte de Roncy, and they were French Protestants, who for conscience sake had left their fatherland and taken shelter in England. They had lived there during four reigns, and the Comte had been created Earl of Lifford, while the sister was governess to Caroline's children. They were, as Dr. Doran says, " hard-worked, ill-paid Court drudges; too ill-paid, even, to appear decently clad "—a fact not redounding to the Queen's credit, and difficult to understand, as she by no means lacked liberality, and about this very time sent a donation of £1,000 to the Provost of Queen's College, Oxford, for its rebuilding and adornment. "Every night in the country, and thrice a week when the King and Queen were in town, this couple passed an hour or two with the King and Queen before they retired to bed." * They must have had a pleasant time of it, according to Lord Hervey, who narrates how "the King walked about, and talked to the brother of armies, or to the sister of genealogies, while the Queen knotted and yawned, till from yawning she came to nodding, and from nodding to snoring."

The Duke of Grafton mentioned by Lord Hervey —described by Swift as " a very pretty gentleman, has been much abroad in the world, jealous for the constitution of his country; a tall, black man, about twenty-five years of age; almost a slobberer, and without one good quality "—was violently in love with the Princess Amelia, who by no means disapproved of his attentions. " They are said to have hunted together two or three times a week; and on one occasion, having stayed out unusually late and lost their attendants, had gone together to a private house in Windsor Forest, which so exasperated the Queen that, but for Sir Robert Walpole, she would have complained to his Majesty." †

Meanwhile Anne, Princess Royal, the goddaughter of the late Queen of England, had in 1733 attained her twenty-third year, and had not yet found an eligible suitor, very much to her own dissatisfaction. She was blessed with but a moderate amount of beauty, according to Lord

* Dr. Doran.　　　　　　† Mrs. Matthew Hall.

Hervey, who said that her personal attractions consisted in "a lively, clean look and a very fair complexion, though she was marked a good deal with the small-pox ; the fault of her person was that of being very ill-made, and a great propensity to fat." Nor was her disposition remarkable for amiability. She was haughty and imperious, and altogether thoughtless of the feelings of others so long as her own whims were gratified. When but a child, she used to make one of her ladies-in-waiting stand by her bedside and read aloud until she felt disposed to sleep. This duty was so prolonged one evening that the unlucky lady fainted from fatigue. The next night the Queen called her daughter to her, and bade her read aloud. The Princess unwillingly complied, and would have taken a seat, but the Queen signified that she should stand. She read on, till, overcome with weariness, she paused, and would fain have retired. "Go on," said Queen Caroline, "it entertains me." In a few minutes more there was another silence. "Continue, continue," quoth the Queen, "I am not yet tired of listening." Fairly tired out, Anne burst into tears, and confessed her intense fatigue. "If you feel so faint from one evening of such employment," said her mother, "what must your attendants feel, upon whom you force the same discipline night after night? Be less selfish, my child, in future, and do not indulge in luxuries purchased at the cost of weariness and ill-health to others."

The ambition of the Princess Royal was sorely mortified by the existence of her brothers, who stood between her and the crown. "I would die to-morrow to be Queen to-day ! " she said once to her mother ; and she was femininely unreasonable enough to bear the Prince of Wales a lasting

grudge for having ever been born—a circumstance
which could hardly be considered under his own
control. She had once nearly attained the dignity
she so coveted; for the Duc de Bourbon proposed
her as a bride to the young Louis XV., and a
contract was entered into between the two
reigning families ; but when it was remembered
that a conversion to Catholicism was an indis-
pensable adjunct of the nuptials, the negociations
were brought abruptly to an end. This had
occurred seven years ago, when Anne was but
sixteen, and no eligible suitor had since made his
appearance, until William Charles Henry, Prince
of Orange, solicited her hand.

The most fervent of his panegyrists could not
accuse the royal suitor of over much beauty.
" He resembled Alexander the Great," says Dr.
Doran drily, " only in having a wry neck and a
halt in his gait;" but Lord Hervey is much
more diffuse concerning him. According to this
chronicler, the suitor of the Princess Royal was a
dwarf, "as much deformed as it was possible for
a human creature to be," poor, "his estate not
clear £12,000 a year," and the coming marriage
was "a miserable match, both in point of man
and fortune." It was altogether not a cheering
prospect for the lady; but, as Lord Hervey remarks, she had to choose, not "between this
Prince and any other, but between a husband
and no husband, between an indifferent settlement and no settlement at all; and whether she
would be wedded to this piece of deformity in
Holland, or die an ancient maid immured in her
royal convent of St. James's." The Princess
deliberated the position carefully; and then, "as
she apprehended the consequences of not being
married at all must one time or other be more

than even the being so married, she very prudently submitted to the present evil to avoid a greater in posterity" *—an admirably matter of fact way of looking at it. The King and Queen were not anxious to recognize this Dutch Adonis as their son-in-law; but they left their daughter perfectly free to follow her own inclination. The Queen, however, aware that Anne knew nothing more of her future husband than could be gathered from the flattering portrait sent to her, recommended her not to be too hasty in accepting her unseen suitor. The Princess received this caution with little gratitude, and declared that her mind was made up. Her father, vexed with her obstinacy, told her, in his usual fashion of going straight to the point, that the Prince "was the ugliest man in Holland." "I do not care," returned Anne, "how ugly he may be. If he were a Dutch baboon I would marry him!" "Nay, then, have your way," said the King, speaking in the strong Westphalian accent that was always more perceptible when he was annoyed; "have your way. You will find him *baboon* enough, I promise you!"

The Princess being resolute, the marriage was finally determined upon; and a message was sent to Parliament, acquainting them "that the object of the King was to strengthen the Protestant succession by this alliance with a family and name always dear to this nation."† A dowry of £80,000 was voted; and on the 7th November, 1733, the bridegroom elect arrived at Greenwich, and proceeded to Somerset House. He did not meet with any very flattering reception. The King maintained that "the Prince of Orange was a nothing

* Lord Hervey.
† "Royal Princesses of England," by Mrs. Matthew Hall.

till he had married his daughter, and that being her husband made him everything,"* and allowed no public honours to be paid him; the Tower guns were not fired; and the public guard was not turned out.

The Queen sent Lord Hervey to call upon her future son-in-law with her compliments; and on his return begged to be told "without disguise what sort of hideous animal she was to prepare herself to see." Her informant could give her a grain of comfort. He assured her that, though no Adonis, the Prince was not so bad as he had expected; for though his shape was as unfortunate as it could be, his countenance was "far from disagreeable, and his address sensible, engaging, and noble." The peer continued by expressing a fear that the Princess must be in much anxiety; but " the Queen told him that in that he was mistaken; she was in her own apartment at her harpsichord with some of the opera people, and that she had been as easy all that afternoon as she had ever seen her all her life."† "For my part," added the Queen, "I never said the least word to encourage her to this marriage, or to dissuade her from it; the King left her, too, absolutely at liberty to accept or reject it; but as she thought the King looked upon it as a proper match, and one which, if she would bear his person, he should not dislike, she said she was resolved if it was a monkey she would marry him."

The marriage was to have taken place at once; but, directly after his arrival, the bridegroom-elect was attacked with a dangerous fever, and the ceremony was perforce postponed. "During this tedious and dangerous illness," says Lord Hervey,

* Lord Hervey.
† "Royal Princesses of England," by Mrs. Matthew Hall.

" no one of the royal family went to see him. The King thought it below his dignity, and the rest, whatever they thought, were not allowed to do it." The Princess Royal exhibited a phlegmatic calm worthy of her future country. " She appeared precisely the same under all contingencies ; and whether the lover were in or out of England, in life or out of it, seemed to this strong-minded lady to be one and the same thing."*

The recovery of the Prince was long and tedious. Not until January was he able to travel by easy stages to Bath, to drink the waters, and he remained there more than a month before his health was sufficiently re-established to proceed to Oxford, where he was solemnly complimented by the University. Early in March he returned to London, and the long deferred preparations for the wedding were resumed, to the relief of the irascible Duchess of Marlborough, who had been infinitely annoyed by a boarded gallery, along which the procession was to pass, which had been erected directly in front of her windows, excluding the light, in preparation for the ceremony, and which had remained during the four months of the postponement of the marriage. " I wish," Duchess Sarah had repeatedly remarked, as she surveyed the obstruction, " the Princess would oblige me by taking away her *orange chest!* "

In spite of the unflatteringly cool demeanour of his lady-love, the bridegroom made her some magnificent presents. " I must tell you," writes Mrs. Delany to her sister on the 2nd March, 1734, " the presents the Prince of Orange has prepared for his Princess—a necklace of rose diamonds ; the five middle diamonds are half the necklace, two of which are worth four thousand pound, her ear-

* Dr. Doran.

rings of proportionate value; a green diamond to
hang as a bob to her necklace of a vast size, and
five loops for her stays, the finest that he could
get in England. He presented her before his
sickness with pearls much finer than any of the
Queen's."

There was now no longer any cause for delay;
and accordingly the ill-favoured groom and the
admirably self-contained bride were united " in
the French chapel," St. James's, by the Bishop of
London, on the evening of the 24th March. The
ceremony was gorgeous and imposing, though the
tranquillity of the proceedings was marred by a
squabble between Lord Hervey and the Irish peers
concerning their precedence, which ended in the
former "leaving out altogether their names from
his list, and saying, that if they were not satisfied,
they might walk through the procession in any
order they pleased on the day after the wedding ! "*
The chapel was brilliantly lighted " with thirty-
six branches, each holding twelve large wax
candles, and one hundred and twenty-six sconces,
each holding three smaller wax candles."† A
throne was placed for the King and Queen, chairs
of state for the bride and bridegroom, " the aisles
on each side of the altar, and the two side galleries,
were hung with crimson velvet, trimmed with
broad gold lace and fringe,"‡ and " the area, or
haut-pas, near the altar, was covered with fine
purple cloth, on which their Majesties stood
during the ceremony."§ The Prince of Orange,
who must, as Dr. Doran remarks, have looked
very much like Riquet à la Houppe, and his whole
suite, were " as magnificent as gold and silver
varied in brocade, lace, and embroidery could make

* "Royal Princesses of England."   † *Ibid.*
‡ *Ibid.*   § *Ibid.*

them, and the jewels he gave the Princess of immense value, particularly the necklace, which was so large that twenty-two diamonds made the whole round of her neck."* The bride, wearing her coronet, was "in virgin robes of silver tissue, having a train six yards long, which was supported by ten dukes' and earls' daughters, all of whom were attired in robes of silver tissue."† During the ceremony, the Queen and her younger daughters manifested "undisguised and unaffected concern;"‡ but we are told the King "behaved very well," which probably means that he displayed more imperturbability than his consort. After the conclusion of the rite, the newly-married pair seated themselves on their chairs of state to hear the anthem, the music of which had been composed for the occasion by Handel, and then the whole of the brilliant assembly returned in procession to the palace. "As soon as they arrived at the door of the lesser drawing-room, the company stopped; but their Majesties, the Prince of Wales, the Duke, the bride and bridegroom, and the Princess went in, when the Prince of Orange and Princess Royal knelt, and asked their Majesties' blessing."§

The whole of the royal family supped in public at midnight; and then followed an extraordinary ceremony that in the nineteenth century is considered more honoured in the breach than in the observance. "It was the custom when royalty was united in the bonds of matrimony for the whole Court to enter the nuptial chamber and pay their respects to the young couple when in bed."‖ The Queen had always sincerely pitied her

---

* Lord Hervey.   † Ibid.
‡ Ibid.   § "Royal Princesses of England."
    ‖ "John, Lord Hervey." Vide "Temple Bar."

daughter's fate in being united to so ill-favoured
a consort; but her equanimity was completely
overthrown when her new son-in-law appeared in
the room. "In his silver tissue night-dress, his
ugliness, and his deformity, he struck her as the
impersonation of a monster."* Indeed, Lord
Hervey declares "the appearance he made was
indescribable; from the shape of his brocaded
gown and the make of his back, he looked behind
as if he had no head, and before as if he had no
neck and legs." Caroline actually cried with
disgust and vexation, and could not restrain her
feelings when speaking of the spectacle. "Ah,
mon Dieu!" she said subsequently to Lord
Hervey, using the French that was her ordinary
tongue; "quand je voyais entrer ce monstre pour
coucher avec ma fille, j'ai pensé m' évanouir; je
chancelais auparavant, mais ce coup-la m'
assommée. Dites-moi, my lord Hervey, avez-
vous bien remarqué et consideré ce monstre dans
ce moment? et n'aviez-vous pas bien pitié de la
pauvre Anne? Bon Dieu! c'est trop sotte en moi,
mais j'en pleure encore." "Madam," said Lord
Hervey, by way of consolation, "in half a year
all persons are alike, the figure of the body one's
married to, like the prospect of the place one lives
at, grows so familiar to one's eyes, that one looks
at it mechanically without regarding either the
beauties or deformities that strike a stranger."
"One may," said the not very much comforted
Queen, "and I believe one does, grow blind at
last; but you must allow, my dear Lord Hervey,
there is a great difference, as long as one sees, in
the manner of one's growing blind."

A drawing-room was held the day after the
wedding, at which Mrs. Delany was present, and

* Dr. Doran.

of which she thus writes the following day to her sister :—

"The Princess of Orange's wedding-dress was the prettiest thing that ever was seen—a corps de robe, that is, in *plain English*, a stiff-bodied gown. The eight peers' daughters that held up her train were in the same sort of dress—all white and silver, with great quantities of jewels in their hair, and long locks: some of them were very pretty and well-shaped—it is a most becoming dress. They all wore it yesterday, except the Princess, and she was in a manteau and petticoat, white damask, with the finest embroidery of rich embossed gold and festoons of flowers intermixed in their natural colours. On one side of her head she had a green diamond of a vast size, the shape of a pear, and two pearls prodigiously large, that were fastened to wires and hung loose upon her hair; on the other side small diamonds prettily disposed; her earrings, necklace, and bars to her stays, all extravagantly fine, presents of the Prince of Orange to her. The Prince of Orange was in gold stuff embroidered with silver; it looked rich but not showy. The King was in a gold stuff, which made much more show, with diamond buttons in his coat, his star and George shone most gloriously. The Queen's clothes were a green ground flowered with gold and several shades, but grave and very handsome; her head was loaded with pearls and diamonds. The Prince of Wales was fine, as you may suppose, but I hardly ever remember men's clothes. Princess Amelia had white embroidered with gold and scarlet; Princess Caroline, white embroidered with silver, green, and purple. The Prince of Wales dances better than anybody, and the Prince of Orange most surprisingly well considering his shape."

For a week after the marriage the Prince of
Orange was taken by his brother-in-law, the Prince
of Wales, to see all the sights of London. A
bill was passed for his naturalization, followed in
no long time by the settlement of £5,000 a-year
on his wife ; and the Princesses, his sisters-in-law,
found leisure to discuss their elder's chances
of happiness with her singular-looking spouse.
Princess Amelia vowed no power on earth would
have made her wed such a man ; while Princess
Caroline thought the bride had acted prudently
and wisely under the circumstances, and that, had
she been placed in a similar position, she would
have done the same. Indeed, the conduct of the
young wife gave no grounds on which to base
commiseration for her. She seemed to have
suddenly awakened from her frigid impassibility
into a vehement admiration of her husband. " She
made prodigious court to him," says Lord Hervey,
" addressed everything she said to him, and ap-
plauded everything he said to anybody else."

In April, 1734, the Prince and Princess of
Orange set sail for Holland. The Queen cried the
whole of the first three days after parting with
her daughter ; but three weeks had not passed,
Lord Hervey tells us, before—excepting on post-
days—Anne seemed as much forgotten as if she
had been dead for years. " So quick a smoother is
absence," writes the peer, in his moralizing strain,
" of the deepest impressions royal minds are capable of receiving. Impressions that are only
to be preserved by an effort of memory and reflection are indeed, in all human compositions, like
characters written in sand, that if they are not
perpetually retained by our senses they are seldom
of any great duration, and are easily effaced though
ever so strongly marked."

Many congratulatory addresses to their Majesties followed the marriage; among them one from the House of Lords to the Queen, which was rendered disagreeable rather than pleasant to her from the fact that it was presented by Lord Chesterfield.

"Caroline had never seen this peer since the time he was dismissed from her husband's household, when she was Princess of Wales. He had not been presented at Court since the accession of the present sovereign, and the Queen was therefore resolved to treat as an utter stranger the man who had been impertinent enough to declare he designed that the step he took should be considered as a compliment to the Queen. The latter abhorred him nevertheless, for his present attempt to turn the compliment addressed to her by the Lords into a joke."* She declared he should see how little his insolence affected her, and that he should find "it was as little in his power for his presence to embarrass her as for his raillery behind her back to pique her, or his consummate skill in politics to distress the King or his ministers."† She received the deputation—Lords Chesterfield, Scarborough, and Hardwicke—in her chamber, only her children and Lord Hervey being present. "Lord Chesterfield's speech was well written and well got by heart, and yet delivered with a faltering voice, a face as white as a sheet, and every limb trembling with concern. The Queen's answer was quiet and natural, and delivered with the same ease that she would have spoken to the most indifferent person in her circle."‡

* Dr. Doran.   † Lord Hervey.   ‡ *Ibid.*

CHAPTER III.

The Excise Bill—Caroline's great influence—Her support of
Walpole—Resignation of Lady Suffolk—Arrival of the
Princess of Orange—Her conversation with Lord Hervey—
Her wish to remain in England—Her reluctant farewell—
King's treatment of the Prince of Wales—Return of the
Princess of Orange—Her final departure—Queen's liking for
Lord Hervey—Her conversations with him—Her power over
the King—Her ill-health—Her endurance—The importance
of her life—Her opinion of a second marriage—Departure of
the King for Hanover—Caroline appointed Regent—King's
extraordinary letters—Lord Hervey's imaginary diary—His
drama of Court life—The King's return—His ill-humour—
Lord Hervey's account of an evening with the King and
Queen—Conversation of the Queen and Sir Robert Walpole
—Her remark on the Triple Alliance.

A PROOF of the exceeding esteem and deference
accorded to Queen Caroline—which, indeed, could
hardly have been greater had she been Queen-
Regent of England—is afforded by the fact that
when Sir Robert Walpole's excise scheme was in
debate, a party of the lords delegated Lord Stair
to present himself to the Queen at Kensington,
and remonstrate with her on what they called
" this unconstitutional and destructive measure."

Lord Stair was confident enough, but utterly
devoid of tact; and he performed his mission so
awkwardly, abusing Caroline's favourite, Walpole,
and entering into matters connected purely with
the domestic life of royalty, that the Queen's
patience, long-suffering as it was, became at
length exhausted, and she interrupted his tirade.
She was " superb in her rebuke—superb in its
matter and manner—superb in her dignity and in
the severity with which she crushed Lord Stair
beneath her fiery sarcasms and her withering

contempt. She ridiculed his assertions, and told him he had become traitor to his own country and the betrayer of his own constituents. She mocked his complacent assurances that his object was not personal, but patriotic. She professed her intense abhorrence of having the private dissensions of noblemen ripped open in her presence, and bade him learn better manners than to speak, as he had done, of 'the King's servants to the King's wife.'" *

"My conscience," pleaded Lord Stair, in answer to her reproof; but Caroline cut him short—" Ne me parlez point de conscience, milord; vous me faites évanouir," and the baffled peer left the presence after entreating her to keep what had passed a secret—an entreaty that the Queen respected until she found Lord Stair himself had divulged all, when, as she said, she took " la première occasion d'égosiller tout."

This Excise Bill caused no small commotion in its day, and on the first evening of its debate the discussion lasted till one in the morning ; and when Lord Hervey hastened to the palace at its conclusion, to carry news to their Majesties, the King kept him talking in the Queen's bedchamber until three, entirely oblivious of the fatigue and hunger of his informant.

" When," says Dr. Doran, " the clamour against the Bill rose to such a pitch that all England, the army included, seemed ready to rise against it, Walpole offered himself as a personal sacrifice, if the service and interests of the King would be promoted by his surrender of office and power. It is again illustrative of the influence of Caroline that this offer was made to her and not to the King. He was in truth the Queen's minister,

* Dr Doran.

and nobly she stood by him. When Walpole made the offer in question, Caroline declared that she could not be so mean, so cowardly, or so ungrateful as to abandon him ; and she infused the same spirit into the King. The latter had intended, from the first, to reign and govern, and be effectively his own minister ; but Caroline so wrought upon him that he thought he had of himself reached the conviction that it was necessary for him to trust in a minister, and that Walpole was the fittest man for such an office. And so he grew to love the very man whom he had been wont to hold in his heart's extremest hate. He would even occasionally speak of him as a 'noble fellow,' and, with tears in his eyes, would listen to an account of some courageous stand Walpole had made in the House against the enemies of the Government, and he would add the while a running commentary of sobs."

The Queen's resolution to stand by her minister was thoroughly disinterested and generous ; for her power by no means depended on the success or fall of the Premier. As Lord Hervey remarks, "had he retired, Caroline would have placed before the King the names of a new ministry, and the Administration would not have hung together a moment after it had outlived her liking." She exerted herself to the utmost in favour of the Bill ; but the public opposition was so strong that, in spite of courtly favour, Walpole withdrew his measure—not before both he and his royal mistress had incurred the obloquy of the mob, who hung in effigy the minister and a nameless female figure, well understood by all to represent the Queen.

Shortly after, the resignation of Mrs. Howard, now the Countess of Suffolk, was announced ; the

King seeming rather relieved than otherwise that
"that old deaf woman," as he unflatteringly
styled his quondam enchantress, was preparing to
quit his Court. She was succeeded as Mistress
of the Robes by the Countess of Tankerville;
and the change had scarcely been effected when,
in the middle of July, the Princess of Orange re-
appeared in England, barely three months after
she had quitted it. Her husband had gone to
join the camp of Prince Eugene, and Anne, who
disliked Holland cordially, was only too glad of
an excuse for returning home. Her unlooked-for
appearance annoyed her father, and was not
productive of much satisfaction to her mother.
The Princess had not returned inclined to make
herself peculiarly agreeable; and she did not
hesitate to cause it to be generally known when
her father's behaviour annoyed her.

"Was there ever anything so unaccountable,"
she said one day, shrugging her shoulders, and
speaking to Lord Hervey, who was leading her to
her own apartment after the drawing-room, "as
the temper of papa? He has been snapping
and snubbing every mortal for this week, because
he began to think Philipsburg would be taken; and
this very day, that he actually hears it is taken, he
is in as good humour as I ever saw him in my life.
To tell you the truth," she added in French," "I
find *that* so whimsical, and (between ourselves) so
utterly foolish, that I am more enraged by his good,
than I was before by his bad, humour."

"Madam," replied Lord Hervey, "he may be
about Philipsburg as David was about the child,
who, whilst it was sick, fasted, lay upon the earth,
and covered himself with ashes; but the moment
it was dead, got up, shaved his beard, and drank
wine."

"It may be like David," retorted Anne, "but I am sure it is not like Solomon." The King had a quite erroneous idea that his eldest daughter loved him better than any of his other children. He did not know what an unutterable bore she found him. "I wish," she said sympathetically, on hearing of Lady Suffolk's withdrawal, "I wish with all my heart he would take somebody else, that mamma might be a little relieved from the occasion of seeing him for ever in her room." She was expecting ere long to become a mother, and was inwardly resolved that her child's birth should take place in England, so that the infant should be *English-born;* "for, as her brothers were unmarried, she thought she might yet stand in the line of inheritance to the throne." * Her husband, however, wished her to return home, and the Queen insisted on her obeying him. Anne found excuses for delay after delay, but at length very reluctantly set forth. "The last thing she thought of was the success of the opera, and the triumph of Handel. She recommended both to the charge of Lord Hervey, and then went on her way to Harwich, sobbing."† Her mother and her gentle sister, Caroline, left behind at Kensington Palace, were found by Lord Hervey after her departure, sitting together, drinking chocolate, and crying. He had just succeeded in partially consoling them when the gallery door opened, and the Queen rose from her seat, saying, "The King here already!" It was not his Majesty who entered, but the Prince of Wales. The Queen saw her mistake, and "detesting the exchange of the son for the daughter, she burst out anew into tears, and

* "Royal Princesses of England."   † Dr. Doran.

cried out, 'Oh, God! this is too much!'"* The
King himself entered directly afterwards, and,
passing by his son without speaking, took her
hand and led her out to walk with him. This
uncompromising cut was George's usual treatment
of his son. "Whenever the Prince was in a
room with him," says Lord Hervey, "it put one
in mind of stories that one has heard of ghosts
which appear to part of the company and were
invisible to the rest; and in this manner, wherever the Prince stood, though the King passed
him ever so often, or ever so near, it always
seemed as if the King thought the Prince filled a
void space."

The Queen and the Princess might have spared
their lamentations, for on the following day
(October 22nd) the Princess of Orange unexpectedly re-appeared. When she had proceeded
as far as Colchester, she had found letters from
her husband, stating that he was unable to be at
the Hague as soon as he expected; and she had
at once started on her return to Kensington.
"Tears and kisses," says Dr. Doran, "were her
welcome from her mother, and smiles and an
embrace formed the greeting from her father."
She remained in England till November, and then
once more unwillingly started on her tardy return
home. She put to sea, but suffered, or feigned to
suffer, so much, that she bade the captain land
her again, and declared she should not be fit for
the voyage for another ten days. This behaviour
caused wonderful confusion. "Her father, and
indeed the Queen also, insisted on her repairing
to Holland by way of Calais, as her husband had
thoughtfully suggested. She was compelled to
pass through London, much to the King's annoy-

* Lord Hervey.

ance ; but he declared that she should not stop, but proceed at once over London Bridge to Dover. He added, that she should never again come to England in the same condition of health. His threat was partly founded on the expense, her visit having cost him £20,000." * Forced to submit, the disappointed Princess unwillingly returned to her foreign home, and in due time became the mother of a son.

The Queen meantime was constantly occupied with her multitudinous duties; and, whenever she found any well-earned leisure, was pleased to devote it to conversation with her favourite, Lord Hervey. So constantly were this peer and his royal mistress together that Caroline used to say, laughingly, "It is well I am so old, or I should be talked of because of this creature." He used to ride by her while she drove, on a hunter she had given him, and discuss many things, of which politics were not the least important, with her. Shrewd as she was, it was hardly to be expected that a Princess brought up in one of the despotic little Courts of Germany, should thoroughly appreciate the advantages of the English Constitution. She gave her opinions on that point at great length to Lord Hervey. " I have heard her," says that nobleman, " at different times speak with great indignation against the assertors of the people's rights ; have heard her call the King, not without some despite, the humble servant of Parliament—the pensioner of his people—a puppet of sovereignty that was forced to go to them for every shilling he wanted, that was obliged to court them that were always abusing him, and could do nothing of himself. . . . At other times she was more on her guard.

* Dr. Doran.

I have heard her say she wondered how the English could imagine that any sensible Prince would take away their liberty if he could. 'Mon Dieu!' she cried, 'what a figure would this poor island make in Europe if it were not for its government. It is its excellent free government that makes all its inhabitants industrious, as they know that what they get nobody can take from them—it is its free government, too, that makes foreigners send their money thither, because they know it is secure, and that the Prince cannot touch it; and since it is its freedom to which this kingdom owes everything that makes it great, what Prince who had his senses, and knew that his own greatness depended on the greatness of the country over which he reigned, would wish to take away what made both him and them considerable.' 'I had as lief,' she added, 'be Elector of Hanover as King of England if the government was the same. Quel diable, that had anything else, would take you all, or think you worth having, if you had not your liberties? Your island might be a very pretty thing in that case for Bridgeman and Kent to cut out into gardens; but for the figure it would make in Europe it would be of no more consequence here in the West than Madagascar in the East; and for this reason, as impudent and as insolent as you all are with your troublesome liberty, your Princes, if they are sensible, will rather bear with your impertinences than cure them—a way that would lessen their influence in Europe full as much as it would increase their power at home.'"

"It was at a hunting party," says Dr. Doran, "that Lord Hervey endeavoured to convince the Queen that for England to go to war for the purpose of serving the empire would be a disastrous course to take. He could not convince her in a long conversation, and thereupon, the chase being over, he sat down and penned a political pamphlet, which he called a letter, which was 'as long as a President's message,' and which he forwarded to the Queen. If Caroline was not to be persuaded by it, she, at least, thought none the worse of the writer, who had spared no argument to support the cause in which he boldly pleaded."

There is a curious circumstance connected with these opinions of the Queen. "What is very surprising," says Lord Hervey, "yet what I know to be true, the arguments of Sir Robert Walpole [in favour of non-intervention in the disagreements of Continental governments] conveyed through the Queen to the King, so wrought upon him that they quite changed the colour of his Majesty's sentiments, though they did not tinge the channel through which they flowed "—a fact, testifying, as Mrs. Oliphant observes, "at once to the Queen's faithfulness to her political adviser, even when she did not agree with him, and the powerful nature of her agency." It is, says the same writer, "a singular instance surely of candid dealing, and that rarest of all forms of truthfulness, the perfectly honest transmission by one mind of the arguments of another."

The health of the Queen, though she had as yet scarcely passed middle age, was by no means strong, and it was not the custom of her house to take any care of their physical well-being. The King, who had an excellent constitution, disliked intensely being ill himself or seeing anyone else so. When he *was* indisposed, he would rise from his bed to hold a levee, even if he had to return to it immediately afterwards; and he always expected others to follow his example. The Queen submitted to the Spartan-like régime with the wonderful endurance of a brave woman. When she was suffering from gout, she had, as Horace Walpole tells us, "more than once dipped her whole leg in cold water to be able to attend the King." In this autumn of 1733 she "was labouring under cold, cough, and symptoms of fever, in addition to having been weakened by loss of blood, a process she had recently undergone twice;"* but the King insisted on dragging her from Kensington to London for his birthday, and, not content with that fatigue, took her to the opera to hear Farinelli. At the morning drawing-room on this birthday "she found herself so near swooning, that she was obliged to send her chamberlain to the King, begging him to retire, 'for she was unable to stand any longer.'"† Nevertheless, "at night he brought her into a still greater crowd at the ball, and there kept her till eleven o'clock."‡

"Sir Robert Walpole frequently, and never more urgently than at this time, impressed upon her the necessity of being careful of her own health. He addressed her as though she had been Queen Regent of England—as she certainly was governing sovereign—and he described to her in such pathetic terms the dangers which England would, and Europe might, incur, if any fatal accident deprived her of life, and the King were to fall under the influence of any other woman, that the poor Queen, complaining and coughing, with head heavy, and aching eyes half closed with pain, cheeks flushed, pulse quick, spirits low, and breathing oppressed, burst into tears, alarmed at

* Dr. Doran. † *Ibid.* ‡ Lord Hervey.

the picture, and with every disposition to do her
utmost for the benefit of her health, and the well-
being of the body politic.

" It was the opinion of Caroline, that in case
of her demise the King would undoubtedly marry
again, and she had often advised him to take such
a step. She affected, however, to believe that a
second wife would not be able to influence him to
act contrary to the system which he had adopted
through the influence of herself and Walpole." *

In 1735 the King set forth on a visit to Hanover, where he always felt more at his ease than in
England, and Caroline ruled as Regent.   George
wrote to her perpetually ; and his letters, always
in French, " were filled," says Lord Hervey,
" with an hourly account of everything he saw,
heard, thought, or did, and crammed with minute
trifling circumstances, not only unworthy of a
man to write, but even of a woman to read ; most
of which I saw, and almost all of them I heard
reported by Sir Robert Walpole, to whose perusal
few were not committed, and many passages were
transmitted to him by the King's own order ; who
used to tag several paragraphs with ' Montrez ceci
et consultez le gros homme.'   Among many
extraordinary things and expressions these letters
contained was one in which he desired the Queen
to contrive, if she could, that the Prince of
Modena, who was to come at the latter end of the
year to England, might bring his wife with him."
He wished much to have the pleasure of paying
his addresses to this lady ; " un plâisir," he wrote
to his wife, " que je suis sûr, ma cherè Caroline,
vous serez bien aise de me procurer, quand je
vous dis combien je la souhaite ! "

During this summer, Lord Hervey was absent

* Dr. Doran.

230 LIVES OF THE PRINCESSES OF WALES.

from Court for a time; "but we may perhaps," says Dr. Doran, "learn from one of his letters, addressed to the Queen while he was resting in the country from his light labours, the nature of his office and the way in which Caroline was served. The narrative is given by the writer as part of an imaginary post-obit diary, in which he describes himself as having died on the day he left her, and as having been repeatedly buried in the various dull country houses by whose proprietors he was hospitably received." He thus continues:—

"But whilst my body, Madam, was thus disposed of, my spirit (as when alive), was still hovering, though invisible, round your Majesty, anxious for your welfare, and watching to do you any little service that lay within my power.

"On Monday, whilst you walked, my *shade* still turned on the side of the sun to guard you from its beams.

"On Tuesday morning, at breakfast, I brushed away a fly that had escaped Teed's observation, and was just going to be the taster of your chocolate.

"On Wednesday, in the afternoon, I took off the chilliness of some strawberry-water your Majesty was going to drink as you came in hot from walking; and at night I hunted a bat out of your bedchamber, and shut a sash just as you fell asleep, which your Majesty had a little indiscreetly ordered Mrs. Purcel to leave open.

"On Thursday, in the drawing-room, I took the forms and voices of several of my acquaintances, made strange faces, put myself into awkward postures, and talked a good deal of nonsense, whilst your Majesty entertained me very gravely, *recommended* me very graciously, and laughed at me internally very heartily.

"On Friday, being post-day, I proposed to get

the best pen in the other world for your Majesty's use, and slip it invisibly into your standish just as Mr. Shaw was bringing it into your gallery for you to write; and accordingly I went to Voiture, and desired him to hand me his pen; but when I told him for whom it was designed, he only laughed at me for a blockhead, and asked me if I had been at Court for four years to so little purpose as not to know that your Majesty had a much better of your own.

"On Saturday I went on the shaft of your Majesty's chaise to Richmond; as you walked there I went before you, and with an invisible wand I brushed the dew and the worms out of your path all the way, and several times uncrumpled your Majesty's stocking.

"Sunday.—This very day, at chapel, I did your Majesty some service, by tearing six leaves out of the parson's sermon and shortening his discourse six minutes."

It was probably during this same absence that Lord Hervey wrote the sketch of the manner in which the news of his death would be received at Court, which, somewhat abridged, is here subjoined:—

"THE DEATH OF LORD HERVEY; OR, A MORNING AT COURT."

A Drama.

ACT I.

Scene :—The Queen's Gallery. *Time,* Nine in the Morning.

Enter THE QUEEN, PRINCESS EMILY, PRINCESS CAROLINE, followed by LORD LIFFORD (a Frenchman), and MRS. PURCEL.

QUEEN.—Mon Dieu, quelle chaleur! en verité on étouffe. Pray, open a little these windows.

LORD LIFFORD.—Has-a your Majesty hear-a de news?

QUEEN.—What news, my dear lord?

LORD L.—Dat my Lord Hervey, as he was coming last night to *tone*, was rob and murdered by highwaymen, and tron in a ditch.

P. CAROLINE.—Eh, grand Dieu!

QUEEN (striking her hand upon her knee).— Comment, est il veritablement mort? Purcel, my angel, shall I not have a little breakfast?

MRS. PURCEL.—What would your Majesty please to have?

QUEEN.—A little chocolate, my soul, if you give me leave; and a little sour cream and some fruit.
                                [*Exit* MRS. PURCEL.

QUEEN (to Lord Lifford).—Eh, bien! my Lord Lifford, dites nous un peu comment cela est arrivé. I cannot imagine what he had to do to be putting his nose there.

LORD L.—Madame, on sçavait quelque chose de cela de Mon Maran qui d'abord qu 'il a vu de voleurs s'est enfui et venu à grand galoppe à Londrès, and after dat a waggoner take up de body and put it in his cart.

QUEEN (to Princess Emily).—Are you not ashamed, Amalie, to laugh?

P. EMILY.—I only laughed at the cart, mamma.

QUEEN.—Ah, that is a very fade plaisanterie.

P. EMILY.—But if I may say it, mamma, I am not very sorry.

QUEEN.—Fi donc! Eh bien, my Lord Lifford! My God, where is this chocolate, Purcel?

(*Re-enter* Mrs. Purcel, with the chocolate and fruit.)

QUEEN (to Mrs. Purcel).—Well, I am sure

Purcel now is very sorry for my Lord Hervey : have you heard it?

Mrs. P.—Yes, Madam ; and I am always sorry when your Majesty loses anything that entertains you.

Queen.—Look you there, now, Amalie ; I swear now Purcel is a thousand times better as you.

P. Emily.—I did not say I was not sorry for mamma ; but I am not sorry for him.

Queen.—And why not?

P. Emily.—What, for that creature !

P. Caroline.—I cannot imagine why one should not be sorry for him : I think it very dure not to be sorry for him. I own he used to laugh malapropos sometimes, but he was mightily mended ; and for people that were civil to him, he was always ready to do anything to oblige them ; and for my part I am sorry, I assure.

P. Emily.—Mamma, Caroline is duchtich : for my part, I cannot paroître.

Queen.—Ah, ah ! You can paroître and be duchtich very well sometimes ; but this is no paroître ; and I think you are very great brutes. I swear now he was very good, poor my Lord Hervey ; and with peoples' lives that is no jest. My dear Purcel, this is the nastiest fruit I have ever tasted ; is there none of the Duke of Newcastle's ? or that old fool Johnstone's ? Il était bien joli quelquefois, my Lord Hervey, was he not, Lifford?

Lord L. (taking snuff).—Yes, ended he was very pretty company sometimes.

(P. Emily shrugs her shoulders and laughs again.)

Queen (to Princess Emily).—If you did not think him company, I am sorry for your taste. (To Princess Caroline).—My God, Caroline, you will twist off the thumbs of your gloves. Mais, my Lord Lifford, qui vous a conté tout ça des voleurs, du ditch, et des waggoners?

LORD L.—I have hear it at St. James's, et tout le monde en parle.

QUEEN (to Mrs. Purcel).—Have you sent, Purcel, to Vickers about my clothes?

MRS. P.—He is here, if your Majesty pleases to see the stuffs.

QUEEN.—No, my angel. I must write now. Adieu, adieu, my Lord Lifford.

ACT II.

Scene.—The Queen's dressing-room. The QUEEN is discovered at her toilet, cleaning her teeth; Mrs. PURCEL dressing her Majesty's head. The PRINCESSES, Lady BURLINGTON and Lady PEMBROKE, Ladies of the Bed-chamber, and Lady SUNDON, Women of the Bedchamber, standing round. Morning prayers saying in the next room.

1ST PARSON (behind the scenes).—From pride, vain-glory, and hypocrisy, from envy, hatred, and malice, and all uncharitableness—

2ND PARSON.—Good Lord deliver us!

QUEEN.—I pray, my good Lady Sundon, shut a little that door; those creatures pray so loud one cannot hear oneself speak. (Lady Sundon goes to shut the door.) So, so, not quite so much; leave it enough open for those parsons to think we may hear, and enough shut that we may not hear quite so much. (To Lady Burlington.) What do you say, Lady Burlington, to poor Lord Hervey's death? I am sure you are very sorry.

LADY P. (sighing and lifting up her eyes).—I swear it is a terrible thing.

LADY B.—I am just as sorry as I believe he would have been for me.

QUEEN.—I am sure you have not forgiven him his jokes upon Chiswick.

* * * * *

[*Enter* LORD GRANTHAM.

* * * * *

QUEEN . . . . . But what news do you bring us, my Lord Grantham?

LORD G.—Your Majesty has hear de news of poor my Lord Hervey?

QUEEN.—Ah, mon cher, my Lord, c'est une veillesse; il y a cent ans qu'on le sçait.

LORD G.—I have just been talking of him to Sir Robert. Sir Robert is prodigiously concerned; he has seen Monsieur—how you call?—Marant.

QUEEN.—Maran vous voudrez dire. I pray, my good child, take away all these things, and let Sir Robert come in.

(Lord Grantham brings in Sir Robert Walpole, and all but Sir Robert and the Queen go out.)

QUEEN.—Come, come, my good Sir Robert, sit down. Well, how go matters?

SIR R.—Everything very well, Madam, pure and well. I have just had intelligence out of the city —all is very quiet there.

QUEEN.—But we must hang some of these villains.

SIR R.—We will if we can, Madam. . . . . But what news from Hanover, Madam?

QUEEN.—There is a letter of five-and-forty pages from the King; I have not time now, but there are some things in it that I must talk to you about.

SIR R.—I have had a long letter, too, from Horace.

QUEEN.—Oh! Mon Dieu! Not about his silly ladder-story again. My good Sir Robert, I am so tired and so sick of all that nonsense, that I cannot bear to talk or think of it any more. Apropos poor my Lord Hervey, I swear I could cry!

SIR R.—Your Majesty knows that I had a great partiality for him; and really, Madam, whatever faults he might have, there was a great deal of good stuff in him. I shall want him, and your Majesty will miss him.

QUEEN.—Oh! So I shall. . . . . . Adieu, my good Sir Robert; I believe it is late. I must go a moment into the drawing-room; do you know who is there?

SIR R.—I saw the Duke of Argyle, Madam.

QUEEN,—Oh, Mon Dieu! I am so weary of that Felt-Marshall and his tottering head, and his silly stories about the bishops, that I could cry whenever I am obliged to entertain him. And who is there more?

SIR R.—There is my Lord President, Madam.

QUEEN.—Oh, that's very well. I shall talk to him about his fruit, and some silly council at the Cockpit, and the Plantations; my Lord President loves the Plantations. . . . . But who is there beside? Adieu, adieu, my good Sir Robert; I must go, though you are to-day excellent conversation.

ACT III.

Scene changes to great drawing-room. All the courtiers ranged in a circle.

Enter the QUEEN, led by Lord GRANTHAM, followed by the PRINCESSES and all her train. Queen curtsies very slightly. Drawing-room bows and curtsies very low.

QUEEN (to the Duke of Argyle).—Where have been, my Lord? One has not had the pleasure to see you a great while, and one always misses you.

DUKE OF A.—I have been in Oxfordshire, Madam, and so long that I was asking my father, Lord Selkirk, how to behave. I know nobody that knows the ways of a Court so well, or that has known them so long.

LORD SELKIRK.—My God! my Lord, I know nobody knows them better than the Duke of Argyle.

DUKE OF A.—All I know, father, is as your pupil; but I told you I was grown a country gentleman.

QUEEN (laughing).—Ha! ha! ha! You are always so good together, and my Lord Selkirk is always so lively. (Turning to Lord President.) I think, my Lord, you are a little of a country gentleman, too—you love Chiswick mightily; you have very good fruit there, and are very curious in it; you have very good plums.

LORD PRESIDENT.—I like a plum, Madam, mightily; it is a very pretty fruit.

QUEEN.—The greengage, I think, is very good.

LORD PRESIDENT.—There are three of that sort, Madam; there is the true greengage, and there is the Drap d' Or, that has yellow spots; and there is the Reine Claude, that has red spots.

QUEEN.—Ah, ah! One sees you are very curious, and that you understand these things perfectly well; upon my word, I did not know you were so deep in these things. You know the plums as Solomon did the plants, from the cedar to the hyssop.

QUEEN (to 1st Court Lady).—I believe you found it very dusty?

1ST COURT LADY.—Very dusty, Madam.

QUEEN (to 2nd Court Lady).—Do you go soon into the country, Madam?

2ND COURT LADY.—Very soon, Madam.

QUEEN (to 3rd Court Lady).—The town is very empty, I believe, Madam.

3RD COURT LADY.—Very empty, Madam.

QUEEN (to 4th Court Lady).—We have had the finest summer for walking in the world.

4TH COURT LADY.—Very fine, Madam.

*   *   *   *   *

[*Enter* Lord GRANTHAM, in a hurry.

LORD GRANTHAM.—Ah, dere is my Lord Hervey in your Majesty's gallery; he is in de frock and de bob, or he should have come in.

QUEEN.—Mon Dieu! My Lord Grantham, you are mad!

LORD G.—He is dere, all so live as he was; and has play de trick to see as we should all say.

QUEEN.—Then *he* is mad. Allons voir qu'est ce que c'est tout ceci.   [*Exeunt* Queen.

The King returned from Hanover somewhat unexpectedly on Sunday, the 26th of October following. "The Queen and her Court had just left the little chapel in the palace of Kensington, when intimation was given to her Majesty that the King, who had left Hanover on the previous Wednesday, was approaching the gate. Caroline, at the head of her ladies and gentlemen of her suite, hastened down to receive him; and, as he alighted from his ponderous coach, she took his hand and kissed it. This ceremony performed by the Regent, a very unceremonious, hearty, and honest kiss was impressed on his lips by the wife. The King endured the latter without emotion, and then, taking the Queen-regent by the fingers, he led her upstairs in a very stately and formal manner. In the gallery there was a grand presentation, at which his Majesty exhibited much ill-humour, and conversed with everybody but the Queen." *

The cause of all this ill-humour was a certain Madame Walmoden, with whom he had fallen in love, whom he had basely tempted from her husband, and whom he had been compelled to leave behind him at Herrenhausen. Never too well-pleased to return from Hanover, where he ruled as autocrat, to England, where he was but the chief magistrate of the state, he this time came back in so ruffled a frame of mind as to be well-nigh unbearable. "No English or even French cook could dress a dinner; no English confectioner set out a dessert; no English player could act; no English coachman could drive, or English jockey ride; no Englishman knew how to come into a room, nor any Englishwoman how to dress herself. Whereas at Hanover all these things were in the utmost perfection." † "It was observed," says Dr. Doran, "that his behaviour to Caroline had never been so little tinged with outward respect as now. She bore his ill-humour with admirable patience; and her quiet endurance only the more provoked the petulance of the little and worthless King." During his absence she had caused some valueless pictures to be removed from Kensington, and replaced with really good ones; but George immediately commanded that the innovation should be at once done away

* Dr. Doran.   † Lord Hervey.

with, and all the old daubs restored. "I suppose," said he snappishly to Lord Hervey, who was trying to defend the Queen's taste, "I suppose you assisted the Queen with your fine advice when she was pulling my house to pieces, and spoiling all my furniture. Thank God, at least, she has left the walls standing!" Lord Hervey meekly inquired if the two Vandykes which the Queen had substituted for "two sign-posts," should remain. The King was pleased to observe he didn't care whether they stayed or not; "but," he remarked, "for the picture with the dirty frame over the door, and the three nasty little children, I will have them taken away, and the old ones restored. I will have it done, too, to-morrow morning before I go to London, or else I know it will not be done at all." Not, as we may guess, without some suspicion of laughter in his voice, Lord Hervey next asked if his Majesty would have "his gigantic fat Venus restored too?" His Majesty signified that he would, for he liked his fat Venus much better than what had been put in its place. Having thus countermanded all his wife's orders, he found time to rail at his ministers for leaving town "to torment a poor fox that was generally a much better beast than any of them that pursued him;" and then finally grumbled himself off to bed.

Unfortunately the following morning found him in no better humour. He entered the gallery, where the Queen and Princesses were taking chocolate, with the Duke of Cumberland standing by. This was too good an opportunity for self-assertion to be lost. "He snubbed the Queen, who was drinking chocolate, for being always stuffing; the Princess Amelia for not hearing him; the Princess Caroline for being grown fat; the

Duke of Cumberland for standing awkwardly; and then he carried the Queen out to walk, to be re-snubbed in the garden." * What Caroline had to endure from her choleric little lord may be gathered from Lord Hervey's description of one evening:—

"About nine o'clock every night the King used to return to the Queen's apartment from that of his daughter's, where, from the time of Lady Suffolk's disgrace, he used to pass these evenings he did not go to the opera or play at quadrille, constraining them, tiring himself, and talking to Lady Deloraine . . . who was always of the party.

"At his return to the Queen's side, the Queen used often to send for Lord Hervey to entertain them till they retired, which was generally at eleven. One evening, among the rest, as soon as Lord Hervey came into the room, the Queen, who was knotting while the King walked backwards and forwards, began jocosely to attack Lord Hervey upon an answer just published to a book of his friend Bishop Hoardley's upon the Sacrament, in which the Bishop was very ill-treated; but before she had uttered half what she had a mind to say, the King interrupted her, and told her she always loved talking of such nonsense and things she knew nothing about; adding that if it were not for such foolish people loving to talk of those things when they were written, the fools who wrote upon them would never think of publishing their nonsense and disturbing the Government with impertinent disputes that nobody of any sense ever troubled himself about. The Queen bowed, and said, ' Sir, I only did it to let Lord Hervey know that his friend's book

* Lord Hervey.

had not met with that general approbation he had intended.' 'A pretty fellow for a friend!' said the King, turning to Lord Hervey. 'Pray what is it that charms you to him?' . . .

"Lord Hervey, in order to turn the conversation, told the King that he had that day been with a Bishop of a very different stamp . . . who had carried us to Westminster Abbey to show us a pair of old brass gates to Henry VII.'s chapel. . . . Whilst ord Hervey was going on with a particular detail and encomium on these gates—the Queen asking many questions about them, and seeming extremely pleased with the description—the King stopped the conversation short by saying, 'My lord, you are always putting some of these fine things in the Queen's head, and then I am to be plagued with a hundred plans and workmen.' Then turning to the Queen, he said, 'I suppose I shall see a pair of these gates to Merlin's Cave * to complete your nonsense there.' 'Apropos,' said the Queen, 'I hear the Craftsman † has abused Merlin's Cave.' 'I am very glad of it,' interrupted the King; 'you deserve to be abused for such childish, silly stuff, and it is the first time I ever knew the scoundrel to be in the right.'

"This the Queen swallowed too, and began to talk on something else, till the conversation, I know not by what transition, fell on the ridiculous expense it was to people, by the money given to servants, to go and stay two or three days with their acquaintance in the country; upon which the Queen said she had found it a pretty large expense this summer to visit her friends even in town. 'That is your own fault,' said the King,

* A grotto built by the Queen at Richmond.
† The Opposition newspaper.

'for my father, when he went to people's houses in town never was fool enough to be giving away his money.' The Queen pleaded for her excuse that she had only done what Lord Grantham had told her she was to do; to which his Majesty replied that my Lord Grantham was a pretty director; that she was always asking some fool or other what she was to do; and that none but a fool would ask another fool's advice. The Queen then appealed to Lord Hervey, whether it was not now as customary to give money in town as in country. *He knew it was not, but said it was.* He added, too, that to be sure, were it not so for particulars (private persons), it would certainly be expected from her Majesty. To which the King said, 'Then she may stay at home as I do. You do not see me running into every puppy's house to see his new chairs and stools; nor is it for you,' said he, addressing himself to the Queen, 'to be running your nose everywhere, and trotting about the town to every fellow that will give you some bread-and-butter, like an old girl that loves to go abroad, no matter where, or whether it be proper or no.' The Queen coloured, and knotted a good deal faster during this speech than she had done before, whilst the tears came into her eyes, but she said not one word. Lord Hervey (who cared not whether he provoked the King's wrath himself or not, provided he could have the merit to the Queen of diverting his Majesty's ill-humour from her) said to the King, that as the Queen loved pictures, there was no way of seeing a collection but by going to people's houses. 'And what matter whether she saw a collection or not?' replied the King. 'The matter, sir, is that she satisfies her own curiosity, and obliges the people whose house she honours with her presence.' 'Supposing,' said the King, 'she had a curiosity to see a tavern, would it be fit for her to satisfy it? and yet the innkeeper would be very glad to see her.' 'If the innkeepers,' replied Lord Hervey, 'were used to be well received by her Majesty in her palace, I should think the Queen's seeing them at their own houses would give no additional scandal.' The King then, instead of answering Lord Hervey, turned to the Queen, and with a good deal of vehemence, poured out an unintelligible torrent of German, to which the Queen made not one word of reply, but knotted on till she caught her thread, then snuffed the candles that stood on the table before her, and snuffed one of them out; upon which the King, in English, began a new dissertation upon her Majesty, and took her awkwardness for his text."

The Queen suffered keenly under such outbursts of temper; but she was too proud to acknowledge it, even to her favourite, Lord Hervey, and the latter knew it; and accordingly, " when, on the following morning, she remarked that he had looked at her the evening before as if he thought she had been going to cry, the courtier protested that he had neither done the one nor thought the other, but had expressly directed his eyes on another object, lest if they met hers, the comicality of the scene should have set both of them laughing."* During his sojourn in Hanover the King had caused pictures of all the extravagant Court revels in which he had indulged with Madame Walmoden to be painted, all the figures therein represented being portraits of the veritable revellers. Five of these pictures, with his own peculiar notions of good taste, he had caused to

* Dr. Doran.

be hung in the Queen's dressing-room; and occasionally he would vary the evening's amusement by taking up a candle from the Queen's table, and exhibiting these pictures to Lord Hervey, graphically narrating the circumstances connected with each scene, and naming all the persons represented. "During which lecture Lord Hervey, while peeping over his Majesty's shoulders at those pictures, was shrugging up his own, and now and then stealing a look to make faces at the Queen, who, a little angry. a little peevish, and a little tired at her husband's absurdity, and a little entertained with his lordship's grimaces, used to sit and knot in a corner of the room, sometimes yawning, and sometimes smiling, and equally afraid of betraying those signs, either of her lassitude or mirth."* The King had promised Madame Walmoden to return to her by the 29th of the next May, and this fact, coming to the knowledge of Caroline, "gave her," says Dr. Doran, "more pain than all the royal fits of ill-humour together." Verily, she had much to bear; for Sir Robert Walpole, when she once alluded to the matter, "assured her coarsely and calmly that nothing was more natural; that she was herself old and past the age of pleasing; and that, in fact, there was nothing else to be looked for. He had the incredible audacity to propose to her, at the same time, that she should send for a certain Lady Tankerville, 'a handsome, good-natured, simple woman,' to make a balance on the side of England to the attractions of Hanover. We are not told that Lady Tankerville, whose recommendation was that she would be 'a safe fool,' had done anything to warrant the minister's selection of her. Caroline laughed, Sir Robert

* Lord Hervey.

said, 'and took the proposal extremely well.'
But her laugh, Lord Hervey wisely remarks, was
no sign of her satisfaction with so presumptuous
and injurious an address." *   In spite of all she
endured, the Queen could yet make witty remarks
on passing events.   Speaking of the Triple
Alliance, she said, " It always put her in mind
of the ʳouth Sea Scheme, which the parties concerned entered into, not without knowing the
cheat, but hoping to make advantage of it, everybody designing, when he had made his own
fortune, to be the first in scrambling out of it,
and each thinking himself wise enough to be
able to leave his fellow adventurers in the lurch."

* Mrs. Oliphant.

CHAPTER IV.

Marriage of the Prince of Wales—King's return to Hanover—
His prolonged absence—The Queen and Walpole—Her letter
to the King—His reply—His return—A stormy voyage—
Letter of Princess Amelia—The Queen's birthday—Dissen-
sions between the King and Prince of Wales—Queen's
estrangement from her son—Her illness—Her imprudence—
King's want of consideration—Affection of the Princess
Caroline—Queen's injunction concerning the Prince of Wales
—Her state pronounced hopeless—Her superstition regard-
ing Wednesday—Her farewells to her children—Her last
gift to the King—His extraordinary conduct—His grief—
His irritability—Queen's interview with Sir Robert Walpole
—With the Archbishop of Canterbury—Her death—Her
funeral—Behaviour of the King—Character of the Queen—
Verses on her death—Her children—Death of the King.

In the April of the year following (1736), the
marriage of the Prince of Wales and the Princess
Augusta of Saxe-Gotha, of which an account is
given in the biography of the latter lady, took
place ; and in the following month, the King, in
spite of Sir Robert Walpole's opposition, set sail
for Hanover in fulfilment of his promise. Mortify-
ing as his disgraceful conduct must have been to
the Queen, there must, nevertheless, have been a
slight degree of relief mingled with her vexation ;
for his Majesty's temper had not increased in
suavity during these latter months. On Caroline
one day gently urging a somewhat more courteous
treatment of the Bishops, he turned upon her with
the amiable remark :—" I am sick to death of all
this foolish stuff, and wish, with all my heart,
that the devil may take all your bishops, and the
devil take your minister, and the devil take the
parliament, and the devil take the whole island,
provided I can get out of it and go to Hanover."

But perhaps, on the whole, his absence was less bearable than his presence. " Bitter were Caroline's feelings," says Dr. Doran, " when she found his return protracted beyond the usual period. For the King to be absent on his birthday was a most unusual occurrence, and Caroline felt that the rival must have some power indeed. who could thus restrain him from indulgence in old habits. She was, however, as proud as she was pained. She began to grow cool in her ceremony and attentions to the King. She abridged the ordinary length of her letters to him, and the usual four dozen pages were shortened into some seven or eight. Her immediate friends, who were, aware of this circumstances, saw at once that her well-known judgment and prudence were now in default. They knew that to attempt to insinuate reproach to the King would arouse his anger, and not awaken his sleeping tenderness. They feared lest her power over him should become altogether extinct, and that his Majesty would soon as little regard his wife by force of habit as he had long ceased to do by readiness of inclination. It was Walpole's conviction that the King's respect for her was too firmly fixed to be ever shaken. Faithless himself, he reverenced the fidelity and sincerity which he knew were in her ; and if she could not rule by the heart, it was certain that she might still continue supreme by the head—by her superior intellect. Still, the minister recognised the delicacy and danger of the moment, and, in an interview with Caroline, he made it the subject of as extraordinary a discussion as was ever held between minister and royal mistress—between man and woman. Walpole reminded her of faded charms and growing years, and he expatiated on the impossibility of her ever being able to establish supremacy in the King's regard by power of her personal attractions ! It is a trait of her character worth noticing, that she listened to these unwelcome, but almost unwarrantably expressed, truths with immovable patience. But Walpole did not stop here. He urged her to resume her long letters to the King, and to address him in terms of humility, submissiveness, duty, and tender affection ; and he set the climax on what one might almost be authorised to consider his impudence, by recommending her to invite the King to bring Madame Walmoden with him to England. At this counsel the tears *did* spring into the eyes of Caroline." Most women, royal or simple, would have marked their sense of the insult by instant dismissal of the offender ; but the Queen had so schooled herself in almost unnatural self-restraint that she bore the counsel unresistingly, and further, actually acted upon it. She wrote to the King what has well been called "the most singular letter that ever wife wrote to a husband."* In order, she wrote, to remove the occasion of his constant absences, she was prepared to take Madame Walmoden into her service. George answered this communication with one of the most extraordinary productions that ever issued from a royal or any other pen. " He extols," says Lord Hervey, " the Queen's merit towards him in the strongest expression of his sense of all her goodness to him, and the gratitude he feels towards her. He commands her understanding, her temper, and, in short, leaves nothing unsaid that can demonstrate the opinion he has of her head and the value he sets upon her heart." " Mais," he continues, " vous voyez mes passions, ma chère Caroline. Vous connaissez

* Dr. Doran.

mes faiblesses, il n'y a rien de caché dans mon cœur pour vous, et plût á Dieu que vous pourriez me corriger avez la même facilité que vous m'approfondissez! Plût á Dieu que je pourrais vous imiter autant que je sais vous admirer, que que je pourrais apprendre de vous imiter toutes les vertus que vous me faites voir, sentir, et aimer!" Sir Robert Walpole, who saw this letter, told Lord Hervey it was so well written that "if the King would only write to women instead of strutting and talking to them, he believed his Majesty would get the better of all the men in the world."* Chacun à son gout!

The return journey of the King was fixed for the 7th of December; but he came alone, his enchantress remaining, after all the discussions, at Hanover. He passed the Hague, where his daughter Anne, the Princess of Orange, lay almost at the point of death; but he did not consider it worth while to pause and enquire after her well-being. He was to embark at Helvoetsluys on the 11th; and the day following such a storm raged that all in England concluded that, if he had indeed put to sea, he must necessarily be lost. Guns had been heard in the distance at Harwich, which people set down to signals of distress from the royal fleet; bets were offered and taken on the event, and much excitement prevailed concerning the fate of the missing monarch. The Queen affected to make light of all gloomy forebodings, and amused, or feigned to amuse herself, by reading "Rollin." "Walpole began to discuss the prospects of the royal family, the probable conduct of the possible new sovereign, the little regard he would have for his mother, the fatherless guardian he would be over his brother and

* "John, Lord Hervey." *Vide* "Temple Bar," October, 1878.

sisters, and the bully and dupe he would prove, by turns, of all with whom he came in contact. Lord Hervey and Queen Caroline discussed the same delicate question; and the latter, fancying that her son already assumed, in public and in her presence, the swagger of a new greatness, and that he was bidding for popularity, would not listen to Lord Hervey's assurances that she would be able to rule him as she had done his father."* The Prince himself declared his conviction that his father had perished, and the Queen grew hourly more anxious; when a courier who had been sent over at peril of his life, arrived to tell her Majesty that the King was still in safety at Helvoetsluys, waiting for fair weather.

Fair weather did come, and continued just long enough for the King to embark, and then suddenly gave place to a worse storm than the preceding one. The ships which had left Helvoetsluys with that bearing the King reached different harbours by ones and twos, scattered, tossed, and injured by the tempest. All they could tell was, that the whole convoy had started together, that a fearful storm had arisen, and Sir Charles Wager, who commanded the royal yacht, had signalled to all to seek their own safety; that all had been separated, and that when last seen the King's ship was tacking, and, it was hoped, *might* have returned to shore in safety. "Christmas Day at St. James's," says Dr. Doran, "was the very gloomiest of festive times, and the evening was solemnly spent in round games of cards. The Queen, indeed, did not know of the disasters which had happened to the royal fleet; but there was uncertainty enough touching the fate of her royal husband to make even the reading of "Rollin"

* Dr. Doran.

appear more decent than playing at basset and cribbage. Meanwhile, the ministers and Court officials stood round the royal table, and discoursed on trivial subjects, while their thoughts were directed towards their storm-tossed master. On the following morning, Sir Robert Walpole informed her Majesty of the real and graver aspect of affairs. The heart of the tender woman at once melted; and Caroline burst into tears, unrestrainedly. "The next day fell on a Sunday, and she resolved to attend church as usual. In the midst of the service a letter was brought her. She trembled so much that she could not open it; and the Duke of Grafton broke the seal, and announced, "His Majesty is safe!" The missive was from the King, who informed her that he had been driven back to Helvoetsluys after twenty-four hours beating about, and how the whole thing was entirely the fault of Sir Charles Wager, who had insisted on his setting out—a deliberate misrepresentation of the truth, George having himself grown so impatient of the delay as to declare he *would* cross, whether the passage were rough or smooth.

"Be the weather what it may," he asserted, "I am not afraid."

"*I am*," said the admiral, laconically.

Thereupon the King, behaving comically like a spoilt child, remarked—that he wanted to see a storm, and would sooner be twelve hours in one than be shut up for twenty-four hours more at Helvoetsluys.

"Twelve hours in a storm!" retorted Sir Charles, with scant ceremony; "four would do your business for you."

Nevertheless the King *would* go; and very nearly paid for his self-will with his life.

"Sir," said Sir Charles, when they were secure on the Dutch coast once more, "you wished to see a storm; how does your Majesty like it?"
"So well," replied the temporarily subdued King, "that I never wish to see another."
"The joy of Caroline was honest and unfeigned. She declared that her heart had been heavier that day than ever it had been before; that she was still, indeed, anxious touching the fate of one whose life was so precious, not merely to his family, but to all Europe; and that, but for the impatience and indiscretion of Sir Charles Wager, the past great peril would never have been incurred."* She wrote to congratulate her husband on his safety, and received an answer in the elegant French George knew well how to indite.

"In spite," he says, "of all the danger I have incurred in the tempest, my dear Caroline, and notwithstanding all I have suffered, having been ill to an excess which I thought the human body could not bear, I assure you that I would expose myself to it again and again to have the pleasure of hearing the testimonies of your affection with which my position inspired you. This affection which you testify for me, this friendship, this fidelity, the inexhaustible goodness which you show for me, and the indulgence which you have for all my weaknesses, are so many obligations, which I can never sufficiently recompense, can never sufficiently merit, but which I also can never forget."

This letter Caroline showed to Sir Robert Walpole and Lord Hervey, remarking that she was reasonably pleased with it, but not unreasonably proud of it. The Princess Amelia also sent con-

* Dr. Doran.

LIVES OF THE PRINCESSES OF WALES.

gratulations—not to her father, but to Horace
Walpole, who was in his suite:—

"You have been very good and obliging, my
good Mr. Walpole, to take the trouble of writing
to me; and I assure you my joy is too great to
be expressed, that you are all safe at Helvoet.
What mamma underwent ever since Friday last,
can't be imagined—for she never was easy since
she heard that the sloop of the English secretary's
office was come here with so much difficulty, and
that they had left you all at sea. But on Sunday
morning before nine, Sir Robert came to mamma,
to give her the dreadful account of the three men-
of-war being come, and Lord Augustus's ship,
without masts or sails—then you may imagine
what we all felt. We went to church as usual,
and about two the messenger came in, and made
not only mamma and her children happy, but
indeed everybody. The consternation was great
before, and they seemed all to dread to hear
some bad news. But now pray be careful, and
don't get out till you are sure of seeing our
sweet faces, and then we will all make you as
welcome as we can; for I cannot afford any
more to be so frightened, for we are all still half
dead.

"I pitied poor Mrs. Walpole extremely; but I
saw her yesterday, and we thanked God heartily
together that you are all safe. Sir Robert hath
been very childish, for he drank more than he
should upon the arrival of the messenger, and
felt something of the gout that same night; but
he is perfectly well again. I hunted with him
yesterday at Richmond, and he was in excellent
spirits.

"I thank you, dear Horace, for letting me know
so exactly how my sister does—I am very happy

she is so well. Mamma commands me to make
you her compliments; Caroline desires hers to be
given you also; and I remain your sincere friend
upon land, but hate you at sea—for you take my
stomach and rest away, and I lose both eating and
sleeping."

The Queen declared that, even had the King
really perished, she would still have retained Lord
Hervey in her service, and would have implored
Sir Robert Walpole, on her knees, to serve the
new sovereign as he had served the former one.
After five weeks' more delay, George landed at
Lowestoft, and arrived in London on the 15th of
January, happily for all his *entourage* in high
good humour, and expatiating on the admirable
qualities of the Queen with extravagant laudation.
Caroline's birthday this year—the last she was
ever to celebrate—is thus mentioned by Mrs.
Delany:—

"March 3rd, 1737.

"Last Tuesday, being Her Majesty's birthday, I went to pay my devoirs in a new pink-
coloured tabby; I went in the morning with Lady
Sunderland, and at night with Mrs. Pine; there
was a great crowd. The King looked in good
humour. . . He does not go abroad, but passes
the summer at Hampton Court; he was excessively
fine on the birthday, and the Princess Amelia's
clothes very beautiful. There was nothing else
remarkable, but that my Lord Onslow was very
near being demolished; he went to help some
ladys into the foreigners' box, his foot slipped,
and he tumbled backward among all the crowd,
and had like to have beat the Princess Mary off
her seat. He lay sprawling some time before he
could recover himself, and caused much mirth

throughout the assembly; the King and Queen laughed heartily."

This year was embittered to the Queen by the struggle made by the Prince of Wales and his friends on the question of his revenue. "There seems little doubt," says Mrs. Oliphant, "that so far as simple justice went, he had right on his side. In the immense Civil List granted to the King, £100,000 had been tacitly allotted to the Prince as his share : it is true that no express stipulation had been made, but there appears no doubt that such was the understanding. And George II., while Prince of Wales, had himself enjoyed a similar income. He had, however, kept his son on an uncertain allowance—£30,000 before his marriage, and £50,000 after it. The Prince's desire to get possession of the full income intended for him was not, certainly, an unnatural one, though, in times so ticklish, the attempt to extort it by Parliamentary influence, to humiliate the King, and force him into action contrary at once to his pride and his wishes, was as unwise as can well be conceived." The excitement and commotion at Court when the Prince's intentions were heard of was very great, and the King and Queen seemed for once to have changed places—the King taking it, to the general surprise, tolerably quiet, and the Queen betraying much anxiety and depression. "The King," says Lord Hervey, "took the first notice of this business with more temper and calmness than anybody expected he would; and the Queen, from the beginning of the affair to the end of it, was in much greater agitation and anxiety than I ever saw her on any other occasion." The weakness and ill-health she then endured probably helped to undermine the inflexible courage with which she had hitherto faced every trial. "Her concern," says Lord Hervey, "was so great that more tears flowed on this occasion than I ever saw her shed on all other occasions put together. She said she had suffered a great deal from many disagreeable circumstances this last year; the King's staying abroad; the manner in which his stay had been received and talked of here; her daughter the Princess Royal's danger in lying-in; and the King's danger at sea; but that her grief and apprehension at present surpassed everything that she had ever felt before; that she looked on her family from this moment as distracted with divisions of which she could see no hope or end—divisions which would give the common enemies of her family such advantages as might one time or other enable them to get the better of it; and though she had spirits and resolution to struggle with most misfortunes and difficulties, this last, she owned, got the better of her —that it was too much for her to bear; that it not only got the better of her spirits and resolution, but of her appetite and rest, as she could neither eat nor sleep; and that she really feared it would kill her."

Public opinion declared that the Prince was certain to be on the winning side; but, when the debate actually came on, contrary to all expectation, the King gained by a majority of thirty. The *how* of such matters was not much regarded in those days. "Most people," says Lord Hervey, with straightforward calmness, "thought it [the majority] cost a great deal of money; but Sir Robert Walpole and the Queen both told me separately that it cost the King but £900—£500 to one man and £400 to another.

This attempt of the Prince infinitely increased

258 LIVES OF THE PRINCESSES OF WALES.

the animosity of his mother and her favourite
daughter, the gentle Princess Caroline, who was
bitterly angered against him on account of his at-
tempts to influence public opinion against the Queen.
Both Caroline and her child spoke of him in terms
which, though coarse and harsh to us of the nineteenth century, were, we must remember, the
ordinary manner of expression of the time. People
in those days called a spade a spade with alarming
directness; and those of the very highest rank
habitually indulged in language which now-a-days
would not be tolerated in a respectable servant.
The Queen's contempt for her son was as deep as
her indignation, and, it must be confessed, was
not ill-merited.

"I know," she said, "he would sell not only
his reversion in the Electorate, but even in this
kingdom, if the Pretender would give him five or
six hundred thousand pounds in present; but,
thank God! he has neither right nor power to sell
his family—though his folly and his knavery may
sometimes distress them."

" She often wished, with angry tears," says Mrs.
Oliphant, "that Lady Bristol, Lord Hervey's
mother, a violent and foolish woman, could but
have the Prince, whose friend she was, for her
son, and leave to poor Caroline the man whose
almost filial duty was her own chief comfort."

In the August following occurred the birth of
the Prince of Wales' eldest child, the " Lady
Augusta," with all its extraordinary attendant circumstances.*   On the 13th of September Frederick
and his family left St. James's Palace by Royal
order.   That morning, Lord Hervey tells us, " the
Queen, at breakfast, every now and then repeated,

* For a fuller account of this event see life of Augusta of
Saxe-Gotha.

I hope in God I shall never see him again ; and
the King, among many other paternal *douceurs* in
his valediction to his son, said : Thank God :
to-morrow night the puppy will be out of my
house."

Indeed, both George and Caroline constantly
lost their dignity when speaking of their son.
Frederick invariably named his mother as the
instigator of all harsh measures against him—a
fact of which the Queen was well aware.

"My dear lord," she said once to Lord Hervey,
" I will give it you under my hand, if you have
any fear of my relapsing, that my dear first-born
is the greatest ass, and the greatest liar, and the
greatest *canaille*, and the greatest beast, in the
whole world, and that I most heartily wish he was
out of it ! "

"The Queen was a great while," explained the
King, " before her maternal affection would give
him up for a fool, and yet I told her so before he
had been acting as if he had no common sense."

" While this discussion was at its hottest," says
Dr. Doran, " the Queen fell ill of the gout. She
was so unwell, so weary of being in bed, and so
desirous of chatting with Lord Hervey, that she
now, for the first time, broke through the Court
etiquette, which would not admit a man, save
the Sovereign, into the royal bed-chamber. The
noble lord was with her there during the whole
of each day that her confinement lasted. She
was too old, she said, to have the honour of being
talked of for it; and so, to suit her humour, the
old ceremony was dispensed with."

But the Queen was not much longer to struggle
on under the harassing weight of her queenship
and her manifold duties. She had long endured
in silence a disease that was now growing daily

more serious. She knew the King had an unconquerable dislike to any kind of sickness or physical ailment, and she had therefore resolutely refused, when, having a suspicion of her illness, he had begged her to have medical advice.

"Again, and again," says Dr. Doran, "the King had urged her . . . and again and again she had refused, and each time with renewed expressions of displeasure; until at last, the King, contenting himself with expressing a hope that she would not have to repent of her obstinacy, made her a promise never to allude to the subject again without her consent."

She never again mentioned it; and, resolved never to deny a request of her husband, used to commit fearful imprudences, in order to be able to walk with him and attend him whenever he needed her.

"She made it so invariable a rule," says Horace Walpole, "never to refuse a desire of the King, that every morning, at Richmond, she walked several miles with him; and more than once, when she had the gout in her foot, she dipped her whole leg in cold water to be ready to attend him. The pain, her bulk, and the exercise, threw her into such fits of perspiration as routed the gout; but those exertions hastened the crisis of her distemper."

George, with his usual utter want of consideration, insisted on her being present at all the Court ceremonies; and the Queen, in harness to the last, never failed him; but the weary drama of her life was well-nigh played out. In the August of 1737 she was so ill that a report spread in town that she was dead; but though, by one of her violent remedies, she cured herself for the time, she was unable to be present at the christening of her granddaughter, of whom she was one of the sponsors. Still she struggled on, till the morning of Wednesday, the 9th of November, when she suffered so much that she was forced to return to bed when she essayed to rise; " but her courage was great, and the King's pity small, and consequently she rose, after resting some hours, in order to preside at the usual Wednesday's drawing-room. The King had a great dislike to see her absent from this ceremony; without her, he used to say, there was neither grace, gaiety, nor dignity; and, accordingly, she went to this last duty with the spirit of a wounded knight who returns to the field and dies in harness."* She passed Lord Hervey with a serio-comic grumble at her enforced toil, and went through her work with a gracious smile or timely word for each, like the brave woman she was. But even her courage had to fail at last. " Coming back to Lord Hervey, she said, ' I am not able to entertain people.' ' Would to God,' replied Lord Hervey, ' the King would have done talking of the Dragon of Wantley [a farce then playing at Covent Garden] and release you.' At last the King went away, telling the Queen, as he went by, that she had overlooked the Duchess of Norfolk. The Queen made her excuse for having done so to the Duchess of Norfolk, the last person she ever spoke to in public, and then retired, going immediately to bed, where she grew worse every moment."† She was given " snake-root and Sir Walter Raleigh's cordial," ‡ and bled, but the remedies were of no avail. " I have an ill," said the Queen, " which nobody knows of "—a remark taken no notice of at the time. She was lovingly tended all that day by the Princess Caroline,

* Dr. Doran.   † " Lord Hervey's Memoirs."   ‡ *Ibid.*

always her best-loved daughter, who, though in very weak health herself, insisted on watching by her mother until two o'clock in the morning. Then the King took her place as "nurse" in a fashion peculiar to himself. He neither sat up or went to bed; but "lay on the Queen's bed all night in his night-gown, where he could not sleep, nor she turn about easily." *

The following day brought with it no abatement of the Queen's sufferings. "Her illness visibly increased, and George was as visibly affected by it —not so much so, however, as not to be concerned about matters of dress. With the sight of the Queen's suffering before his eyes, he remembered that he had to meet the Foreign Ministers that day, and he was exceedingly particular in directing the pages to see that new ruffles were to be sewn to his old shirt sleeves, whereby he might wear a decent air in the eyes of the representatives of foreign majesty. The Princess Caroline continued to exhibit unabated sympathy for the mother who had perhaps loved her better than any other of her daughters. The Princess was in tears and suffering throughout the day, and almost needed as much care as the royal patient herself; especially after losing much blood by the sudden breaking of one of the small vessels in the nose. It was in this day that, to aid Broxholm, who had hitherto prescribed for the Queen, Sir Hans Sloane and Dr. Hulse were called in." † Thinking it possible that the Prince of Wales might come to the palace on hearing of his mother's condition, Lord Hervey, who then filled the office of Vice-Chamberlain, desired to know how he was to act on such an occasion. The King, to whom he appealed, was sufficiently explicit on the point:—

* Lord Hervey.   † Dr. Doran.

"If the puppy," said George, "in one of his impertinent affected airs of duty and affection, dare to come to St. James's, I order you to go to the scoundrel and tell him I wondered at his impudence for daring to come here; that he has my orders already, and knows my pleasure, and bid him go about his business; for his poor mother is not in a condition to see him act his false, whining, cringing tricks now, nor am I in a humour to bear his impertinence; and bid him trouble me with no more messages, but get out of my house."

In this prohibition Caroline fully concurred. She expected he would call and make inquiries for her.

"Sooner or later," she said, "I am sure one shall be plagued with some message of that sort, because he will think it will have a good air in the world to ask to see me; and perhaps hopes I shall be fool enough to let him come, and give him the pleasure of seeing my last breath go out of my body, by which means he would have the joy of knowing I was dead five minutes sooner than he could know it in Pall Mall."

"I am so far," she continued, after an interval, "from desiring to see him, that nothing but your absolute commands should ever make me consent to it. For what should I see him? For him to tell me a hundred lies, and to give myself, all this time, a great deal of trouble to no purpose? If anything I could say to him would alter his behaviour, I would see him with all my heart, but I know that is impossible. Whatever advice I gave him he would thank me for, he would cry like a calf all the while I was speaking, and swear to follow my directions; and would laugh at me the moment he was out of the room, and do just the contrary of all I bid him the moment I was dead. And, therefore, if I should grow worse, and be weak enough to talk of seeing him, I beg you, sir, to conclude that I doat or rave."

Hard words for a mother's lips to utter; but scarcely too hard to be spoken of the son who sat in Carlton House repeating, " We shall have good news soon, we shall have good news soon; she can't hold out much longer ! "

Meanwhile the physicians, who had been thoroughly puzzled by Caroline's state, had discovered that the true cause of her illness was a rupture, from which she had suffered in secret for years. This discovery of what she had hidden so long was a bitter trial to her fortitude. " She turned her face to the wall and shed tears when she could no longer conceal it—the only tears she shed for herself. But she did not hesitate to give herself over to the painful and useless operations with which doctors of every age and degree of enlightenment torture people who are past help."* Two more doctors—Shipton and Bussier—were called in; and Caroline submitted to all their measures with most uncomplaining patience and resolution. Sometimes even her endurance gave way, and she could not restrain a groan; but she bravely bade them "not heed her silly complaints." " When the hour of her torture came," says Mrs. Oliphant, " she turned wistfully to ask the King if he approved what the surgeons proposed to do; and on receiving his assurance that it was thought necessary, submitted with that resolution which had never failed her. On the Saturday night the Princess Caroline, whom the physicians had insisted on bleeding, lay dressed on a couch in a room adjoining her mother's ; Lord Hervey lay on

* Mrs. Oliphant.

a mattress at the foot of the sofa; the King, to every one's relief, went off to bed; and Princess Amelia watched by the Queen.

The next morning the doctors announced that her Majesty's case was hopeless, and that it was but a question of a days or even hours. The Queen was by far the most composed of all to whom the news was communicated; but she observed that she did not think she would die before Wednesday. "It was her peculiar day," she said. "She had been born on a Wednesday, was married on a Wednesday, first became a mother on a Wednesday, was crowned on Wednesday, and she was convinced she should die on a Wednesday."* Nevertheless, she prepared to take leave of her husband and children at once. "As I have always," she said to the King, " told you my thoughts of things and people as fast as they arise, I have nothing left to communicate to you. The people I love and those I do not, the people I like and dislike, and those I would wish you to be kind to, you know as well as myself; and I am persuaded it would therefore be a useless trouble both to you and me at this time to add any particular recommendations."

To her eldest daughter, Anne, she left no message, nor did she show any desire to see her. To the Princess Amelia she spoke kindly, and affectionately to the Princess Caroline, whom she predicted would follow her in less than a year. Notwithstanding, she committed to her care the two little Princesses, Mary and Louisa. "Poor Caroline, it is a fine legacy I leave you," she said. To her youngest child she spoke in what seems a strangely prophetic spirit—"Louisa, remember I

* Dr. Doran.

die by being giddy and obstinate, in having kept
my disorder in secret." "As for you, William,"
she added, to the Duke of Cumberland, "you
know I have always loved you tenderly, and placed
my chief hope in you; show your gratitude to me
in your behaviour to the King; be a support to
your father, and double your attention to make up
for the disappointment and vexation he must
receive from your profligate and worthless brother.
It is in you only I hope for keeping up the credit
of our family, when your father shall be no more.
Attempt nothing even against your brother, and
endeavour to mortify him in no way but by showing superior merit."

Her son never forgot her words. His maxim
in after life was, Horace Walpole tells us, "to
bear everything from his brother, if he lived to be
King, rather than set an example of disobedience
to the Royal authority."

Then the Queen turned again to her husband,
and drawing from her finger a ruby ring, placed
it on his.

"This is the last thing I have to give you," she
said; "naked I came to you, and naked I go from
you. I had everything I ever possessed from you,
and to you whatever I have I return. My will you
will find a very short one—I give all I have to
you." As he sat sobbing by her, she counselled
him to marry again. "Wiping his eyes and
sobbing between every word, with much ado he
got out this answer: 'Non, j' aurai des
maîtresses.'"* "Eh, mon Dieu!" cried Caroline, "cela n'empêche pas!" As Mrs. Oliphant
says, "Criticism stands confounded before such
an incident. Perhaps it is possible poor Caroline, sick and weary, did not wish for the suc-

* Lord Hervey.

cessor she suggested a life more perfect than
her own had been; and we all know by experience, though we will never allow in theory,
that the near approach of death has as little
moral effect on the mind as that of any other
familiar accident of life."

This scene over, the Queen fell into a deep
sleep, and George, kissing her pale cheeks over and
over again, expressed his conviction that she would
never wake to consciousness again. Throughout
her illness he manifested intense affection for her,
and painful anxiety regarding her state. His only
consolation, when not in her presence, seemed to
be expatiating to any and every one upon her
excellence.

"There is no known or discoverable good
quality which he did not acknowledge in her;
not only the qualities which dignify woman, but
those which elevate men. With the courage and
intellectual strength of the latter, she had the
beauty and virtue of the former. He never tired
of this theme, told it over and over again, and ever
at an interminable length. The most singular
item in this monster dissertation was his cool assurances of his children and friends that she was
the only woman in the world who suited him for a
wife; and that, if she had not been his wife, he
would rather have had her for his mistress than
any other woman he had ever seen or heard of."*

"Poor woman!" he cried, "how she always
found something obliging, agreeable, and pleasing
to say to everybody, and always sent people away
from her better satisfied than they came! With
what grace and politeness and sweetness she maintained her dignity!"

Unfortunately his solicitude for her exhibited
* Dr. Doran.

itself in her presence by increased irritability of manner. It seemed as if the habit of railing at her had become too confirmed to be laid aside even at so grave a moment as the present. " How the devil should you sleep when you will never lie still a moment ? " he asked her roughly, as she turned restlessly in her bed ; " you want to rest, and the doctors tell you nothing can do you so much good, and yet you always move about. Nobody can sleep in that manner, and that is always your way ; you never take the proper method to get what you want, and then you wonder you have it not." Sometimes the Queen, in her weakness and weariness, fixed her eyes on some one spot. " Mon Dieu ! " said George, " what are you looking at ? How on earth can you stare like that ? Your eyes are like those of a calf whose throat has just been cut ! " He perpetually pressed her to eat, and was very angry if she did not. " How is it possible you should know whether you like a thing or not ? " he demanded. At length the doctors had a notice pinned to the curtains of her bed, desiring all present to speak as softly as possible, and so secured her some degree of quiet. She grew steadily worse, but, in spite of the doctors' opinion, lingered on from day to day through all the following week. For the last time she exerted herself to see one of the colleagues of her by-gone life. Sir Robert Walpole was admitted to her room. " Her minister, the man whom she had made and kept supreme in England, came to say his farewell. Perhaps Caroline by that time had slid beyond the power of those arts which she had practised all her life. She spoke to Sir Robert, having little breath to spare, barely what she meant, without considering the King, his temper and his pride. ' My good Sir Robert,' she said, to the kneeling and alarmed minister, who dropped some tears by her bedside, ' you see me in a very indifferent situation. I have nothing to say to you but to recommend the King, my children, and the kingdom to your care.' Even in the presence of the dying, Sir Robert's heart gave a throb of terror as he scrambled up plethoric from his knees. Where was the Queen's usual prudence and ménagement ? Caroline had come to the bare elements, and could now ménager no more."* To George's honour, be it said, he never resented this consignment of his interests to the minister's hands ; but seemed subsequently to have a stronger liking for the Premier for the dead Queen's sake, and reminded Sir Robert that *he* needed no protection, since Caroline had rather begged him to protect the King.

It was not till within a very few days of her death that Dr. Potter, Archbishop of Canterbury, was sent for to see the Queen. Caroline's views had been always more or less broad, and Lady Sundon, formerly Mr. Clayton, was said to have strongly influenced her in that direction. It does not appear that the Queen herself expressed any wish on the subject, but public opinion began to express itself strongly at the absence of all ministers of religion from her bedside. Sir Robert Walpole thought it better not to offend the popular instinct. " Pray, madam," he said coarsely to the Princess Amelia, " let this farce be played : the Archbishop will act it very well. You may bid him be as short as you will. It will do the Queen no hurt, no more than any good ; and it will satisfy all the wise and good fools, who will call us Atheists if we don't pretend to be as great fools as they are." Accordingly, Dr. Potter

* Mrs. Oliphant.

was sent for; and, coming night and morning, prayed with the dying Queen. What passed between them is not known, except that she recommended to his care Dr. Bulter, the clerk of her closet, whose "Analogy" she used to read every morning at breakfast. The sacrament was not administered to her; whether on account of her refusal to see her eldest son or not is doubtful. When the Archbishop came from her room for the last time, eager questioners demanded, "My lord, has the Queen received!" but the prelate only answered the query ambiguously by stating that "her Majesty was in a most heavenly frame of mind."

On Sunday, the 20th, the end came. "How long can this last?" asked the Queen of one of her physicians. "It will not be long," he answered, "before your Majesty will be relieved from this suffering." "The sooner the better," answered the Queen. At ten o'clock that night, when the King was sleeping on the floor at the foot of her bed, and the Princess Amelia lay on a couch in a corner, the death-rattle sounded in Caroline's throat. "I have now got an asthma," she said softly; "open the window." There was a pause. "Pray," murmured the dying Queen. The Princess Amelia opened a book; but she had hardly read ten words when Caroline expired. Princess Caroline, bending over her mother, held a looking-glass to the motionless lips, and finding no breath sully its surface, cried " 'Tis over," and ceased the weeping which had been incessant during the Queen's last moments; while the King kissed his dead wife's face and hands with the tenderest affection.

The funeral of the Queen was called "decently private," but was marked by much pomp and splendour. She was interred in Westminster Abbey, and the Princess Amelia—not the King— was chief mourner. The anthem sung on the occasion, " The ways of Zion do mourn," was, say the chronicles of the time, " set to Musick by Mr. Handell." In after years George ordered that his coffin should be placed close to Caroline's, and that the planks on the sides of each should be withdrawn, that their ashes might mingle together.

In spite of his infatuation for the Walmoden, which continued up to his death, and whom he created Countess of Yarmouth—in spite of his unfaithfulness to her while living, and all the intolerable insults he had made her endure—there is no doubt that the incomprehensible little King loved his wife and regretted her loss as profoundly as was possible to his nature. Immediately after her death, " the sole subject of his conversation was 'Caroline.' He loved to narrate the whole history of her early life and his own; their wedding and their wooing, their joys and vexations. In these conversations he introduced something about every person with whom he had ever been in anything like close connection."* Even to Madame Walmoden he talked of her, described her beauty, her virtues, her good judgment; and was perpetually wondering what Caroline would have advised in certain contingencies. "There was something noble in his remark, on ordering the payment to be continued of all her salaries to her officers and servants, and all her benefactions to benevolent institutions, that, if possible, nobody should suffer by her death but himself. We almost pity the wretched, but imbecile old man too, when we see him bursting into tears at the sight of Walpole, and confessing to him, with a helpless

* Dr. Doran.

shaking of the hands, that he had lost the rock of his support, his warmest friend, his wisest counsellor, and that henceforth he must be dreary, disconsolate, and succourless, utterly ignorant whither to turn for succour or for sympathy."* "I hear," he said, long years after her death, to Baron Brinkman, "I hear you have a portrait of my wife, which was a present from her to you, and that it is a better likeness than any I have got. Let me look at it." The picture was brought, and placed before the King. "It *is* like her," he said, "place it nearer me and leave me till I ring." For two hours the Baron waited ere the summons came. Then, as he entered the chamber, the King, looking up with his eyes full of tears, muttered, "Take it away; take it away! I never yet saw the woman worthy to buckle her shoe." After which he went and breakfasted with Lady Yarmouth.

The character of Queen Caroline presents a striking and puzzling aspect. One recognizes distinctly *power* of no ordinary kind—power of government, of self-repression, of endurance; but the lights and shades are so confused and intermixed that it is difficult to form a just estimate of her real self. Perhaps of no one is it more true that her vices were those of the time, her virtues her own. In an age of such superlative coarseness, refinement of mind and expression was an almost impossible attribute; and the laxity of morals that was then universal may well account for much that is to us strange and repugnant. Religion was little thought of in those days; scepticism and infidelity were rife; and Caroline's life may little accord with an ideal of the nineteenth century; but we must not forget that

* Dr. Doran.

her warmest approval and commendation were
bestowed on Berkeley, for his "Minute Philosopher," in which he ably refutes scepticism. "The
expression of such approval is warrant for the
Queen's sincerity in the cause of true religion. So
delighted was the Queen with this work, that she
procured for its author his nomination to the
Bishopric of Cloyne. Never was reward more
nobly earned, more worthily bestowed, or more
gracefully conferred." * To sum up her character
in the words of Mrs. Oliphant—"Her life was
little spiritual, but it was very human. Her
heart was most stout, resolute, and faithful; and
she had that quality which Queen Katharine
adds as a crowning grace to the excellences of the
good woman—she had a great patience. Never,
perhaps, was there such a wife, and seldom such a
queen."

Among the many verses occasioned by her
death was the following fiercely trenchant
epitaph :—

Here lies unpitied, both by Church and State,
The subject of their flattery and hate ;
Flatter'd by those on whom her favors flow'd,
Hated for favors impiously bestow'd ;
Who aim'd the Church by Churchmen to betray,
And hoped to share in arbitrary sway.
In Tindall's and in Hoadley's paths she trod,
An hypocrite in all but disbelief in God.
Promoted luxury, encouraged vice,
Herself a sordid slave to avarice.
True friendship's tender love ne'er touch'd her heart,
Falsehood appear'd in vice disguised by art.
Fawning and haughty ; when familiar rude ;
And never civil seem'd but to delude.
Inquisitive in trifling, mean affairs,
Heedless of public good or orphans' tears ;
To her own offspring mercy she denied,
And, unforgiving, unforgiven died.

* Dr. Doran.

In reply to this another epitaph was drawn up by some more loyal subject:—

> Here lies, lamented by the poor and great—
> (Prop of the Church and glory of the State)—
> A woman, late a mighty monarch's queen,
> Above all flattery, and above all spleen;
> Loved by the good, and hated by the evil,
> Pursued, now dead, by satire and the devil.
> With steadfast zeal (which kindled in her youth)
> A foe to bigotry, a friend to truth;
> Too generous for the lust of lawless rule,
> Nor Persecution's nor Oppression's tool.
> In Locke's, in Clarke's, in Hoadley's paths she trod,
> Nor fear'd to follow where *they* follow'd God.
> To all obliging and to all sincere,
> Wise to choose friendships, firm to persevere.
> Free without rudeness; great without disdain;
> An hypocrite in nought but *hiding pain.*
> To Courts she taught the rules of just expense,
> Join'd with economy, magnificence;
> Attention to a kingdom's vast affairs,
> Attention to the meanest mortal's cares;
> Profusion might consume, or avarice hoard,
> 'Twas hers to feed, unknown, the scanty board.
> Thus, of each human excellence possess'd,
> With as few faults as e'er attend the best;
> Dear to her lord, to all her children dear,
> And (to the last her thought, her conscience clear)
> Forgiving all, forgiven and approved,
> To peaceful worlds her peaceful soul removed.

Of the children of Caroline, Anne, the eldest—who, on the news of her mother's death, hurried over to England, hoping to gain the influence over the King just dropped by the Queen, and was anything but warmly received by her father—lived only till 1759. She lost her singular-looking consort eight years before. He had grown increasingly ugly ever since his marriage, and she increasingly jealous of him. Her death was not particularly lamentable to her father, who had come to dislike her only less than his detested eldest son. Amelia, the second daughter, died at

an advanced age, unmarried, in 1786. She was
somewhat imperious and despotic in disposition,
but kindly, generous, and charitable, and an
excellent mistress to her servants. Caroline, the
Queen's favourite child, took her mother's
prophecy, uttered on the latter's deathbed, that
in less than a year she would follow her, as
literal fact; and though her death did not occurr
until 1757, lived all her life in the strictest seclusion in St. James's Palace. She was the gentlest
and sweetest of all Caroline's children, and,
perhaps, the most unhappy. Constant inter-
course with the Queen's favourite attendant,
Lord Hervey, had taught her to care for him too
much for her own peace; and his death in 1743
added to the melancholy that clouded her days.
Her chief pleasure was in rendering all the kind-
nesses that lay in her power to his children, for
whom she had almost a motherly affection. She
looked for death eagerly as the ending of a long
and troublous pilgrimage; a feeling evidenced by
her remark when pressed to do something of
which she disapproved—"I would not do it *to die.*"
We are told that "her whole income was dispensed between generosity and charity; and till
her death, by shutting up the current, discovered
the source, the gaols of London did not suspect
that the best support of their wretched inhabitants
issued from the palace." * William, Duke of
Cumberland, unfavourably known in history as
the "Butcher" of Culloden, died in 1765, being
then only forty-four years of age. He was the
favourite son of Caroline, who, says Dr. Doran,
"loved him because he was daring and original;
qualities which he evinced by his replies to her
when she was lecturing him as a wayward child.

* Horace Walpole.

For the same reason was he liked by his grandfather, at whose awkward English the graceless
boy laughed loudly, and mimicked admirably."
He was a thorough soldier, brave, hearty, and
sincere, and was described by George II. in his
will as " the best son that ever lived, and one who
had never given his father cause to be offended."

Of Caroline's two younger daughters, Mary and
Louisa, the elder married Frederick, the Elector
of Hesse Cassel, who treated her with unmitigated
brutality, and rendered her life well-nigh unbearable, until his death released her from her thraldom.
She died in 1772, aged forty-nine. Louisa, the
youngest, was wedded to Frederick V. of Denmark
in 1743. " Her career, in many respects, resembled that of her mother. She was married to
a King who kept a mistress in order that the
world should think he was independent of all
influence on the part of his wife. She was basely
treated by this King; but not a word of complaint
against him entered into the letters which this
spirited and sensible woman addressed to her
relations. Indeed, she had said at the time of
her marriage that, if she should become unhappy,
her family should never know anything about it.
She died, in the flower of her age, a terrible death,
as Walpole calls it, and after an operation which
lasted an hour. The cause of it was the neglect
of a slight rupture, occasioned by stooping
suddenly when *enceinte,* the injury resulting from
which she had imprudently and foolishly concealed."* She wrote most touching farewell
letters to her father and family. The King manifested what was, for him, considerable concern on
hearing of her death. " This has been a fatal
year to my family," he said. " I lost my eldest

* Dr. Doran.

son, but I was glad of it. Then the Prince of Orange died, and left everything in confusion. Poor little Edward [Duke of York] has been cut open for an imposthume in his side; and now the Queen of Denmark is gone! I know I did not love my children when they were young; I hated to have them coming into the room; but now I love them as well as most fathers."

Of all the children of George and Caroline, one only—the Princess Amelia—passed the age of fifty. The King survived his wife twenty-three years, dying October 25th, 1760, and was buried, according to his wish, by the side of her whom he had really loved as much as he was capable of doing, and who had loved him so faithfully and well.

AUGUSTA OF SAXE-GOTHA.

AUGUSTA OF SAXE-GOTHA.

CHAPTER I.

Description of Frederick Prince of Wales—Queen Caroline's scheme for his marriage—Lady Diana Spencer—Augusta of Saxe-Gotha—Mission of Lord Delaware—Journey of the Princess—Meeting of Frederick and Augusta—A royal water-party—Augusta's reception at St. James's—Criticisms upon her—Marriage of the Prince and Princess—Congratulations of the Lord Mayor—Augusta's visit to the theatre—Her feigned illness—Her visit to the City—Her attendance at the Lutheran chapel—The Queen's opinion of her—Her childishness — Lady Archibald Hamilton — Extraordinary conduct of the Prince—Danger of the Princess—Birth of the Lady Augusta—Visits of the Queen to the Princess of Wales—Christening of the Royal infant—Removal of the Prince and Princess to Kew—Princess Caroline's opinion of Frederick—Birth of George III.—Birthday of the Prince of Wales—Birth of the Duke of York—Of Princess Elizabeth—Visit of Frederick to St. Bartholomew's Fair—Leicester House—Reconciliation of the King and Prince—Birth of the Duke of Gloucester—Of the Duke of Cumberland—Anecdotes of Prince George—Royal theatricals—Princess Elizabeth—Reception of Vertue at Carlton House—Birth of Princess Louisa—Of Prince Frederick—His christening—Visit of the Prince and Princess to Spitalfields—The Princess's birthday.

In the beginning of the year 1736, the marriage of the heir-apparent of the English crown, Frederick, Prince of Wales, began to be publicly discussed. He was now nine and twenty years of age, and the public were of opinion that it was high time for him to form a suitable alliance, and set up an establishment of his own. He was a favourite with the lower and middle classes, in spite of his numerous faults, of which perhaps they were hardly aware; and the undisguised dislike and contempt manifested for him by his father may have served to fan the flame of the popular liking.   That he had little sterling worth is undoubtedly true; but a certain ready courtesy and genial good-humour went far towards attracting the sympathies of the people.   Lord Hervey writes of him in the following by no means favourable terms; but it must be remembered that that peer was the special *protégé* and partizan of the Queen, and would therefore be disposed to paint Frederick in the most unflattering tints :—

"The Prince's character at his first coming over, though little more respectable, seemed much more amiable than, upon his opening himself further and being better known, it turned out to be; for though there appeared nothing in him to be admired, yet there seemed nothing in him to be hated—neither anything great nor anything vicious; his behaviour was something that gained one's good wishes, though it gave one no esteem for him; for his best qualities, whilst they prepossessed one the most in his favour, always gave one a degree of contempt for him at the same time; his carriage, whilst it seemed engaging to those who did not examine it, appearing mean to those who did; for though his manners had the show of benevolence, from a good deal of natural or habitual civility, yet his cajoling everybody, and almost in an equal degree, made those things which might have been thought favours, if more judiciously or sparingly bestowed, lose all their weight. . . . He was indeed as false as his capacity would allow him to be, and was more capable in that walk than in any other, never having the least hesitation from principle or fear of future detection in telling any lie that served his present purpose.   He had a much weaker understanding, and, if possible, a more obstinate temper, than his father; that is, more tenacious of opinions he had once formed, though less capable of ever forming right ones. Had he had one grain of merit at the bottom of his heart, one should have had some compassion for him in the situation to which his miserable, poor head soon reduced him; for his case, in short, was this: he had a father that abhorred him, a mother that despised him, sisters that betrayed him, a brother set up against him, and a set of servants that neglected him, and were neither of use nor capable of being of use to him, nor desirous of being so."

In the days of Frederick's childhood, it had always been a favourite scheme of Queen Caroline and her sister-in-law, the Queen of Prussia, that he should wed one of the latter's daughters. Now that the children whose matrimonial prospects had been thus discussed were grown to maturity, the project was revived. Sir Charles Hotham was sent by George II. to propose the alliance to the King of Prussia. The King of England suggested " that his eldest son, Frederick, should marry the eldest daughter of the King of Prussia, and that his second daughter should marry the same King's eldest son. To these terms the Prussian monarch would not agree, objecting that if he gave *his* eldest daughter to the Prince of Wales, he must have the eldest, and not the second, daughter of George and Caroline for the Prince of Prussia. Caroline would have agreed to these terms, but George would not yield; the proposed inter-marriages were broken off, and the Courts were estranged for years." *

This match having been frustrated, it was

* Dr. Doran.

necessary to find another royal lady for Frederick's bride. The King, like the people, had become convinced that the suitable time had arrived for his son's marriage, and Walpole was anxious it should take place without delay, as there were rumours that the Prince of Wales had accepted from the Duchess of Marlborough the hand of her favourite granddaughter, Lady Diana Spencer, with a dowry of £100,000, and that the wedding was to take place privately in the Duchess's lodge at Richmond.

The Queen advised her husband to review the Princesses of the little duchy of Saxe-Gotha; and while the King was in Hanover, it was contrived that he should meet the Princess Augusta, daughter of the late Duke, Frederick II., and sister of the reigning Serenity. He was pleased to approve of the lady, and wrote to Caroline, telling her to bid her son prepare for his marriage. The Queen communicated the intelligence to the Prince, who answered philosophically that "whoever his Majesty thought a proper match for his son would be agreeable to him."

Accordingly Lord Delware, a "long, lank, awkward, and unpolished" peer, as Dr. Doran tells us, was despatched to ask the hand of the young Princess in marriage. "The match was straightway resolved upon; and as the young lady knew very little of French and less of English, it was suggested to her mother that a few lessons in both languages would not be thrown away. The Duchess of Saxe-Gotha, however, was wiser in her own conceit than her officious counsellors; and remembering that the Hanoverian family had been a score of years and more upon the throne of England, she very naturally concluded that the people all spoke or understood

German, and that it would really be needlessly
troubling the child to make her learn two
languages, to acquire a knowledge of which would
not be worth the pains spent upon the labour." *
The young Princess, who was but seventeen,
having been born November 19th, 1719, started
from Gotha on the 17th of April on her voyage
to become the bride of the heir of England. She
had not one lady with her, and must have felt
strangely desolate and friendless as she thus
quitted the country of her youth. She embarked
at Helvoetluys on board the royal yacht William
and Mary, which had been sent thither to convey
her to England, and arrived at Greenwich on the
25th. On disembarking "she excited general
admiration by her fresh air, good humour, and
tasteful dress. It was St. George's Day ; no in-
auspicious day whereon landing should be made in
England by the young girl of seventeen, who was to
be the mother of the first king born and bred in
England since the birthday of James II." †
None of the Royal family had troubled themselves to be present to welcome the bride-elect;
and she was conveyed, in solitary state, from the
Hospital, where she had landed, to the Queen's
House in the park, in one of her Majesty's coaches,
heartily cheered by crowds of people who were
anxious to see the future Princess of Wales ; and
she appeared, in the quaint phraseology of some
chronicler of the day, "highly delighted with the
joy of the people expressed at her arrival, and
had the goodness to show herself for above half
an hour from the gallery towards the park." By
and by the bridegroom arrived alone, bearing the
greetings of his father, mother, brother, and
sisters, who sent "their compliments, and hoped

* Dr. Doran. † *Ibid.*

she was well!"—a sufficiently unimpassioned welcome to the poor young bride. What passed at this first interview between the Princess and her future husband, Court chroniclers are too discreet to record, but the following day, Monday, the 26th, he again repaired to Greenwich, and they dined together in public—that is to say, in a room overlooking the park, the windows of which were thrown open to "oblige the curiosity of the people," as the news of the day had it; and then the Prince, leading her to the waterside, helped her into his newly-flagged and ornamental barge, and "gave her the diversion" of proceeding up the river as far as the Tower and back again, "preceded," as the minute narrators of the time tell us, "by a band of music." All the craft upon the river saluted the royal pair as they passed, and hung out flags and bunting, and little boats full of anxious sight-seers thronged the water. Returned to Greenwich, they supped, as they had dined, in public, and Frederick, kissing her hand, took leave, promising to return the next morning—a promise he subsequently broke, and allowed her to come alone to his father's palace.

This formidable journey to the home of her future husband's relatives was taken on the Tuesday morning by Augusta, who drove in one of the royal carriages as far as Lambeth; whence, taking boat, she crossed to Whitehall, where she entered one of the Queen's state chairs, and was borne to St. James's Palace. Alighting at the garden entrance, she was met by the Prince of Wales, who checked her when she would have knelt, drew her to him, and kissed her twice upon the lips; then, taking her hand, led her into the presence of a "numerous and splendid Court beyond expression." The King, Queen, Duke of

Cumberland, and the Princesses, were all in waiting to receive her. His Majesty had been impatiently awaiting her arrival, and had grown somewhat · irritable in consequence; but the behaviour of the Princess mollified him. As soon as she gained the Royal presence, " she threw herself," says Lord Hervey, " all along on the floor, first at the King's and then at the Queen's feet." This Oriental-like obeisance was so gratifying to George that when she would have knelt and kissed his hand, he put his arm round her, and kissed her on both cheeks; and the Queen and the Royal family followed suit. Her tact and *savoir-faire* won the bride many encomiums; " she behaved with a propriety and ease which won the admiration of Walpole and the sneers of old ladies who criticised her." * Lord Hervey was not one of the favourably impressed, but then he rarely *was* favourably impressed with anyone. "Her person," says the hypercritical peer, " from being very ill-made, a good deal awry, her arms long, and her motions awkward, had, in spite of all the finery of jewels and brocade, an ordinary air, which no trappings could cover or exalt."

The bride-elect dined with the Prince of Wales and the Princesses ; and, possibly by way of making her feel at home, the brother and sisters squabbled fiercely as to the etiquette to be observed at the meal. The Prince declared the Princesses ought to be seated on stools, instead of chairs, like himself and the bride; the Princesses refused to enter the dining-room until chairs were placed for them. One would have thought that on the eve of the wedding they might have found some more suitable subject of conversation than a ludicrous dispute touching their dignity.

* Dr. Doran.

This meal over, at eight in the evening, the wedding procession set out for the chapel. The bride, " in her hair," and wearing, as Princess of Wales, a crown with one bar, and a profusion of diamonds, was attired in white, over which came a gorgeous robe of crimson velvet, trimmed with row after row of ermine. Her train was borne by four bridesmaids, Lady Caroline Lennox, daughter of the Duke of Richmond, Lady Caroline Fitzroy, daughter of the Duke of Grafton, Lady Caroline Cavendish, daughter of the Duke of Devonshire, and Lady Sophia Fermor, daughter of the Earl of Pomfret—" all," say the chronicler, " in virgin habits of silver like the Princess, and adorned with diamonds not less in value than from £20,000 to £30,000 each."

The Duke of Cumberland gave the bride away ; the Lord and Vice-Chamberlains of the House-hold—the Duke of Grafton and Lord Hervey— attending them. " The Countess of Effingham and the other ladies of the household left the Queen's side to swell the following of the bride. The Lord Bishop of London, Dean of the Chapel Royal, officiated on this occasion ; and when he pronounced the two before him to have become as one, the trumpets blazoned forth their edition of the event, the drums rolled a deafening peal, a clash of instruments followed, and above all boomed the thunder of the cannon in the park, telling in a million echoes of the conclusion of the irrevocable compact. A little ceremony followed in the King's drawing-room, which was in itself appropriate, and which seemed to have heart in it. On the assembling thereof of the entire bridal party, the newly-married couple went, once more hand in hand, and kneeling before the King and his consort, who were seated

at the upper end of the room, the latter solemnly
gave their blessing to their children and bade
them be happy."*

The remainder of the proceedings shall be given
in the words of a newswriter of the period. "At
half an hour after ten, their Majesties sat down to
supper in ambigu, the prince and duke being on
the King's right hand, and the Princess of Wales
and the four princesses on the Queen's left. Their
Majesties returning to the apartments of the
Prince of Wales, the bride was conducted to
her bedroom and the bridegroom to his
dressing-room, where the duke undressed him,
and his Majesty did his Royal Highness the
honour to put on his shirt. The bride was undressed by the princesses; and being in bed in a
rich undress, his Majesty came into the room, and
the prince following soon after in a night-gown of
silver stuff, and a cap of the finest lace, the
quality were admitted to see the bride and bridegroom sitting up in bed, and surrounded by all
the Royal family. His Majesty was dressed in a
gold brocade, turned up with silk, and embroidered
with large flowers in silver and colours, as was the
waistcoat; the buttons and stars were diamonds.
Her Majesty was in a plain yellow silk, robed and
faced with pearls, diamonds, and other jewels of
immense value. The Dukes of Newcastle, Grafton, and St. Albans, the Earl of Albemarle, Colonel
Pelham, and many other noblemen, were in gold
brocades of from three to five hundred pounds a
suit. The Duke of Marlborough was in a white
velvet and gold brocaded tissue. The waistcoats
were universally brocades with large flowers. It
was observed most of the rich clothes were of the
manufactures of England, and in honour of our

* Dr. Doran.

own artists. The few which were French did not come up to those in goodness, richness, or fancy, as was seen by the clothes worn by the Royal family, which were all of the British manufacture. The cuffs of the sleeves were universally deep and open, the waists long, and the plaits more sticking out than ever. The ladies were principally in brocades of gold and silver, and wore their sleeves much lower than had been done for some time."

The day after the wedding the Lord Mayor and Aldermen came to the palace to congratulate the newly-married pair, and were very graciously received. "I curled, powdered, dressed," writes the aggrieved Mrs. Delany, "and went to Mrs. Montague at one; from thence to Court, where we were touz'd and hunched about to make room for citizens in their fur gowns, who came to make their compliments to the royal pair. They received them under their canopy. With great difficulty we made our curtsey to the Princess of Wales, but as for the Prince you might as well have made your compliments to him at *Henley!* It was actually more crowded than the day we went to be presented." An address of congratulation to the King on the royal marriage was moved in the House of Commons by Mr. Lyttleton, and seconded by Pitt, afterwards first Earl of Chatham, who then made his maiden speech. He was so laudatory of the Prince, and implied so much censure of the King, that he excited the deep and lasting enmity of his Majesty, who certainly would have come up to Dr. Johnson's idea of a good hater. Verses on the event, epithalamia, and complimentary odes, of course abounded. Of these perhaps the lines of Whitehead, the poet laureate, are the best:—

Such was the age, so calm the earth's repose,
When Maro sung, and a new Pollio rose.
Oh ! from such omens may again succeed
Some glorious youth to grace the nuptial bed :
Some future Scipio good as well as great,
Some young Marcellus with a better fate ;
Some infant Frederick, or some George, to grace
The rising records of the Brunswick race.

Horace Walpole, writing from Oxford early in
May, says, " I believe the Princess will have more
beauties bestowed upon her by the occasional
poets than even a painter would afford her. They
will cook up a new Pandora, and in the bottom of
the box enclose Hope—that all they have said is
true. A great many, out of excess of good
breeding, who have heard that it was rude to
talk Latin before women, proposed complimenting
her in English ; which she will be much the better
for. I doubt most of them, instead of fearing
their compositions should not be understood,
should fear they should ; they wish they don't
know what to be read by they don't know who."

On the 3rd of this month the Prince, who was
anxious to show his bride to the public, and had
taken her to many shows and sights, accompanied
her to Drury Lane Theatre. A riot broke out among
the footmen, who considered themselves entitled
to enter the gallery gratis ; they forced open the
doors, prevented the Riot Act being read, and
provoked a struggle in which many people were
severely wounded, the audience separating hastily,
and the Prince and Princess leaving in the midst
of the uproar. Towards the end of the month the
King departed for Hanover, leaving directions
that there would be apartments provided for the
Prince and Princess of Wales in whatever palace
the Queen Regent resided. Frederick, rightly
conjecturing that this mandate was merely to

prevent the possibility of his setting up a rival
" young Court," made up his mind to disregard it.
Accordingly, when the Queen proposed a change
of residence, he made apparently extensive preparations to follow her ; then the poor little bride,
well-tutored by her lord, fell ill, and the Prince
pronounced her unfit to move. The Queen, with
much show of interest, visited her daughter-in-
law; but the Princess—whose indisposition
seemed chameleon-like in its rapid changes, inasmuch as it was first measles, then a rash, and
finally a cold—was carefully domiciled in a
darkened room, and well instructed in her rôle ;
and Frederick gained his ends, with which he was
all the more pleased, as he had an exceeding
jealousy of his mother's appointment as Regent,
and would never be present when she opened the
commission if he could avoid it.

On Lord Mayor's Day the Prince and Princess
visited the City, and, say the journals of the day,
" when they were in Cheapside, were pleased to
visit Saddler's Hall, and accept a glass of wine,
and permit the Company to kiss their hands, and
His Royal Highness to salute the ladies there."
In consequence of this mark of condescension, the
Court of Assistants of the Worshipful Company
waited on the Royal pair on the 18th of November,
presented the Prince with the freedom of the Company in a gold box, and asked permission for his
portrait and that of the Princess to be hung in
Saddler's Hall.

It was in this first year of her wifehood that
Augusta produced a considerable sensation amongst
her new relatives by receiving the sacrament at
the German Lutheran chapel. The *letter* at least
of religion was much considered in those days,
and she was seriously remonstrated with. She

wept, pleaded conscientious scruples, and refused all injunctions and commands, until it was intimated to her that if she proved obstinate, the affair might result in her being sent back to her home, when she reluctantly gave way. Such a display of firmness on her part was the more surprising, as she was, in most things, entirely the slave and tool of her husband, who used to instigate her to acts of grave disrespect to the Queen, whom he had a malevolent pleasure in annoying. Her Majesty, when at Kensington, used regularly to attend divine service in the chapel, and was always in her place before prayers began. The Prince incited his wife always to enter the chapel a few minutes late, when she was obliged, in order to reach her own place, to push in front of the Queen, between her and her Prayer Book. Caroline bore this in silence some three or four times, and then directed Sir William Toby, the Princess's chamberlain, to conduct his mistress to her place by another entrance, so that this confusion might be avoided. This the Prince would not allow, and ordered the Princess, if she found the Queen had arrived before her, to quit the chapel.

"For the Princess," says Dr. Doran, "the Queen had nothing but a feeling which partook mostly of a compassionate regard. She knew her to be really harmless, and thought her to be very dull company; which, for a woman of Caroline's intellect and power of conversation, she undoubtedly was. The woman of cultivated mind yawned wearily at the truisms of the commonplace young lady, and made an assertion with respect to her which bespoke a mind more coarse than cultivated. 'Poor creature,' said Caroline, of her young daughter-in-law; 'were she to spit in my face, I should only pity her for being under such a fool's direction, and wipe it off.' The fool, of course, was the speaker's son. The young wife, it must be confessed, was something childish in her ways. Nothing pleased her better than to play half through the day with a large, jointed doll. This she would dress and undress, and nurse and fondle at the windows of Kensington Palace, to the amusement and wonder, rather than to the edification, of the servants in the palace and the sentinels beneath the windows. The Princess Caroline almost forgot her gentle character in chiding her sister-in-law, and desiring her 'not to stand at the window during these operations on her baby.' The Princess Caroline did not found her reproach upon the impropriety of the action, but upon that of allowing it to be witnessed by others. The lower people, she said, thought everything ridiculous that was not customary, and the thing would draw a mob about her, and make *la canaille* talk disagreeably ! "

This account of the young Princess of Wales playing with her doll recalls the memory of another royal lady, Marie Caroline de Bourbon, Duchesse de Berri, who, married when a mere child, brought some of her mimic children with her to Paris, and amused herself with them after she had attained the dignity of wifehood, " until," says Sala, prettily, " there came to her another doll to dandle, of real flesh and blood, and with eyes that moved without any string-pulling."

Frederick took advantage of the simplicity of his young wife's character to induce her to apply for leave to give a situation in her household to Lady Archibald Hamilton—a lady who, despite her mature years and her ten children, had had her name mixed up in a by no means reputable manner with that of the Prince. He assured the Princess that all injurious reports concerning them were false, and Augusta, believing his assertions, did as she was bidden, and received Lady Archibald as Lady of the Bedchamber, privy purse, and Mistress of the Robes, with a salary of £900 a year.

In the summer of 1737 the Prince of Wales announced to his parents that in less than a month his wife expected to become a mother. This announcement the Queen disbelieved. " The wish was father to the thought." She was anxious that the succession should fall to her favourite son, William, Duke of Cumberland, and considered Frederick quite capable of deceiving the world with a spurious child. She declared, that if his communication were actually the fact, she would not fail to be with the Princess at her accouchement. " I will positively be present," she said, speaking in the broad fashion of the day. " It can't be got through as soon as one can blow one's nose ; and I am resolved to be satisfied that the child is hers."

The Queen had a strong will, and usually carried out her resolutions ; but on this occasion she was destined to be foiled by one whom she deemed so contemptible an opponent, her own son. A peremptory order was issued that the birth of the expected infant should take place at Hampton Court, where the King and Queen were then living ; but Frederick, offended by the command, and only too ready to annoy his mother, inwardly resolved the mandate should be disobeyed. Twice he brought the Princess to London, believing the critical moment at hand ; and twice returned to Hampton Court. At length, on the night of the 31st of July, the Prince and Princess, after dining with the royal family, retired to their own apartments. It became evident that the accouchement of the Princess was imminent; and the Prince insisted on at once setting out for London. Augusta, who had hitherto been eager to carry out her husband's wishes in all points, no matter how unreasonable they were, now implored to be left in peace, and entreated him to think of what she must suffer should he carry out his project; but Frederick refused to listen to such supplications. He ordered his coach to be brought to one of the side entrances of the palace; and commanded Desnoyers, a dancing-master, and Bloodworth, an attendant, to carry her downstairs. The unhappy lady, in imminent peril of her life, reiterated her prayers to be allowed to remain; and was answered by Frederick with the exclamation, "Courage! courage! ah, quelle sottise!" and the assurance, uttered, says Lord Hervey, "with the encouragement of a toothdrawer, or the consolatory tenderness of an executioner, that it would be over in a minute." She was hurried into the coach, accompanied by Lady Archibald Hamilton, and two female attendants. The Prince, only pausing to impress secrecy on those of his attendants who remained at the palace, followed; Vriad, his valet, mounted the box, Bloodworth, Desnoyers, and two or three more attendants, got up behind, and the coach set off at a gallop for St. James's, which was more than twice the distance of the Prince's residence at Kew.

On their arrival, they found the whole palace in confusion; no preparations had been made, and there was not even a bed for the Princess. No sheets could anywhere be found; but Frederick and Lady Archibald Hamilton aired a couple of tablecloths as substitutes. A few officers of

State—the Lord President, Wilmington, and the
Lord Privy Seal, Godolphin—were hastily summoned; and shortly before eleven was born what
Lord Hervey unflatteringly designates as " a little
rat of a girl, about the bigness of a good large
toothpick-case." " Perhaps," says Dr. Doran,
"it was the confusion which reigned before and
at her birth which had some influence on her
intellects in after life. She was an extremely
pretty child, not without some mental qualifica-
tions; but she became remarkable for making
observations which inflicted pain and embarrass-
ment on those to whom they were addressed."

While all this confusion was going on, the
royal family were unsuspectingly engaged in their
usual evening occupations. The King and Princess
Amelia were playing commerce; the Queen was
at quadrille; and Princess Caroline and Lord
Hervey were having a game at cribbage. Soon
after ten they all retired, without having an idea
what had taken place. The first intimation came
at two the following morning, when Mrs. Tich-
borne, one of the Queen's dressers, entered her
majesty's room with a message from the Prince
acquainting his mother with the Princess's condition. Caroline prepared to hurry at once to her
daughter-in-law's room; and her indignation was
great when she heard of the Prince's sudden
flight. She at once prepared to start for St.
James's, and, accompanied by the two Princesses,
and attended by her ladies and two noblemen, set
out with such alacrity that she reached the palace
shortly after four. She spoke little to the Prince,
who came to meet her; but addressed herself
kindly and gently to the Princess, expressed a
fear that her sufferings had been great, and a hope
that she was now doing well; to which the latter,

undoubtedly influenced by her husband, answered rather flippantly that she had hardly suffered at all. The newly-born infant was put into the Queen's arms, and Caroline, looking at it, exclaimed in French after a moment's silence, " May the good God bless you, poor little creature! here you are arrived in a most disagreeable world." Then her Majesty turned to sternly rebuke those who had aided the Prince in his ill-advised journey. " She directed her indignation by turns upon all; but she let it descend with peculiar heaviness upon Lady Archibald Hamilton, and made it all the more pungent by the comment, that, considering Lady Archibald's mature age, and her having been the mother of ten children, she had years enough, and experience enough, and offspring enough, to have taught her better things and greater wisdom. To all these winged words the lady attacked answered no further than by turning to the Prince, and repeating, ' You see, sir! ' as though she would intimate that she had done all she could to turn him from the evil of his ways, and had gained only unmerited reproach for the exercise of a virtue, which, in this case, was likely to be its own and its only reward! "* The Queen, after thus speaking her mind, passed on to the apartments of Lord Hervey, where she partook of the chocolate he had provided, and acknowledged that she believed the little Princess to be veritably her granddaughter—chiefly because she *was* of the weaker sex ; forgetting that in England a girl could inherit as well as a boy, and that the little daughter of the Princess of Wales as effectually barred the Duke of Cumberland from the throne as if she had been a son.

* Dr. Doran.

Nine days later the Queen and the Princesses again visited the Princess of Wales. The Prince met them at the door of his wife's room, but never uttered a word during the time his mother remained. She stayed an hour; and when, before taking leave, she observed she was afraid she was troublesome, neither the Prince nor Princess contradicted her. As she left the palace, the Prince led her downstairs, and, says Lord Hervey, " to make the mob believe that he was never wanting in any respect, he kneeled down in the dirty street, and kissed her hand. As soon as this operation was over, he put her Majesty into the coach, and then returned to the steps of his own door, leaving his sisters to get through the dirt and the mob by themselves as they could. Nor did there come to the Queen any message, either from the Prince or Princess, to thank her afterwards for the trouble she had taken, or for the honour she had done them in this visit." This was the last time Caroline and her son ever met.

The little Princess was christened on the 29th of August, at eight o'clock in the evening, by the Archbishop of Canterbury, who named her Augusta, her sponsors by proxy being the King and Queen and the Duchess Dowager of Saxe-Gotha. The font and flagons used for the ceremony were those that for centuries had figured at royal christenings, and were brought specially from the Tower for the occasion.

"The royal infant was in a magnificent cradle, elevated on steps beneath a canopy of state, and was afterwards laid in the nurse's lap upon a rich cushion embroidered with silver. The Princess of Wales had on an exceedingly rich stomacher, adorned with jewels, and sat upon her bed of state, with the pillows richly adorned with fine

lace embroidered with silver. The Prince of
Wales was present, and richly dressed, attended
by the Lords of his Bedchamber."*

Frederick, probably merely to annoy his parents,
directed that his daughter should be known as the
" Lady Augusta," according to the old English
usage, and that her style should be " Her Royal
Highness," though well aware that his own sisters
were never so known till the accession of their
father to the throne.

Having satisfactorily gained his own way, at
the risk of his wife's life and that of her babe, he
was now not unwilling to make peace with the
King and Queen, and accordingly he addressed
them in badly spelt and rather ungrammatical
French notes, and influenced his wife to do the
same. His parents, however, who, whatever might
be the faults on their side, had certainly now just
cause for resentment, were not inclined to condone
his offence. But they were neither hasty nor un-
dignified in their manner of expressing their displeasure. Until the 10th of September the Prince
received no communication from them; but on
that day a message, conveyed by the Dukes of
Grafton and Richmond, and the Earl of Pembroke,
was brought to him, intimating that "the whole
tenor of the Prince's conduct for a considerable
time had been so entirely void of all real duty,
that their Majesties had long had reason to be
highly offended with him; and, until he withdrew
his regard and confidence from those by whose
instigation and advice he was directed and encouraged in his unwarrantable behaviour to his
Majesty and the Queen, and until he should return to his duty, he should not reside in a palace
belonging to the King, which his Majesty would

* Mrs. Matthew Hall.

not suffer to be made the resort of those who, under the appearance of an attachment to the Prince, fomented the divisions which he had made in his family, and thereby weakened the common interest of the whole." It was further added that the King desired " the Prince should leave St. James's, with all his family, when it could be done without prejudice or inconvenience to the Princess; and that, for the present, his Majesty would leave the care of his granddaughter to the Princess until a proper time called upon him to consider of her education." In obedience to this mandate, the Prince and Princess left St. James's on the 14th of September for Kew, not being allowed to take a single article of furniture with them, it being alleged that the things having been purchased by his Majesty for the Prince's marriage, belonged to the King. They had no sooner taken up their abode at Kew, than Lord Carteret, Sir William Wyndham, and Mr. Pulteney, came to pay their respects to the Prince—a proceeding intensely irritating to the King, who consoled himself by remarking that " they would soon be tired of the puppy, who was, moreover, a scoundrel and a fool ; and who would talk more fiddle-faddle to them in a day than any old woman talks in a week." Frederick still continued to address explanatory notes to the King and Queen; but as they were all couched in terms of deliberate disrespect to his mother, the King refused to be mollified by their representations. The Princess also wrote, apparently sincerely anxious to lessen the breach, thanking the Queen for standing godmother to the little Augusta, and endeavouring to palliate her husband's behaviour. " I am deeply afflicted," she says, in a note dated September 17th, " at the manner in which the Prince's conduct has been represented to your Majesties, especially with regard to the two journeys which we made from Hampton Court to London the week previous to my confinement. . . . Is it credible, that if I had gone twice to London with the design and in the expectation of being confined there, I should have returned to Hampton Court? I flatter myself that time and the good offices of your Majesty will bring about a happy change in a situation of affairs, the more deplorable for me inasmuch as I am the innocent cause of it." This letter, delivered to the Queen as she was going into chapel, was replied to by one which, while it treated the Princess as blameless, by no means excused the Prince. Both the father and son published copies of the correspondence which had passed at the time of the Prince's expulsion from St. James's; and, on Thursday, September 22nd, when the Prince and Princess of Wales received at Carlton House the congratulations of the Lord Mayor and Corporation on the birth of the "Lady Augusta," copies of the message from the King commanding his retirement from St. James's were distributed among the company by the lords of the Prince's council.

Shortly after, as Carlton House was undergoing some repairs, the Prince and Princess rented Norfolk House, in St. James's Square, which was only let to them by the Duke and Duchess after they had obtained the approval of the King. Here they established themselves for some little time, the Prince allying himself with the chiefs of the Opposition, and studying economy with a thoroughness that rather diminished his popularity.

"He reduced," says a writer of the day, "the number of his inferior servants, which made him many enemies among the lower sort of people, and farmed all his tables, even that of the Princess and himself "—*i.e.*, caused them to be supplied at so much a head. These retrenchments, with the diminishing of his stud, did not raise him in the public favour he was ever anxious to obtain. He was garrulous concerning his conduct when he should become King. He intended his mother to be "fleeced, flayed, and minced; " his sister Amelia to be imprisoned; and his sister Caroline to be left to starve ; while he always affected great kindness of feeling for his brother William, Duke of Cumberland, and ignored the younger Princesses, Mary and Louisa, altogether. The Princess Caroline was not more favourably inclined to her brother than he was to her.

"On one occasion," says Dr. Doran, "as Desnoyers, the dancing-master, had concluded his lesson to the young Princesses, and was about to return to the Prince, who made of him a constant companion, the Princess Caroline bade him inform his patron, if the latter should ever ask him what was thought of his conduct by her, that it was her opinion that he and all who were with him, except the Princess of Wales, deserved hanging. Desnoyers delivered this message, with the assurance of respect given by one who acquits himself of a disagreeable commission to one whom he regards.

" ' How did the Prince take it ? ' asked Caroline, when next Desnoyers appeared at Hampton Court.

" ' Well, Madam,' said the dancing-master, ' he first spat in the fire, and then observed, " Ah, ah! Desnoyers, you know the way of that Caroline. That is just like her. She is always like that." '

" ' Well, M. Desnoyers,' remarked the Princess, ' when next you see him again, tell him that I think his observation is as foolish as his conduct.'

" The exception made by the Princess Caroline of

the Princess of Wales, in the censure distributed by the former, was not undeserved. She was the mere tool of her husband, who made no confidante of her, but kept her in the most complete ignorance of all that was happening around her, and much of which immediately concerned her." The Prince was wont to declare that he would never prove himself so great a simpleton as his father, or allow his consort to rule or influence him.

On June 4th, 1738, at Norfolk House, the Princess became the mother of a son, afterwards George III. The birth of the royal infant had not been expected until two months later, and the day after his birth he was so ill that his death was hourly expected; but, contrary to general expectation, he gradually recovered, and, when a month old, was christened George William Frederick, his sponsors being the King of Sweden, the Duke of Saxe-Gotha, and the Queen of Prussia.

"In consequence of the delicacy of the infant Prince at the time of his birth, the greatest care was necessary in choosing for him a nurse. The wife of one of the gardeners at the palace was chosen for that important trust, who, besides being a perfectly healthful and careful person, possessed much kindness of heart. She loved her nursling, not so much on account of his exalted station, as from his being a little fragile creature, whom it gladdened her sight to behold improving and thriving whilst under her charge. The babe returned her love; his affection for his devoted attendant seemed to 'grow with his growth and strengthen with his strength,' for he became fonder of her every day; and even years after, when he had become a man and a king, he did not regret the gratitude he owed to her who had so tenderly cherished him in his feeble state of infantine helplessness. And on many occasions, when she was in distress or poverty, she applied to the Prince, confident of receiving from him relief and kindness; nor was she disappointed in her expectations."*

"After much persuasion," writes Mrs. Delany to her sister, on January 23rd, 1739, "and many debates within myself, I consented to go with Lady Dysart to the Prince's birthday, humbly drest in my pink damask, white and gold handkerchief, plain green ribbons, and Lady Sunderland's buckles for my stays. 'Twas a *good foil* for those that were there. I never saw so much finery without any mixture of trumpery in my life. Lady Huntingdon's, as the most extraordinary, I must describe first:—Her petticoat was black velvet embroidered with chenille, the pattern a *large stone vase* filled with *ramping flowers* that spread almost over a breadth of the petticoat from the bottom to the top; between each vase of flowers was a pattern of gold shells, and foliage embossed, most heavily rich; the gown was white satin, embroidered also with chenille mixed with gold ornaments, *no vases* on the *sleeve,* but *two or three on the tail;* it was a most laboured piece of finery, the pattern much properer for a stucco staircase than the apparel of a lady,—a mere shadow that tottered under every step she took under the load. The next fine lady was Mrs. Spencer; her clothes, green paduasoy covered all over, the gown as well as petticoat, with a very fine and very pretty trimming; it was well made; she looked genteel and easy, and had all the Dowager Duchess of Marlborough's jewels, which made her look quite magnificent. Lady Dysart was white and gold, and looked as handsome as ever I saw her; Miss

* " Early Days of English Princes." Mrs. Russell Grey.

Carteret in an uncut blue velvet, and *all* my Lady Carteret's jewels; Lady Carteret in the same clothes she made for the Prince's wedding, white and gold and colours; the Princess was in white satin, the petticoat covered with a gold trimming like embroidery, faced and robed with the same. Her head and stomacher a rock of diamonds and pearls; her looks pleased me better than her dress; there appeared in them such strong marks of contentment and good humour. She spoke *to everybody*, and so did the Prince. The ball began at eight; I never saw a ball at Court well-managed before. The Prince and Princess sat under the State, their attendants on stools on the right and left hand; benches were placed for the rest of the company, the first row of which was kept for the dancers. The best dancers were Lady Catherine Hanmer, Lady Dysart, and Miss Wyndham; nothing extraordinary among the men; much finery, chiefly brown with gold or silver embroidery, and rich waistcoats. Lord Carteret was there morning and night. 'Tis now strongly reported that there is going to be a reconciliation between the King and Prince, but the truth of that is doubted. Lord Townshend has thrown up, nobody knows why. The Prince began the ball with the Duchess of Bedford; after one minuet he sat down. When two country-dances were over, the Princess went to quadrille with Lady Archibald Hamilton, Lady Westmoreland, and Lady Chesterfield; the Prince in another room to whist with Lord Baltimore, Lady Blandford, and Lady Carteret. At half an hour after eleven the Prince and Princess gave over cards and went away. The dancing broke up at the same time, and all the company, I believe, was gone by half an hour after twelve, which I think was very orderly, considering how many people there were to get at their equipages. I got home a little after twelve."

The year following Mrs. Delany again attended on Frederick's birthday, accompanied by Lady Dysart and a Miss Dashwood.

" I was curled," she says, "powdered, and decked with silver ribbon, and was told by critics in the art of dress that I was well dressed. Lady Dysart was in a scarlet damask gown, facings and robings embroidered with gold and colours, her petticoat white satin, all covered with embroidery of the same sort, very fine and handsome. . . . The Princess's clothes were white satin, the petticoat, robings, and facings covered with a rich gold net, and upon that flowers in their natural colours embroidered, her head crowned with jewels; and her behaviour (as it always is) affable and obliging to everybody. The Prince was in old clothes, and not well; he was obliged to go away very early. The Duchess of Bedford's clothes were the most remarkably fine, though finery was so common it was hardly distinguished, and my little pretension to it, you may imagine, was easily eclipsed by such superior brightness. The Duchess of Bedford's petticoat was green paduasoy, embroidered very richly with gold and silver, and a few colours; the pattern was festoons of shells, coral, corn, cornflowers, and seaweeds; everything in different works of gold and silver except the flowers and coral, the body of the gown white satin, with a mosaic pattern of gold facings, robings and train the same as the petticoat; there was abundance of embroidery, many people in gowns and petticoats of different colours. The men were as fine as the ladies, but we had no Lord Clanricard. My

Lord Baltimore was in light brown and silver, his coat lined quite *throughout* with ermine. His lady looked like a *frightened owl*, her locks strutted out and most furiously greased, or rather gummed and powdered; Lady Percival was very fine in white satin, embroidered with gold and silver; Lady Carteret feuille mort uncut velvet, trimmed with silver flowers, grave and handsome; Miss Carteret flowered silk with coloured flowers, and glittering with all her mama's jewels; she danced with a very good air, her person is really fine; but my Lady Carteret's agreeable countenance and easy air pleased me more than younger beauties. Miss Fortescue looked like Cleopatra in her bloom; I thought her the *handsomest* woman at the ball; she was in pink and silver, and very well drest. The Duchess of Queensberry was remarkably fine *for her*, had powder, and was tolerably dressed; she had put on all her best airs, and certainly showed she had *still a right* to be called ' beautiful.' My Lord Carlisle, his lady, son, and two daughters, were all excessively fine. But I grow sick of the word ' fine ' and all its appurtenances, and I am sure you have enough of it. The ball began at nine, and I left them smartly engaged at the hour of twelve."

Meanwhile the Princess's nursery had been increased by two inmates—Edward, born March 14th, 1739, and Elizabeth, born the following year. In a highly laudatory poem, addressed to the Prince of Wales, the poet Thomson thus alludes to these Royal olive branches:—

But more enchanting than the Muses' song,
    United Britons thy dear offspring hail;
The city triumphs through her growing throng,
    The shepherd tells his transport to the dale;

The sons of roughest toil forget their pain,
And the glad sailor cheers the midnight main.

Can aught from fair Augusta's gentle blood,
    And thine, thou friend of liberty ! be born;
Can aught save but is lovely, generous, good ;
    What will, at once, defend us and adorn ?
From thence, prophetic joy ! new Edward's eyes, (*sic*)
New Henries, Annas, and Elizas rise.

The Prince amused himself about this time by
a visit to St. Bartholomew's Fair, of which proceeding a minute account was given by a journalist
of the day. "The multitude behind," we are
told, "was impelled violently forwards, and a
broad blaze of red light, issuing from a score of
flambeaux, steamed into the air. Several voices
were loudly shouting, 'Room there for Prince
Frederick ! make way for the Prince !' and there
was that long sweep heard to pass over the ground
which indicates the approach of a grand and cere-
monious train. Presently the pressure became
much greater, the voices louder, the light stronger,
and, as the train came onward, it might be seen
that it consisted, firstly, of a party of yeomen of
the guards clearing the way ; then several more of
them bearing flambeaux, and flanking the procession ; while in the midst of all appeared a tall,
fair, and handsome young man, having something
of a plump foreign visage, seemingly about four
and thirty years of age, dressed in a ruby-coloured
frock-coat, very richly guarded with gold lace, and
having his long flowing hair curiously curled over
his forehead and at the sides, and finished with a
very large bag and courtly queue behind. The
air of dignity with which he walked ; the blue
ribbon and star and garter with which he was
decorated ; the small, three-cornered, silk Court

hat which he wore, while all around him were un-
covered; the numerous suite, as well of gentlemen
as of guards, which marshalled him along; the
obsequious attention of a short, stout person, who,
by his flourishing manner, seemed to be a player;
all these particulars indicated that the amiable
Frederick, Prince of Wales, was visiting Bartholomew Fair by torchlight, and that Manager Rich
was introducing his Royal guest to all the amuse-
ments of the place."

Leicester House, the whilom residence of George
and Caroline, was taken by the Royal pair, in
addition to their own town residence of Carlton
House; and thus for the second time within thirty
years a younger and rival Court was established in
opposition to the Crown. The enmity between
father and son was, however, soon to be ostensibly
done away with; for the reports of Jacobitism
and wide-spread dissatisfaction in favour of the
Stuarts grew so alarming that a not very sincere
reconciliation took place between the King and his
heir. The latter was induced, after considerable
persuasion, to write to his father, who thereupon
appointed the next day to receive him and five
gentlemen of his Court. The King said nothing
more than, "How does the Princess do? I hope
she is well;" and Frederick, having answered the
query, and kissed the royal hand, retired. This,
however, was looked on as a satisfactory reconciliation; and shortly afterwards the whole of the
re-united royal family went together to visit the
Duchess of Norfolk, on which auspicious occasion
" the streets were illuminated and bonfired." The
courtiers were charmed to be able to attend both
Courts without giving offence to either; the Prince
gained another £50,000 a-year by his exercise of

filial duty; and there was much outward gaiety and rejoicing, the royal pair themselves passing in great state through the city to dine at Greenwich, taking boat to the Tower.

Two more children, William, afterwards Duke of Gloucester, and Henry, afterwards Duke of Cumberland, were born in 1743 and 1745. George, the eldest son, had outgrown the delicacy of his infancy, and occupied a prominent place in the hearts of both parents. On his first birthday the throng flocking to congratulate the Prince and Princess found the royal child guarded by a corps of sixty little boys, sons of notable citizens, dressed as soldiers, who, on their arrival at the palace, had marched, drums beating and colours flying, to the drawing-room, where their baby-colonel awaited them, decked out in a fine hat and feather. When only six years old he was entrusted to the care of Dr. Ayscough, who, according to the fashion of the time, found innumerable virtues to eulogise in his princely pupil. The Bishop of Salisbury gave a pleasing account of his sight of the future King one evening when he was invited to dine with the Prince and Princess of Wales at Cliefden, their place on the banks of the Thames. It was merely a family party, and the children, coming in at dessert, were made to recite various poems for the Bishop's gratification. Occasionally the young Prince acted as page to his royal parents. " When the Prince and Princess of Wales were at dinner, Prince George and his brother Edward used to stand apart and wait upon their father and mother, who were wont to talk to them the while, half in earnest, half in joke, as lord and lady of old might have done to a couple of damoiseaux, whom the lord was to instruct in the school of arms and the lady in that of love." *

The well-known actor, Quin, was engaged to teach the young Prince elocution; and, when still very young, George, his sisters Augusta and Elizabeth, and his brother Edward, with some of their playmates, acted the tragedy of "Cato," on the 4th of January, 1749, in the presence of their parents and a large audience. It was rather a lugubrious play to have been selected, but the royal actors performed their parts in—of course—a highly creditable manner; and a prologue and epilogue were written expressly for their benefit. Before the curtain rose Prince George came forward, and thus delivered himself;—

> To speak with freedom, dignity, and ease,
> To learn those arts which may hereafter please,
> Wise authors say—let youth in earlier age
> Rehearse the poets' labours on the stage.
> Nay, more! a nobler end is still behind—
> The poets' labours elevate the mind;
> Teach our young hearts with gen'rous fire to burn,
> And feel the virtuous sentiments we learn.
> T' attain those glorious ends what play so fit,
> As that where all the powers of human wit
> Combine to dignify great Cæsar's name,
> To deck his tomb, and consecrate his fame?
> Where Liberty, O name for ever dear!
> Breathes forth in every line, and bids us fear
> Nor pains nor death to guard our sacred laws,
> But bravely perish in our country's cause.
> Patriots indeed! Nor why that honest name,
> Through every time and action still the same,
> Should thus superior to my years be thought,
> Know 'tis the first great lesson I was taught.
> What, though a boy! it may with pride be said,
> A boy in *England* born—in England bred;
> Where freedom well becomes the earliest state,
> For there is love of liberty innate.

* "Pages on Pages." *Vide* "Temple Bar," August, 1874.

Yet more : before my eyes those heroes stand,
Whom the great William brought to bless this land,
To guard with pious care that gen'rous plan
Of power well moulded, which he first began.
But while my great forefathers fire my mind,
The friends, the joy, the glory of mankind,
Can I forget that there is one more dear ?
But he is present, and I must forbear.

The epilogue was a dialogue between Prince
Edward and the "Lady Augusta," which must
have been much more amusing to the young reciters
than their brother's solemn peroration :—

PRINCESS AUGUSTA.

The prologue's filled with such fine phrases,
George will alone have all the praises;
Unless we can (to get in vogue)
Contrive to speak our epilogue.

PRINCE EDWARD.

George has, 'tis true, vouchsafed to mention
His future gracious intention
In such heroic strains, that no man
Will e'er deny his soul in *Roman*.
But what have you or I to say to
The pompous sentiments of Cato ?
George is to have imperial sway ;
Our task is only to obey ;
And trust me I'll not thwart his will,
But be his faithful *Juba* still—
Though, sister, now the play is over,
I wish you'd get a better lover.

PRINCESS AUGUSTA.

Why, not to underrate your merit,
Others would court with different spirit ;
And I perhaps might like another
A little better than a brother.
Could I have one of *England's* breeding,
But 'tis a point they are all agreed in,
That I must wed a foreigner
Across the seas,—the Lord knows where,—
Yet, let me go where 'er I will,
England shall have my wishes still.

PRINCE EDWARD.

In England born, my inclination,
Like yours, is wedded to the nation;
And future times, I hope, will see
The General, in reality.
Indeed, I wish to serve this land,
It is my father's strict command;
And none he ever gave will be
More cheerfully obeyed by me.

The little Princess Elizabeth, one of the royal actresses, had suffered ill health from infancy, and was insignificant in appearance and slightly deformed, but with mental powers far superior to her brothers and sisters. "Her figure," says Walpole, "was so very unfortunate that it would have been difficult for her to be happy; but her parts and application were extraordinary. I saw her act in Cato, at eight years old (when she could not stand alone, but was forced to lean against the side scene), better than any of her brothers and sisters. She had been so unhealthy that, at that age, she had not been taught to read, but had learnt the part of Lucia by hearing the others study their parts. She went to her father and mother, and begged she might act. They put her off as gently as they could; she desired leave to repeat her part, and when she did, it was with so much sense that there was no denying her."

On his twelfth birthday Prince George and his eldest sister were present at a boat race, when the future King gave a silver cup to be rowed for. The scene was a pretty one; the royal children, in a magnificent barge, built in the Italian style; the watermen in Chinese dresses; and the water crowded by pleasure boats and crafts of all kind. George was so pleased with the sight that he gave another prize to be contested in like manner soon after.

The Prince of Wales, in spite of his dissolute habits and unworthy life, had considerable taste for art and literature, and was honestly anxious that his children should be intelligently educated in such matters. In the summer of 1749 Vertue, the engraver, was summoned to Carlton House; and, on arriving, found the Prince and Princess at table, while their two eldest sons acted as pages, each with a napkin over his arm. " After they had stood awhile in silence, the Prince said to them, ' This is Mr. Vertue. I have many curious works of his, which you shall see after dinner.' Carlton House was a store of art treasures. The Prince, with Luke Schaub in attendance, and Vertue accompanying, went though them all. He spoke much and listened readily, and parted only to have another art-conference in the following month. The illustrious couple were then seated in a pavilion in Carlton House garden. The Prince showed both knowledge and curiosity with respect to art; and the party adjourned to Leicester House, where Mr. Vertue was shown all the master pieces, with great affability on the part of Frederick and his consort. The royal couple soon after exhibited themselves to the admiring people, through whom they were carried in two chairs over Leicester Fields back to Carlton House. Thence the party repaired to Kew, and the engraver, after examining the pictures, dined with them though, he says, ' being entertained there at dinner was not customary to any person that came from London.' " *

Another daughter, Louisa Anne, had been born

* " Leicester Fields." *Vide* " Temple Bar," June, 1874.

on the 8th of March, 1748 ; and in May, 1750, the
Princess became the mother of her youngest son.
The birth took place at Leicester House, half an
hour after midnight. "Then the Prince, the ladies,
and some of us," writes Bubb Dodington in his
diary, "sat down to breakfast in the next room, then
went to prayers downstairs. The christening was
performed in the palace by the Bishop of Oxford,
Prince George acting as godfather, and naming
the child Frederick William. "Nobody of either
sex," says Bubb Dodington, "was admitted into
the room but the actual servants, except Chief
Justice Willes and Sir Luke Schaub." The
Princess's recovery must have been rapid, for on the
28th of June the same chronicler records, "Lady
Middlesex, Lord Bathurst, Mr. Breton, and I
waited on their Royal Highnesses to Spitalfields,
to see the manufactory of silk, and to Mr. Carr's
shop, in the morning. In the afternoon the same
company, with Lady Torrington in waiting, went
in private coaches to Norwood Forest, to see a
settlement of gipsies. We returned and went to
Bettesworth, the conjuror, in hackney coaches.
Not finding him we went in search of the little
Dutchman, but were disappointed ; and concluded
the particularities of the day by supping with Mrs.
Cannon, the Princess's midwife." Verily, a
curious expedition for the heir to the throne and
his consort !

In the autumn of the same year the Prince and
Princess visited some factories in Gloucestershire ;
receiving addresses from the weavers and wool-
combers, and replying very graciously ; and we
catch another glimpse of the royal children through
an entry in Bubb Dodington's diary, recording
how he had witnessed their performance of "Jane

Gray." Domestic differences occasionally arose in the royal household ; as on one of the birthdays of the Princess of Wales, when, as we learn from Mrs. Delany's written gossip, " there was a very full Court, and great confusion in getting in and out at Leicester House ; the Princess's ladies were affronted by the Princess of Wales.' The story told on their side is this ;—the Princesses, attended by their ladies, went to Leicester House, and were immediately carried into the room to the Princess of Wales before the drawing-room began ; and all the ladies of both stayed in the outward room. As soon as notice was given that the Princess and her sisters were going into the drawing-room, the Princess of Wales's ladies went on, and shut the door upon the other ladies; saying, 'Their Princesses were not there.' "

END OF VOL. II.

Printed by Remington & Co., 134, New Bond Street, W.